A MIDSUMMER NIGHT'S DREAM

THE GRAPHIC NOVEL
William Shakespeare

PLAIN TEXT VERSION

Script Adaptation: John McDonald
American English Adaptation: Joe Sutliff Sanders
Character Designs & Artwork: Jason Cardy & Kat Nicholson
Lettering: Jim Campbell
Design & Layout: Jenny Placentino

Editor in Chief: Clive Bryant

A Midsummer Night's Dream: The Graphic Novel
Plain Text Version

William Shakespeare

First US Edition

Published by: Classical Comics Ltd

Acknowledgments: Every effort has been made to trace copyright holders of
material reproduced in this book. Any rights not acknowledged here will be
acknowledged in subsequent editions if notice is given to Classical Comics Ltd.

Images on page 135 reproduced with the kind permission of The Shakespeare Birthplace Trust.

All enquiries should be addressed to:
Classical Comics Ltd.
PO Box 7280
Litchborough
Towcester
NN12 9AR
United Kingdom
Tel: 0845 812 3000

info@classicalcomics.com
www.classicalcomics.com

ISBN: 978-1-907127-29-8

Printed in Singapore. The paper used in the production of this book is a natural,
recyclable product made from wood grown in sustainable forests.

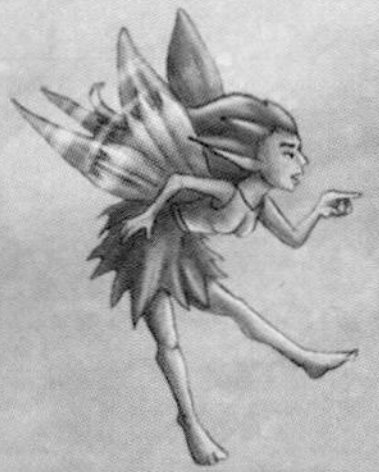

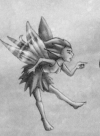

Contents

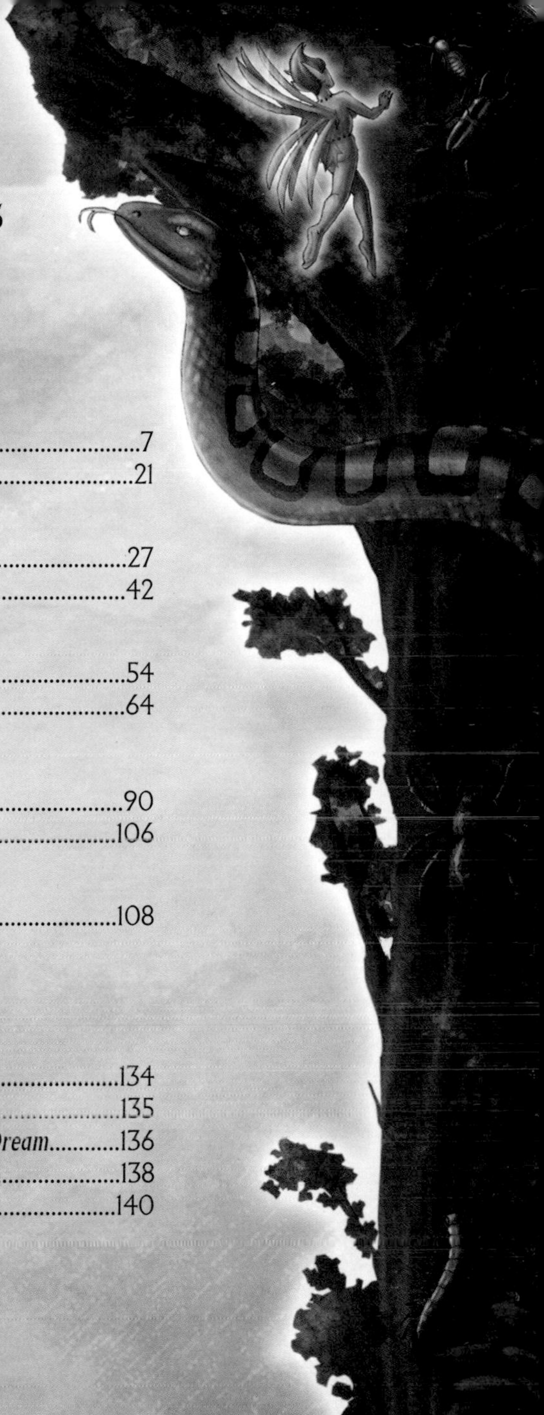

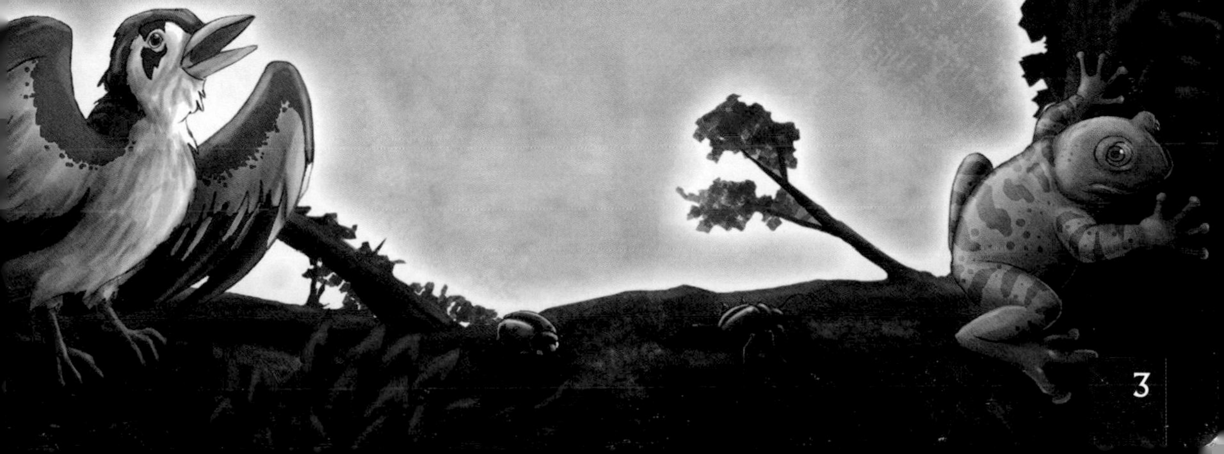

Dramatis Personæ

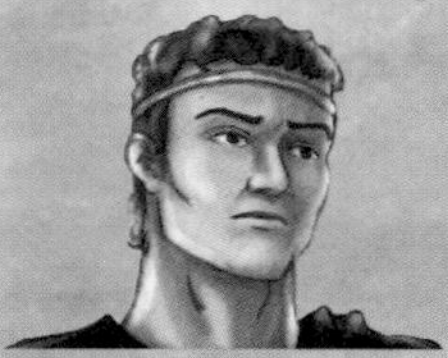

Theseus
Duke of Athens

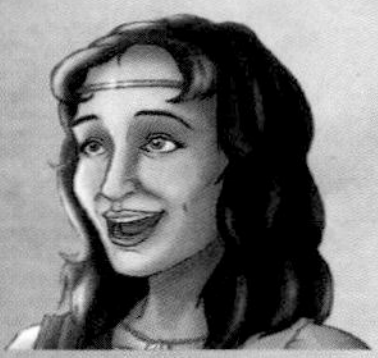

Hippolyta
Queen of the Amazons

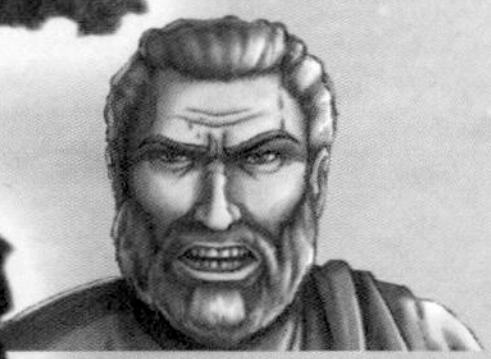

Egeus
Hermia's Father

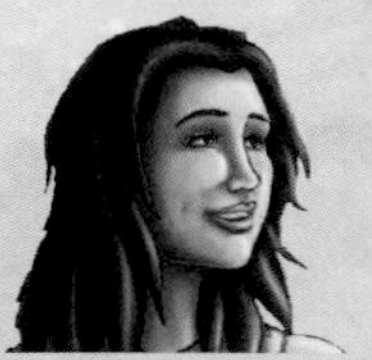

Hermia
Egeus's Daughter,
in love with Lysander

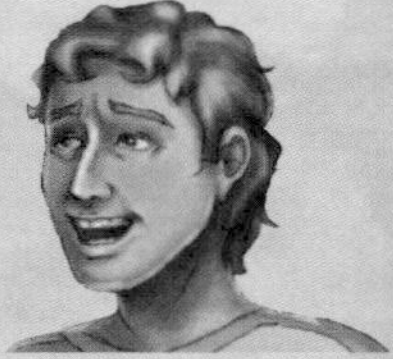

Lysander
In love with Hermia

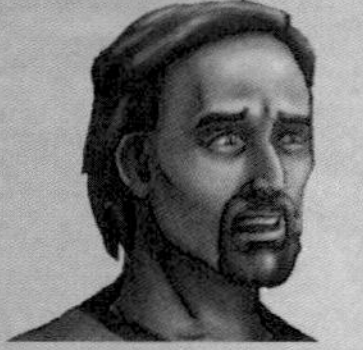

Peter Quince
A Carpenter

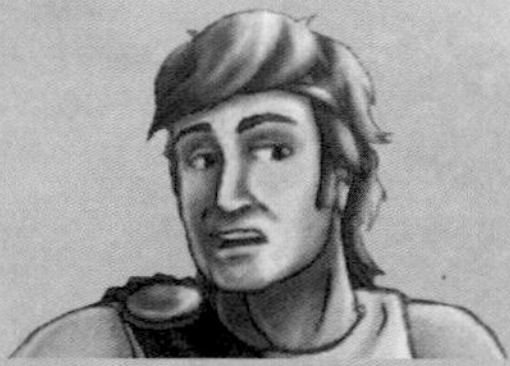

Nick Bottom
A Weaver

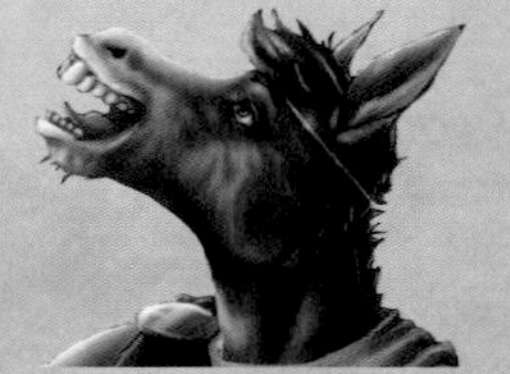

Nick Bottom
(Transformed)

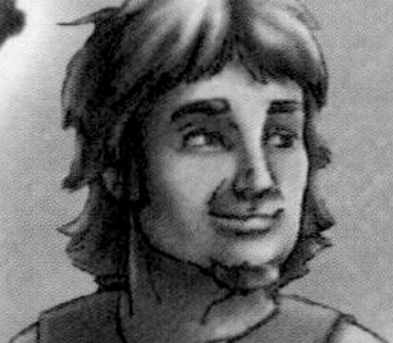

Snug
A Joiner

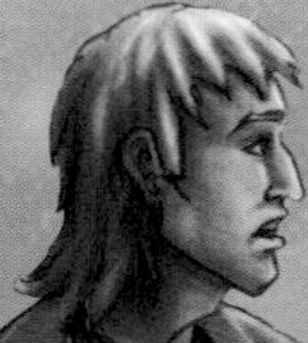

Robin Starveling
A Tailor

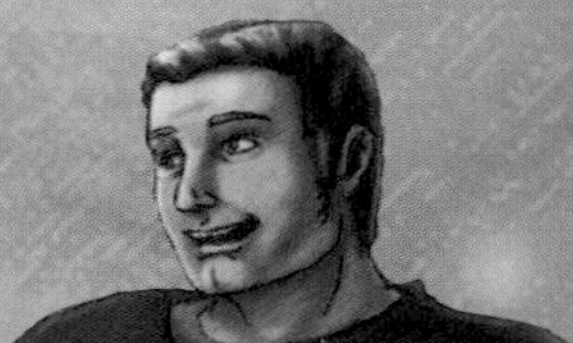

Tom Snout
A Tinker

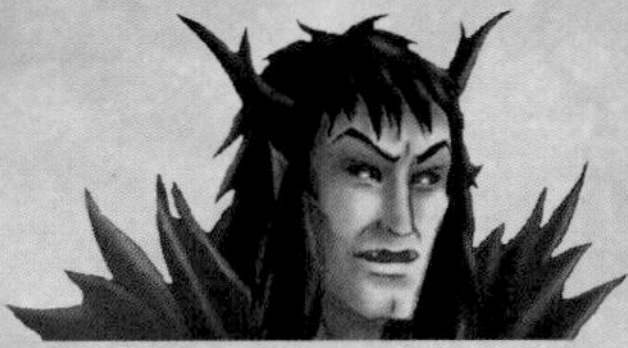

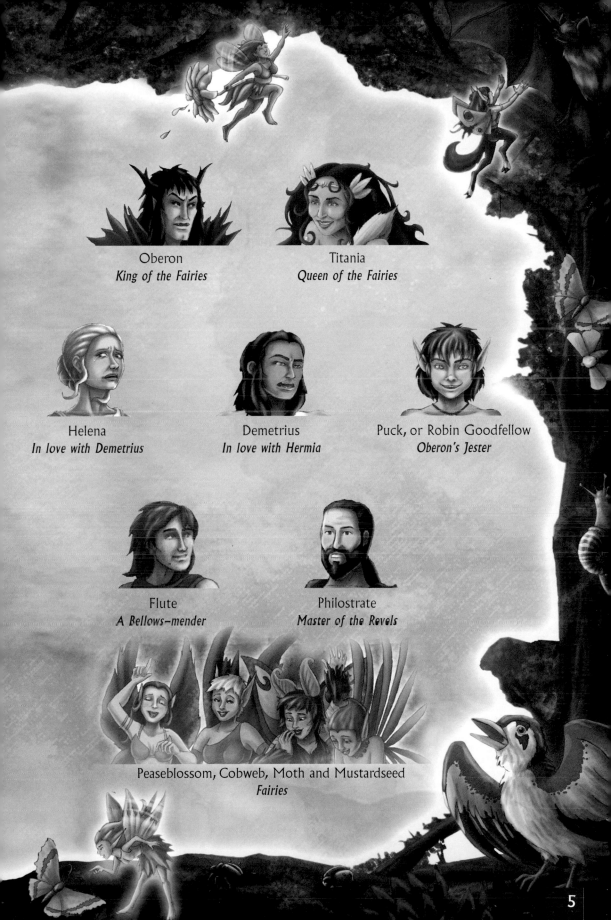

Oberon
King of the Fairies

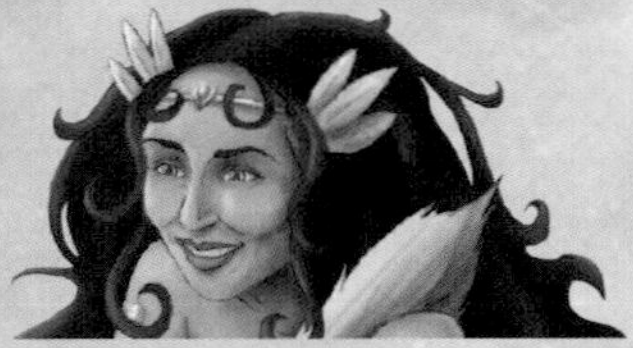

Titania
Queen of the Fairies

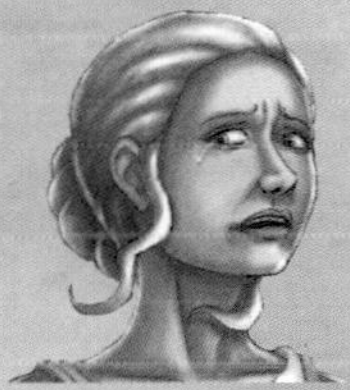

Helena
In love with Demetrius

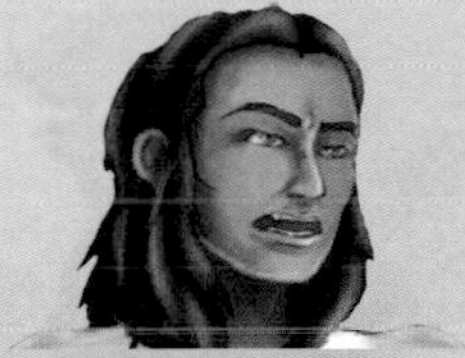

Demetrius
In love with Hermia

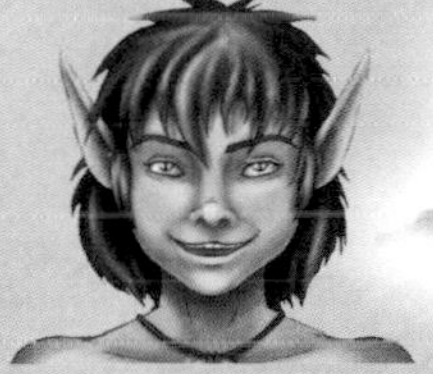

Puck, or Robin Goodfellow
Oberon's Jester

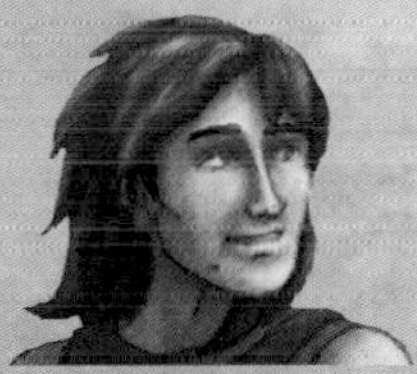

Flute
A Bellows-mender

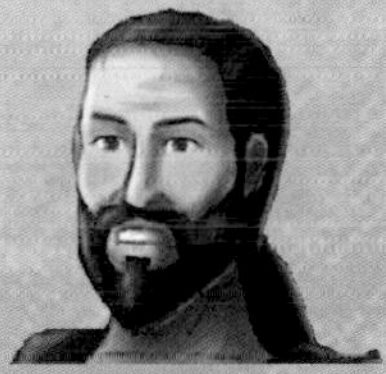

Philostrate
Master of the Revels

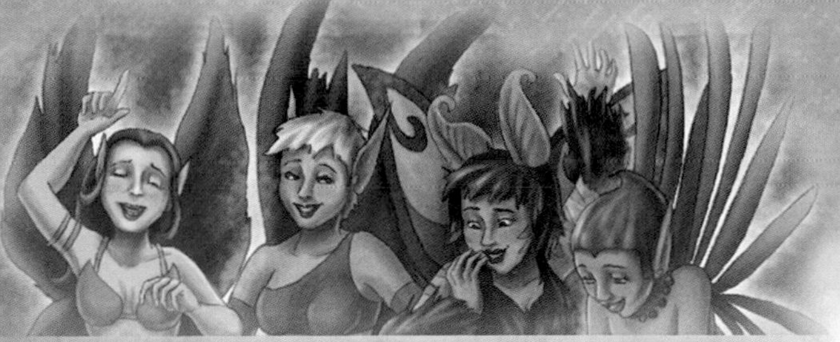

Peaseblossom, Cobweb, Moth and Mustardseed
Fairies

A Midsummer Night's Dream

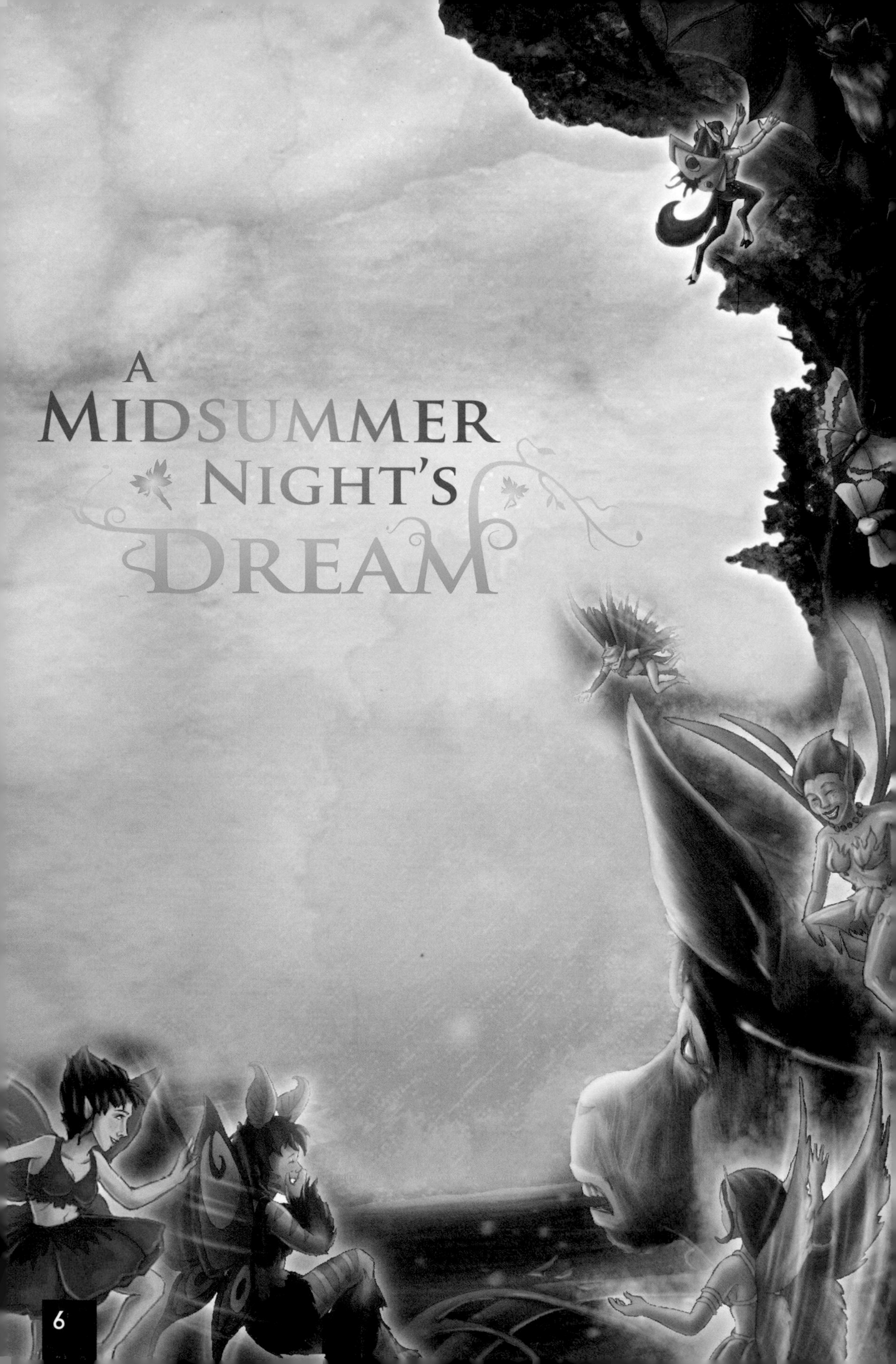

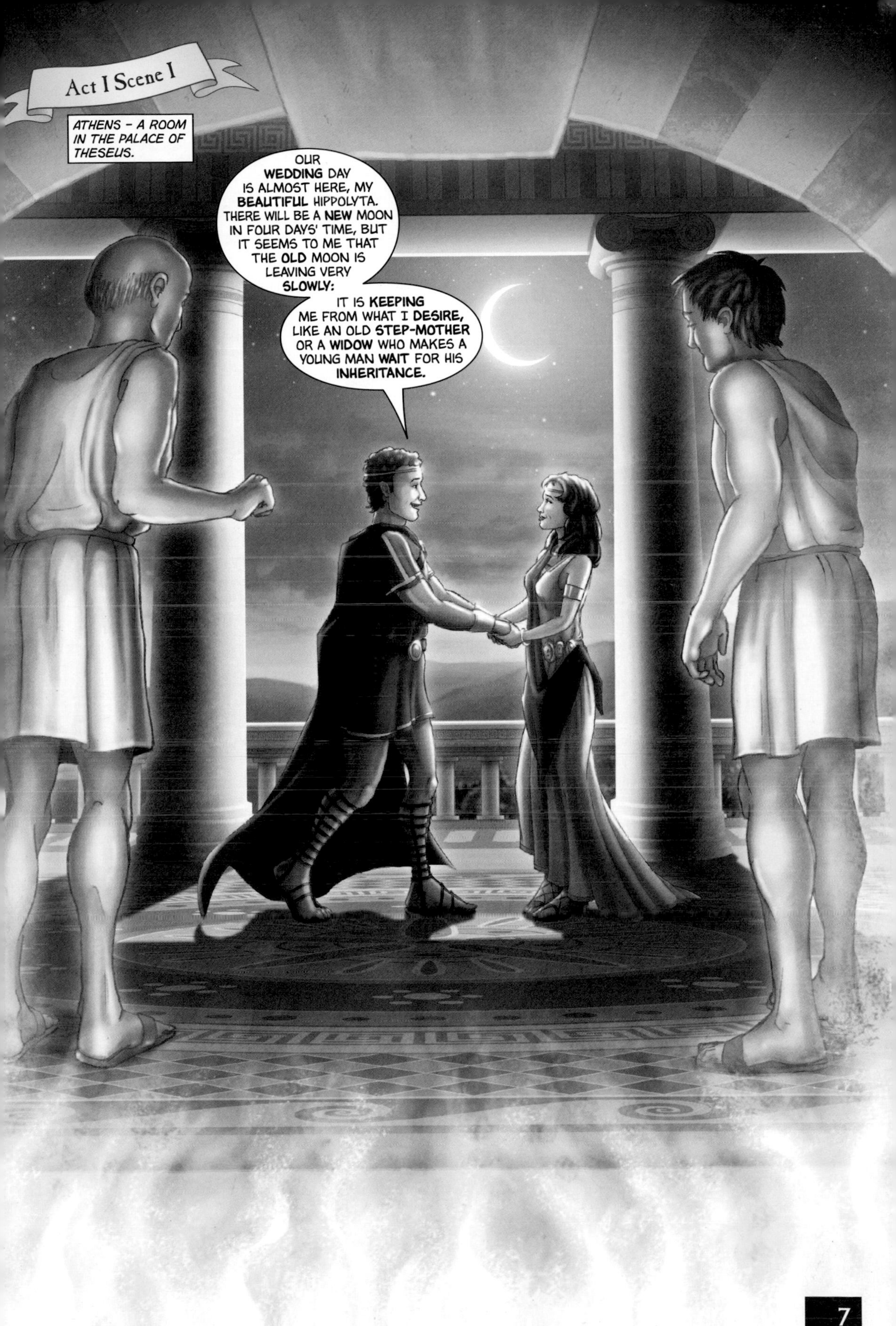
Act I Scene I
ATHENS – A ROOM IN THE PALACE OF THESEUS.
OUR WEDDING DAY IS ALMOST HERE, MY BEAUTIFUL HIPPOLYTA. THERE WILL BE A NEW MOON IN FOUR DAYS' TIME, BUT IT SEEMS TO ME THAT THE OLD MOON IS LEAVING VERY SLOWLY:
IT IS KEEPING ME FROM WHAT I DESIRE, LIKE AN OLD STEP-MOTHER OR A WIDOW WHO MAKES A YOUNG MAN WAIT FOR HIS INHERITANCE.

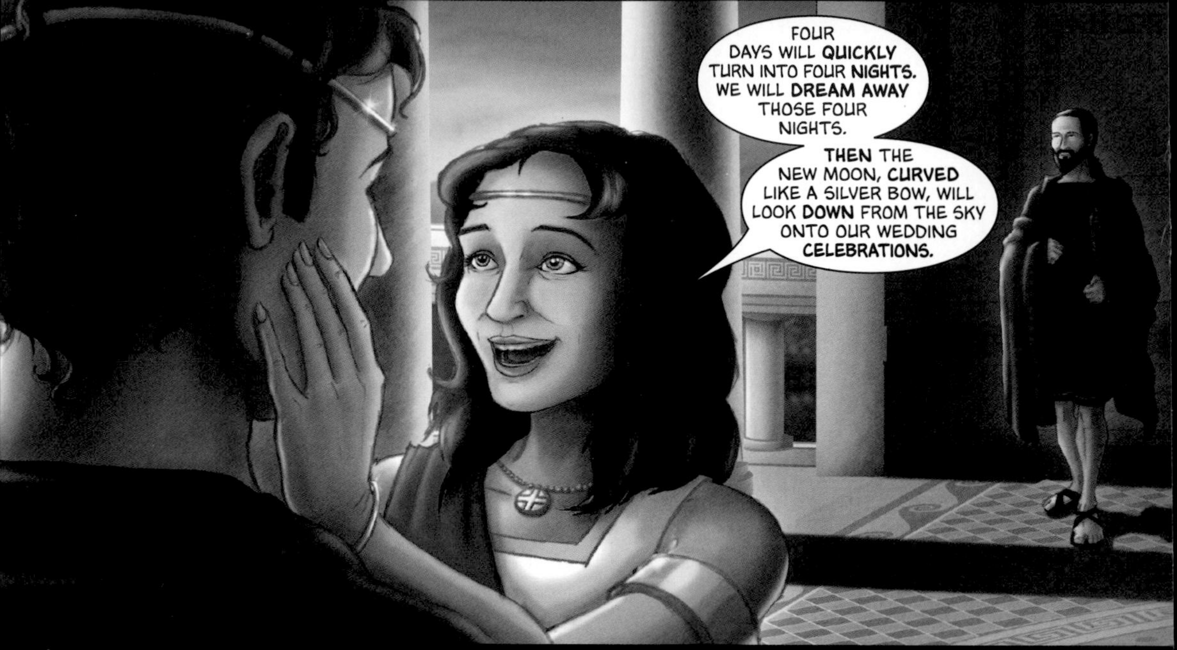
FOUR DAYS WILL QUICKLY TURN INTO FOUR NIGHTS. WE WILL DREAM AWAY THOSE FOUR NIGHTS.
THEN THE NEW MOON, CURVED LIKE A SILVER BOW, WILL LOOK DOWN FROM THE SKY ONTO OUR WEDDING CELEBRATIONS.

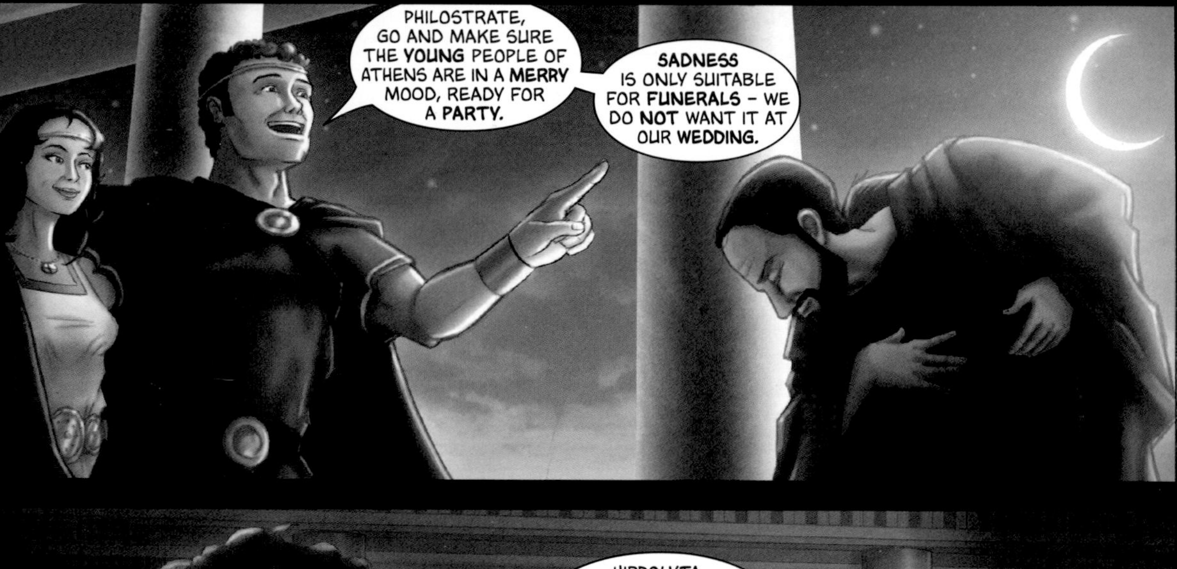
PHILOSTRATE, GO AND MAKE SURE THE YOUNG PEOPLE OF ATHENS ARE IN A MERRY MOOD, READY FOR A PARTY.
SADNESS IS ONLY SUITABLE FOR FUNERALS - WE DO NOT WANT IT AT OUR WEDDING.

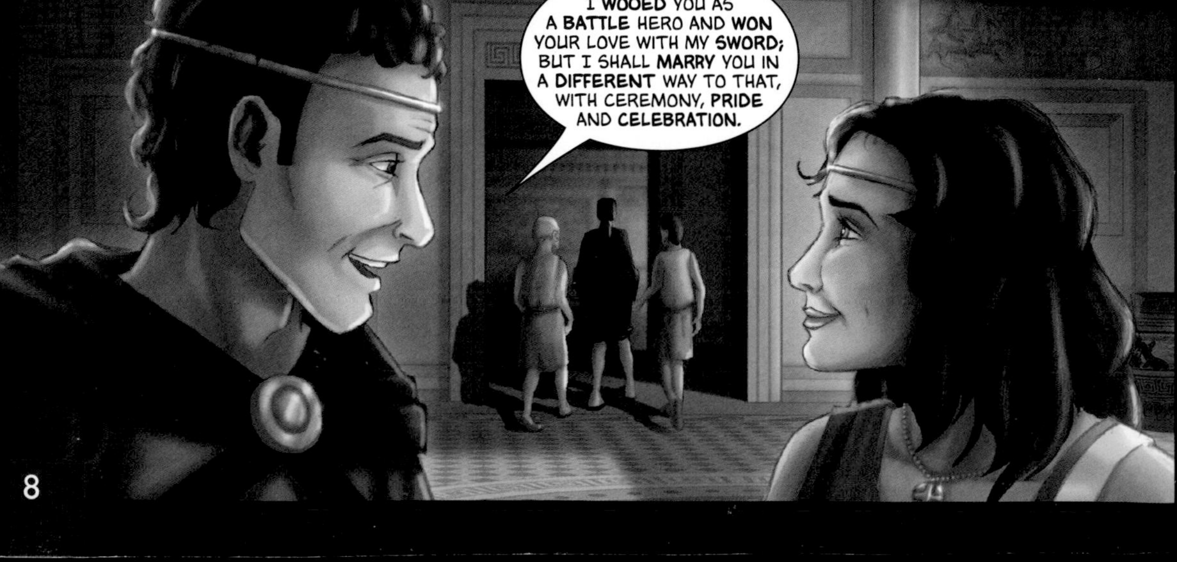
HIPPOLYTA, I WOOED YOU AS A BATTLE HERO AND WON YOUR LOVE WITH MY SWORD; BUT I SHALL MARRY YOU IN A DIFFERENT WAY TO THAT, WITH CEREMONY, PRIDE AND CELEBRATION.

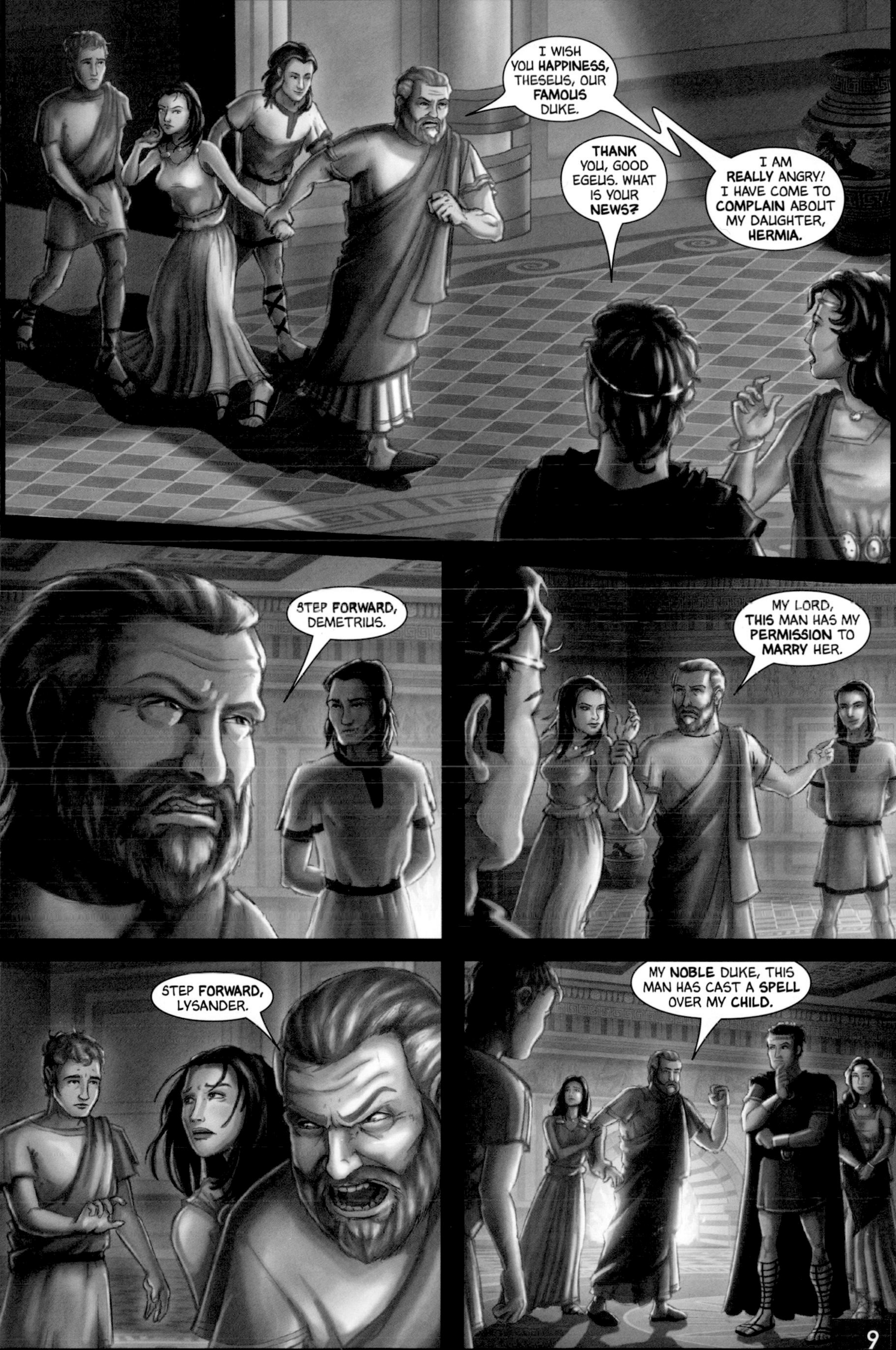
I WISH YOU HAPPINESS, THESEUS, OUR FAMOUS DUKE.
THANK YOU, GOOD EGEUS. WHAT IS YOUR NEWS?
I AM REALLY ANGRY! I HAVE COME TO COMPLAIN ABOUT MY DAUGHTER, HERMIA.
STEP FORWARD, DEMETRIUS.
MY LORD, THIS MAN HAS MY PERMISSION TO MARRY HER.
STEP FORWARD, LYSANDER.
MY NOBLE DUKE, THIS MAN HAS CAST A SPELL OVER MY CHILD.

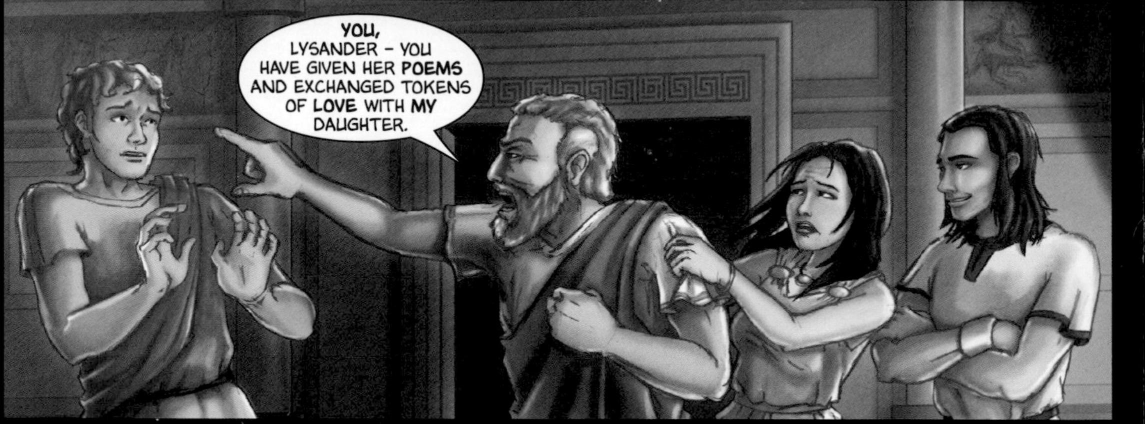
YOU, LYSANDER - YOU HAVE GIVEN HER POEMS AND EXCHANGED TOKENS OF LOVE WITH MY DAUGHTER.

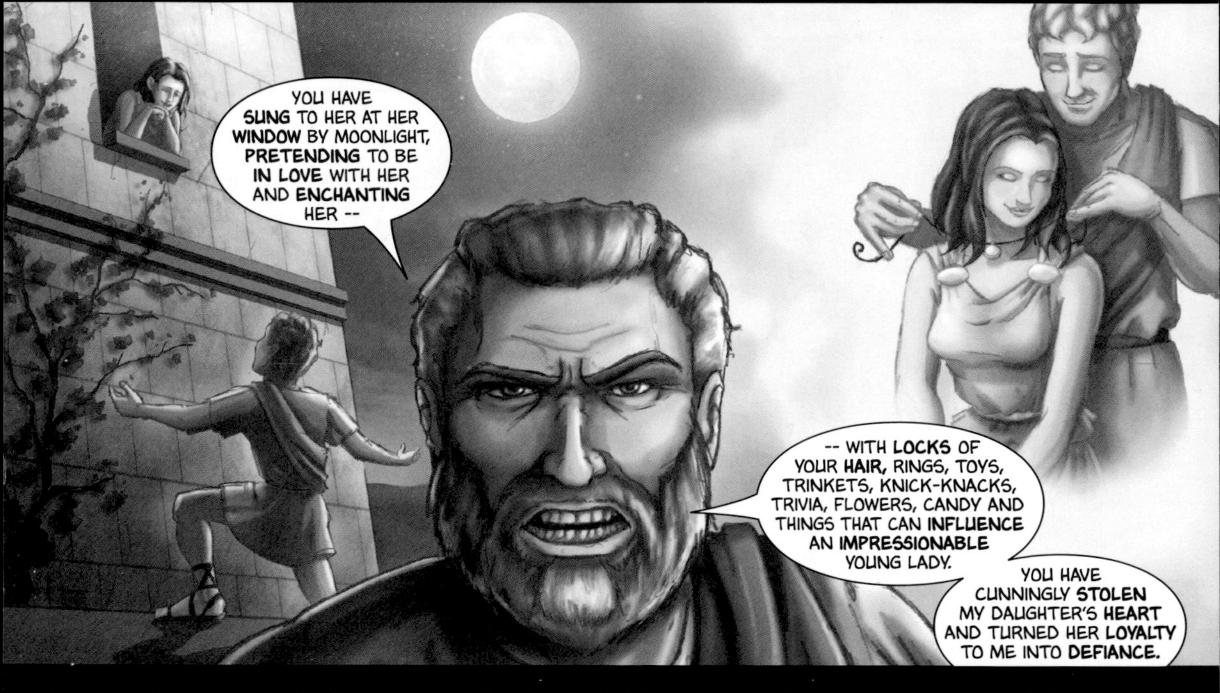
YOU HAVE SUNG TO HER AT HER WINDOW BY MOONLIGHT, PRETENDING TO BE IN LOVE WITH HER AND ENCHANTING HER --
-- WITH LOCKS OF YOUR HAIR, RINGS, TOYS, TRINKETS, KNICK-KNACKS, TRIVIA, FLOWERS, CANDY AND THINGS THAT CAN INFLUENCE AN IMPRESSIONABLE YOUNG LADY.
YOU HAVE CUNNINGLY STOLEN MY DAUGHTER'S HEART AND TURNED HER LOYALTY TO ME INTO DEFIANCE.

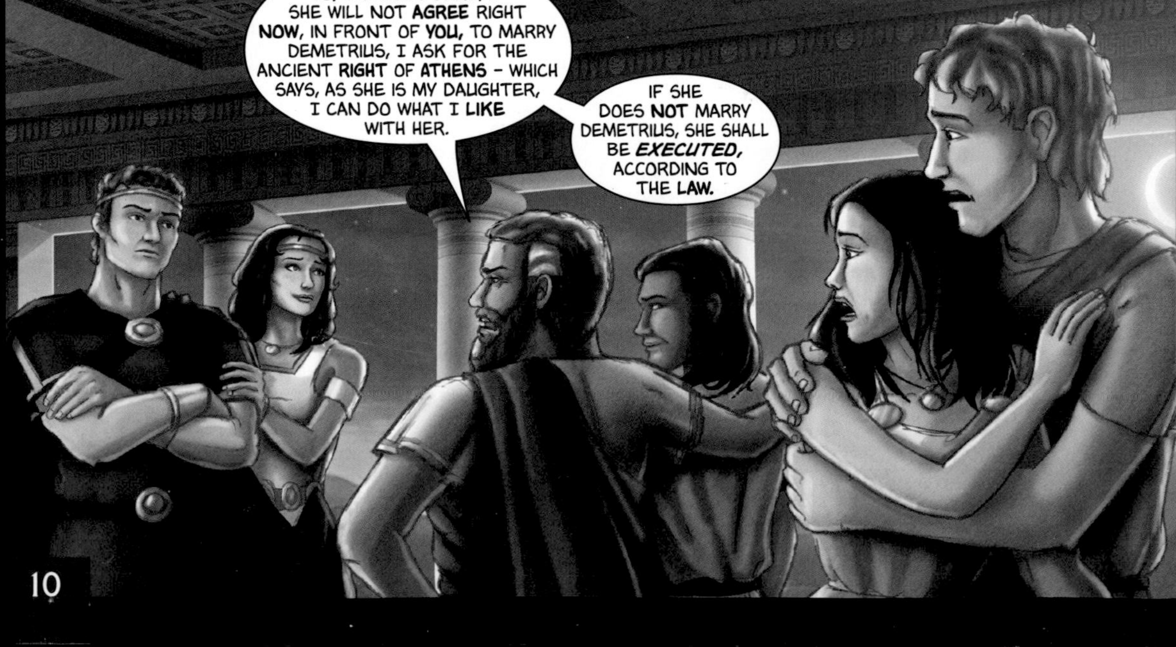
SO, GRACIOUS DUKE, IF SHE WILL NOT AGREE RIGHT NOW, IN FRONT OF YOU, TO MARRY DEMETRIUS, I ASK FOR THE ANCIENT RIGHT OF ATHENS - WHICH SAYS, AS SHE IS MY DAUGHTER, I CAN DO WHAT I LIKE WITH HER.
IF SHE DOES NOT MARRY DEMETRIUS, SHE SHALL BE EXECUTED, ACCORDING TO THE LAW.

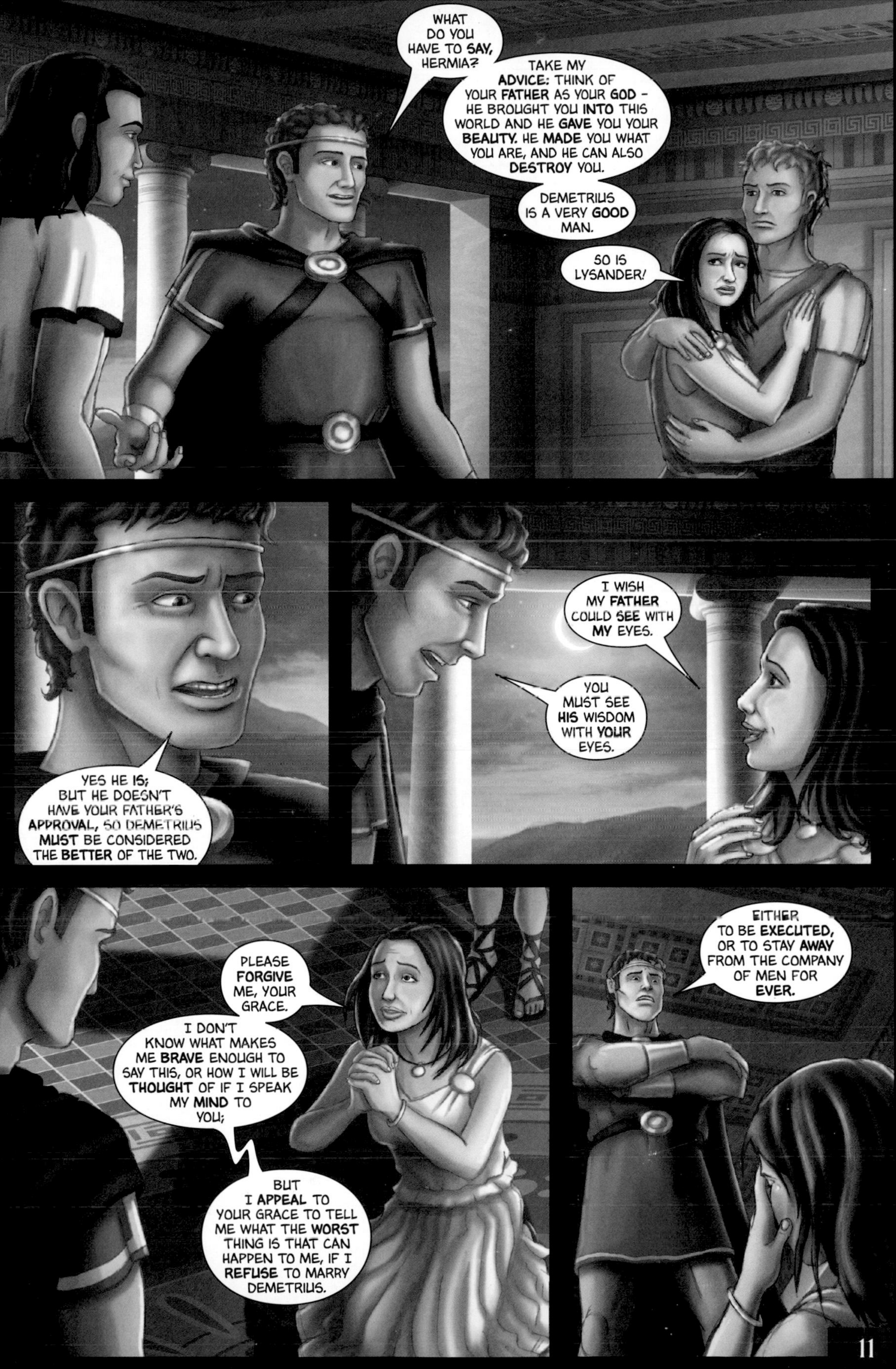
WHAT DO YOU HAVE TO SAY, HERMIA?
TAKE MY ADVICE: THINK OF YOUR FATHER AS YOUR GOD – HE BROUGHT YOU INTO THIS WORLD AND HE GAVE YOU YOUR BEAUTY. HE MADE YOU WHAT YOU ARE, AND HE CAN ALSO DESTROY YOU.
DEMETRIUS IS A VERY GOOD MAN.
SO IS LYSANDER!
YES HE IS; BUT HE DOESN'T HAVE YOUR FATHER'S APPROVAL, SO DEMETRIUS MUST BE CONSIDERED THE BETTER OF THE TWO.
I WISH MY FATHER COULD SEE WITH MY EYES.
YOU MUST SEE HIS WISDOM WITH YOUR EYES.
PLEASE FORGIVE ME, YOUR GRACE.
I DON'T KNOW WHAT MAKES ME BRAVE ENOUGH TO SAY THIS, OR HOW I WILL BE THOUGHT OF IF I SPEAK MY MIND TO YOU;
BUT I APPEAL TO YOUR GRACE TO TELL ME WHAT THE WORST THING IS THAT CAN HAPPEN TO ME, IF I REFUSE TO MARRY DEMETRIUS.
EITHER TO BE EXECUTED, OR TO STAY AWAY FROM THE COMPANY OF MEN FOR EVER.

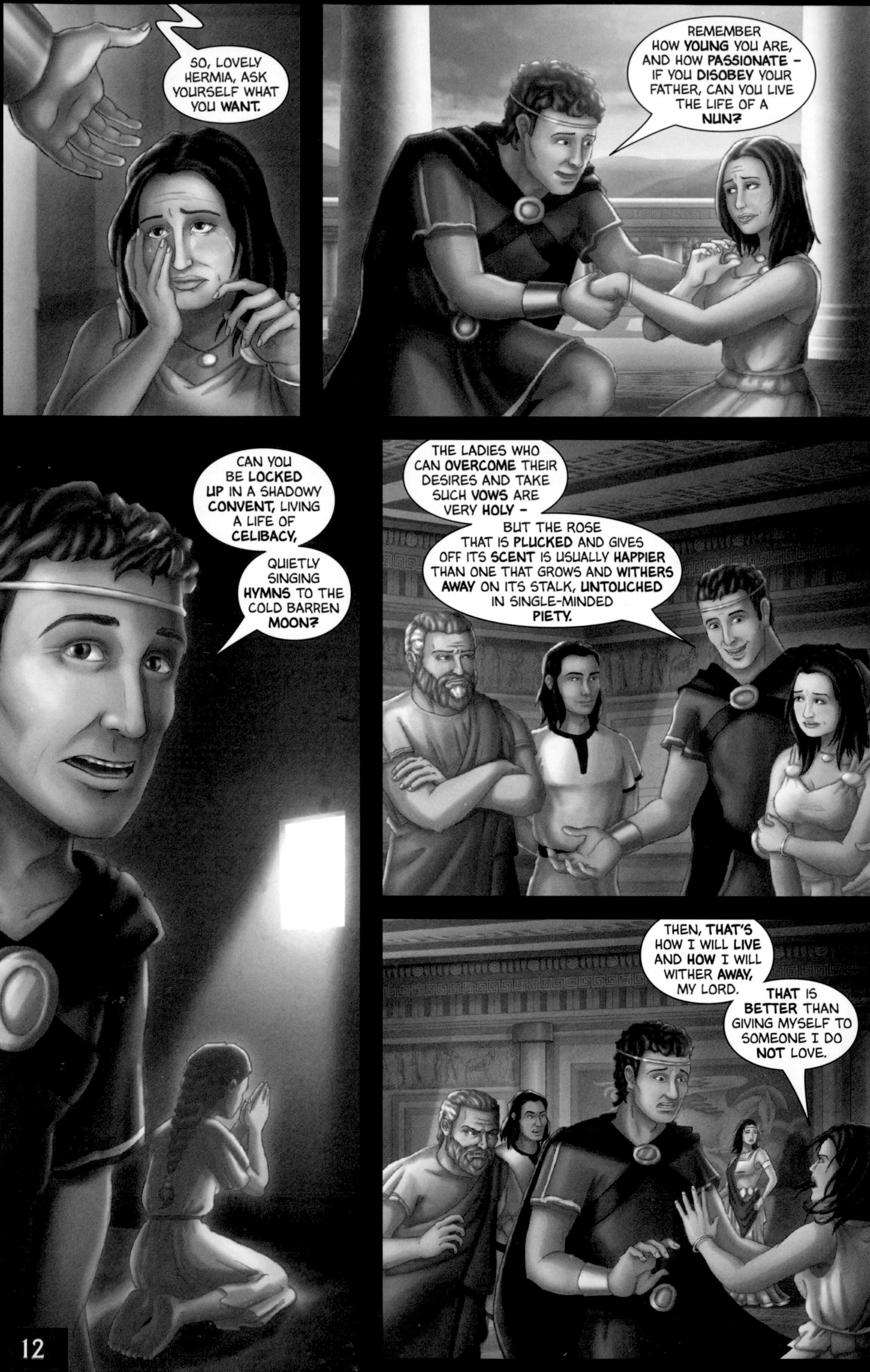

SO, LOVELY HERMIA, ASK YOURSELF WHAT YOU **WANT.**
REMEMBER HOW **YOUNG** YOU ARE, AND HOW **PASSIONATE** – IF YOU **DISOBEY** YOUR FATHER, CAN YOU LIVE THE LIFE OF A **NUN?**
CAN YOU BE **LOCKED UP** IN A SHADOWY **CONVENT,** LIVING A LIFE OF **CELIBACY,**
QUIETLY SINGING **HYMNS** TO THE COLD BARREN **MOON?**
THE LADIES WHO CAN **OVERCOME** THEIR DESIRES AND TAKE SUCH **VOWS** ARE VERY **HOLY** –
BUT THE ROSE THAT IS **PLUCKED** AND GIVES OFF ITS **SCENT** IS USUALLY **HAPPIER** THAN ONE THAT GROWS AND **WITHERS AWAY** ON ITS STALK, **UNTOUCHED** IN SINGLE-MINDED **PIETY.**
THEN, **THAT'S** HOW I WILL **LIVE** AND **HOW** I WILL WITHER **AWAY,** MY LORD.
THAT IS **BETTER** THAN GIVING MYSELF TO SOMEONE I DO **NOT** LOVE.

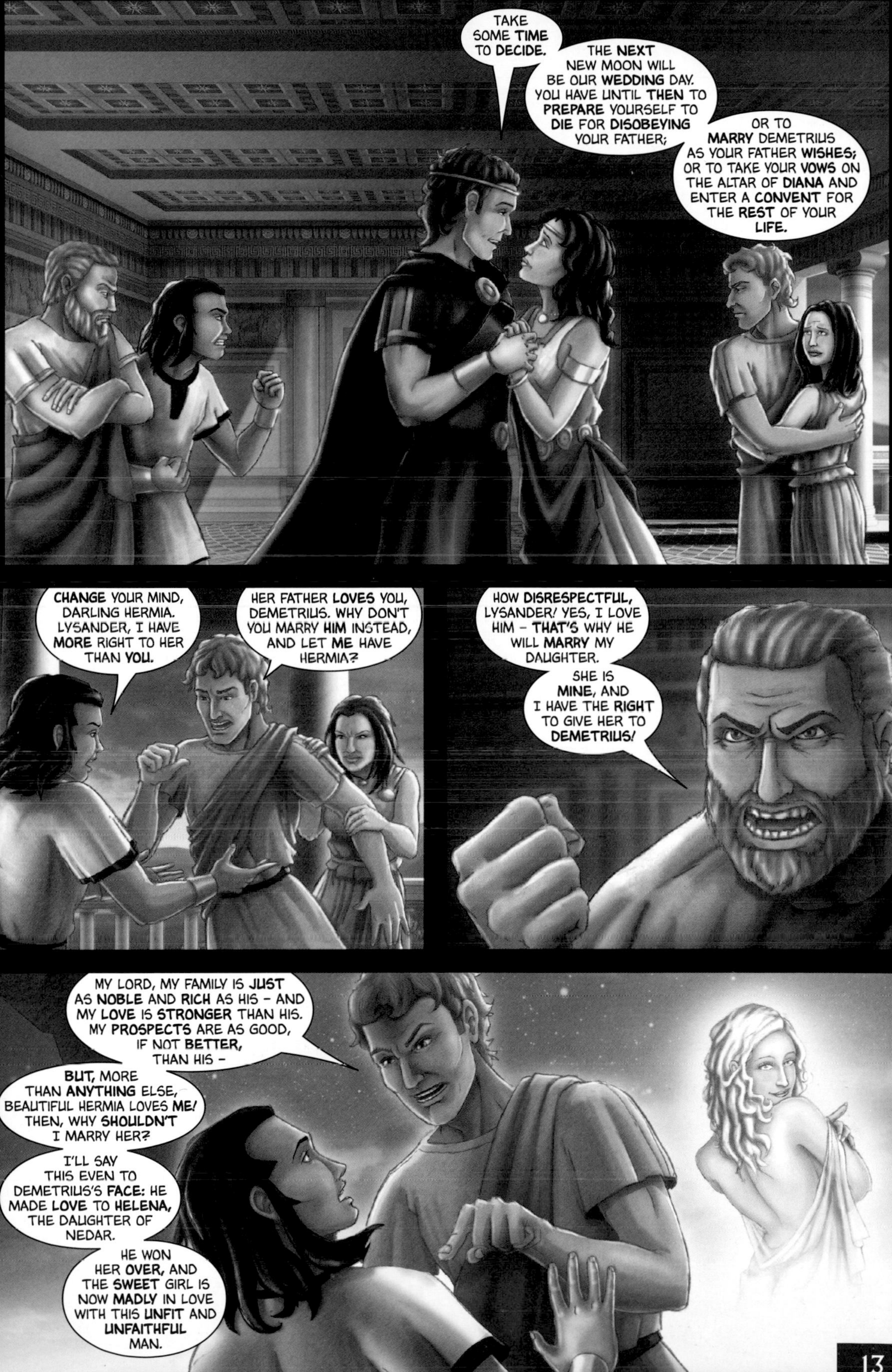
TAKE SOME TIME TO DECIDE.
THE NEXT NEW MOON WILL BE OUR WEDDING DAY. YOU HAVE UNTIL THEN TO PREPARE YOURSELF TO DIE FOR DISOBEYING YOUR FATHER;
OR TO MARRY DEMETRIUS AS YOUR FATHER WISHES; OR TO TAKE YOUR VOWS ON THE ALTAR OF DIANA AND ENTER A CONVENT FOR THE REST OF YOUR LIFE.
CHANGE YOUR MIND, DARLING HERMIA. LYSANDER, I HAVE MORE RIGHT TO HER THAN YOU.
HER FATHER LOVES YOU, DEMETRIUS. WHY DON'T YOU MARRY HIM INSTEAD, AND LET ME HAVE HERMIA?
HOW DISRESPECTFUL, LYSANDER! YES, I LOVE HIM – THAT'S WHY HE WILL MARRY MY DAUGHTER.
SHE IS MINE, AND I HAVE THE RIGHT TO GIVE HER TO DEMETRIUS!
MY LORD, MY FAMILY IS JUST AS NOBLE AND RICH AS HIS – AND MY LOVE IS STRONGER THAN HIS. MY PROSPECTS ARE AS GOOD, IF NOT BETTER, THAN HIS –
BUT, MORE THAN ANYTHING ELSE, BEAUTIFUL HERMIA LOVES ME! THEN, WHY SHOULDN'T I MARRY HER?
I'LL SAY THIS EVEN TO DEMETRIUS'S FACE: HE MADE LOVE TO HELENA, THE DAUGHTER OF NEDAR.
HE WON HER OVER, AND THE SWEET GIRL IS NOW MADLY IN LOVE WITH THIS UNFIT AND UNFAITHFUL MAN.

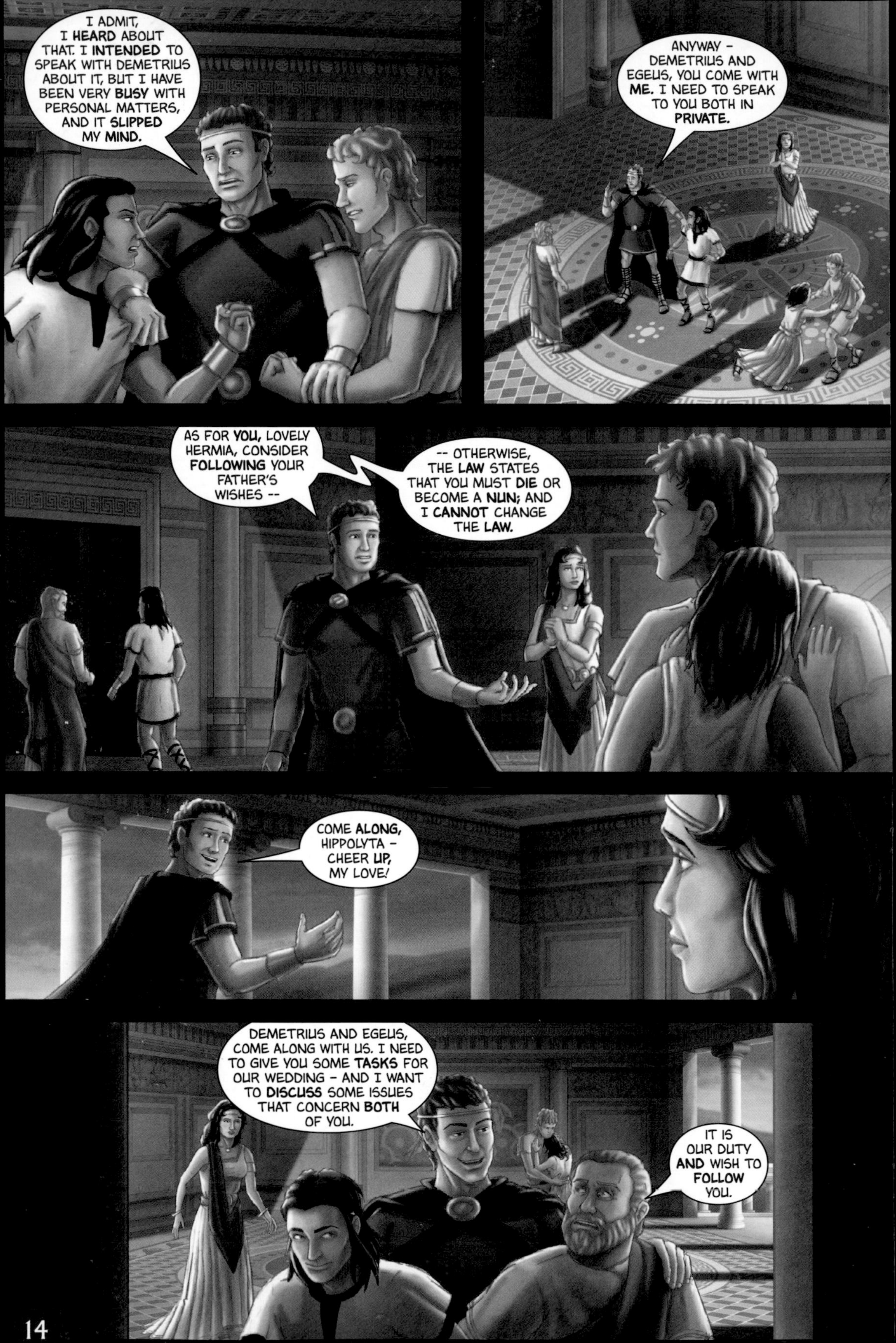
I ADMIT, I HEARD ABOUT THAT. I INTENDED TO SPEAK WITH DEMETRIUS ABOUT IT, BUT I HAVE BEEN VERY BUSY WITH PERSONAL MATTERS, AND IT SLIPPED MY MIND.
ANYWAY – DEMETRIUS AND EGEUS, YOU COME WITH ME. I NEED TO SPEAK TO YOU BOTH IN PRIVATE.
AS FOR YOU, LOVELY HERMIA, CONSIDER FOLLOWING YOUR FATHER'S WISHES --
-- OTHERWISE, THE LAW STATES THAT YOU MUST DIE OR BECOME A NUN; AND I CANNOT CHANGE THE LAW.
COME ALONG, HIPPOLYTA – CHEER UP, MY LOVE!
DEMETRIUS AND EGEUS, COME ALONG WITH US. I NEED TO GIVE YOU SOME TASKS FOR OUR WEDDING – AND I WANT TO DISCUSS SOME ISSUES THAT CONCERN BOTH OF YOU.
IT IS OUR DUTY AND WISH TO FOLLOW YOU.

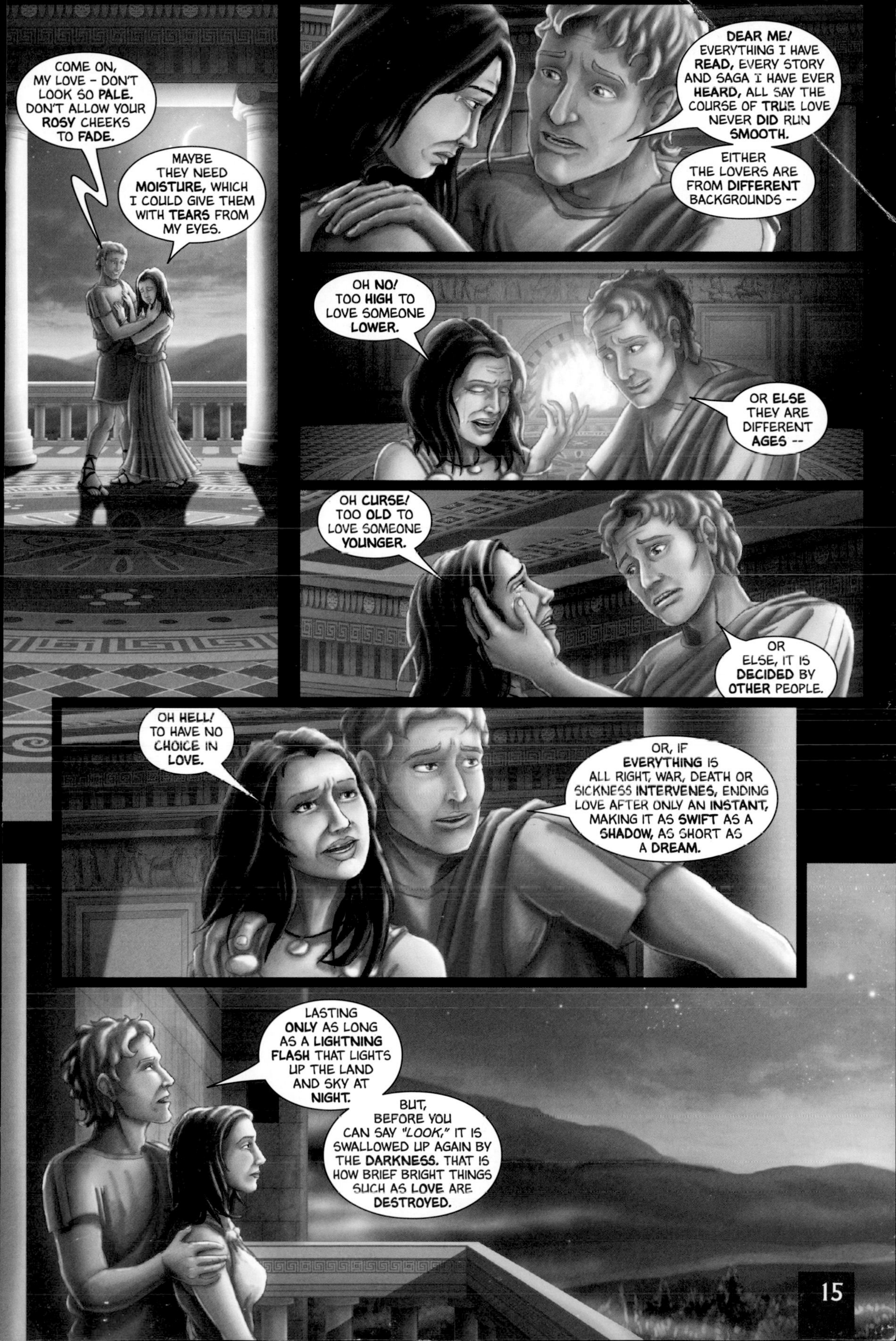
COME ON, MY LOVE - DON'T LOOK SO PALE. DON'T ALLOW YOUR ROSY CHEEKS TO FADE.
MAYBE THEY NEED MOISTURE, WHICH I COULD GIVE THEM WITH TEARS FROM MY EYES.
DEAR ME! EVERYTHING I HAVE READ, EVERY STORY AND SAGA I HAVE EVER HEARD, ALL SAY THE COURSE OF TRUE LOVE NEVER DID RUN SMOOTH.
EITHER THE LOVERS ARE FROM DIFFERENT BACKGROUNDS --
OH NO! TOO HIGH TO LOVE SOMEONE LOWER.
OR ELSE THEY ARE DIFFERENT AGES --
OH CURSE! TOO OLD TO LOVE SOMEONE YOUNGER.
OR ELSE, IT IS DECIDED BY OTHER PEOPLE.
OH HELL! TO HAVE NO CHOICE IN LOVE.
OR, IF EVERYTHING IS ALL RIGHT, WAR, DEATH OR SICKNESS INTERVENES, ENDING LOVE AFTER ONLY AN INSTANT, MAKING IT AS SWIFT AS A SHADOW, AS SHORT AS A DREAM.
LASTING ONLY AS LONG AS A LIGHTNING FLASH THAT LIGHTS UP THE LAND AND SKY AT NIGHT.
BUT, BEFORE YOU CAN SAY "LOOK," IT IS SWALLOWED UP AGAIN BY THE DARKNESS. THAT IS HOW BRIEF BRIGHT THINGS SUCH AS LOVE ARE DESTROYED.

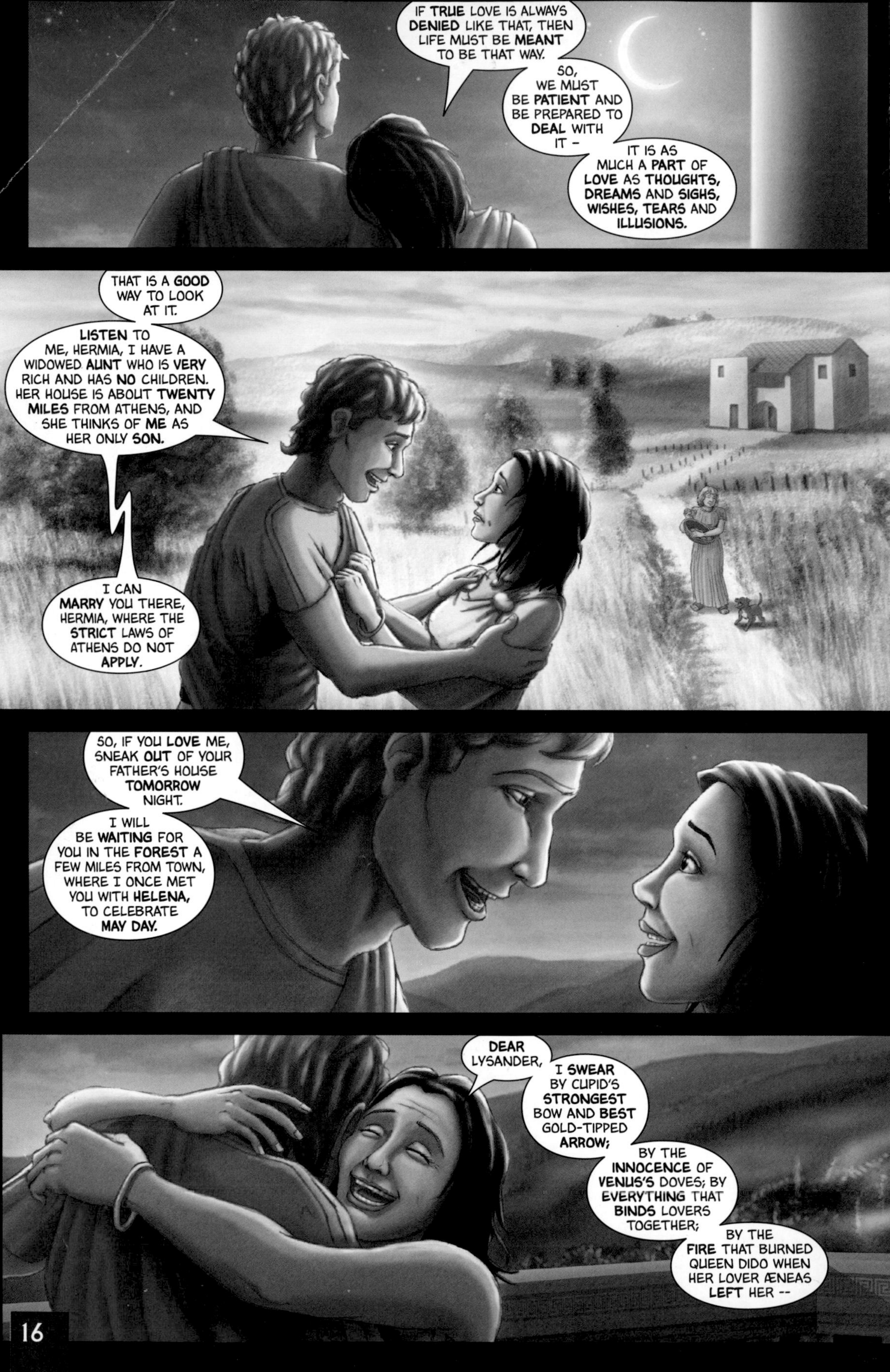
IF TRUE LOVE IS ALWAYS DENIED LIKE THAT, THEN LIFE MUST BE MEANT TO BE THAT WAY.
SO, WE MUST BE PATIENT AND BE PREPARED TO DEAL WITH IT –
IT IS AS MUCH A PART OF LOVE AS THOUGHTS, DREAMS AND SIGHS, WISHES, TEARS AND ILLUSIONS.
THAT IS A GOOD WAY TO LOOK AT IT.
LISTEN TO ME, HERMIA, I HAVE A WIDOWED AUNT WHO IS VERY RICH AND HAS NO CHILDREN. HER HOUSE IS ABOUT TWENTY MILES FROM ATHENS, AND SHE THINKS OF ME AS HER ONLY SON.
I CAN MARRY YOU THERE, HERMIA, WHERE THE STRICT LAWS OF ATHENS DO NOT APPLY.
SO, IF YOU LOVE ME, SNEAK OUT OF YOUR FATHER'S HOUSE TOMORROW NIGHT.
I WILL BE WAITING FOR YOU IN THE FOREST A FEW MILES FROM TOWN, WHERE I ONCE MET YOU WITH HELENA, TO CELEBRATE MAY DAY.
DEAR LYSANDER,
I SWEAR BY CUPID'S STRONGEST BOW AND BEST GOLD-TIPPED ARROW;
BY THE INNOCENCE OF VENUS'S DOVES; BY EVERYTHING THAT BINDS LOVERS TOGETHER;
BY THE FIRE THAT BURNED QUEEN DIDO WHEN HER LOVER ÆNEAS LEFT HER --

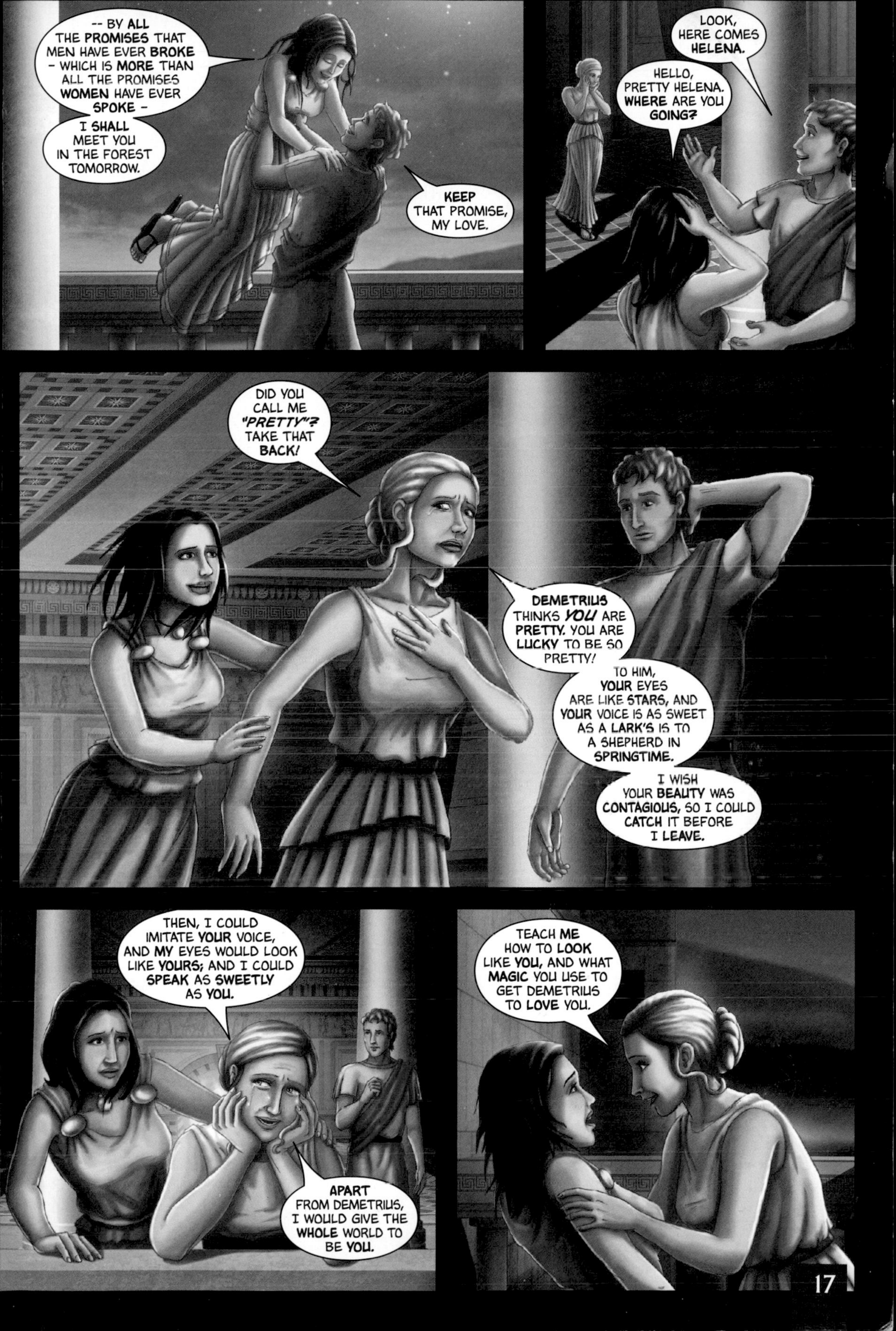
-- BY ALL THE PROMISES THAT MEN HAVE EVER BROKE - WHICH IS MORE THAN ALL THE PROMISES WOMEN HAVE EVER SPOKE -
I SHALL MEET YOU IN THE FOREST TOMORROW.
KEEP THAT PROMISE, MY LOVE.
LOOK, HERE COMES HELENA.
HELLO, PRETTY HELENA. WHERE ARE YOU GOING?
DID YOU CALL ME "PRETTY"? TAKE THAT BACK!
DEMETRIUS THINKS YOU ARE PRETTY. YOU ARE LUCKY TO BE SO PRETTY!
TO HIM, YOUR EYES ARE LIKE STARS, AND YOUR VOICE IS AS SWEET AS A LARK'S IS TO A SHEPHERD IN SPRINGTIME.
I WISH YOUR BEAUTY WAS CONTAGIOUS, SO I COULD CATCH IT BEFORE I LEAVE.
THEN, I COULD IMITATE YOUR VOICE, AND MY EYES WOULD LOOK LIKE YOURS; AND I COULD SPEAK AS SWEETLY AS YOU.
APART FROM DEMETRIUS, I WOULD GIVE THE WHOLE WORLD TO BE YOU.
TEACH ME HOW TO LOOK LIKE YOU, AND WHAT MAGIC YOU USE TO GET DEMETRIUS TO LOVE YOU.

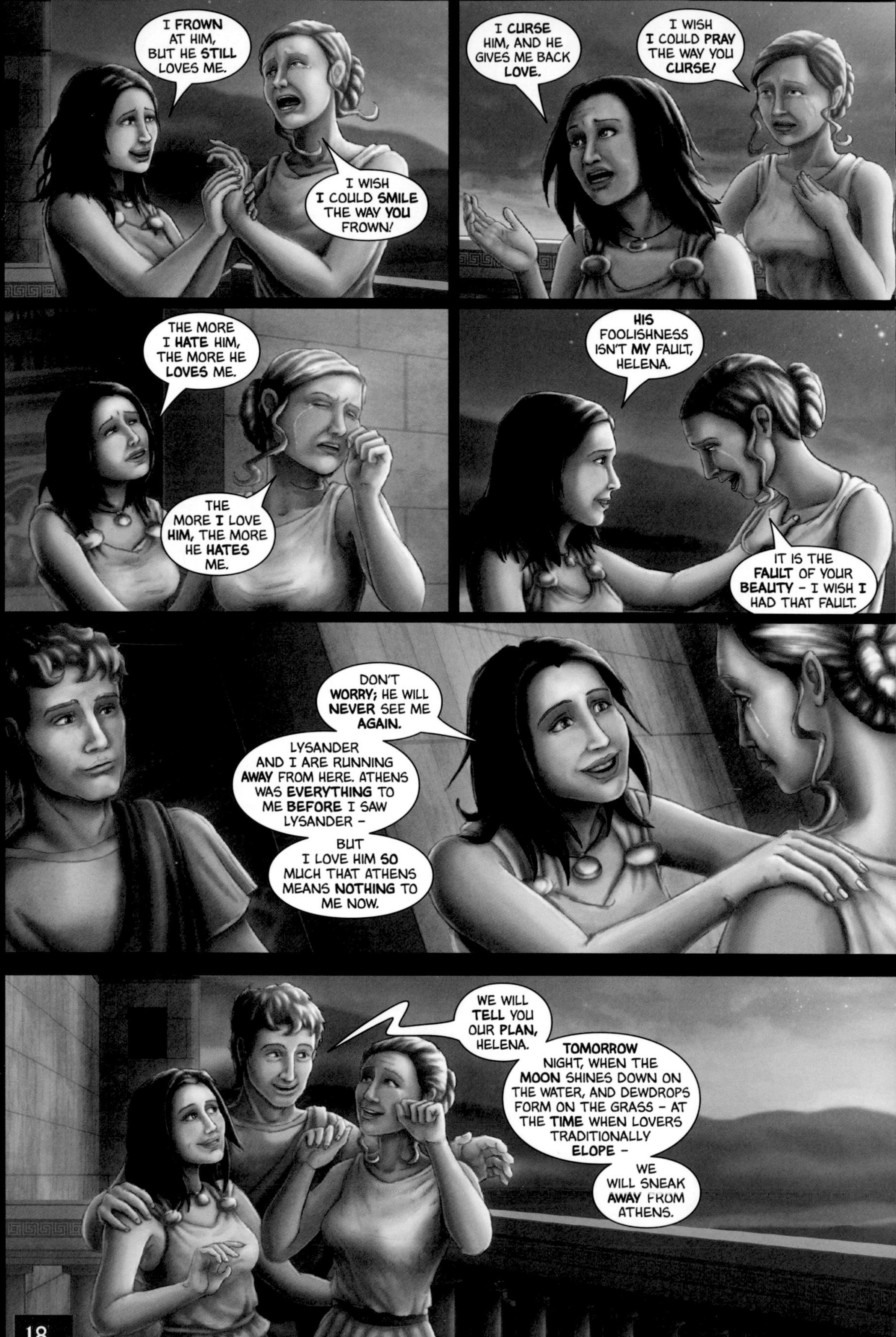
I FROWN AT HIM, BUT HE STILL LOVES ME.
I WISH I COULD SMILE THE WAY YOU FROWN!
I CURSE HIM, AND HE GIVES ME BACK LOVE.
I WISH I COULD PRAY THE WAY YOU CURSE!
THE MORE I HATE HIM, THE MORE HE LOVES ME.
THE MORE I LOVE HIM, THE MORE HE HATES ME.
HIS FOOLISHNESS ISN'T MY FAULT, HELENA.
IT IS THE FAULT OF YOUR BEAUTY – I WISH I HAD THAT FAULT.
DON'T WORRY; HE WILL NEVER SEE ME AGAIN.
LYSANDER AND I ARE RUNNING AWAY FROM HERE. ATHENS WAS EVERYTHING TO ME BEFORE I SAW LYSANDER –
BUT I LOVE HIM SO MUCH THAT ATHENS MEANS NOTHING TO ME NOW.
WE WILL TELL YOU OUR PLAN, HELENA.
TOMORROW NIGHT, WHEN THE MOON SHINES DOWN ON THE WATER, AND DEWDROPS FORM ON THE GRASS – AT THE TIME WHEN LOVERS TRADITIONALLY ELOPE –
WE WILL SNEAK AWAY FROM ATHENS.

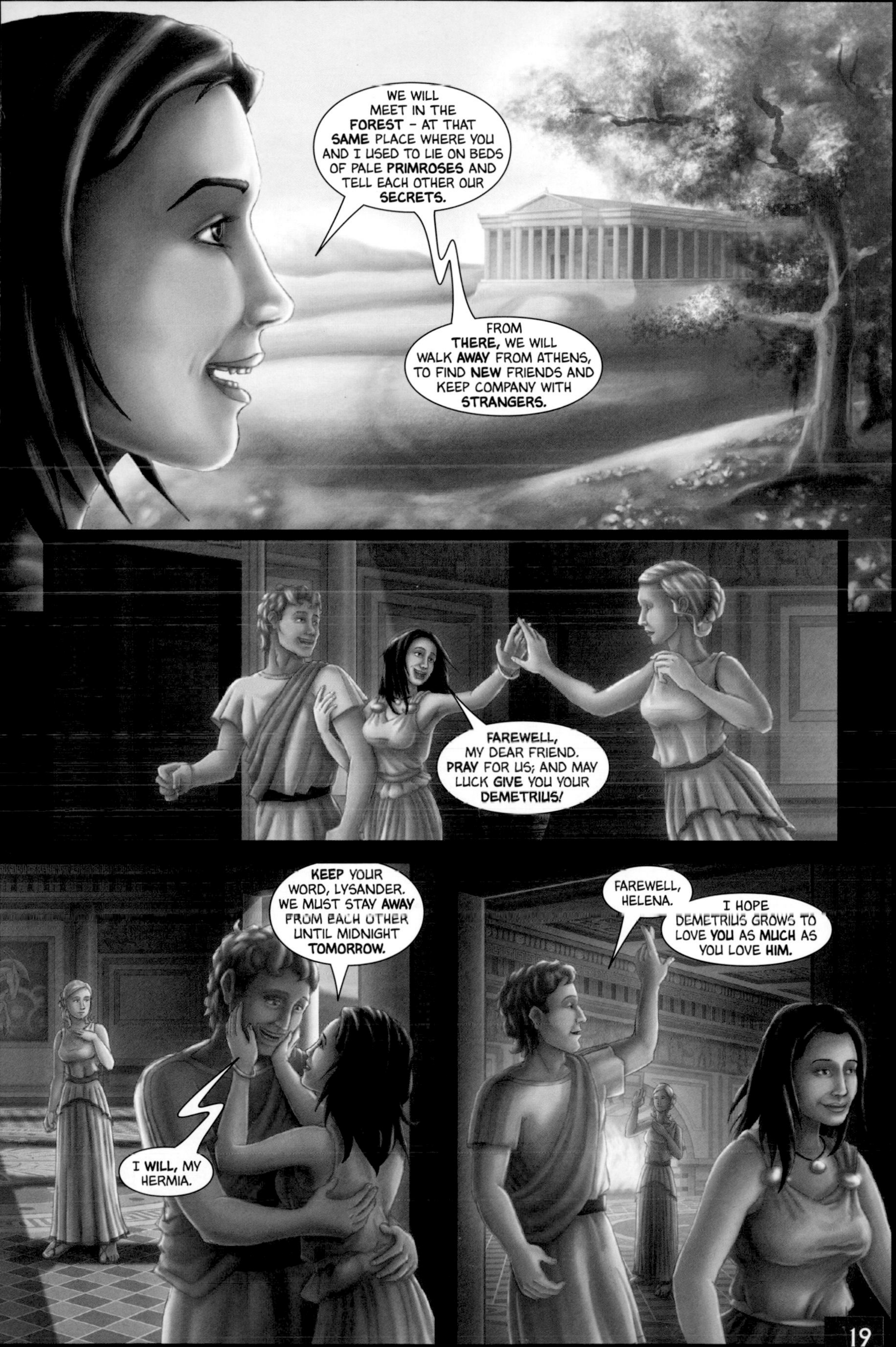
WE WILL MEET IN THE FOREST – AT THAT SAME PLACE WHERE YOU AND I USED TO LIE ON BEDS OF PALE PRIMROSES AND TELL EACH OTHER OUR SECRETS.
FROM THERE, WE WILL WALK AWAY FROM ATHENS, TO FIND NEW FRIENDS AND KEEP COMPANY WITH STRANGERS.
FAREWELL, MY DEAR FRIEND. PRAY FOR US; AND MAY LUCK GIVE YOU YOUR DEMETRIUS!
KEEP YOUR WORD, LYSANDER. WE MUST STAY AWAY FROM EACH OTHER UNTIL MIDNIGHT TOMORROW.
I WILL, MY HERMIA.
FAREWELL, HELENA.
I HOPE DEMETRIUS GROWS TO LOVE YOU AS MUCH AS YOU LOVE HIM.

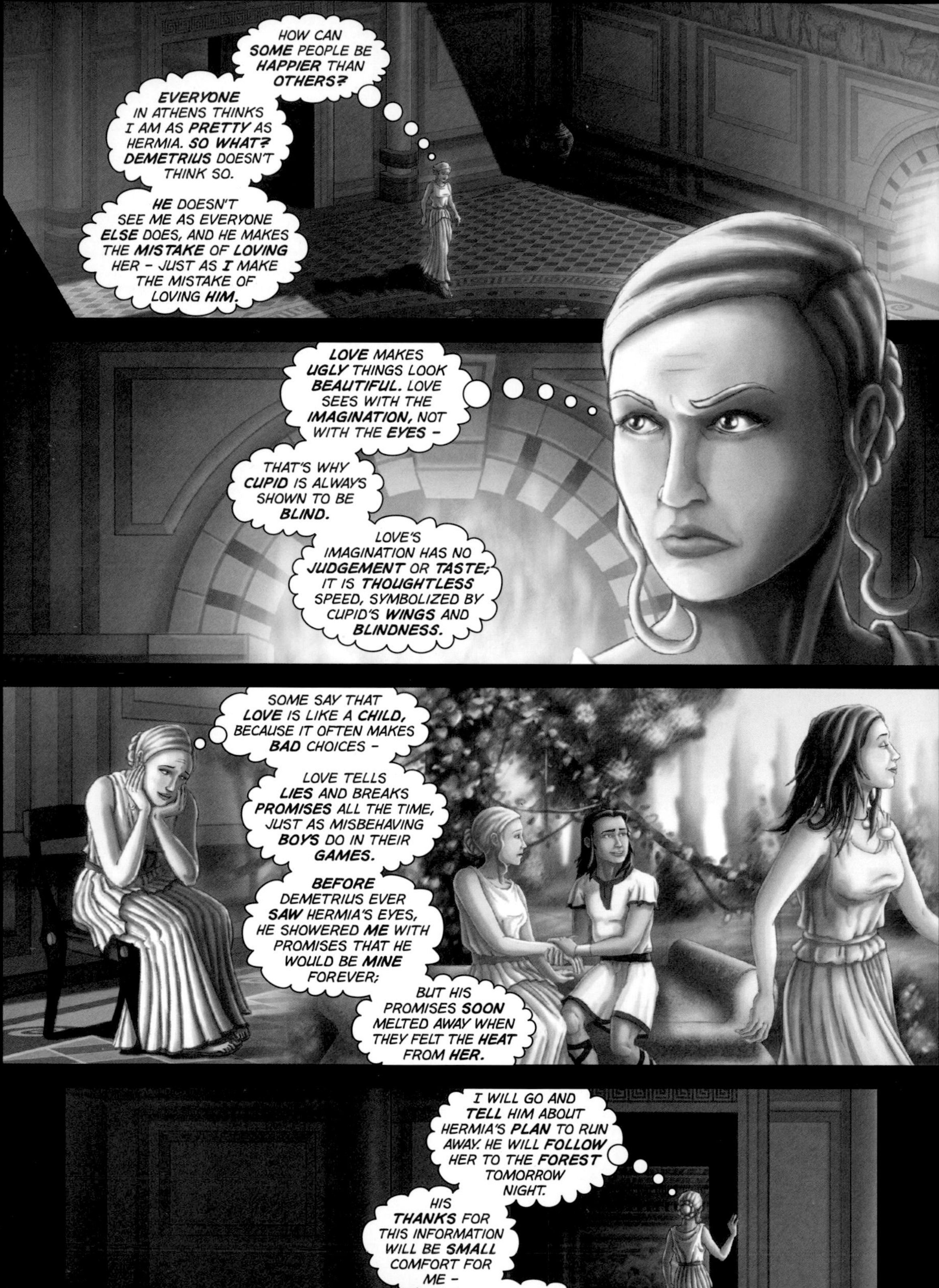
HOW CAN SOME PEOPLE BE HAPPIER THAN OTHERS?
EVERYONE IN ATHENS THINKS I AM AS PRETTY AS HERMIA. SO WHAT? DEMETRIUS DOESN'T THINK SO.
HE DOESN'T SEE ME AS EVERYONE ELSE DOES, AND HE MAKES THE MISTAKE OF LOVING HER – JUST AS I MAKE THE MISTAKE OF LOVING HIM.
LOVE MAKES UGLY THINGS LOOK BEAUTIFUL. LOVE SEES WITH THE IMAGINATION, NOT WITH THE EYES –
THAT'S WHY CUPID IS ALWAYS SHOWN TO BE BLIND.
LOVE'S IMAGINATION HAS NO JUDGEMENT OR TASTE; IT IS THOUGHTLESS SPEED, SYMBOLIZED BY CUPID'S WINGS AND BLINDNESS.
SOME SAY THAT LOVE IS LIKE A CHILD, BECAUSE IT OFTEN MAKES BAD CHOICES –
LOVE TELLS LIES AND BREAKS PROMISES ALL THE TIME, JUST AS MISBEHAVING BOYS DO IN THEIR GAMES.
BEFORE DEMETRIUS EVER SAW HERMIA'S EYES, HE SHOWERED ME WITH PROMISES THAT HE WOULD BE MINE FOREVER;
BUT HIS PROMISES SOON MELTED AWAY WHEN THEY FELT THE HEAT FROM HER.
I WILL GO AND TELL HIM ABOUT HERMIA'S PLAN TO RUN AWAY. HE WILL FOLLOW HER TO THE FOREST TOMORROW NIGHT.
HIS THANKS FOR THIS INFORMATION WILL BE SMALL COMFORT FOR ME –
BUT IT WILL EASE MY PAIN TO SEE HIM GO, AND THEN COME BACK AGAIN.

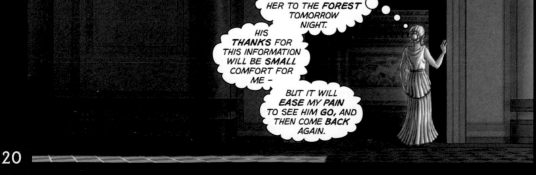

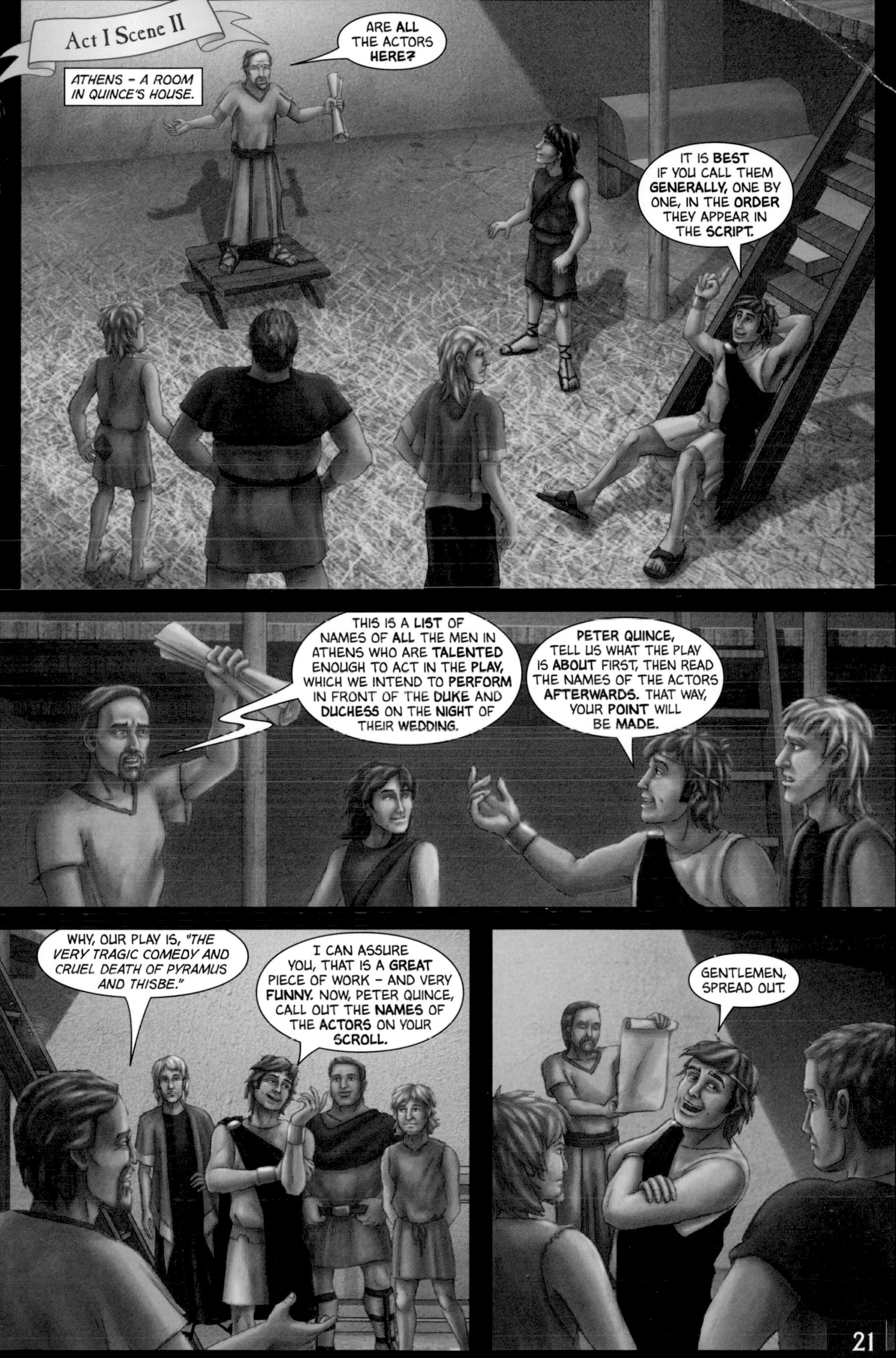
Act I Scene II
ATHENS - A ROOM IN QUINCE'S HOUSE.
ARE ALL THE ACTORS HERE?
IT IS BEST IF YOU CALL THEM GENERALLY, ONE BY ONE, IN THE ORDER THEY APPEAR IN THE SCRIPT.
THIS IS A LIST OF NAMES OF ALL THE MEN IN ATHENS WHO ARE TALENTED ENOUGH TO ACT IN THE PLAY, WHICH WE INTEND TO PERFORM IN FRONT OF THE DUKE AND DUCHESS ON THE NIGHT OF THEIR WEDDING.
PETER QUINCE, TELL US WHAT THE PLAY IS ABOUT FIRST, THEN READ THE NAMES OF THE ACTORS AFTERWARDS. THAT WAY, YOUR POINT WILL BE MADE.
WHY, OUR PLAY IS, "THE VERY TRAGIC COMEDY AND CRUEL DEATH OF PYRAMUS AND THISBE."
I CAN ASSURE YOU, THAT IS A GREAT PIECE OF WORK - AND VERY FUNNY. NOW, PETER QUINCE, CALL OUT THE NAMES OF THE ACTORS ON YOUR SCROLL.
GENTLEMEN, SPREAD OUT.

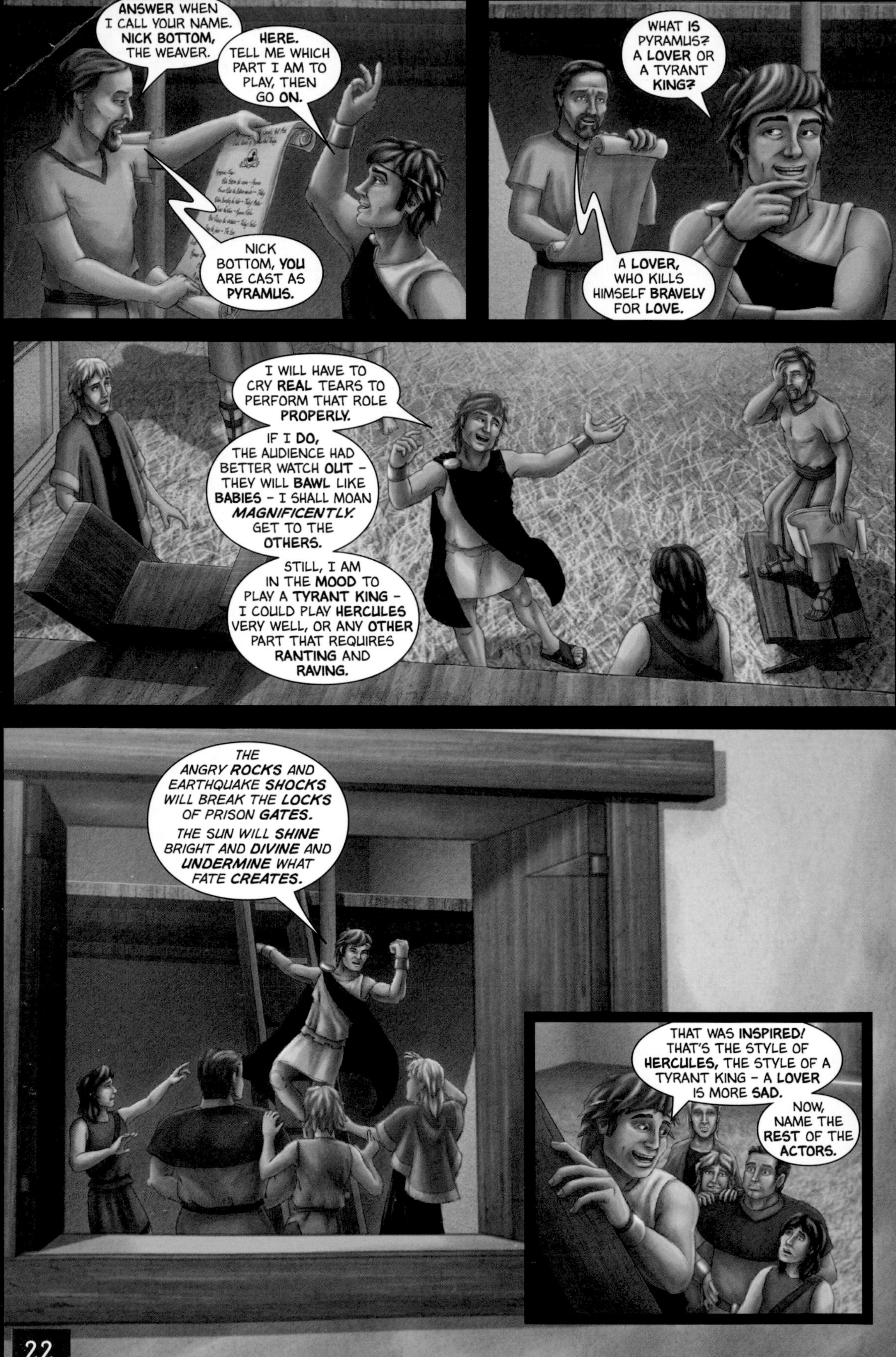
ANSWER WHEN I CALL YOUR NAME. NICK BOTTOM, THE WEAVER.
HERE. TELL ME WHICH PART I AM TO PLAY, THEN GO ON.
NICK BOTTOM, YOU ARE CAST AS PYRAMUS.
WHAT IS PYRAMUS? A LOVER OR A TYRANT KING?
A LOVER, WHO KILLS HIMSELF BRAVELY FOR LOVE.
I WILL HAVE TO CRY REAL TEARS TO PERFORM THAT ROLE PROPERLY.
IF I DO, THE AUDIENCE HAD BETTER WATCH OUT – THEY WILL BAWL LIKE BABIES – I SHALL MOAN MAGNIFICENTLY. GET TO THE OTHERS.
STILL, I AM IN THE MOOD TO PLAY A TYRANT KING – I COULD PLAY HERCULES VERY WELL, OR ANY OTHER PART THAT REQUIRES RANTING AND RAVING.
THE ANGRY ROCKS AND EARTHQUAKE SHOCKS WILL BREAK THE LOCKS OF PRISON GATES.
THE SUN WILL SHINE BRIGHT AND DIVINE AND UNDERMINE WHAT FATE CREATES.
THAT WAS INSPIRED! THAT'S THE STYLE OF HERCULES, THE STYLE OF A TYRANT KING – A LOVER IS MORE SAD.
NOW, NAME THE REST OF THE ACTORS.

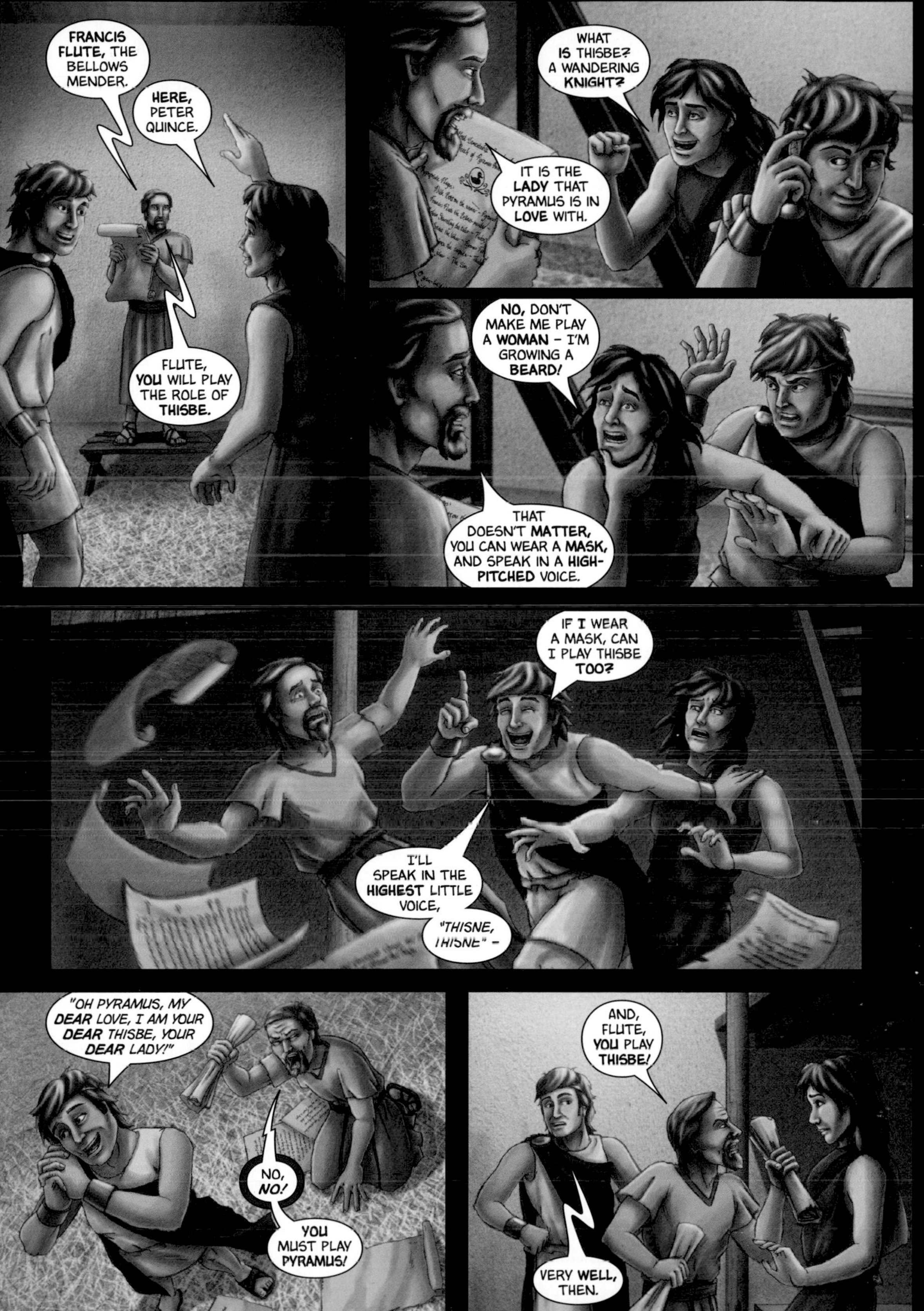
FRANCIS FLUTE, THE BELLOWS MENDER.
HERE, PETER QUINCE.
FLUTE, YOU WILL PLAY THE ROLE OF THISBE.
WHAT IS THISBE? A WANDERING KNIGHT?
IT IS THE LADY THAT PYRAMUS IS IN LOVE WITH.
NO, DON'T MAKE ME PLAY A WOMAN – I'M GROWING A BEARD!
THAT DOESN'T MATTER, YOU CAN WEAR A MASK, AND SPEAK IN A HIGH-PITCHED VOICE.
IF I WEAR A MASK, CAN I PLAY THISBE TOO?
I'LL SPEAK IN THE HIGHEST LITTLE VOICE,
"THISNE, THISNE" –
"OH PYRAMUS, MY DEAR LOVE, I AM YOUR DEAR THISBE, YOUR DEAR LADY!"
NO, NO!
YOU MUST PLAY PYRAMUS!
AND, FLUTE, YOU PLAY THISBE!
VERY WELL, THEN.

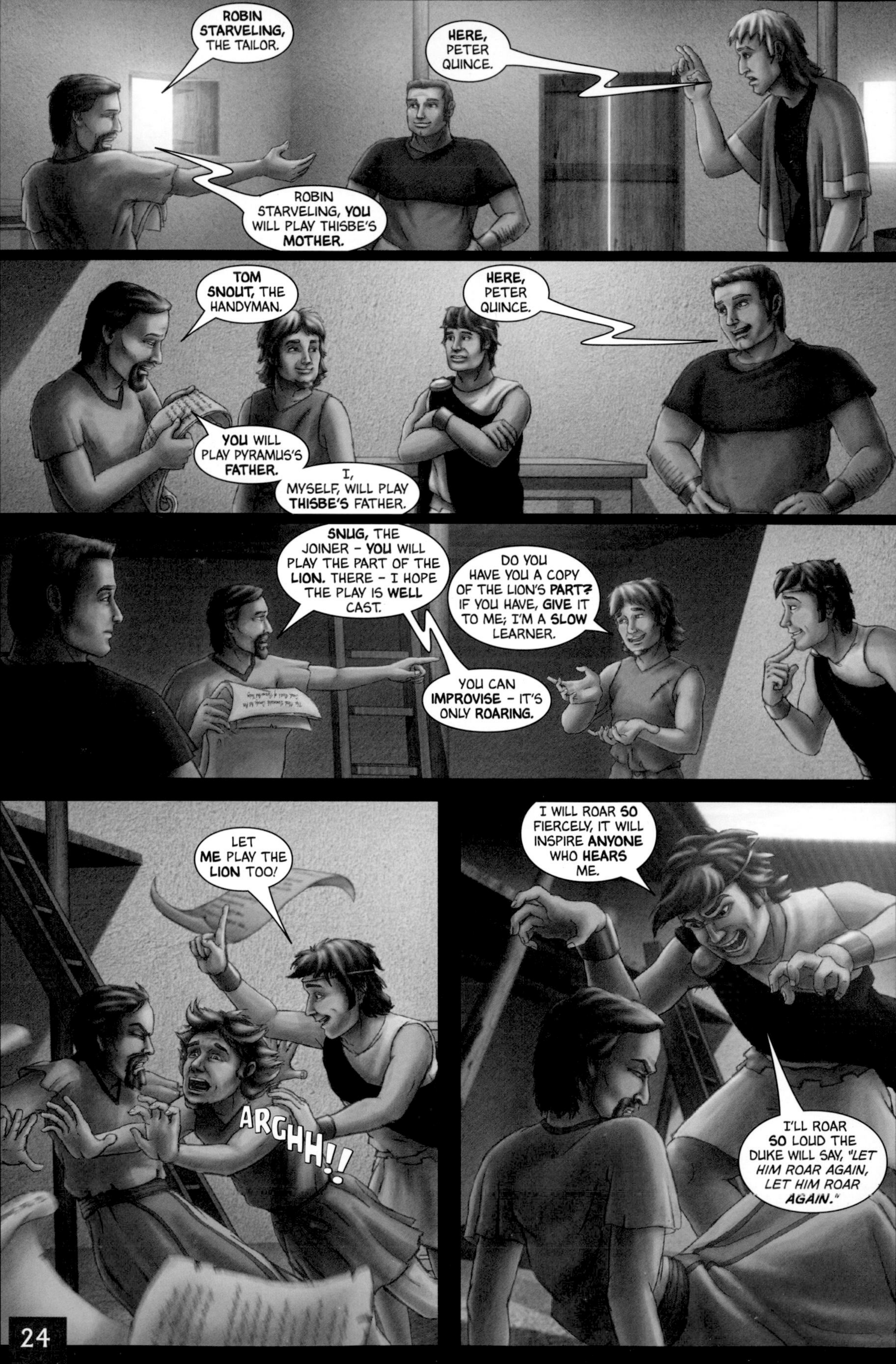
ROBIN STARVELING, THE TAILOR.
HERE, PETER QUINCE.
ROBIN STARVELING, YOU WILL PLAY THISBE'S MOTHER.
TOM SNOUT, THE HANDYMAN.
HERE, PETER QUINCE.
YOU WILL PLAY PYRAMUS'S FATHER.
I, MYSELF, WILL PLAY THISBE'S FATHER.
SNUG, THE JOINER – YOU WILL PLAY THE PART OF THE LION. THERE – I HOPE THE PLAY IS WELL CAST.
DO YOU HAVE YOU A COPY OF THE LION'S PART? IF YOU HAVE, GIVE IT TO ME; I'M A SLOW LEARNER.
YOU CAN IMPROVISE – IT'S ONLY ROARING.
LET ME PLAY THE LION TOO!
ARGHH!!
I WILL ROAR SO FIERCELY, IT WILL INSPIRE ANYONE WHO HEARS ME.
I'LL ROAR SO LOUD THE DUKE WILL SAY, "LET HIM ROAR AGAIN, LET HIM ROAR AGAIN."

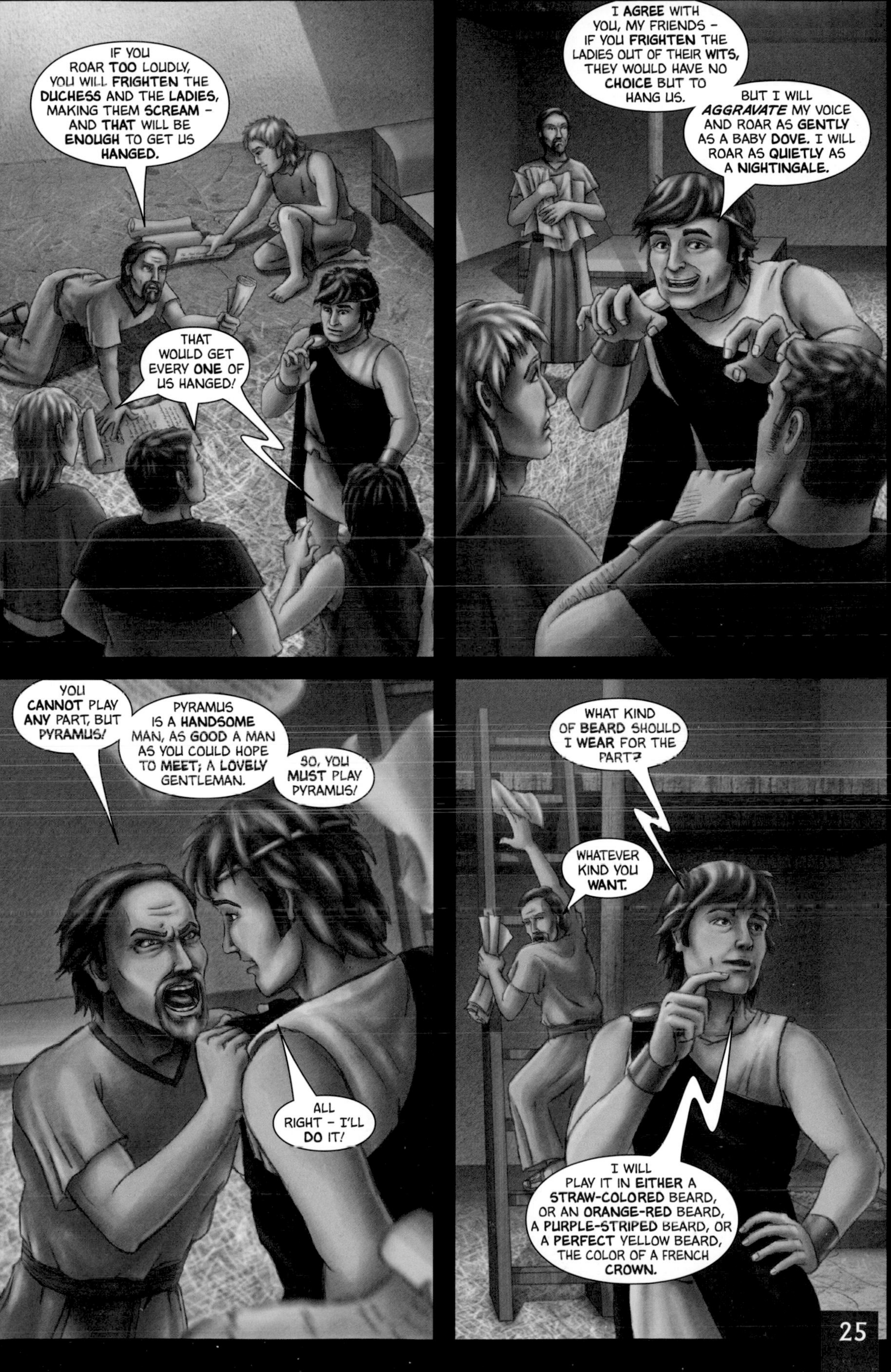
IF YOU ROAR TOO LOUDLY, YOU WILL FRIGHTEN THE DUCHESS AND THE LADIES, MAKING THEM SCREAM – AND THAT WILL BE ENOUGH TO GET US HANGED.
THAT WOULD GET EVERY ONE OF US HANGED!
I AGREE WITH YOU, MY FRIENDS – IF YOU FRIGHTEN THE LADIES OUT OF THEIR WITS, THEY WOULD HAVE NO CHOICE BUT TO HANG US.
BUT I WILL AGGRAVATE MY VOICE AND ROAR AS GENTLY AS A BABY DOVE. I WILL ROAR AS QUIETLY AS A NIGHTINGALE.
YOU CANNOT PLAY ANY PART, BUT PYRAMUS!
PYRAMUS IS A HANDSOME MAN, AS GOOD A MAN AS YOU COULD HOPE TO MEET; A LOVELY GENTLEMAN.
SO, YOU MUST PLAY PYRAMUS!
ALL RIGHT – I'LL DO IT!
WHAT KIND OF BEARD SHOULD I WEAR FOR THE PART?
WHATEVER KIND YOU WANT.
I WILL PLAY IT IN EITHER A STRAW-COLORED BEARD, OR AN ORANGE-RED BEARD, A PURPLE-STRIPED BEARD, OR A PERFECT YELLOW BEARD, THE COLOR OF A FRENCH CROWN.

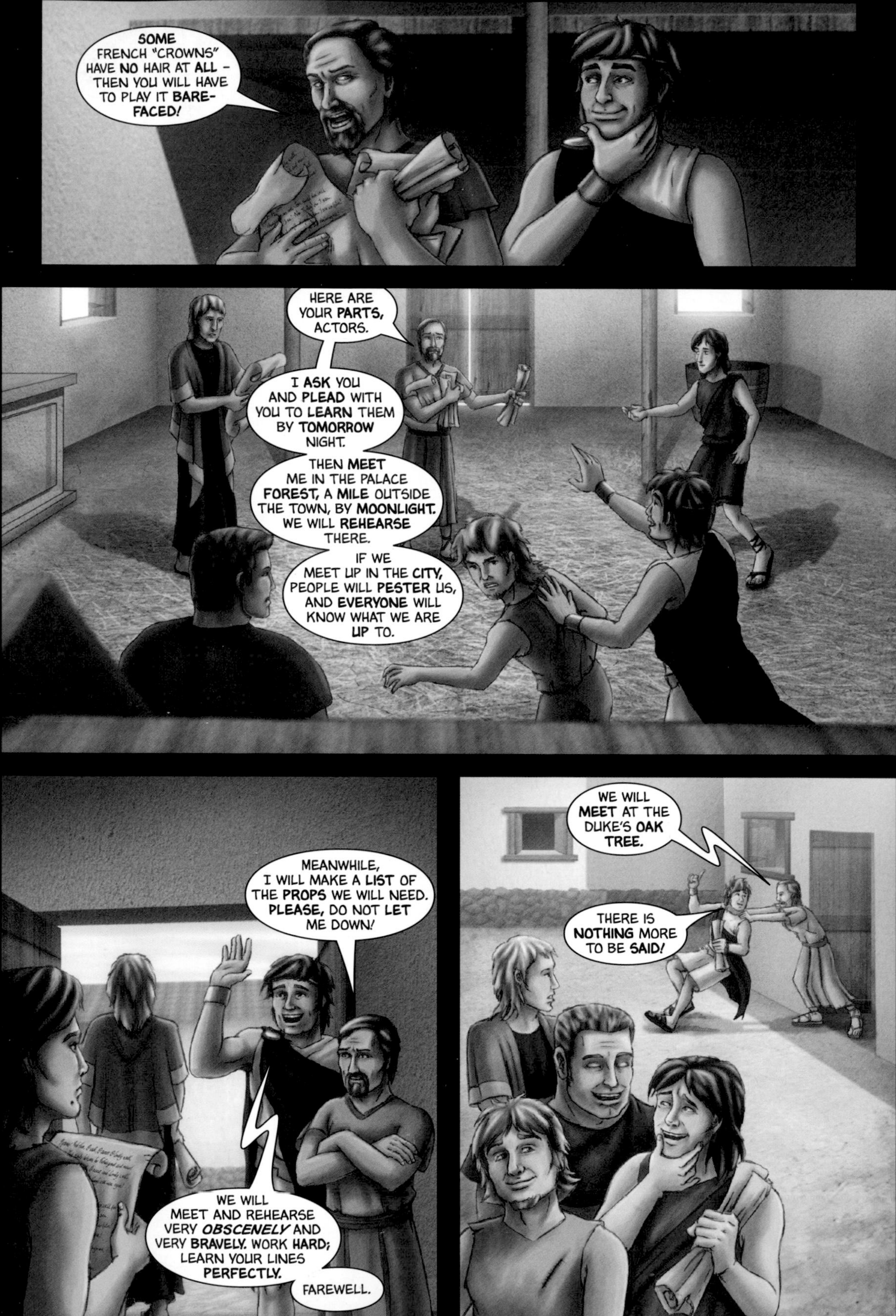
SOME FRENCH "CROWNS" HAVE NO HAIR AT ALL – THEN YOU WILL HAVE TO PLAY IT BARE-FACED!
HERE ARE YOUR PARTS, ACTORS.
I ASK YOU AND PLEAD WITH YOU TO LEARN THEM BY TOMORROW NIGHT.
THEN MEET ME IN THE PALACE FOREST, A MILE OUTSIDE THE TOWN, BY MOONLIGHT. WE WILL REHEARSE THERE.
IF WE MEET UP IN THE CITY, PEOPLE WILL PESTER US, AND EVERYONE WILL KNOW WHAT WE ARE UP TO.
MEANWHILE, I WILL MAKE A LIST OF THE PROPS WE WILL NEED. PLEASE, DO NOT LET ME DOWN!
WE WILL MEET AND REHEARSE VERY OBSCENELY AND VERY BRAVELY. WORK HARD; LEARN YOUR LINES PERFECTLY.
FAREWELL.
WE WILL MEET AT THE DUKE'S OAK TREE.
THERE IS NOTHING MORE TO BE SAID!

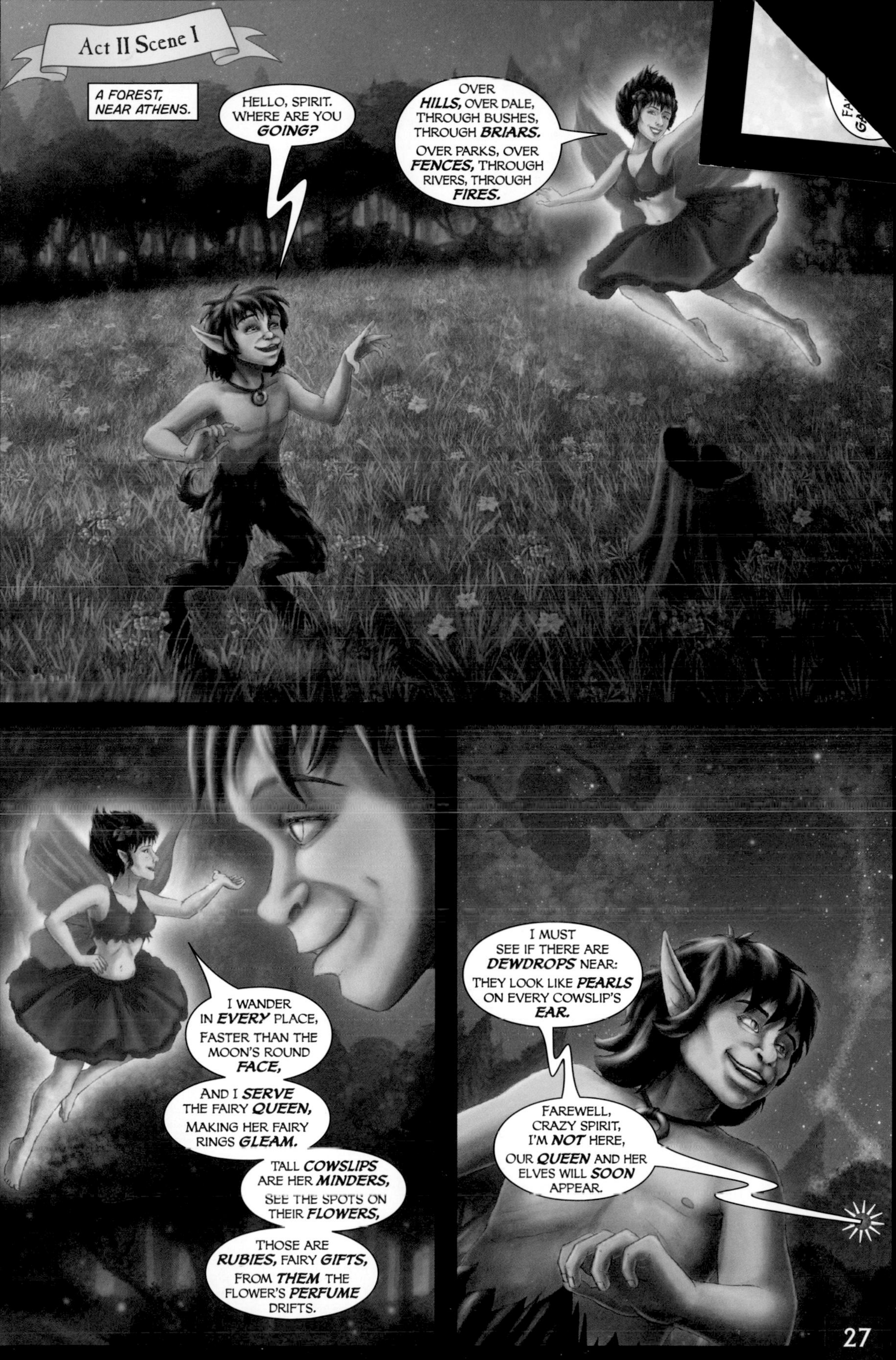

Act II Scene I
A FOREST, NEAR ATHENS.
HELLO, SPIRIT. WHERE ARE YOU GOING?
OVER HILLS, OVER DALE, THROUGH BUSHES, THROUGH BRIARS.
OVER PARKS, OVER FENCES, THROUGH RIVERS, THROUGH FIRES.
I WANDER IN EVERY PLACE,
FASTER THAN THE MOON'S ROUND FACE,
AND I SERVE THE FAIRY QUEEN,
MAKING HER FAIRY RINGS GLEAM.
TALL COWSLIPS ARE HER MINDERS,
SEE THE SPOTS ON THEIR FLOWERS,
THOSE ARE RUBIES, FAIRY GIFTS,
FROM THEM THE FLOWER'S PERFUME DRIFTS.
I MUST SEE IF THERE ARE DEWDROPS NEAR:
THEY LOOK LIKE PEARLS ON EVERY COWSLIP'S EAR.
FAREWELL, CRAZY SPIRIT, I'M NOT HERE,
OUR QUEEN AND HER ELVES WILL SOON APPEAR.

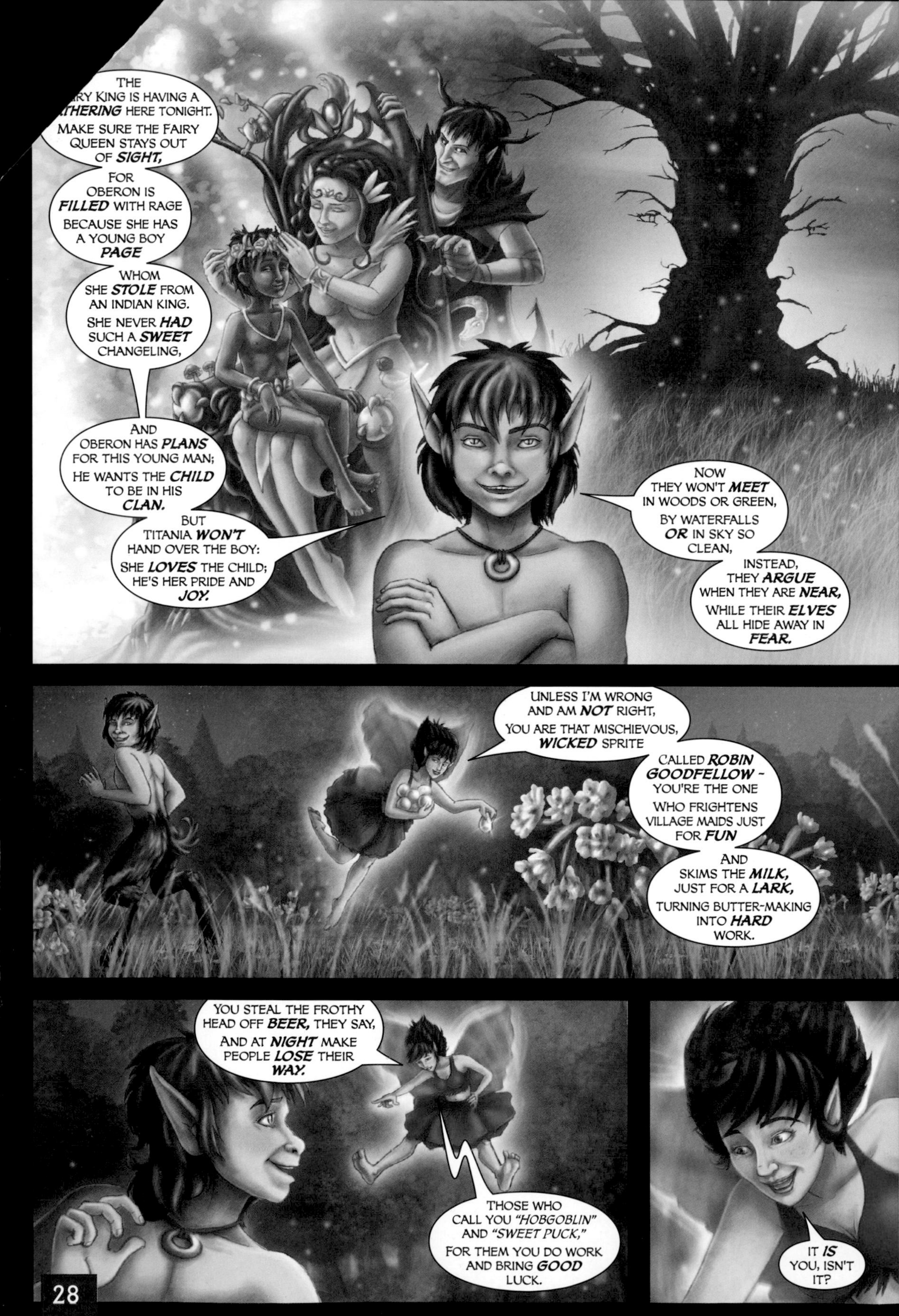

THE IRY KING IS HAVING A THERING HERE TONIGHT. MAKE SURE THE FAIRY QUEEN STAYS OUT OF SIGHT,
FOR OBERON IS FILLED WITH RAGE BECAUSE SHE HAS A YOUNG BOY PAGE
WHOM SHE STOLE FROM AN INDIAN KING. SHE NEVER HAD SUCH A SWEET CHANGELING,
AND OBERON HAS PLANS FOR THIS YOUNG MAN; HE WANTS THE CHILD TO BE IN HIS CLAN.
BUT TITANIA WON'T HAND OVER THE BOY: SHE LOVES THE CHILD; HE'S HER PRIDE AND JOY.
NOW THEY WON'T MEET IN WOODS OR GREEN, BY WATERFALLS OR IN SKY SO CLEAN,
INSTEAD, THEY ARGUE WHEN THEY ARE NEAR, WHILE THEIR ELVES ALL HIDE AWAY IN FEAR.
UNLESS I'M WRONG AND AM NOT RIGHT, YOU ARE THAT MISCHIEVOUS, WICKED SPRITE
CALLED ROBIN GOODFELLOW – YOU'RE THE ONE WHO FRIGHTENS VILLAGE MAIDS JUST FOR FUN
AND SKIMS THE MILK, JUST FOR A LARK, TURNING BUTTER-MAKING INTO HARD WORK.
YOU STEAL THE FROTHY HEAD OFF BEER, THEY SAY, AND AT NIGHT MAKE PEOPLE LOSE THEIR WAY.
THOSE WHO CALL YOU "HOBGOBLIN" AND "SWEET PUCK," FOR THEM YOU DO WORK AND BRING GOOD LUCK.
IT IS YOU, ISN'T IT?

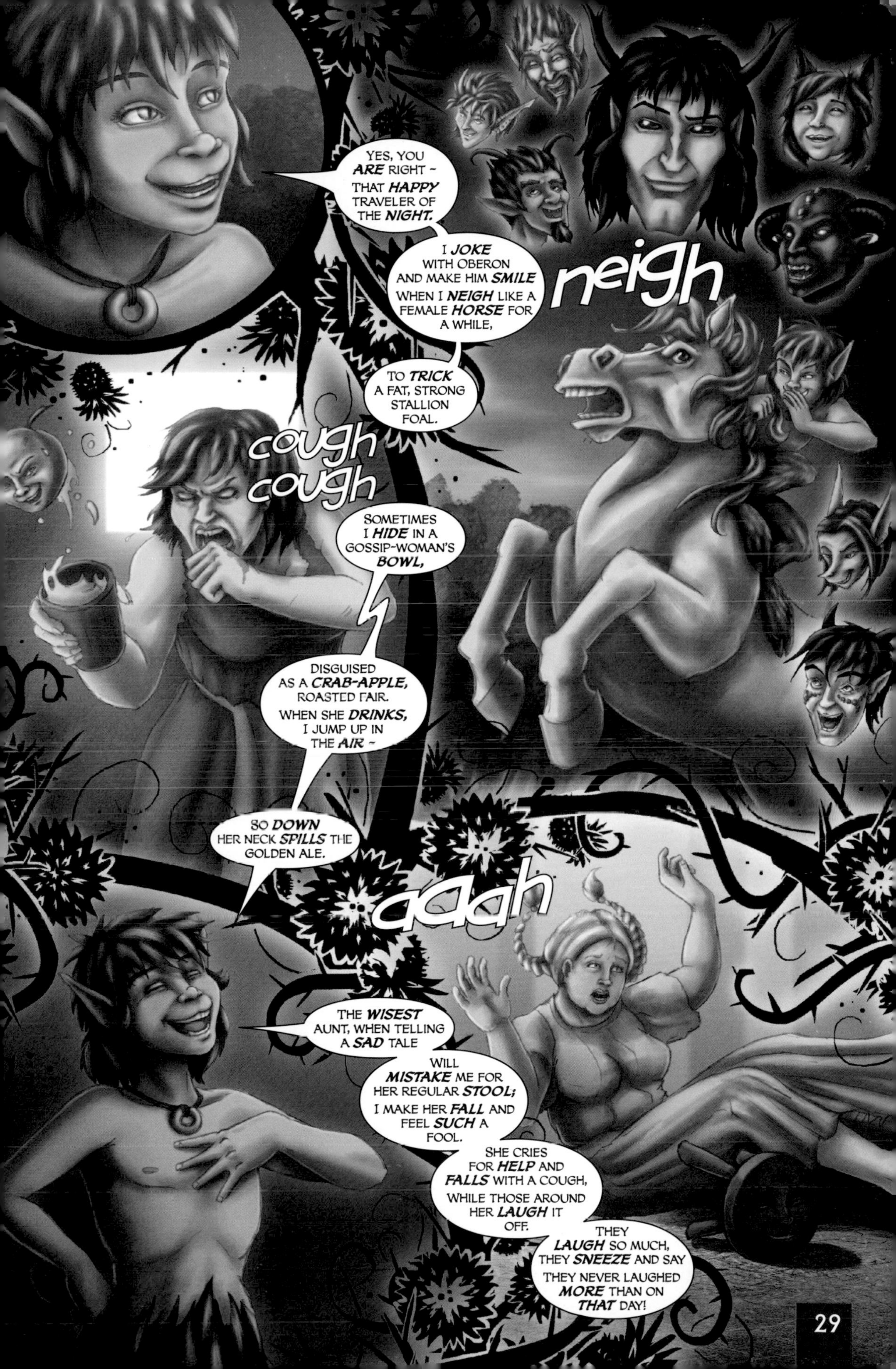
YES, YOU ARE RIGHT - THAT HAPPY TRAVELER OF THE NIGHT.
I JOKE WITH OBERON AND MAKE HIM SMILE WHEN I NEIGH LIKE A FEMALE HORSE FOR A WHILE,
neigh
TO TRICK A FAT, STRONG STALLION FOAL.
cough cough
SOMETIMES I HIDE IN A GOSSIP-WOMAN'S BOWL,
DISGUISED AS A CRAB-APPLE, ROASTED FAIR. WHEN SHE DRINKS, I JUMP UP IN THE AIR -
SO DOWN HER NECK SPILLS THE GOLDEN ALE.
aaah
THE WISEST AUNT, WHEN TELLING A SAD TALE
WILL MISTAKE ME FOR HER REGULAR STOOL; I MAKE HER FALL AND FEEL SUCH A FOOL.
SHE CRIES FOR HELP AND FALLS WITH A COUGH, WHILE THOSE AROUND HER LAUGH IT OFF.
THEY LAUGH SO MUCH, THEY SNEEZE AND SAY THEY NEVER LAUGHED MORE THAN ON THAT DAY!

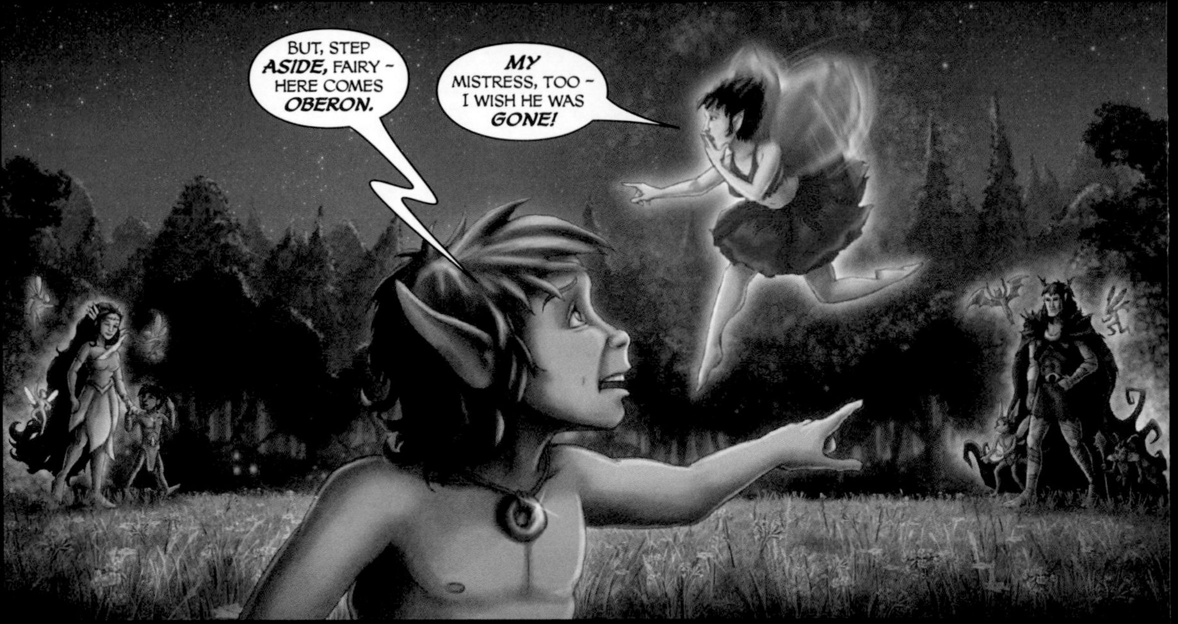
BUT, STEP ASIDE, FAIRY ~ HERE COMES OBERON.
MY MISTRESS, TOO ~ I WISH HE WAS GONE!

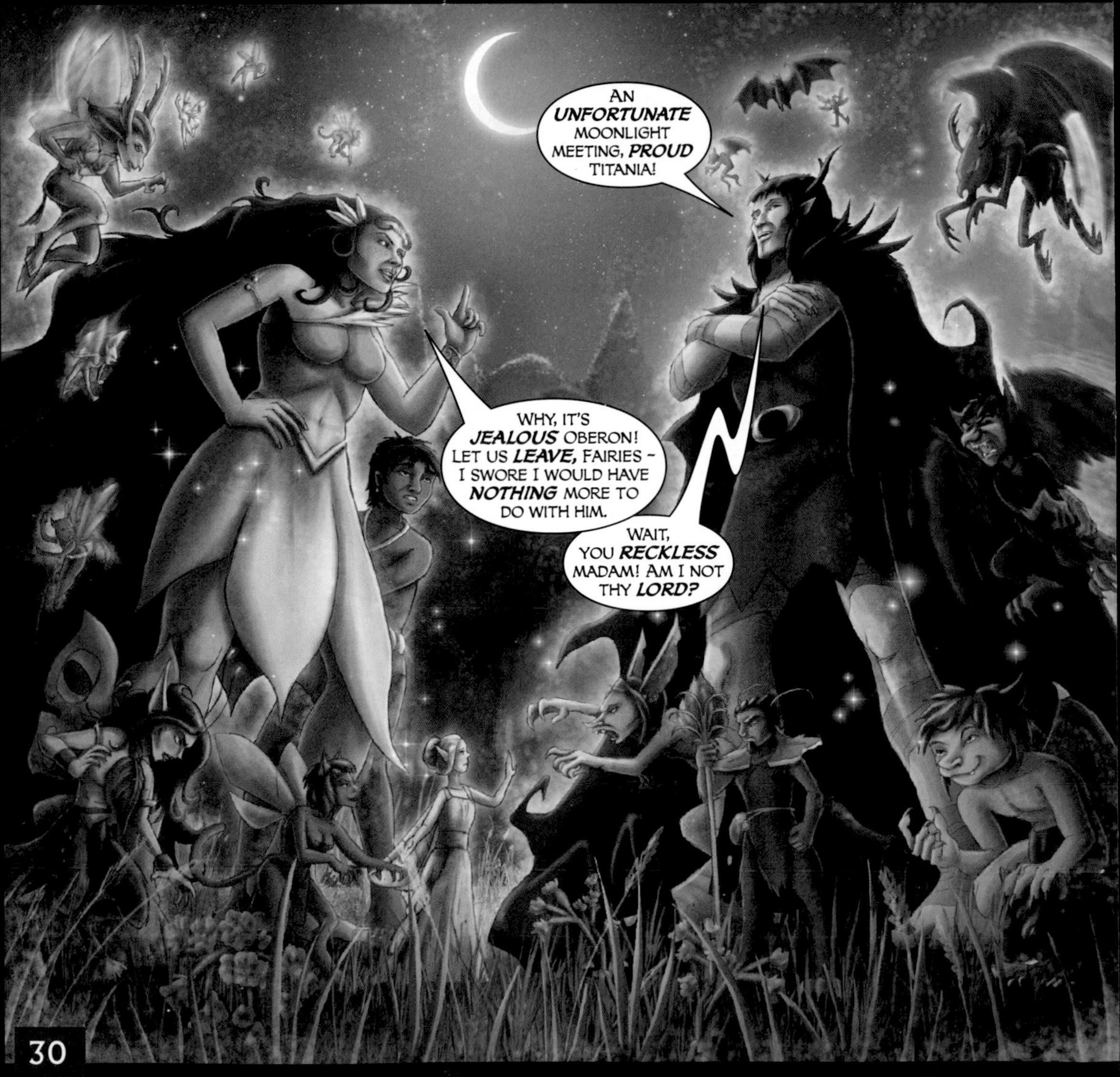
AN UNFORTUNATE MOONLIGHT MEETING, PROUD TITANIA!
WHY, IT'S JEALOUS OBERON! LET US LEAVE, FAIRIES ~ I SWORE I WOULD HAVE NOTHING MORE TO DO WITH HIM.
WAIT, YOU RECKLESS MADAM! AM I NOT THY LORD?

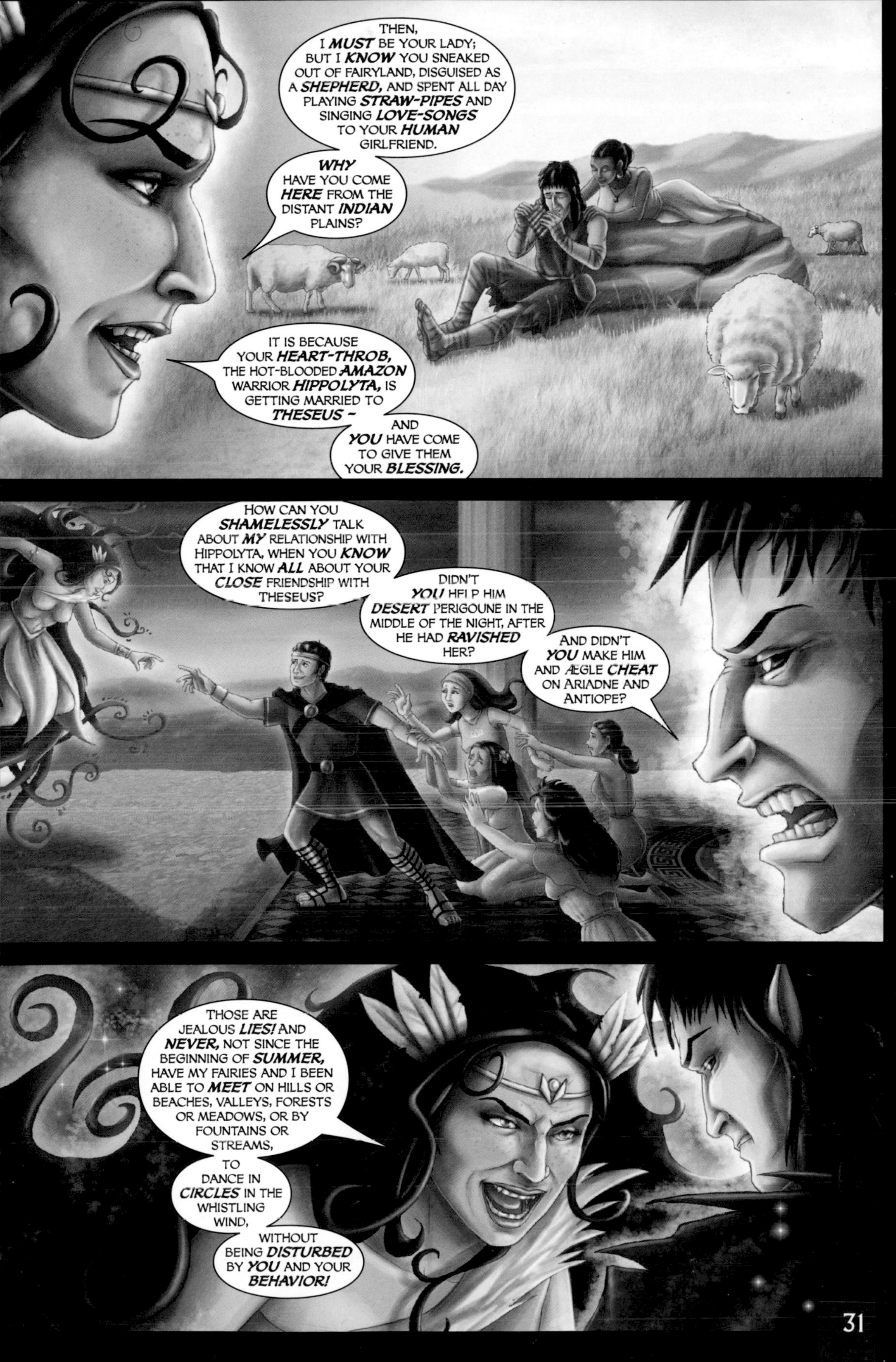
THEN, I MUST BE YOUR LADY; BUT I KNOW YOU SNEAKED OUT OF FAIRYLAND, DISGUISED AS A SHEPHERD, AND SPENT ALL DAY PLAYING STRAW-PIPES AND SINGING LOVE-SONGS TO YOUR HUMAN GIRLFRIEND.
WHY HAVE YOU COME HERE FROM THE DISTANT INDIAN PLAINS?
IT IS BECAUSE YOUR HEART-THROB, THE HOT-BLOODED AMAZON WARRIOR HIPPOLYTA, IS GETTING MARRIED TO THESEUS -
AND YOU HAVE COME TO GIVE THEM YOUR BLESSING.
HOW CAN YOU SHAMELESSLY TALK ABOUT MY RELATIONSHIP WITH HIPPOLYTA, WHEN YOU KNOW THAT I KNOW ALL ABOUT YOUR CLOSE FRIENDSHIP WITH THESEUS?
DIDN'T YOU HELP HIM DESERT PERIGOUNE IN THE MIDDLE OF THE NIGHT, AFTER HE HAD RAVISHED HER?
AND DIDN'T YOU MAKE HIM AND ÆGLE CHEAT ON ARIADNE AND ANTIOPE?
THOSE ARE JEALOUS LIES! AND NEVER, NOT SINCE THE BEGINNING OF SUMMER, HAVE MY FAIRIES AND I BEEN ABLE TO MEET ON HILLS OR BEACHES, VALLEYS, FORESTS OR MEADOWS, OR BY FOUNTAINS OR STREAMS,
TO DANCE IN CIRCLES IN THE WHISTLING WIND,
WITHOUT BEING DISTURBED BY YOU AND YOUR BEHAVIOR!

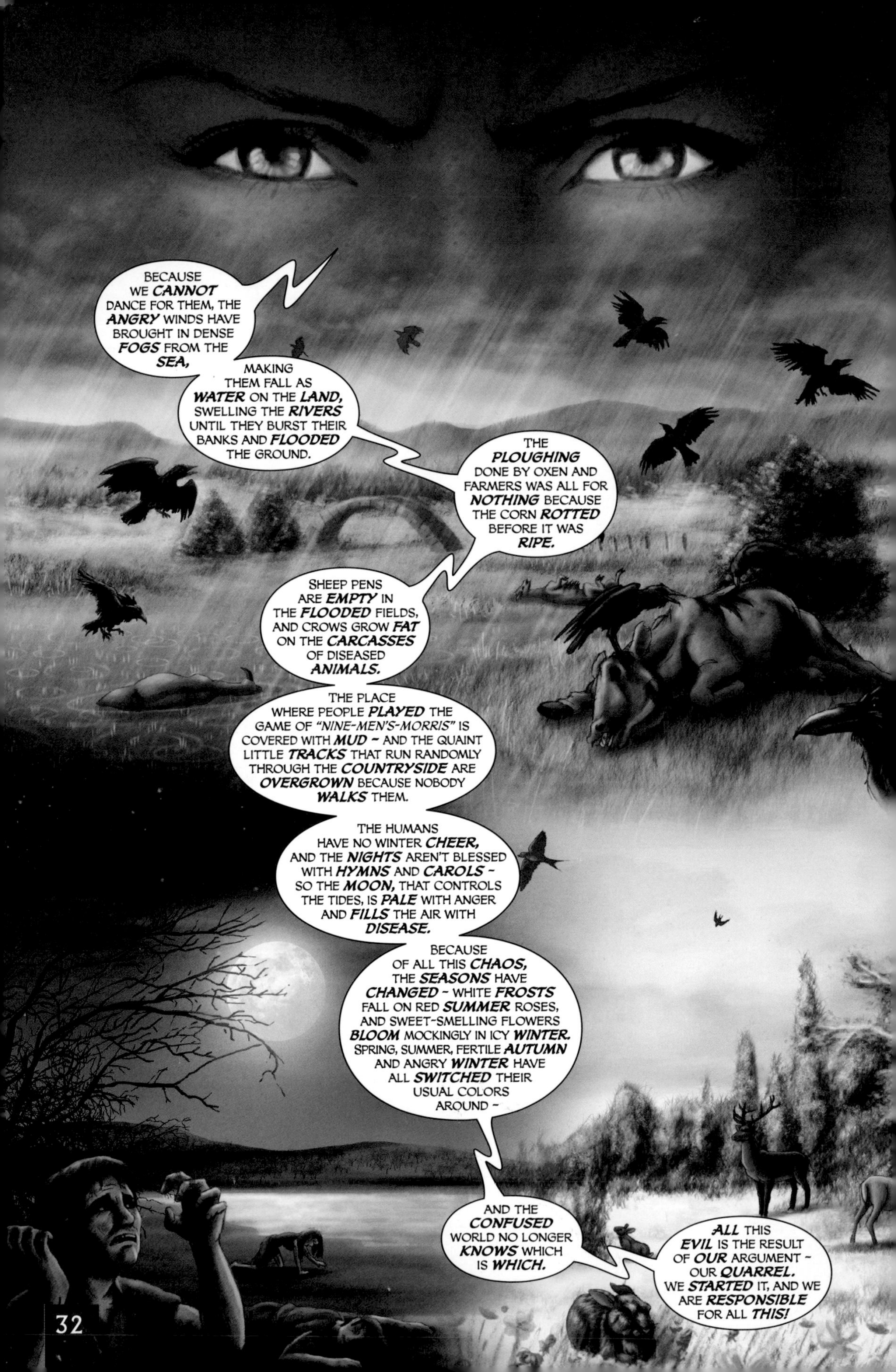

BECAUSE WE CANNOT DANCE FOR THEM, THE ANGRY WINDS HAVE BROUGHT IN DENSE FOGS FROM THE SEA,
MAKING THEM FALL AS WATER ON THE LAND, SWELLING THE RIVERS UNTIL THEY BURST THEIR BANKS AND FLOODED THE GROUND.
THE PLOUGHING DONE BY OXEN AND FARMERS WAS ALL FOR NOTHING BECAUSE THE CORN ROTTED BEFORE IT WAS RIPE.
SHEEP PENS ARE EMPTY IN THE FLOODED FIELDS, AND CROWS GROW FAT ON THE CARCASSES OF DISEASED ANIMALS.
THE PLACE WHERE PEOPLE PLAYED THE GAME OF "NINE-MEN'S-MORRIS" IS COVERED WITH MUD - AND THE QUAINT LITTLE TRACKS THAT RUN RANDOMLY THROUGH THE COUNTRYSIDE ARE OVERGROWN BECAUSE NOBODY WALKS THEM.
THE HUMANS HAVE NO WINTER CHEER, AND THE NIGHTS AREN'T BLESSED WITH HYMNS AND CAROLS - SO THE MOON, THAT CONTROLS THE TIDES, IS PALE WITH ANGER AND FILLS THE AIR WITH DISEASE.
BECAUSE OF ALL THIS CHAOS, THE SEASONS HAVE CHANGED - WHITE FROSTS FALL ON RED SUMMER ROSES, AND SWEET-SMELLING FLOWERS BLOOM MOCKINGLY IN ICY WINTER. SPRING, SUMMER, FERTILE AUTUMN AND ANGRY WINTER HAVE ALL SWITCHED THEIR USUAL COLORS AROUND -
AND THE CONFUSED WORLD NO LONGER KNOWS WHICH IS WHICH.
ALL THIS EVIL IS THE RESULT OF OUR ARGUMENT - OUR QUARREL. WE STARTED IT, AND WE ARE RESPONSIBLE FOR ALL THIS!

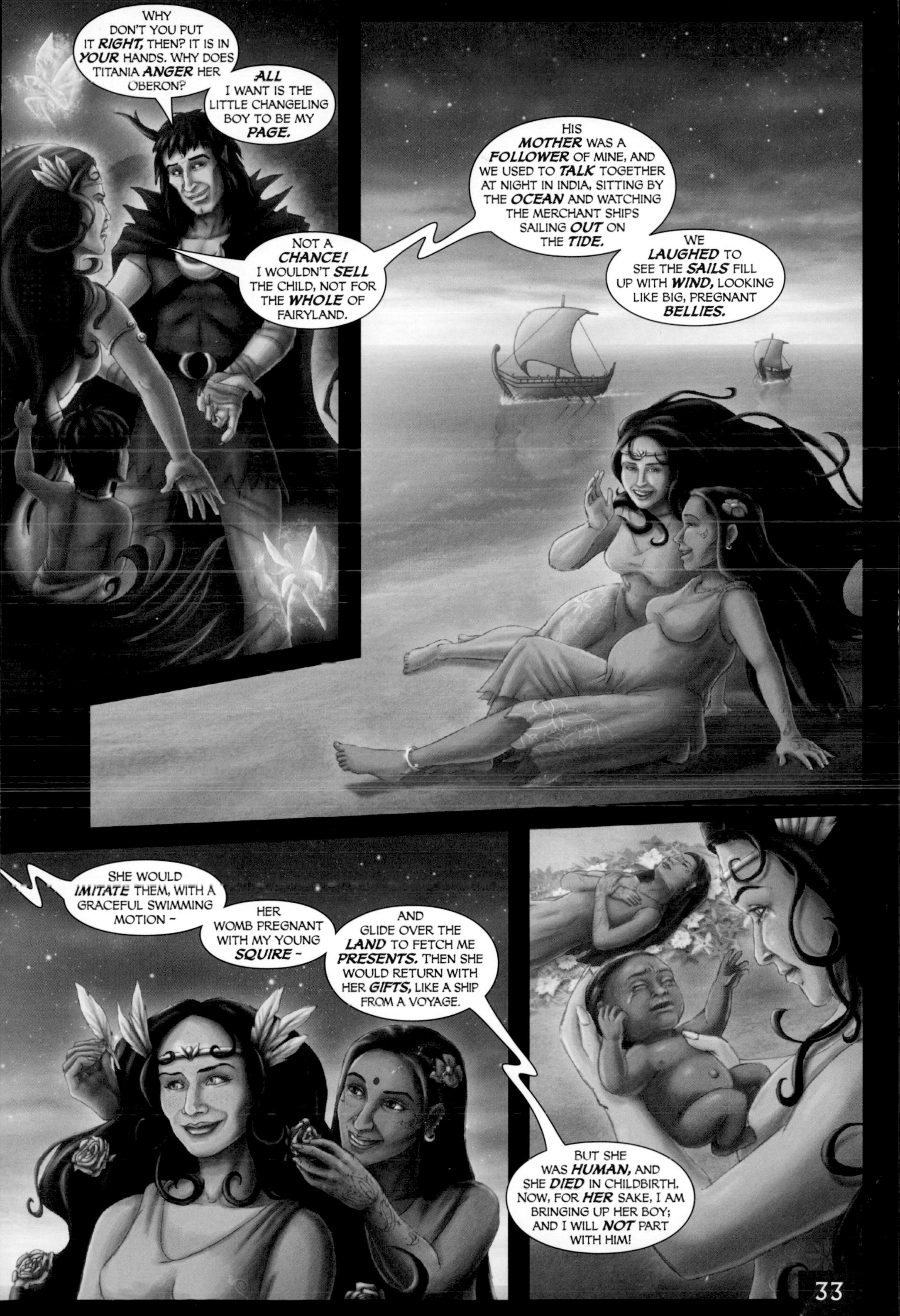
WHY DON'T YOU PUT IT RIGHT, THEN? IT IS IN YOUR HANDS. WHY DOES TITANIA ANGER HER OBERON?
ALL I WANT IS THE LITTLE CHANGELING BOY TO BE MY PAGE.
NOT A CHANCE! I WOULDN'T SELL THE CHILD, NOT FOR THE WHOLE OF FAIRYLAND.
HIS MOTHER WAS A FOLLOWER OF MINE, AND WE USED TO TALK TOGETHER AT NIGHT IN INDIA, SITTING BY THE OCEAN AND WATCHING THE MERCHANT SHIPS SAILING OUT ON THE TIDE.
WE LAUGHED TO SEE THE SAILS FILL UP WITH WIND, LOOKING LIKE BIG, PREGNANT BELLIES.
SHE WOULD IMITATE THEM, WITH A GRACEFUL SWIMMING MOTION ~
HER WOMB PREGNANT WITH MY YOUNG SQUIRE ~
AND GLIDE OVER THE LAND TO FETCH ME PRESENTS. THEN SHE WOULD RETURN WITH HER GIFTS, LIKE A SHIP FROM A VOYAGE.
BUT SHE WAS HUMAN, AND SHE DIED IN CHILDBIRTH. NOW, FOR HER SAKE, I AM BRINGING UP HER BOY; AND I WILL NOT PART WITH HIM!

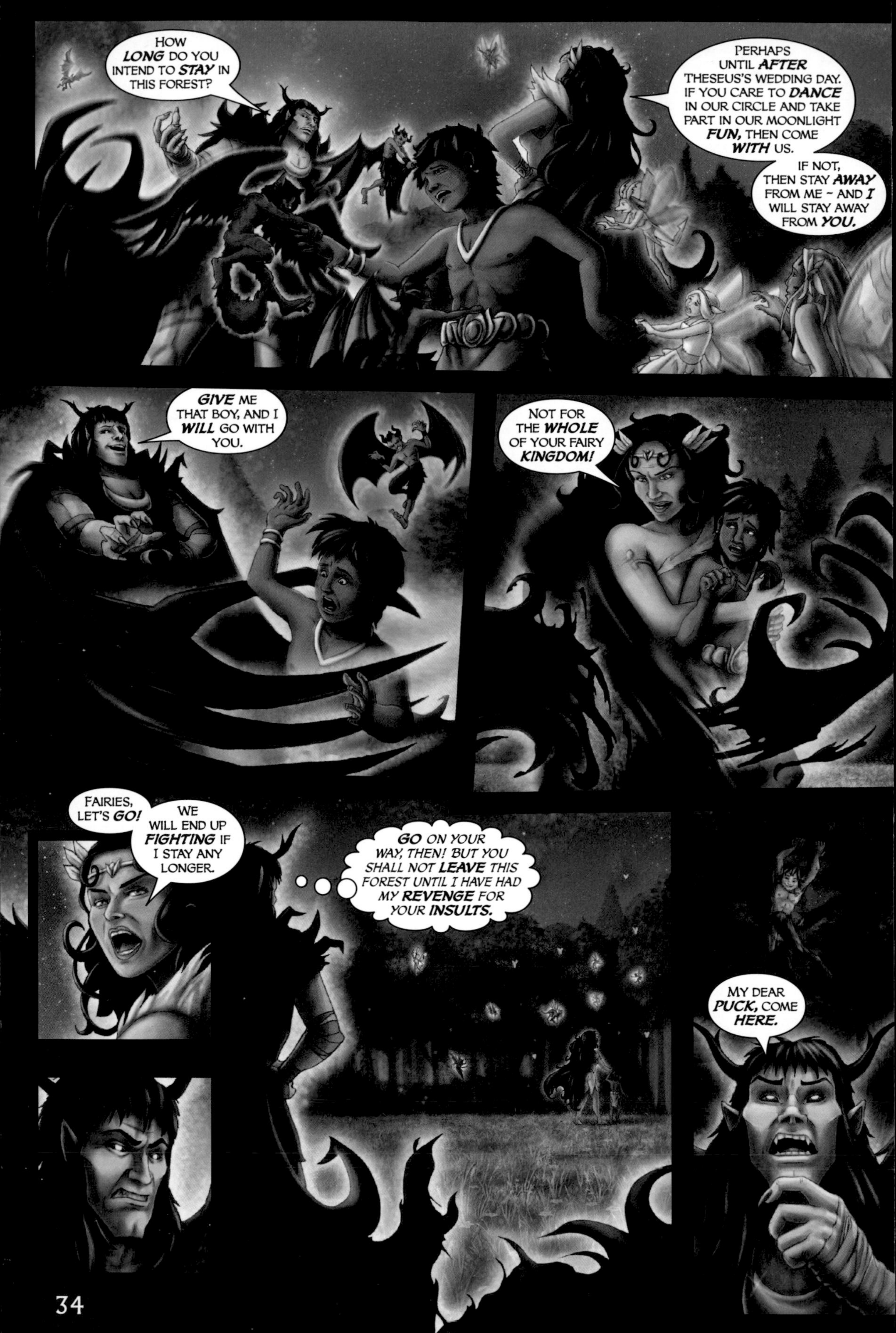
HOW LONG DO YOU INTEND TO STAY IN THIS FOREST?
PERHAPS UNTIL AFTER THESEUS'S WEDDING DAY. IF YOU CARE TO DANCE IN OUR CIRCLE AND TAKE PART IN OUR MOONLIGHT FUN, THEN COME WITH US.
IF NOT, THEN STAY AWAY FROM ME - AND I WILL STAY AWAY FROM YOU.
GIVE ME THAT BOY, AND I WILL GO WITH YOU.
NOT FOR THE WHOLE OF YOUR FAIRY KINGDOM!
FAIRIES, LET'S GO!
WE WILL END UP FIGHTING IF I STAY ANY LONGER.
GO ON YOUR WAY, THEN! BUT YOU SHALL NOT LEAVE THIS FOREST UNTIL I HAVE HAD MY REVENGE FOR YOUR INSULTS.
MY DEAR PUCK, COME HERE.

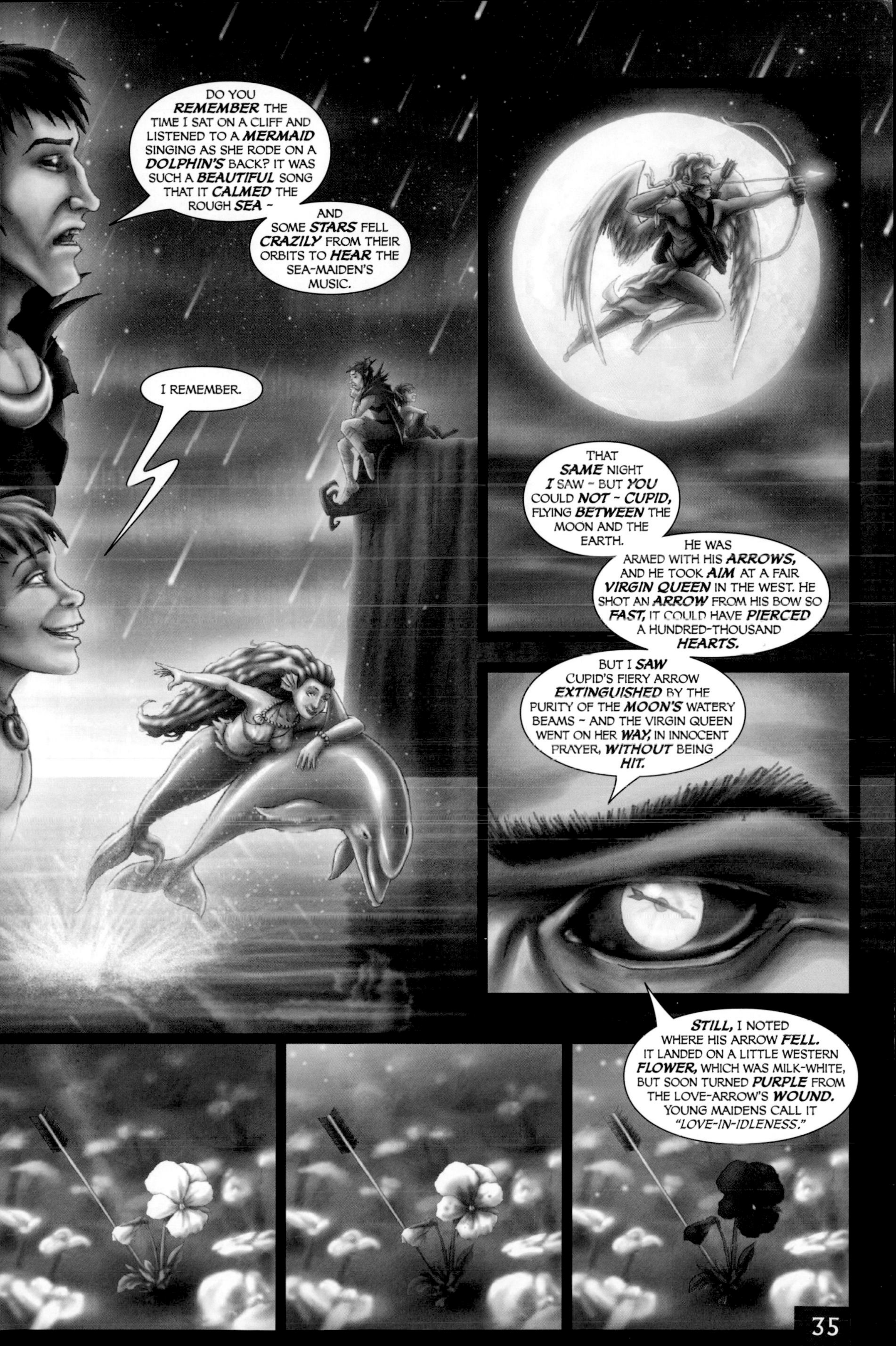

DO YOU REMEMBER THE TIME I SAT ON A CLIFF AND LISTENED TO A MERMAID SINGING AS SHE RODE ON A DOLPHIN'S BACK? IT WAS SUCH A BEAUTIFUL SONG THAT IT CALMED THE ROUGH SEA -
AND SOME STARS FELL CRAZILY FROM THEIR ORBITS TO HEAR THE SEA-MAIDEN'S MUSIC.
I REMEMBER.
THAT SAME NIGHT I SAW - BUT YOU COULD NOT - CUPID, FLYING BETWEEN THE MOON AND THE EARTH.
HE WAS ARMED WITH HIS ARROWS, AND HE TOOK AIM AT A FAIR VIRGIN QUEEN IN THE WEST. HE SHOT AN ARROW FROM HIS BOW SO FAST, IT COULD HAVE PIERCED A HUNDRED-THOUSAND HEARTS.
BUT I SAW CUPID'S FIERY ARROW EXTINGUISHED BY THE PURITY OF THE MOON'S WATERY BEAMS - AND THE VIRGIN QUEEN WENT ON HER WAY, IN INNOCENT PRAYER, WITHOUT BEING HIT.
STILL, I NOTED WHERE HIS ARROW FELL. IT LANDED ON A LITTLE WESTERN FLOWER, WHICH WAS MILK-WHITE, BUT SOON TURNED PURPLE FROM THE LOVE-ARROW'S WOUND. YOUNG MAIDENS CALL IT "LOVE-IN-IDLENESS."

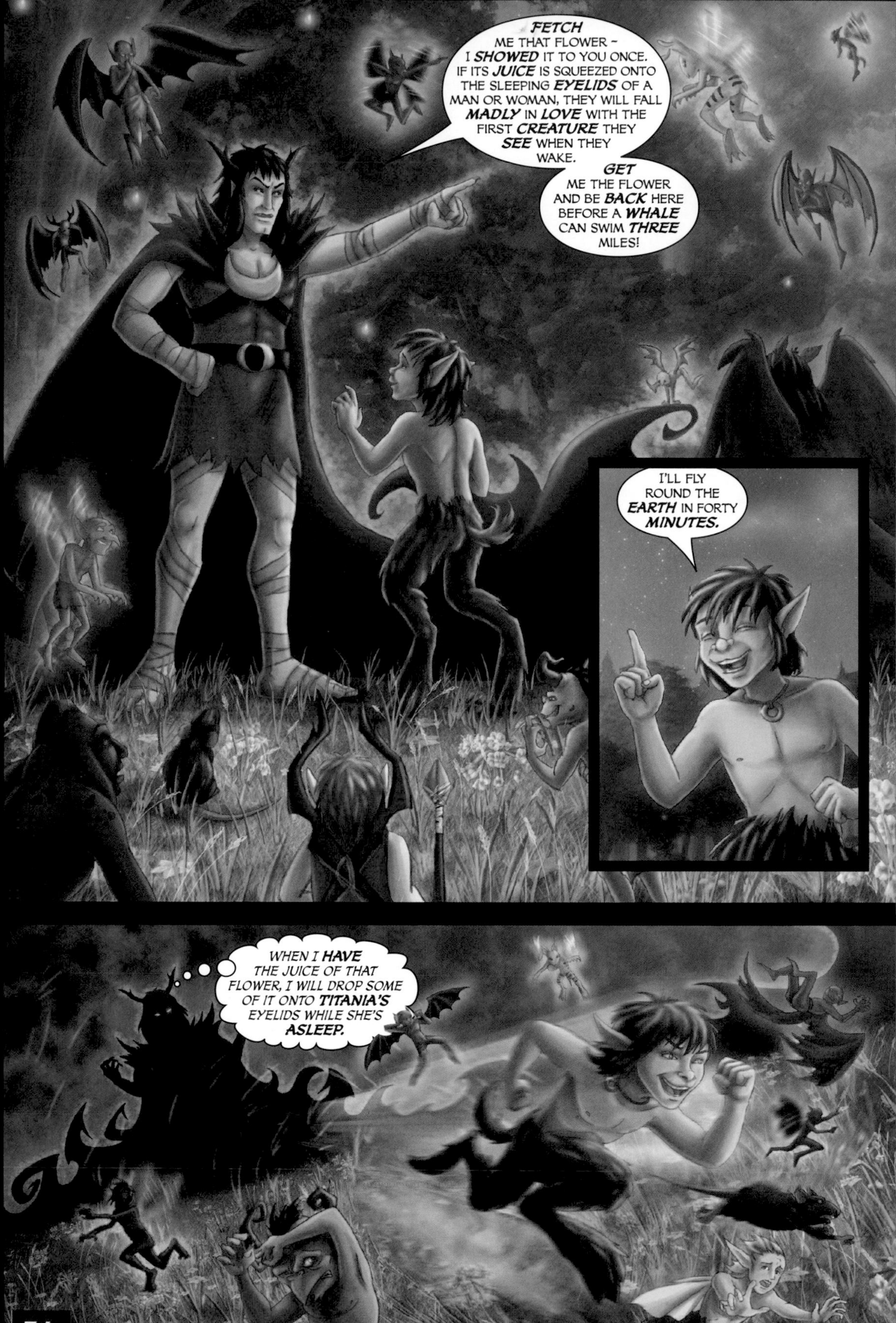
FETCH ME THAT FLOWER – I SHOWED IT TO YOU ONCE. IF ITS JUICE IS SQUEEZED ONTO THE SLEEPING EYELIDS OF A MAN OR WOMAN, THEY WILL FALL MADLY IN LOVE WITH THE FIRST CREATURE THEY SEE WHEN THEY WAKE.
GET ME THE FLOWER AND BE BACK HERE BEFORE A WHALE CAN SWIM THREE MILES!
I'LL FLY ROUND THE EARTH IN FORTY MINUTES.
WHEN I HAVE THE JUICE OF THAT FLOWER, I WILL DROP SOME OF IT ONTO TITANIA'S EYELIDS WHILE SHE'S ASLEEP.

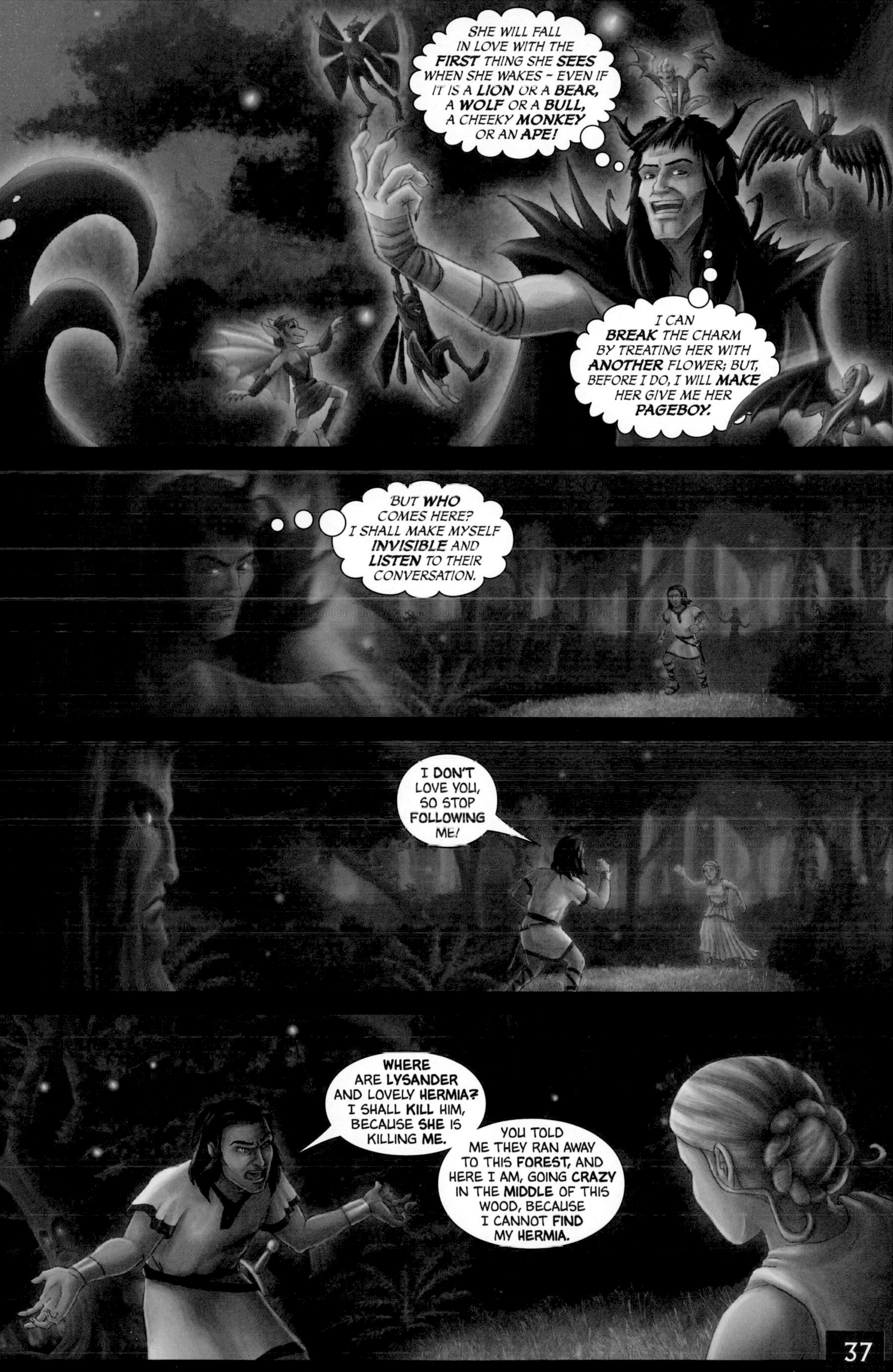
SHE WILL FALL IN LOVE WITH THE FIRST THING SHE SEES WHEN SHE WAKES - EVEN IF IT IS A LION OR A BEAR, A WOLF OR A BULL, A CHEEKY MONKEY OR AN APE!
I CAN BREAK THE CHARM BY TREATING HER WITH ANOTHER FLOWER; BUT, BEFORE I DO, I WILL MAKE HER GIVE ME HER PAGEBOY.
BUT WHO COMES HERE? I SHALL MAKE MYSELF INVISIBLE AND LISTEN TO THEIR CONVERSATION.
I DON'T LOVE YOU, SO STOP FOLLOWING ME!
WHERE ARE LYSANDER AND LOVELY HERMIA? I SHALL KILL HIM, BECAUSE SHE IS KILLING ME.
YOU TOLD ME THEY RAN AWAY TO THIS FOREST, AND HERE I AM, GOING CRAZY IN THE MIDDLE OF THIS WOOD, BECAUSE I CANNOT FIND MY HERMIA.

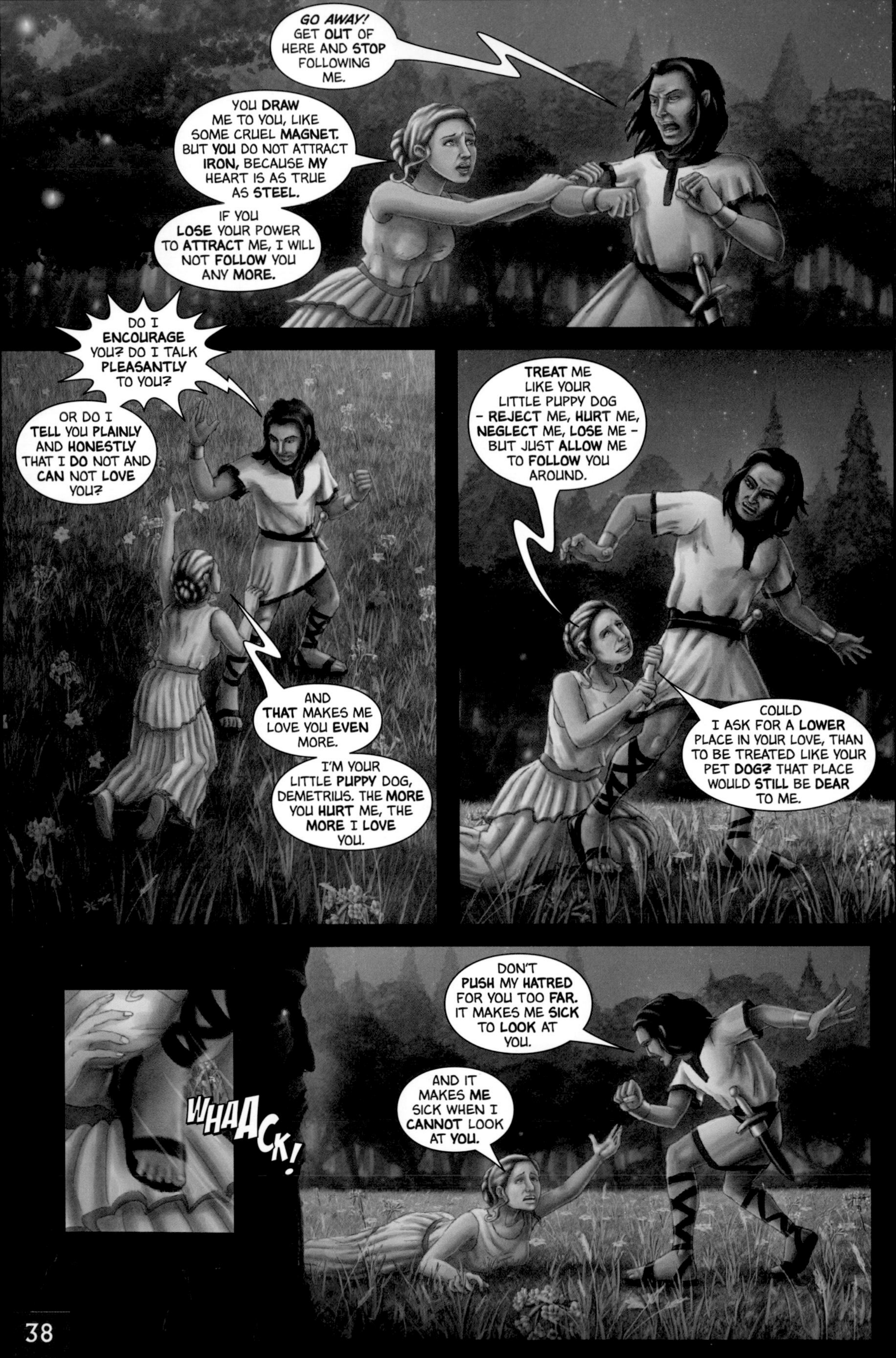
GO AWAY! GET OUT OF HERE AND STOP FOLLOWING ME.
YOU DRAW ME TO YOU, LIKE SOME CRUEL MAGNET. BUT YOU DO NOT ATTRACT IRON, BECAUSE MY HEART IS AS TRUE AS STEEL.
IF YOU LOSE YOUR POWER TO ATTRACT ME, I WILL NOT FOLLOW YOU ANY MORE.
DO I ENCOURAGE YOU? DO I TALK PLEASANTLY TO YOU?
OR DO I TELL YOU PLAINLY AND HONESTLY THAT I DO NOT AND CAN NOT LOVE YOU?
AND THAT MAKES ME LOVE YOU EVEN MORE.
I'M YOUR LITTLE PUPPY DOG, DEMETRIUS. THE MORE YOU HURT ME, THE MORE I LOVE YOU.
TREAT ME LIKE YOUR LITTLE PUPPY DOG – REJECT ME, HURT ME, NEGLECT ME, LOSE ME – BUT JUST ALLOW ME TO FOLLOW YOU AROUND.
COULD I ASK FOR A LOWER PLACE IN YOUR LOVE, THAN TO BE TREATED LIKE YOUR PET DOG? THAT PLACE WOULD STILL BE DEAR TO ME.
WHAACK!
DON'T PUSH MY HATRED FOR YOU TOO FAR. IT MAKES ME SICK TO LOOK AT YOU.
AND IT MAKES ME SICK WHEN I CANNOT LOOK AT YOU.

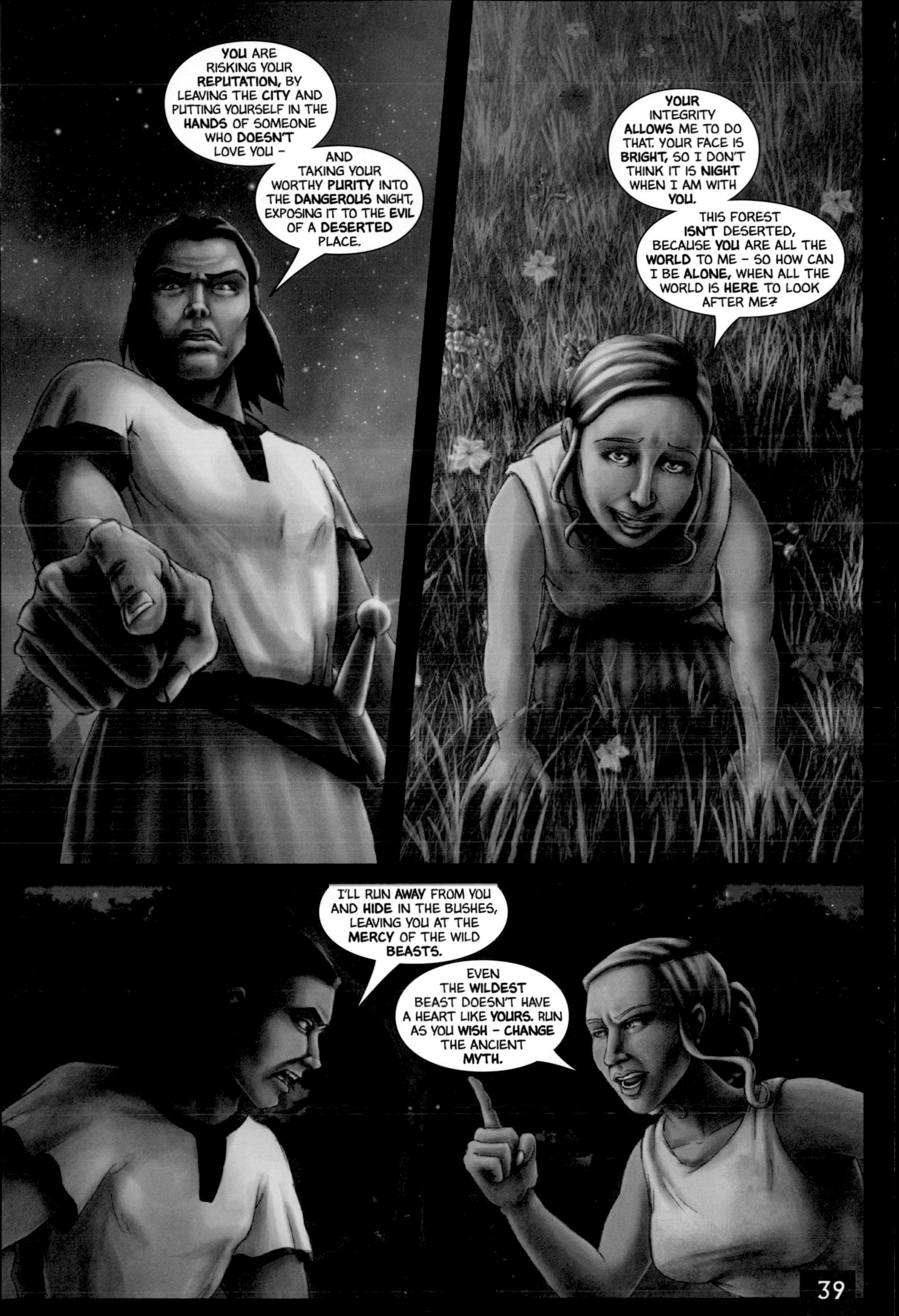
YOU ARE RISKING YOUR REPUTATION, BY LEAVING THE CITY AND PUTTING YOURSELF IN THE HANDS OF SOMEONE WHO DOESN'T LOVE YOU –
AND TAKING YOUR WORTHY PURITY INTO THE DANGEROUS NIGHT, EXPOSING IT TO THE EVIL OF A DESERTED PLACE.
YOUR INTEGRITY ALLOWS ME TO DO THAT. YOUR FACE IS BRIGHT, SO I DON'T THINK IT IS NIGHT WHEN I AM WITH YOU.
THIS FOREST ISN'T DESERTED, BECAUSE YOU ARE ALL THE WORLD TO ME – SO HOW CAN I BE ALONE, WHEN ALL THE WORLD IS HERE TO LOOK AFTER ME?
I'LL RUN AWAY FROM YOU AND HIDE IN THE BUSHES, LEAVING YOU AT THE MERCY OF THE WILD BEASTS.
EVEN THE WILDEST BEAST DOESN'T HAVE A HEART LIKE YOURS. RUN AS YOU WISH – CHANGE THE ANCIENT MYTH.

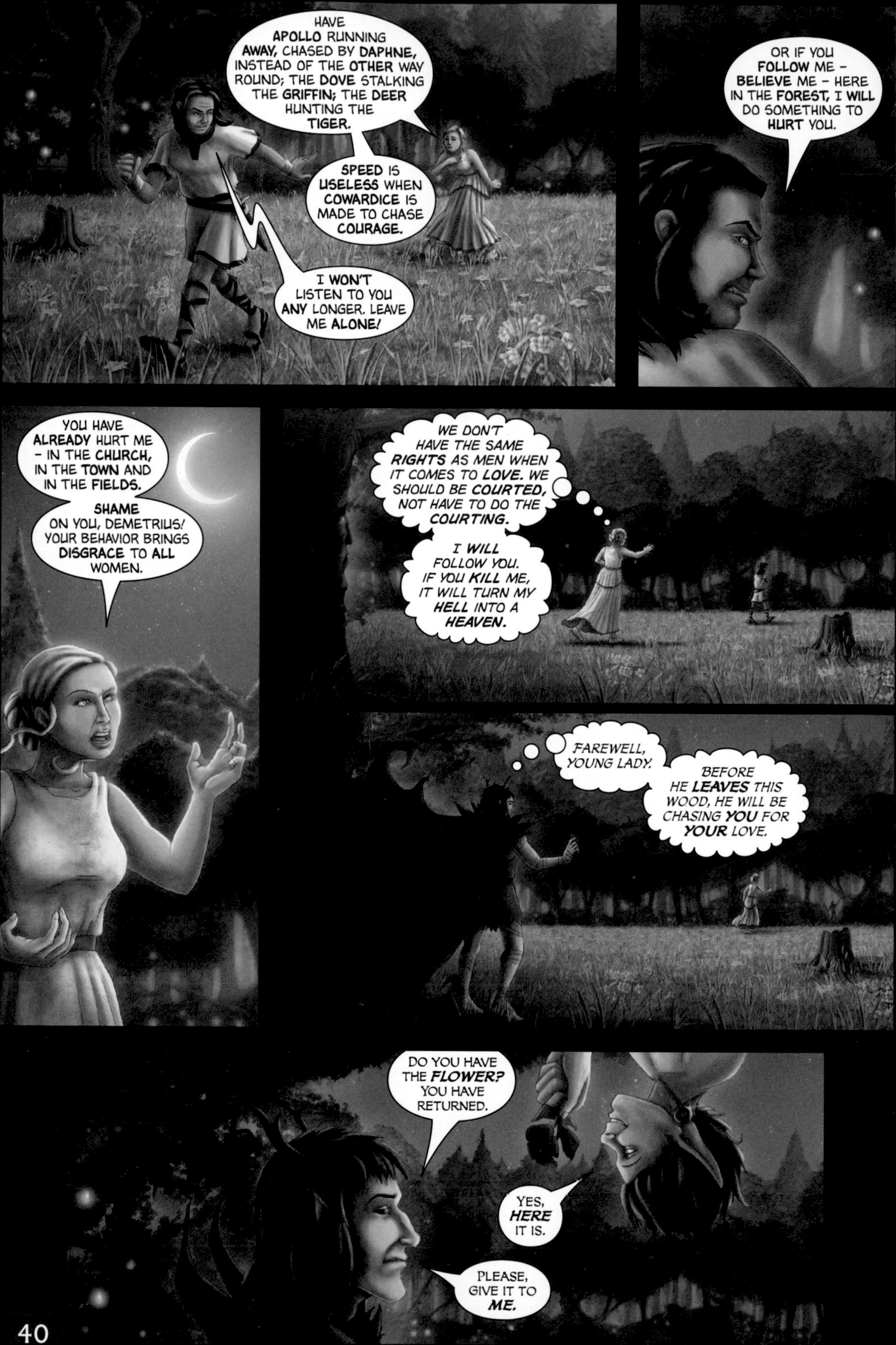
HAVE APOLLO RUNNING AWAY, CHASED BY DAPHNE, INSTEAD OF THE OTHER WAY ROUND; THE DOVE STALKING THE GRIFFIN; THE DEER HUNTING THE TIGER.
SPEED IS USELESS WHEN COWARDICE IS MADE TO CHASE COURAGE.
I WON'T LISTEN TO YOU ANY LONGER. LEAVE ME ALONE!
OR IF YOU FOLLOW ME - BELIEVE ME - HERE IN THE FOREST, I WILL DO SOMETHING TO HURT YOU.
YOU HAVE ALREADY HURT ME - IN THE CHURCH, IN THE TOWN AND IN THE FIELDS.
SHAME ON YOU, DEMETRIUS! YOUR BEHAVIOR BRINGS DISGRACE TO ALL WOMEN.
WE DON'T HAVE THE SAME RIGHTS AS MEN WHEN IT COMES TO LOVE. WE SHOULD BE COURTED, NOT HAVE TO DO THE COURTING.
I WILL FOLLOW YOU. IF YOU KILL ME, IT WILL TURN MY HELL INTO A HEAVEN.
FAREWELL, YOUNG LADY.
BEFORE HE LEAVES THIS WOOD, HE WILL BE CHASING YOU FOR YOUR LOVE.
DO YOU HAVE THE FLOWER? YOU HAVE RETURNED.
YES, HERE IT IS.
PLEASE, GIVE IT TO ME.

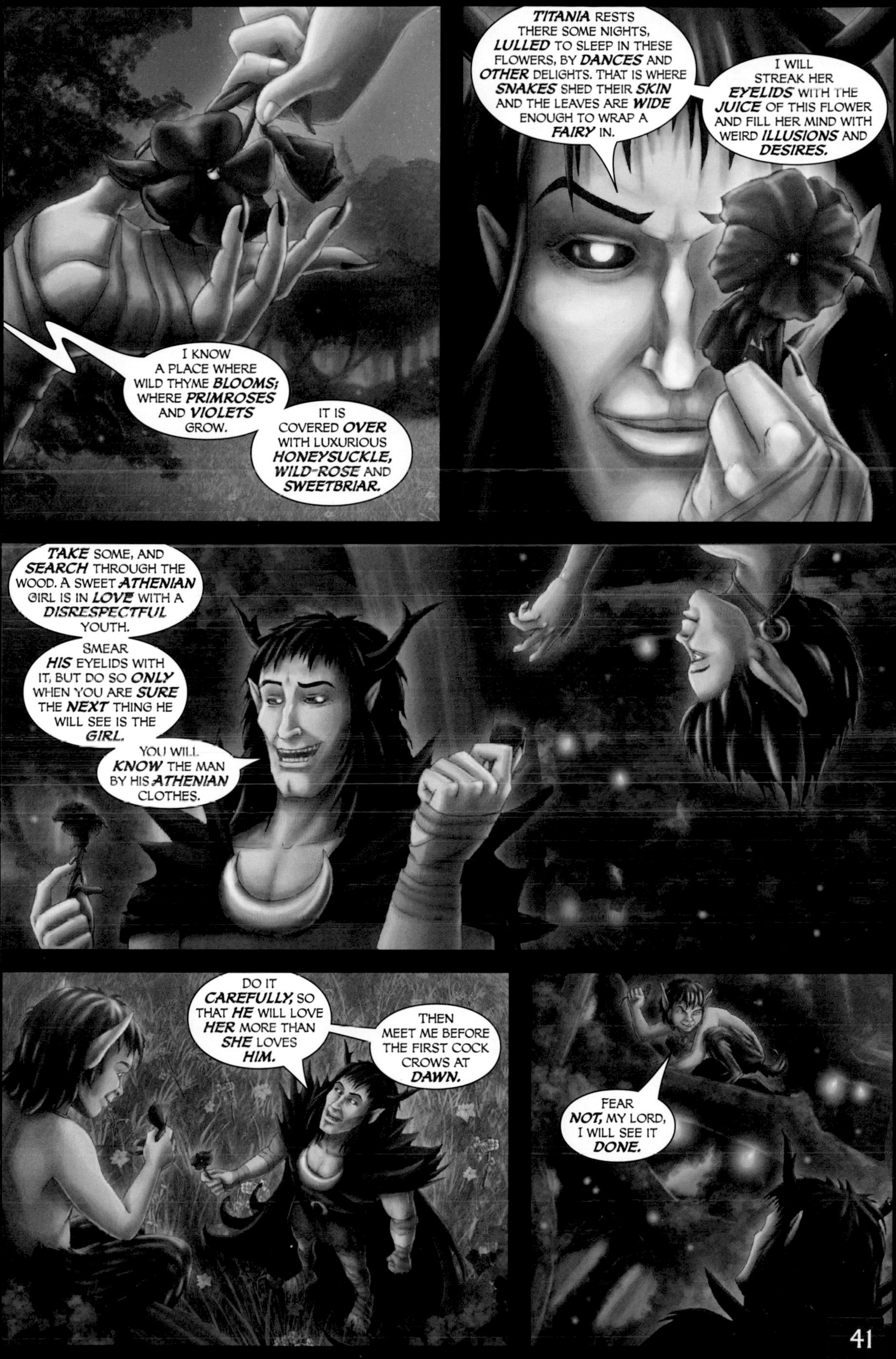
I KNOW A PLACE WHERE WILD THYME BLOOMS; WHERE PRIMROSES AND VIOLETS GROW.
IT IS COVERED OVER WITH LUXURIOUS HONEYSUCKLE, WILD-ROSE AND SWEETBRIAR.
TITANIA RESTS THERE SOME NIGHTS, LULLED TO SLEEP IN THESE FLOWERS, BY DANCES AND OTHER DELIGHTS. THAT IS WHERE SNAKES SHED THEIR SKIN AND THE LEAVES ARE WIDE ENOUGH TO WRAP A FAIRY IN.
I WILL STREAK HER EYELIDS WITH THE JUICE OF THIS FLOWER AND FILL HER MIND WITH WEIRD ILLUSIONS AND DESIRES.
TAKE SOME, AND SEARCH THROUGH THE WOOD. A SWEET ATHENIAN GIRL IS IN LOVE WITH A DISRESPECTFUL YOUTH.
SMEAR HIS EYELIDS WITH IT, BUT DO SO ONLY WHEN YOU ARE SURE THE NEXT THING HE WILL SEE IS THE GIRL.
YOU WILL KNOW THE MAN BY HIS ATHENIAN CLOTHES.
DO IT CAREFULLY, SO THAT HE WILL LOVE HER MORE THAN SHE LOVES HIM.
THEN MEET ME BEFORE THE FIRST COCK CROWS AT DAWN.
FEAR NOT, MY LORD, I WILL SEE IT DONE.

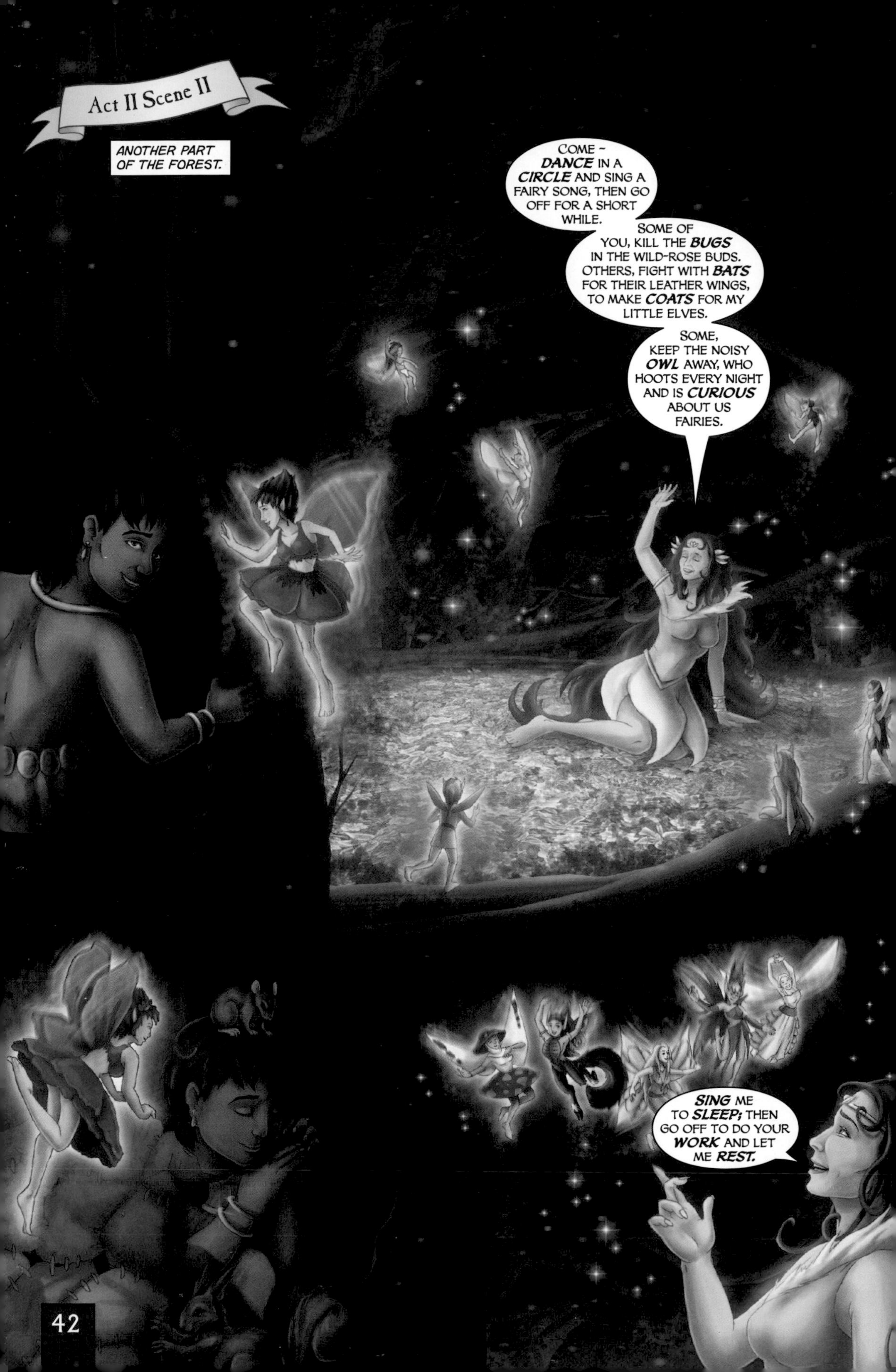
Act II Scene II
ANOTHER PART OF THE FOREST.
COME – DANCE IN A CIRCLE AND SING A FAIRY SONG, THEN GO OFF FOR A SHORT WHILE.
SOME OF YOU, KILL THE BUGS IN THE WILD-ROSE BUDS. OTHERS, FIGHT WITH BATS FOR THEIR LEATHER WINGS, TO MAKE COATS FOR MY LITTLE ELVES.
SOME, KEEP THE NOISY OWL AWAY, WHO HOOTS EVERY NIGHT AND IS CURIOUS ABOUT US FAIRIES.
SING ME TO SLEEP; THEN GO OFF TO DO YOUR WORK AND LET ME REST.

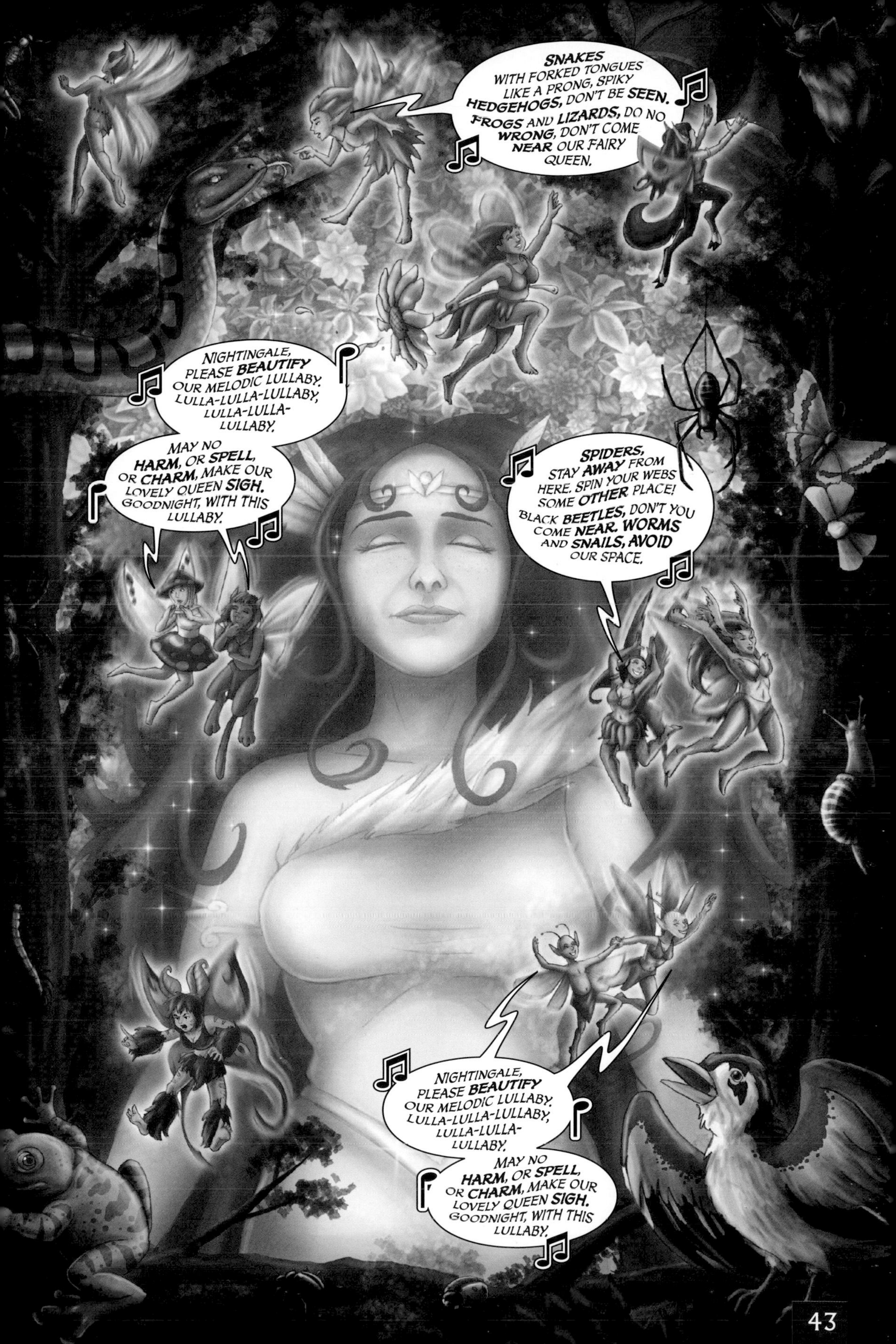
SNAKES WITH FORKED TONGUES LIKE A PRONG, SPIKY HEDGEHOGS, DON'T BE SEEN. FROGS AND LIZARDS, DO NO WRONG, DON'T COME NEAR OUR FAIRY QUEEN.
NIGHTINGALE, PLEASE BEAUTIFY OUR MELODIC LULLABY. LULLA-LULLA-LULLABY, LULLA-LULLA-LULLABY.
MAY NO HARM, OR SPELL, OR CHARM, MAKE OUR LOVELY QUEEN SIGH. GOODNIGHT, WITH THIS LULLABY.
SPIDERS, STAY AWAY FROM HERE. SPIN YOUR WEBS SOME OTHER PLACE! BLACK BEETLES, DON'T YOU COME NEAR. WORMS AND SNAILS, AVOID OUR SPACE.
NIGHTINGALE, PLEASE BEAUTIFY OUR MELODIC LULLABY. LULLA-LULLA-LULLABY, LULLA-LULLA-LULLABY.
MAY NO HARM, OR SPELL, OR CHARM, MAKE OUR LOVELY QUEEN SIGH. GOODNIGHT, WITH THIS LULLABY.

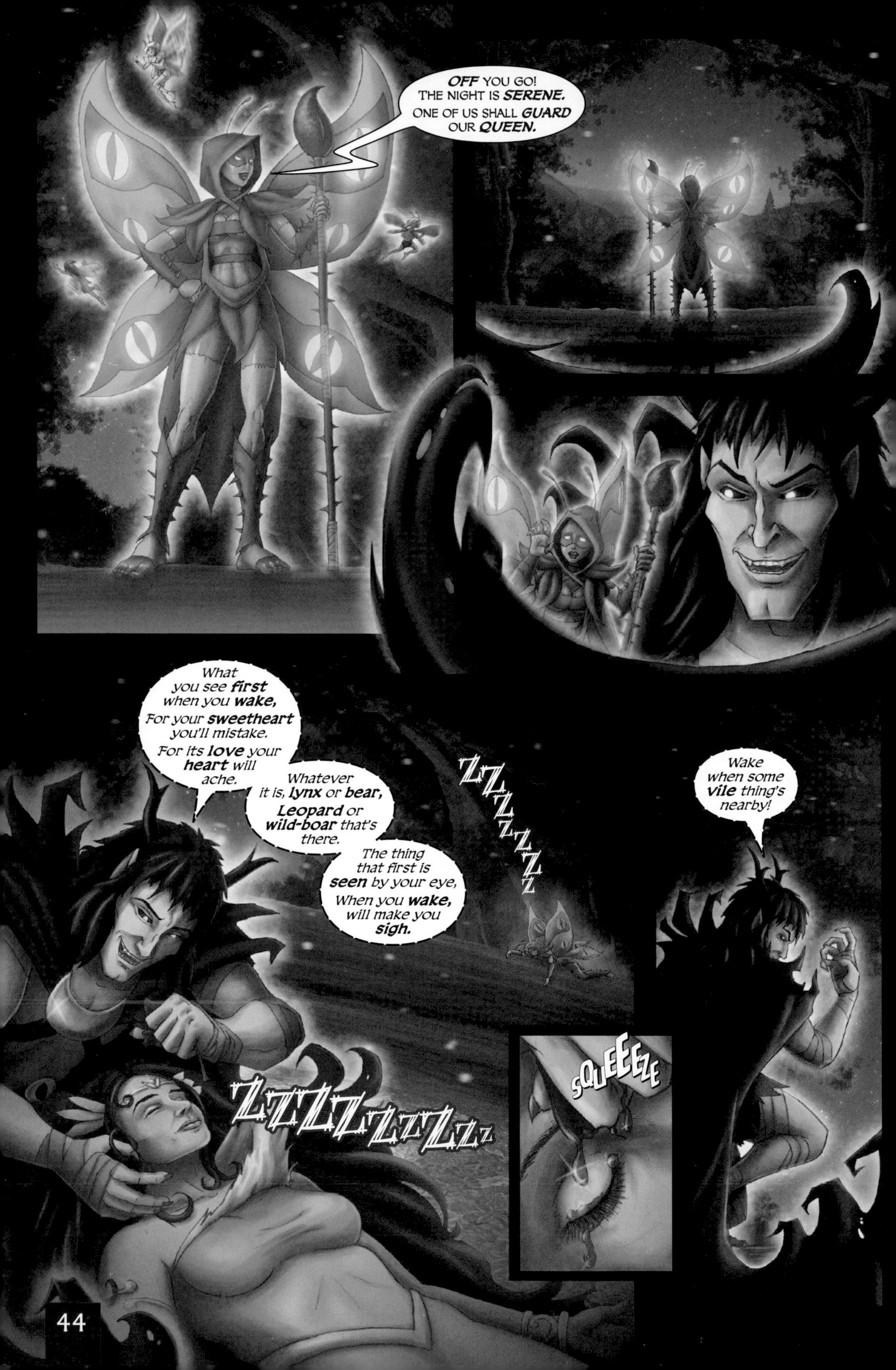

OFF YOU GO! THE NIGHT IS SERENE. ONE OF US SHALL GUARD OUR QUEEN.
What you see first when you wake, For your sweetheart you'll mistake. For its love your heart will ache.
Whatever it is, lynx or bear, Leopard or wild-boar that's there.
The thing that first is seen by your eye, When you wake, will make you sigh.
ZZZZZZZ
ZZZZZZZZZzz
Wake when some vile thing's nearby!
SQUEEEEZE

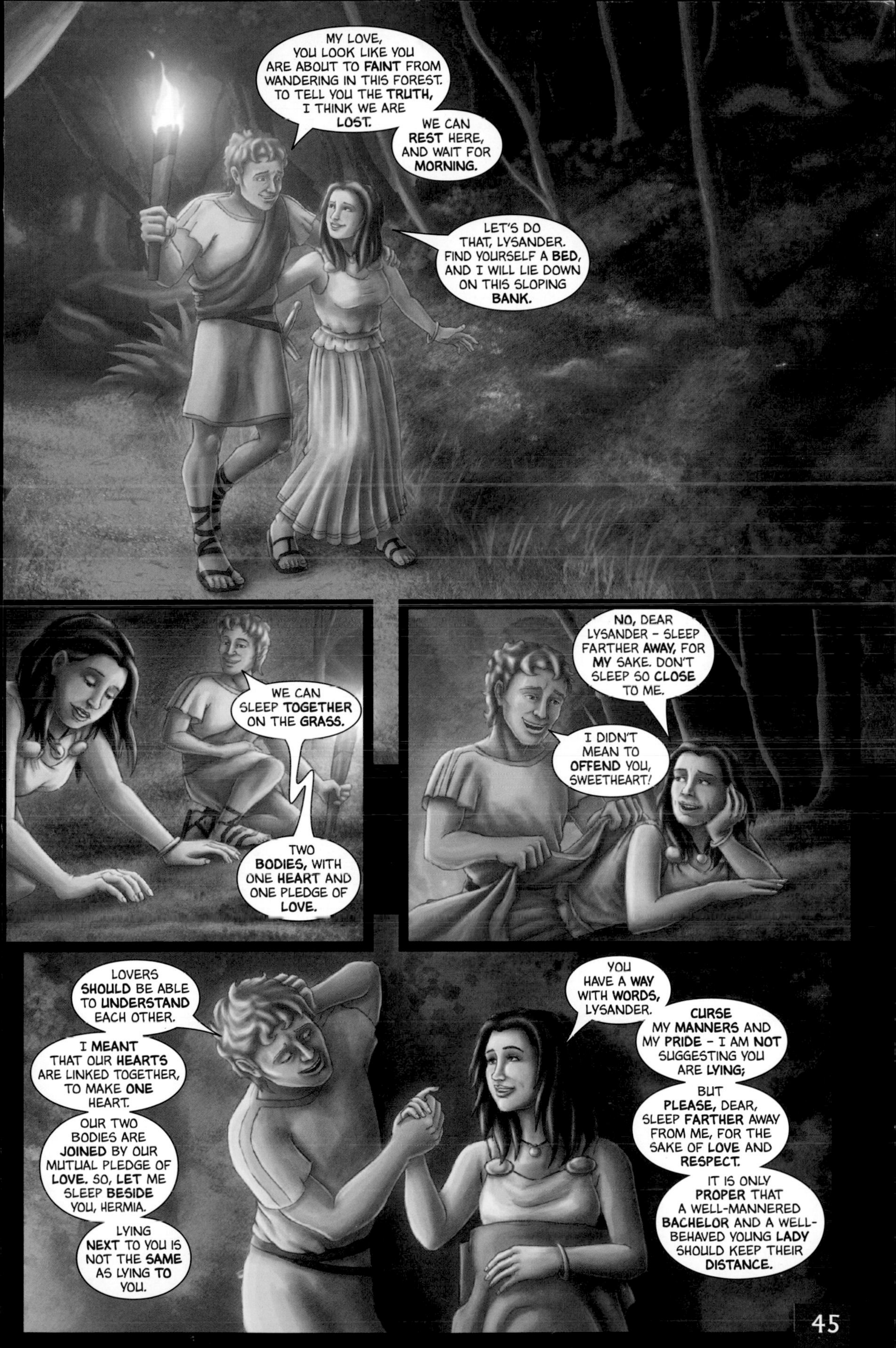

MY LOVE, YOU LOOK LIKE YOU ARE ABOUT TO FAINT FROM WANDERING IN THIS FOREST. TO TELL YOU THE TRUTH, I THINK WE ARE LOST.
WE CAN REST HERE, AND WAIT FOR MORNING.
LET'S DO THAT, LYSANDER. FIND YOURSELF A BED, AND I WILL LIE DOWN ON THIS SLOPING BANK.
WE CAN SLEEP TOGETHER ON THE GRASS.
TWO BODIES, WITH ONE HEART AND ONE PLEDGE OF LOVE.
NO, DEAR LYSANDER – SLEEP FARTHER AWAY, FOR MY SAKE. DON'T SLEEP SO CLOSE TO ME.
I DIDN'T MEAN TO OFFEND YOU, SWEETHEART!
LOVERS SHOULD BE ABLE TO UNDERSTAND EACH OTHER.
I MEANT THAT OUR HEARTS ARE LINKED TOGETHER, TO MAKE ONE HEART.
OUR TWO BODIES ARE JOINED BY OUR MUTUAL PLEDGE OF LOVE. SO, LET ME SLEEP BESIDE YOU, HERMIA.
LYING NEXT TO YOU IS NOT THE SAME AS LYING TO YOU.
YOU HAVE A WAY WITH WORDS, LYSANDER.
CURSE MY MANNERS AND MY PRIDE – I AM NOT SUGGESTING YOU ARE LYING;
BUT PLEASE, DEAR, SLEEP FARTHER AWAY FROM ME, FOR THE SAKE OF LOVE AND RESPECT.
IT IS ONLY PROPER THAT A WELL-MANNERED BACHELOR AND A WELL-BEHAVED YOUNG LADY SHOULD KEEP THEIR DISTANCE.

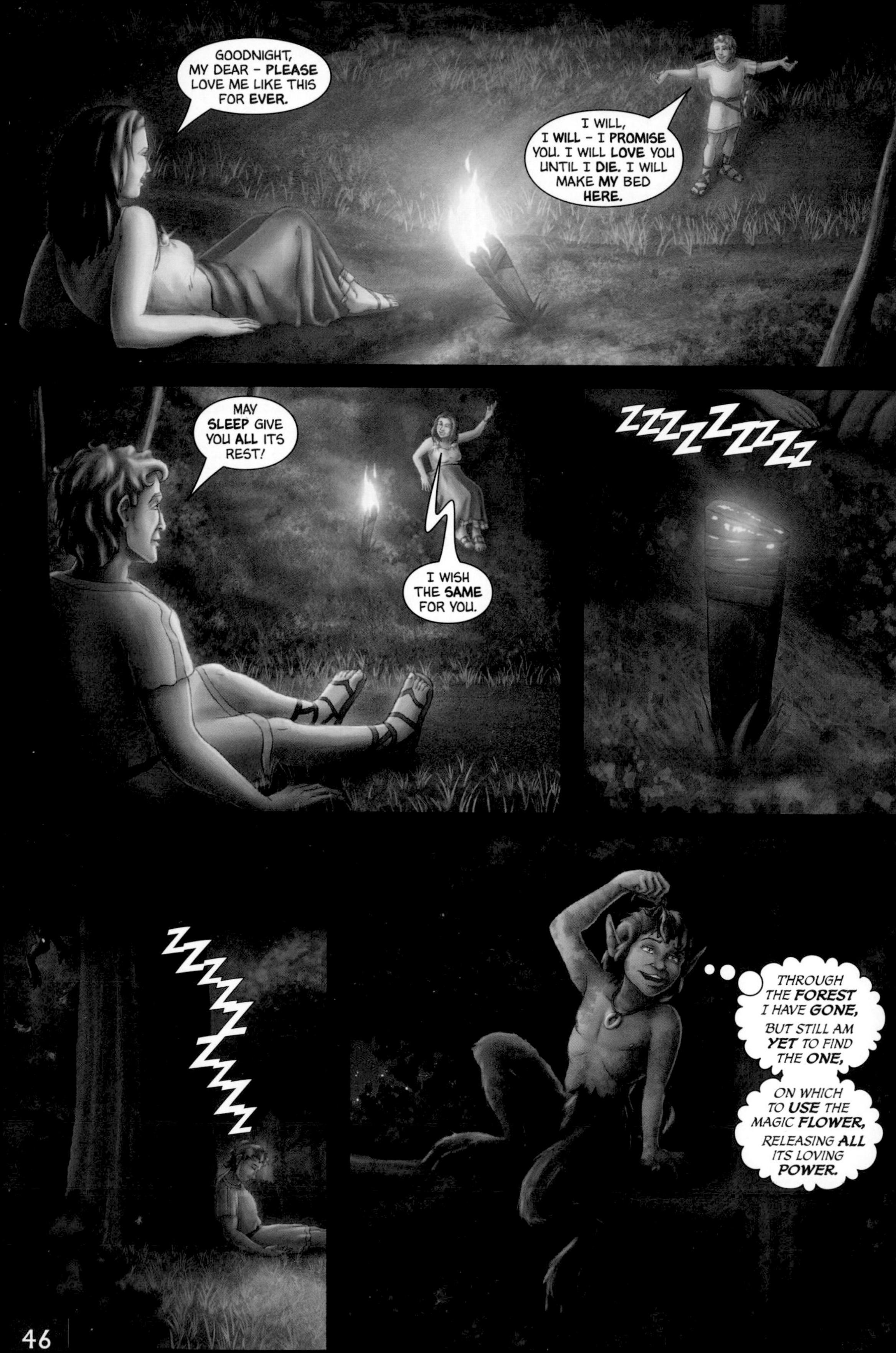

GOODNIGHT, MY DEAR – **PLEASE** LOVE ME LIKE THIS FOR **EVER.**
I WILL, I **WILL** – I **PROMISE** YOU. I WILL **LOVE** YOU UNTIL I **DIE.** I WILL MAKE **MY** BED **HERE.**
MAY **SLEEP** GIVE YOU **ALL** ITS REST!
I WISH THE **SAME** FOR YOU.
ZZZZZZZZZ
ZZZZZZZZ
*THROUGH THE **FOREST** I HAVE **GONE,** BUT STILL AM **YET** TO FIND THE **ONE,***
*ON WHICH TO **USE** THE MAGIC **FLOWER,** RELEASING **ALL** ITS LOVING **POWER.***

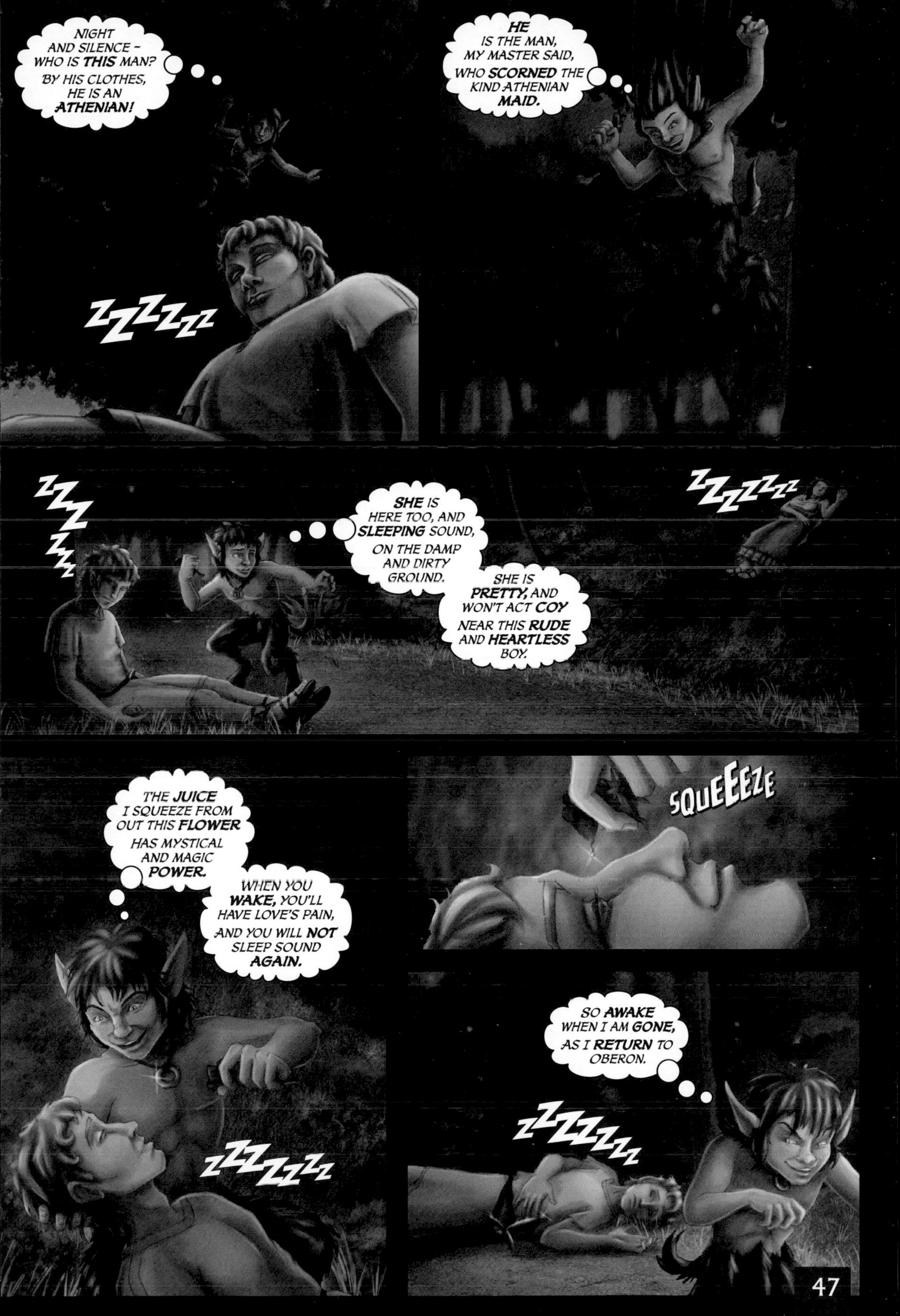
NIGHT AND SILENCE – WHO IS THIS MAN? BY HIS CLOTHES, HE IS AN ATHENIAN!
ZZZZZZ
HE IS THE MAN, MY MASTER SAID, WHO SCORNED THE KIND ATHENIAN MAID.
ZZZZZ
SHE IS HERE TOO, AND SLEEPING SOUND, ON THE DAMP AND DIRTY GROUND.
SHE IS PRETTY, AND WON'T ACT COY NEAR THIS RUDE AND HEARTLESS BOY.
ZZZZZZZ
THE JUICE I SQUEEZE FROM OUT THIS FLOWER HAS MYSTICAL AND MAGIC POWER.
WHEN YOU WAKE, YOU'LL HAVE LOVE'S PAIN, AND YOU WILL NOT SLEEP SOUND AGAIN.
ZZZZZZZ
SQUEEEZE
SO AWAKE WHEN I AM GONE, AS I RETURN TO OBERON.
ZZZZZZZ

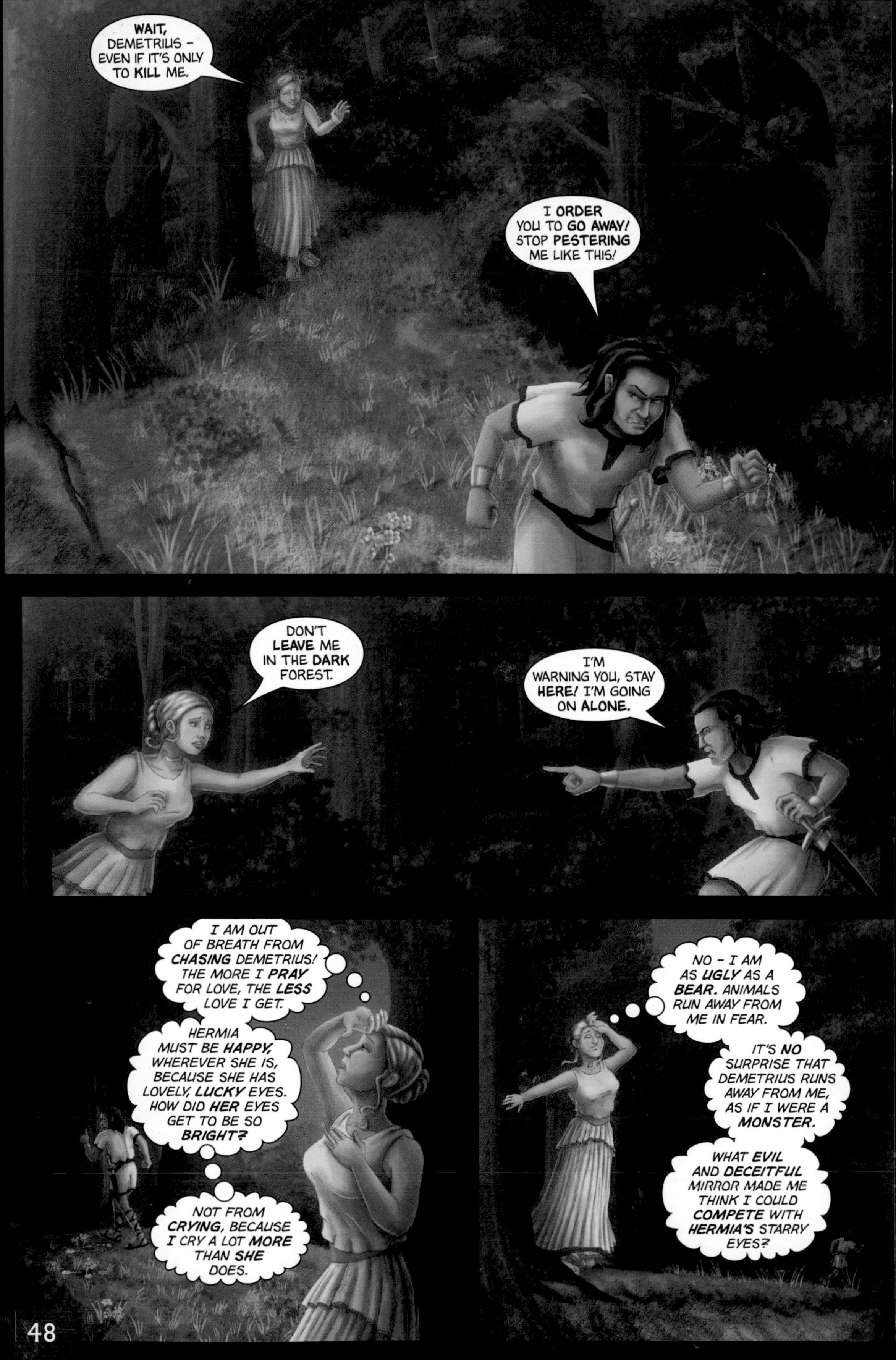
WAIT, DEMETRIUS – EVEN IF IT'S ONLY TO KILL ME.
I ORDER YOU TO GO AWAY! STOP PESTERING ME LIKE THIS!
DON'T LEAVE ME IN THE DARK FOREST.
I'M WARNING YOU, STAY HERE! I'M GOING ON ALONE.
I AM OUT OF BREATH FROM CHASING DEMETRIUS! THE MORE I PRAY FOR LOVE, THE LESS LOVE I GET.
HERMIA MUST BE HAPPY, WHEREVER SHE IS, BECAUSE SHE HAS LOVELY, LUCKY EYES. HOW DID HER EYES GET TO BE SO BRIGHT?
NOT FROM CRYING, BECAUSE I CRY A LOT MORE THAN SHE DOES.
NO – I AM AS UGLY AS A BEAR. ANIMALS RUN AWAY FROM ME IN FEAR.
IT'S NO SURPRISE THAT DEMETRIUS RUNS AWAY FROM ME, AS IF I WERE A MONSTER.
WHAT EVIL AND DECEITFUL MIRROR MADE ME THINK I COULD COMPETE WITH HERMIA'S STARRY EYES?

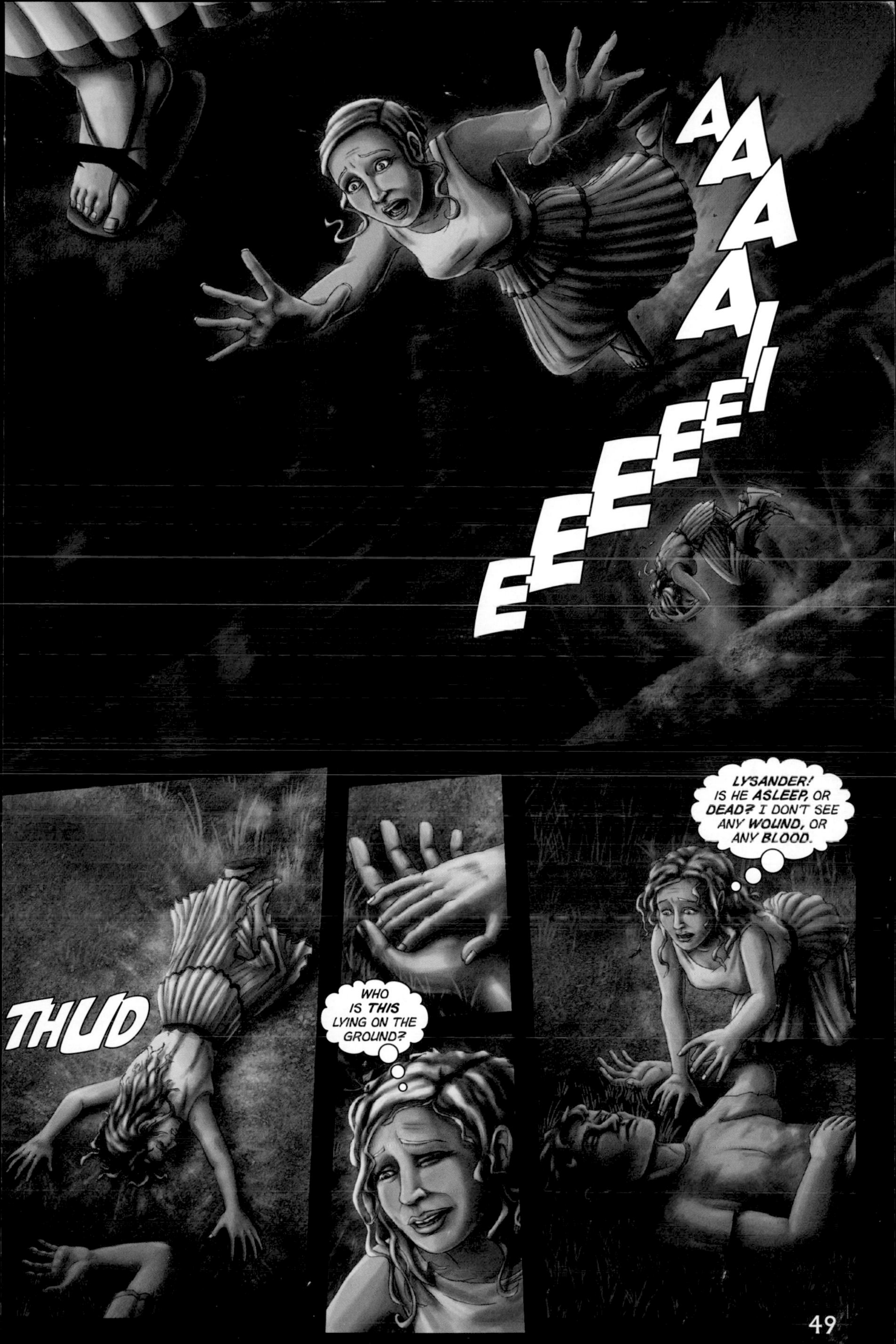
AAAAAIIEEEEEEE
THUD
WHO IS THIS LYING ON THE GROUND?
LYSANDER! IS HE ASLEEP, OR DEAD? I DON'T SEE ANY WOUND, OR ANY BLOOD.

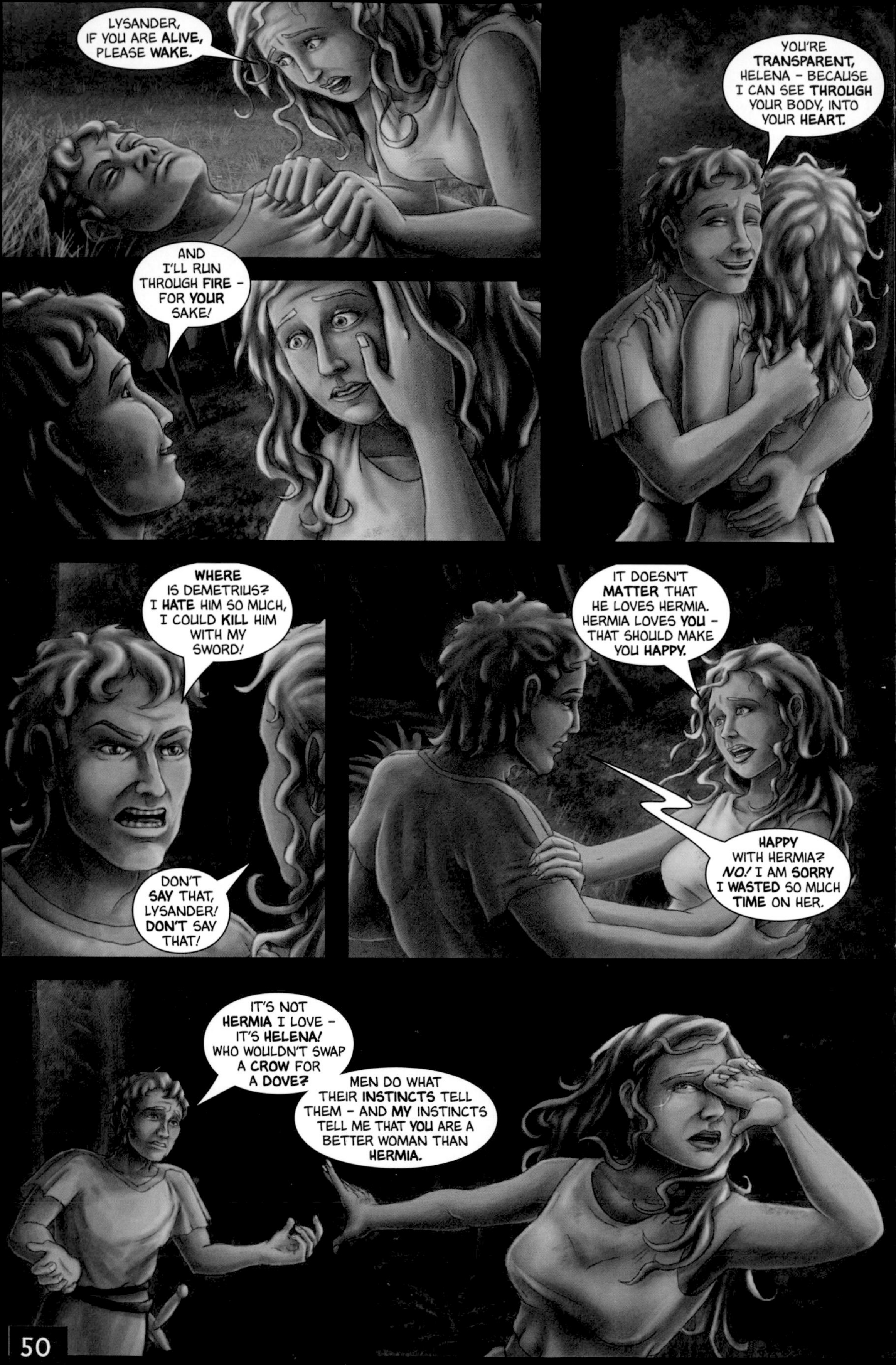
LYSANDER, IF YOU ARE **ALIVE,** PLEASE **WAKE.**
AND I'LL RUN THROUGH **FIRE** – FOR **YOUR** SAKE!
YOU'RE **TRANSPARENT,** HELENA – BECAUSE I CAN SEE **THROUGH** YOUR BODY, INTO YOUR **HEART.**
WHERE IS DEMETRIUS? I **HATE** HIM SO MUCH, I COULD **KILL** HIM WITH MY SWORD!
DON'T **SAY** THAT, LYSANDER! **DON'T** SAY THAT!
IT DOESN'T **MATTER** THAT HE LOVES HERMIA. HERMIA LOVES **YOU** – THAT SHOULD MAKE YOU **HAPPY.**
HAPPY WITH HERMIA? ***NO!*** I AM **SORRY** I **WASTED** SO MUCH **TIME** ON HER.
IT'S NOT **HERMIA** I LOVE – IT'S **HELENA!** WHO WOULDN'T SWAP A **CROW** FOR A **DOVE?**
MEN DO WHAT THEIR **INSTINCTS** TELL THEM – AND **MY** INSTINCTS TELL ME THAT **YOU** ARE A BETTER WOMAN THAN **HERMIA.**

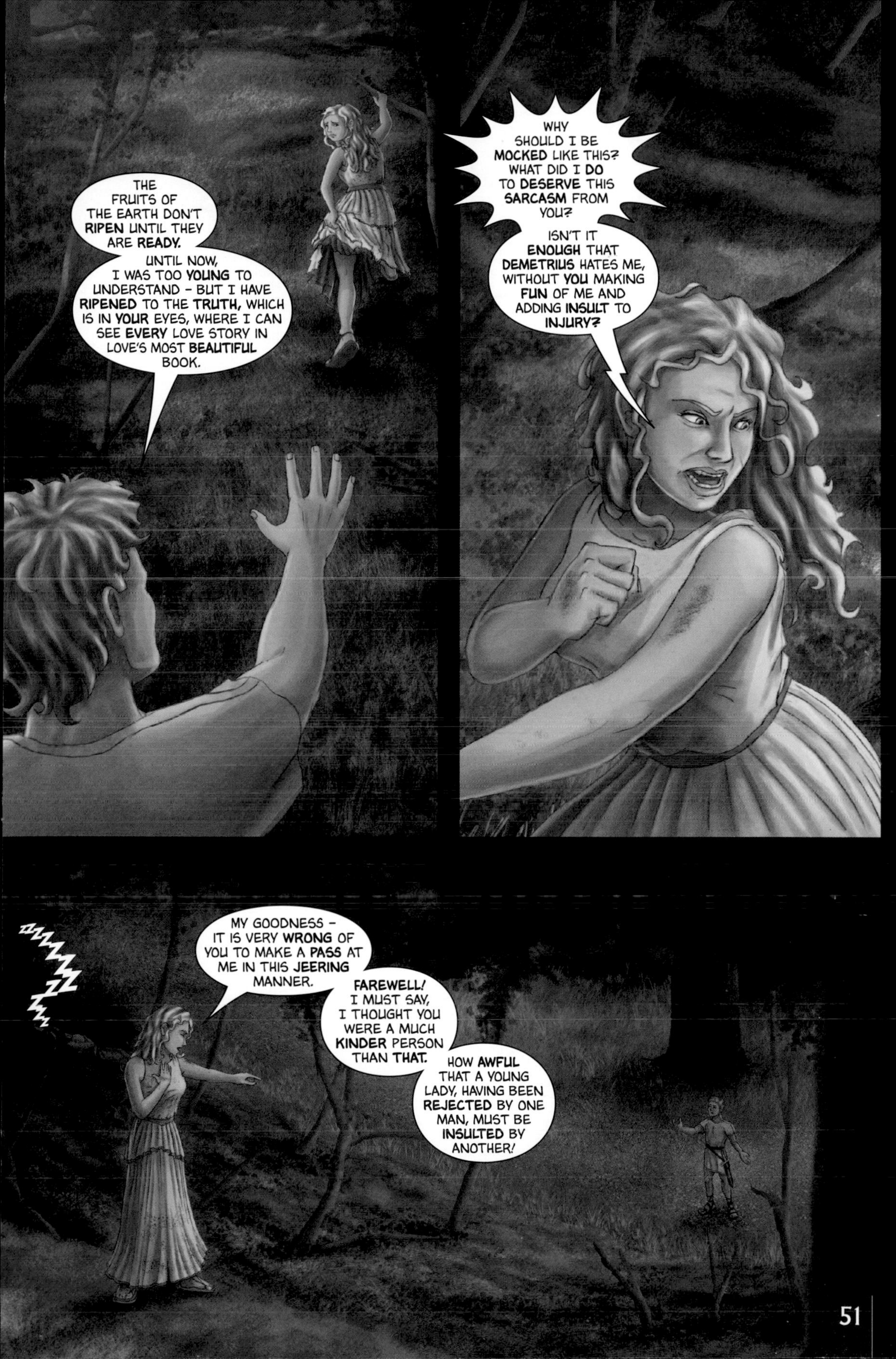

THE FRUITS OF THE EARTH DON'T RIPEN UNTIL THEY ARE READY.
UNTIL NOW, I WAS TOO YOUNG TO UNDERSTAND – BUT I HAVE RIPENED TO THE TRUTH, WHICH IS IN YOUR EYES, WHERE I CAN SEE EVERY LOVE STORY IN LOVE'S MOST BEAUTIFUL BOOK.
WHY SHOULD I BE MOCKED LIKE THIS? WHAT DID I DO TO DESERVE THIS SARCASM FROM YOU?
ISN'T IT ENOUGH THAT DEMETRIUS HATES ME, WITHOUT YOU MAKING FUN OF ME AND ADDING INSULT TO INJURY?
MY GOODNESS – IT IS VERY WRONG OF YOU TO MAKE A PASS AT ME IN THIS JEERING MANNER.
FAREWELL! I MUST SAY, I THOUGHT YOU WERE A MUCH KINDER PERSON THAN THAT.
HOW AWFUL THAT A YOUNG LADY, HAVING BEEN REJECTED BY ONE MAN, MUST BE INSULTED BY ANOTHER!

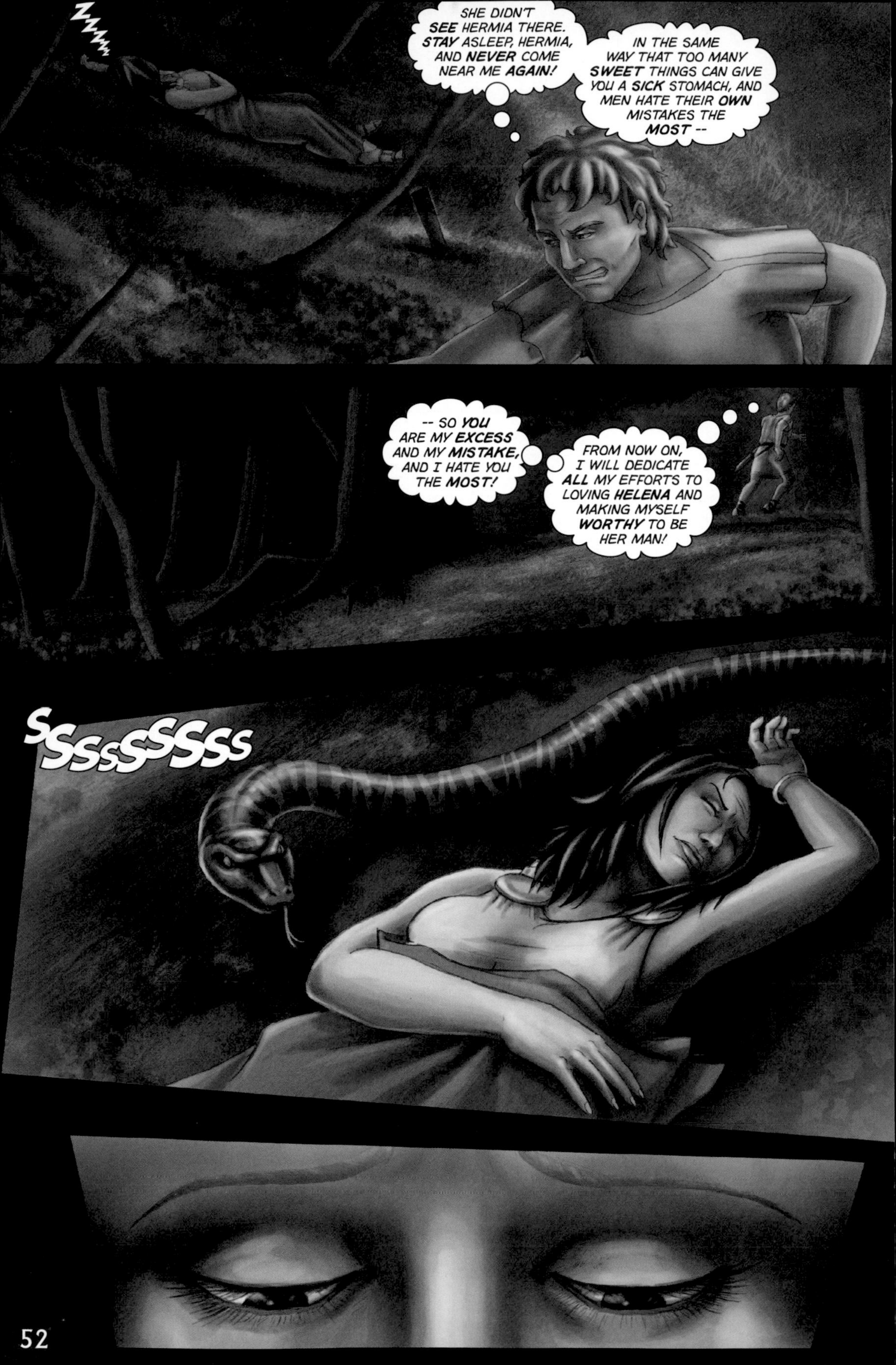

ZZZZZ
SHE DIDN'T SEE HERMIA THERE. STAY ASLEEP, HERMIA, AND NEVER COME NEAR ME AGAIN!
IN THE SAME WAY THAT TOO MANY SWEET THINGS CAN GIVE YOU A SICK STOMACH, AND MEN HATE THEIR OWN MISTAKES THE MOST --
-- SO YOU ARE MY EXCESS AND MY MISTAKE, AND I HATE YOU THE MOST!
FROM NOW ON, I WILL DEDICATE ALL MY EFFORTS TO LOVING HELENA AND MAKING MYSELF WORTHY TO BE HER MAN!
SSSSSSSSS

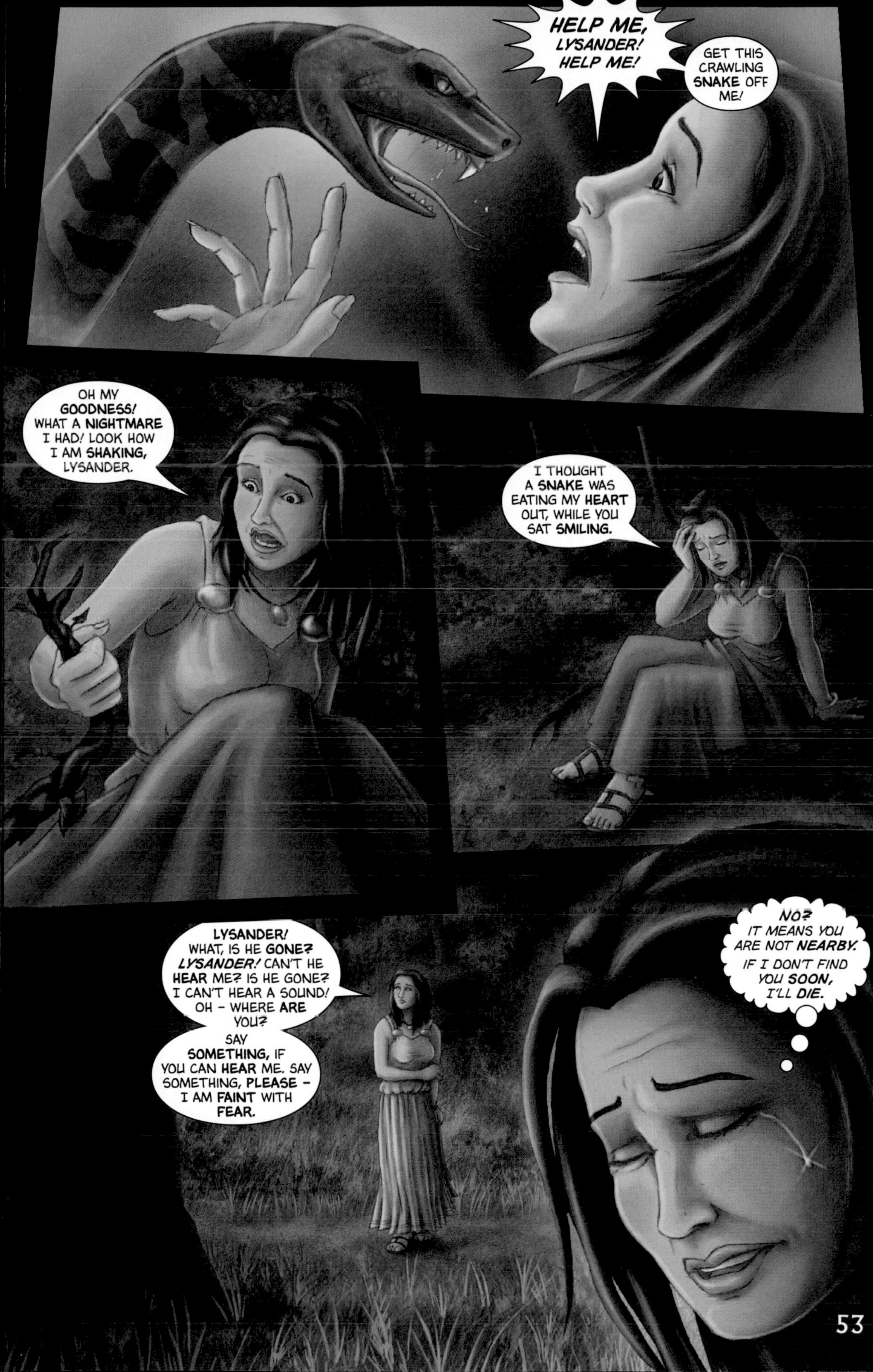
HELP ME, LYSANDER! HELP ME!
GET THIS CRAWLING SNAKE OFF ME!
OH MY GOODNESS! WHAT A NIGHTMARE I HAD! LOOK HOW I AM SHAKING, LYSANDER.
I THOUGHT A SNAKE WAS EATING MY HEART OUT, WHILE YOU SAT SMILING.
LYSANDER! WHAT, IS HE GONE? LYSANDER! CAN'T HE HEAR ME? IS HE GONE? I CAN'T HEAR A SOUND! OH – WHERE ARE YOU?
SAY SOMETHING, IF YOU CAN HEAR ME. SAY SOMETHING, PLEASE – I AM FAINT WITH FEAR.
NO? IT MEANS YOU ARE NOT NEARBY.
IF I DON'T FIND YOU SOON, I'LL DIE.

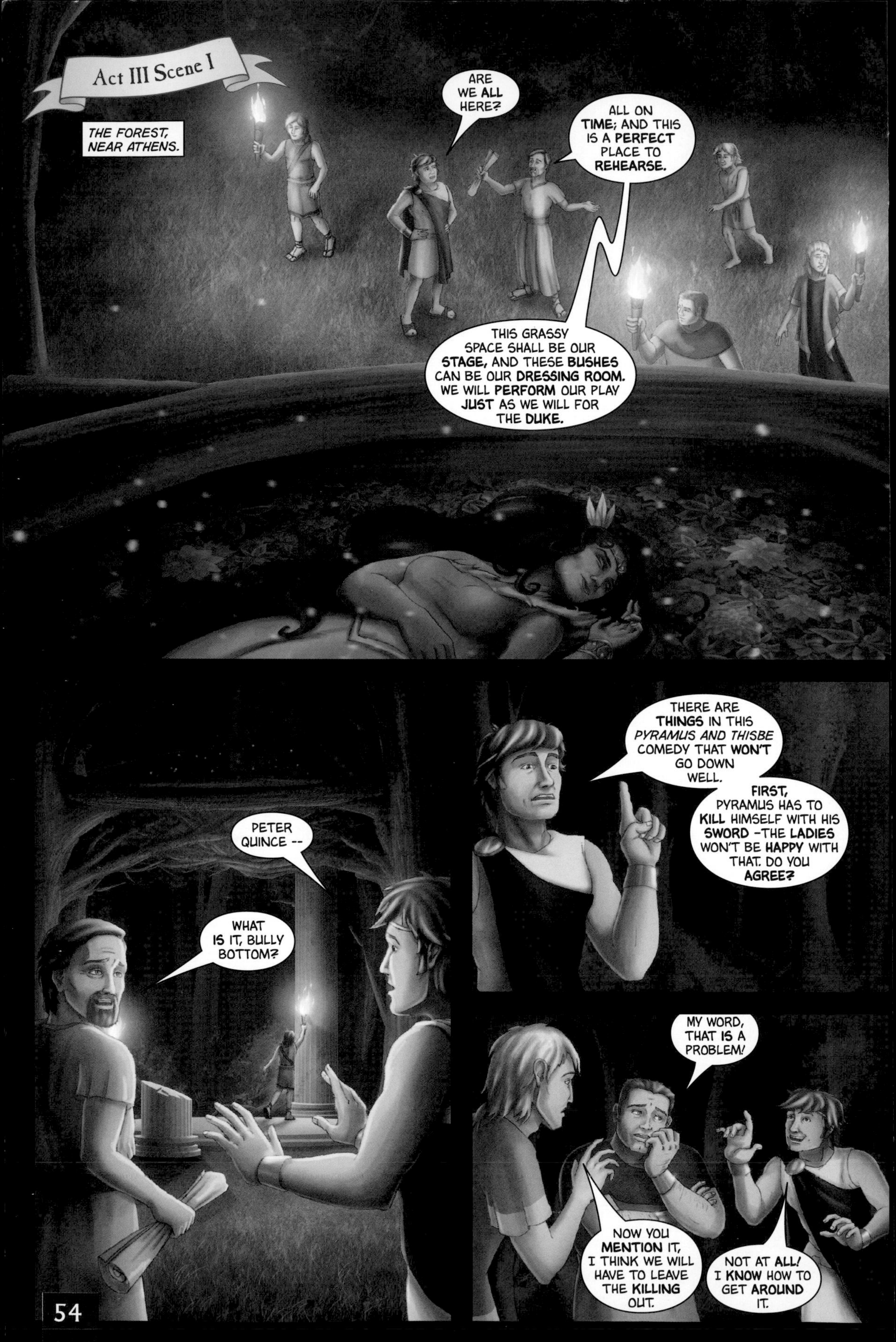
Act III Scene I
THE FOREST, NEAR ATHENS.
ARE WE ALL HERE?
ALL ON TIME; AND THIS IS A PERFECT PLACE TO REHEARSE.
THIS GRASSY SPACE SHALL BE OUR STAGE, AND THESE BUSHES CAN BE OUR DRESSING ROOM. WE WILL PERFORM OUR PLAY JUST AS WE WILL FOR THE DUKE.
PETER QUINCE --
WHAT IS IT, BULLY BOTTOM?
THERE ARE THINGS IN THIS PYRAMUS AND THISBE COMEDY THAT WON'T GO DOWN WELL.
FIRST, PYRAMUS HAS TO KILL HIMSELF WITH HIS SWORD -THE LADIES WON'T BE HAPPY WITH THAT. DO YOU AGREE?
MY WORD, THAT IS A PROBLEM!
NOW YOU MENTION IT, I THINK WE WILL HAVE TO LEAVE THE KILLING OUT.
NOT AT ALL! I KNOW HOW TO GET AROUND IT.

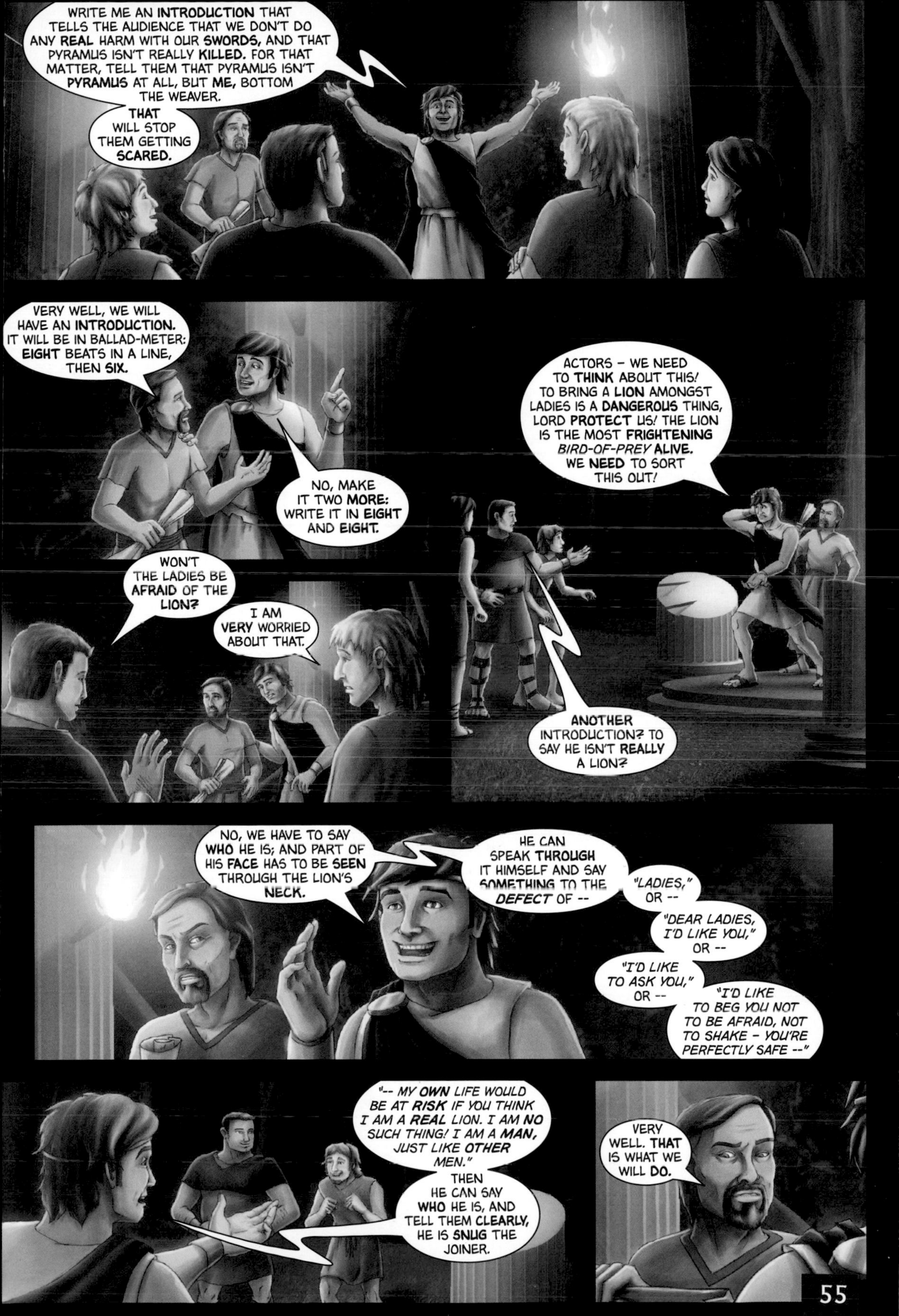

WRITE ME AN INTRODUCTION THAT TELLS THE AUDIENCE THAT WE DON'T DO ANY REAL HARM WITH OUR SWORDS, AND THAT PYRAMUS ISN'T REALLY KILLED. FOR THAT MATTER, TELL THEM THAT PYRAMUS ISN'T PYRAMUS AT ALL, BUT ME, BOTTOM THE WEAVER.
THAT WILL STOP THEM GETTING SCARED.
VERY WELL, WE WILL HAVE AN INTRODUCTION. IT WILL BE IN BALLAD-METER: EIGHT BEATS IN A LINE, THEN SIX.
NO, MAKE IT TWO MORE: WRITE IT IN EIGHT AND EIGHT.
WON'T THE LADIES BE AFRAID OF THE LION?
I AM VERY WORRIED ABOUT THAT.
ACTORS – WE NEED TO THINK ABOUT THIS! TO BRING A LION AMONGST LADIES IS A DANGEROUS THING, LORD PROTECT US! THE LION IS THE MOST FRIGHTENING *BIRD-OF-PREY* ALIVE. WE NEED TO SORT THIS OUT!
ANOTHER INTRODUCTION? TO SAY HE ISN'T REALLY A LION?
NO, WE HAVE TO SAY WHO HE IS; AND PART OF HIS FACE HAS TO BE SEEN THROUGH THE LION'S NECK.
HE CAN SPEAK THROUGH IT HIMSELF AND SAY SOMETHING TO THE *DEFECT* OF --
"LADIES," OR --
"DEAR LADIES, I'D LIKE YOU," OR --
"I'D LIKE TO ASK YOU," OR --
"I'D LIKE TO BEG YOU NOT TO BE AFRAID, NOT TO SHAKE – YOU'RE PERFECTLY SAFE --"
"-- MY OWN LIFE WOULD BE AT RISK IF YOU THINK I AM A REAL LION. I AM NO SUCH THING! I AM A MAN, JUST LIKE OTHER MEN."
THEN HE CAN SAY WHO HE IS, AND TELL THEM CLEARLY, HE IS SNUG THE JOINER.
VERY WELL. THAT IS WHAT WE WILL DO.

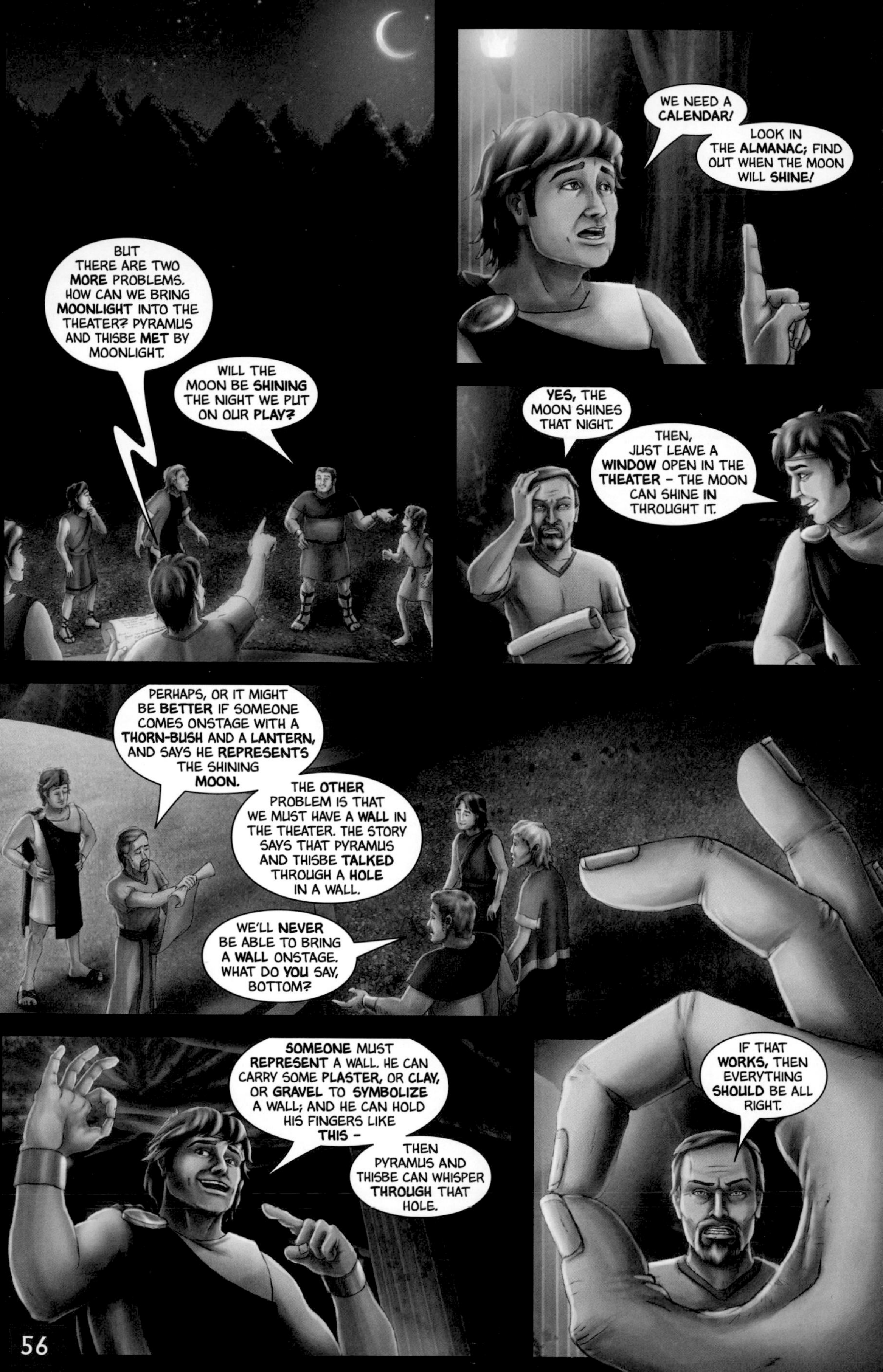
BUT THERE ARE TWO MORE PROBLEMS. HOW CAN WE BRING MOONLIGHT INTO THE THEATER? PYRAMUS AND THISBE MET BY MOONLIGHT.
WILL THE MOON BE SHINING THE NIGHT WE PUT ON OUR PLAY?
WE NEED A CALENDAR!
LOOK IN THE ALMANAC; FIND OUT WHEN THE MOON WILL SHINE!
YES, THE MOON SHINES THAT NIGHT.
THEN, JUST LEAVE A WINDOW OPEN IN THE THEATER - THE MOON CAN SHINE IN THROUGHT IT.
PERHAPS, OR IT MIGHT BE BETTER IF SOMEONE COMES ONSTAGE WITH A THORN-BUSH AND A LANTERN, AND SAYS HE REPRESENTS THE SHINING MOON.
THE OTHER PROBLEM IS THAT WE MUST HAVE A WALL IN THE THEATER. THE STORY SAYS THAT PYRAMUS AND THISBE TALKED THROUGH A HOLE IN A WALL.
WE'LL NEVER BE ABLE TO BRING A WALL ONSTAGE. WHAT DO YOU SAY, BOTTOM?
SOMEONE MUST REPRESENT A WALL. HE CAN CARRY SOME PLASTER, OR CLAY, OR GRAVEL TO SYMBOLIZE A WALL; AND HE CAN HOLD HIS FINGERS LIKE THIS -
THEN PYRAMUS AND THISBE CAN WHISPER THROUGH THAT HOLE.
IF THAT WORKS, THEN EVERYTHING SHOULD BE ALL RIGHT.

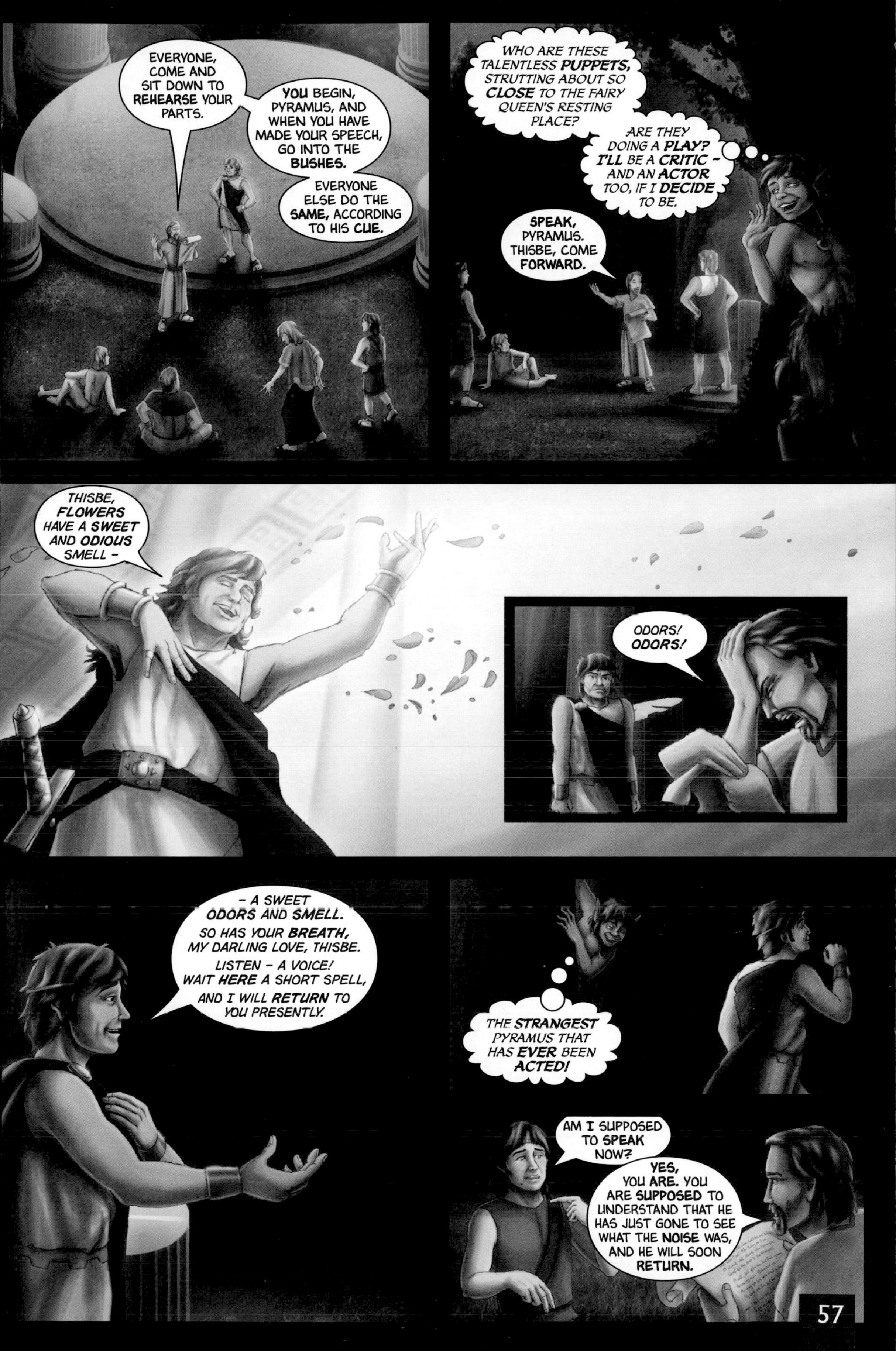
EVERYONE, COME AND SIT DOWN TO REHEARSE YOUR PARTS.
YOU BEGIN, PYRAMUS, AND WHEN YOU HAVE MADE YOUR SPEECH, GO INTO THE BUSHES.
EVERYONE ELSE DO THE SAME, ACCORDING TO HIS CUE.
WHO ARE THESE TALENTLESS PUPPETS, STRUTTING ABOUT SO CLOSE TO THE FAIRY QUEEN'S RESTING PLACE?
ARE THEY DOING A PLAY? I'LL BE A CRITIC – AND AN ACTOR TOO, IF I DECIDE TO BE.
SPEAK, PYRAMUS. THISBE, COME FORWARD.
THISBE, FLOWERS HAVE A SWEET AND ODIOUS SMELL –
ODORS! ODORS!
– A SWEET ODORS AND SMELL. SO HAS YOUR BREATH, MY DARLING LOVE, THISBE.
LISTEN – A VOICE! WAIT HERE A SHORT SPELL, AND I WILL RETURN TO YOU PRESENTLY.
THE STRANGEST PYRAMUS THAT HAS EVER BEEN ACTED!
AM I SUPPOSED TO SPEAK NOW?
YES, YOU ARE. YOU ARE SUPPOSED TO UNDERSTAND THAT HE HAS JUST GONE TO SEE WHAT THE NOISE WAS, AND HE WILL SOON RETURN.

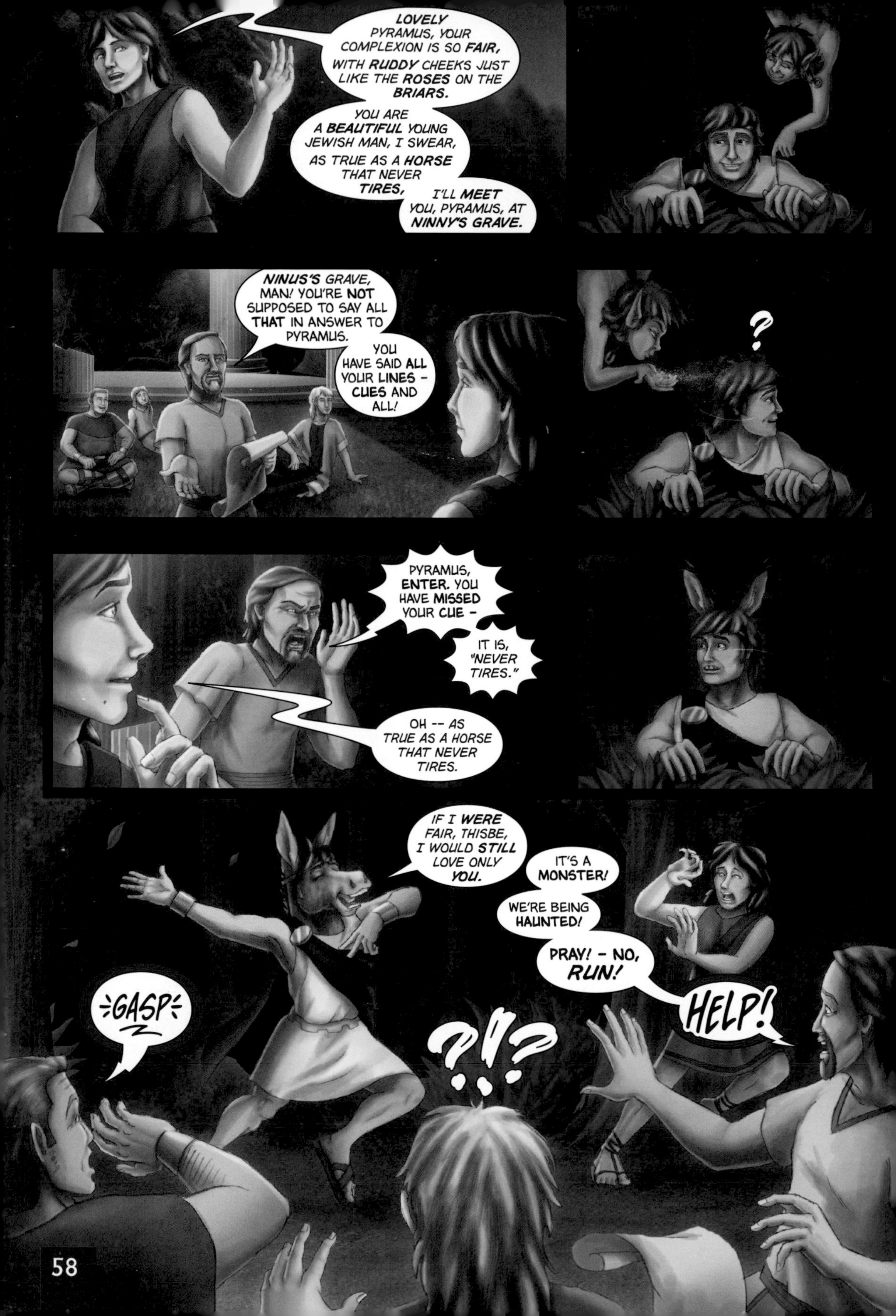
LOVELY PYRAMUS, YOUR COMPLEXION IS SO FAIR, WITH RUDDY CHEEKS JUST LIKE THE ROSES ON THE BRIARS.
YOU ARE A BEAUTIFUL YOUNG JEWISH MAN, I SWEAR, AS TRUE AS A HORSE THAT NEVER TIRES,
I'LL MEET YOU, PYRAMUS, AT NINNY'S GRAVE.
NINUS'S GRAVE, MAN! YOU'RE NOT SUPPOSED TO SAY ALL THAT IN ANSWER TO PYRAMUS.
YOU HAVE SAID ALL YOUR LINES - CUES AND ALL!
?
PYRAMUS, ENTER. YOU HAVE MISSED YOUR CUE -
IT IS, "NEVER TIRES."
OH -- AS TRUE AS A HORSE THAT NEVER TIRES.
IF I WERE FAIR, THISBE, I WOULD STILL LOVE ONLY YOU.
IT'S A MONSTER!
WE'RE BEING HAUNTED!
PRAY! - NO, RUN!
HELP!
GASP
?!?

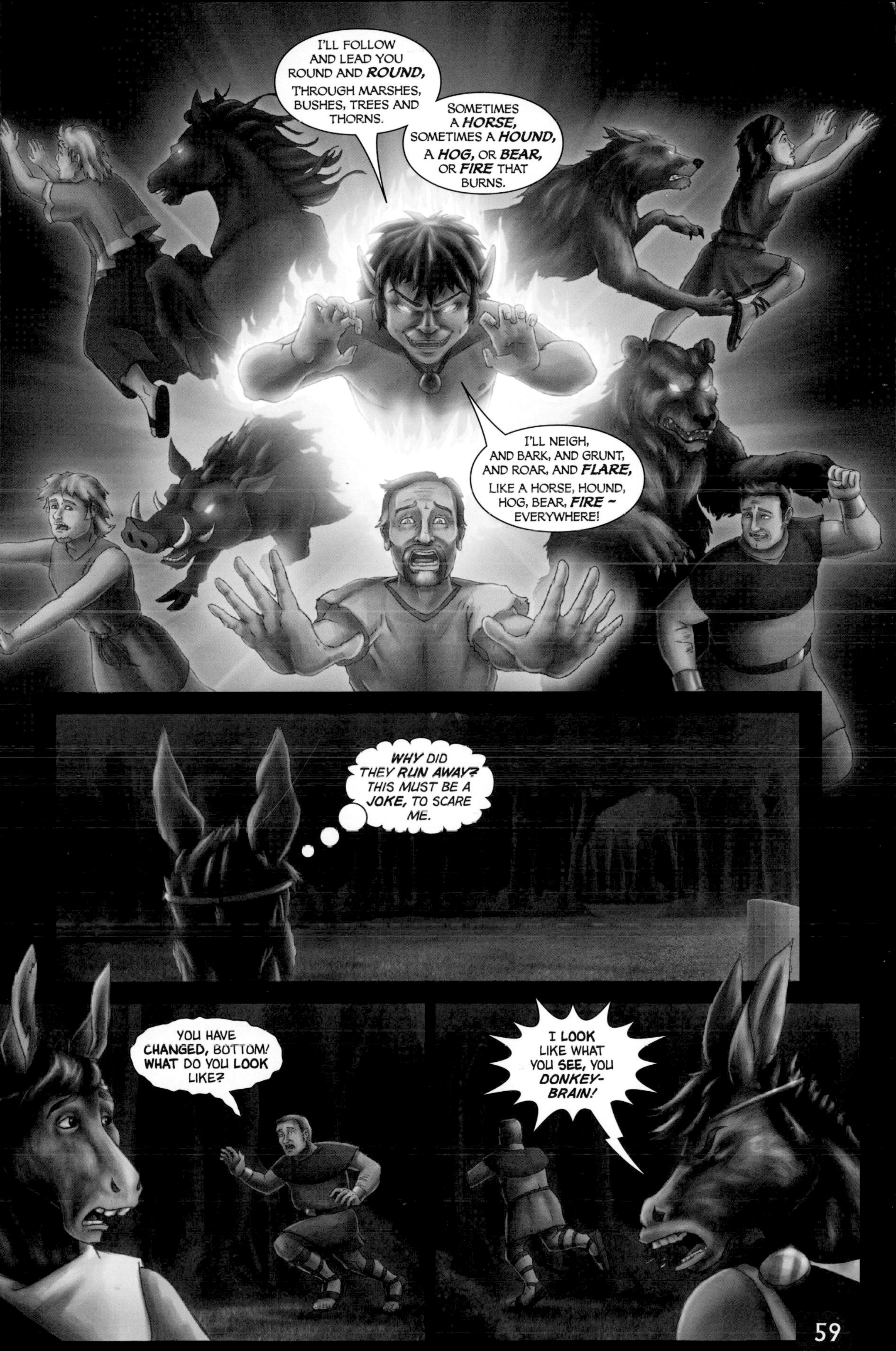
I'LL FOLLOW AND LEAD YOU ROUND AND ROUND, THROUGH MARSHES, BUSHES, TREES AND THORNS.
SOMETIMES A HORSE, SOMETIMES A HOUND, A HOG, OR BEAR, OR FIRE THAT BURNS.
I'LL NEIGH, AND BARK, AND GRUNT, AND ROAR, AND FLARE, LIKE A HORSE, HOUND, HOG, BEAR, FIRE ~ EVERYWHERE!
WHY DID THEY RUN AWAY? THIS MUST BE A JOKE, TO SCARE ME.
YOU HAVE CHANGED, BOTTOM! WHAT DO YOU LOOK LIKE?
I LOOK LIKE WHAT YOU SEE, YOU DONKEY-BRAIN!

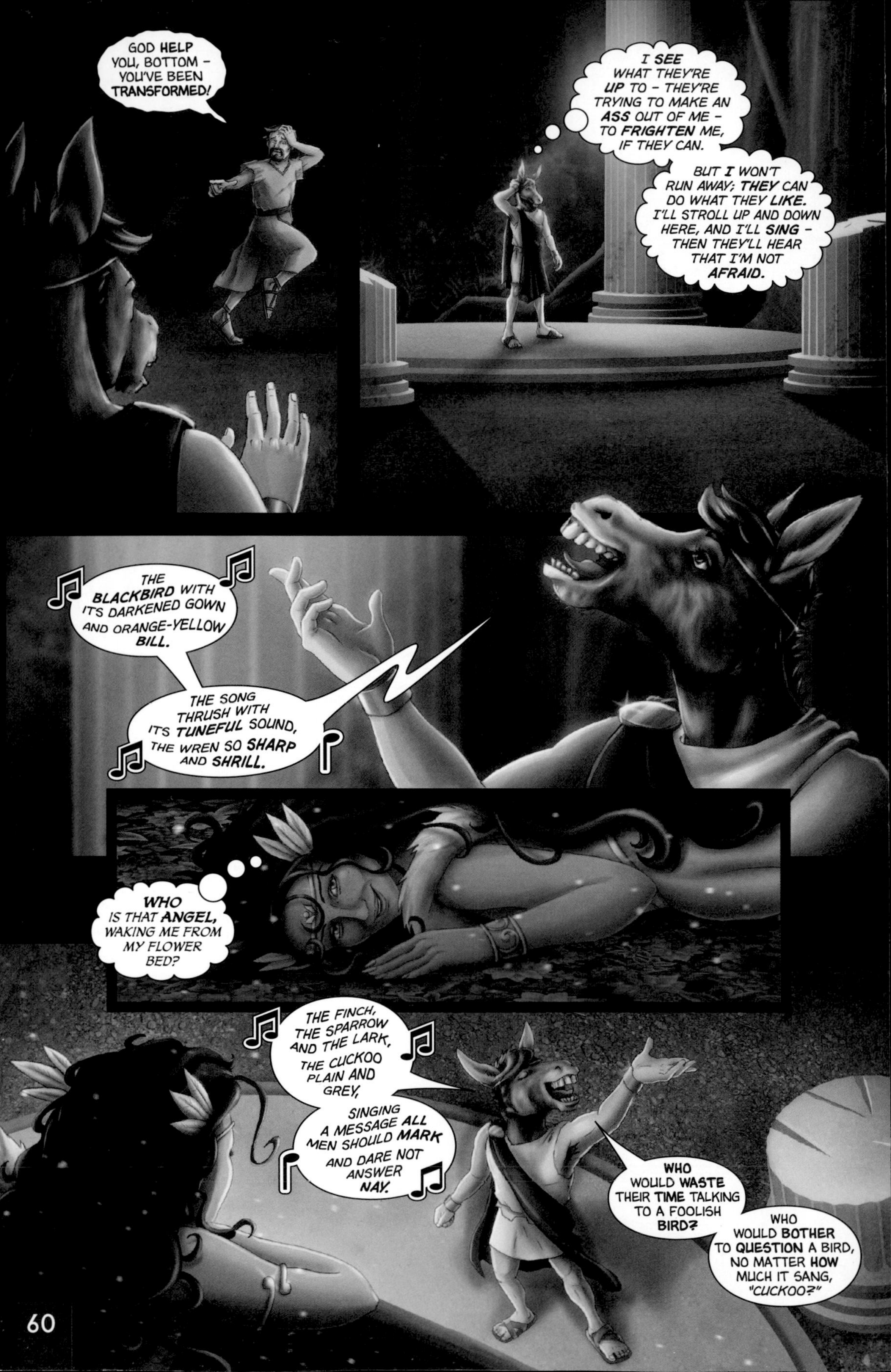
GOD HELP YOU, BOTTOM – YOU'VE BEEN TRANSFORMED!
I SEE WHAT THEY'RE UP TO – THEY'RE TRYING TO MAKE AN ASS OUT OF ME – TO FRIGHTEN ME, IF THEY CAN.
BUT I WON'T RUN AWAY; THEY CAN DO WHAT THEY LIKE. I'LL STROLL UP AND DOWN HERE, AND I'LL SING – THEN THEY'LL HEAR THAT I'M NOT AFRAID.
THE BLACKBIRD WITH IT'S DARKENED GOWN AND ORANGE-YELLOW BILL.
THE SONG THRUSH WITH IT'S TUNEFUL SOUND, THE WREN SO SHARP AND SHRILL.
WHO IS THAT ANGEL, WAKING ME FROM MY FLOWER BED?
THE FINCH, THE SPARROW AND THE LARK, THE CUCKOO PLAIN AND GREY,
SINGING A MESSAGE ALL MEN SHOULD MARK AND DARE NOT ANSWER NAY.
WHO WOULD WASTE THEIR TIME TALKING TO A FOOLISH BIRD?
WHO WOULD BOTHER TO QUESTION A BIRD, NO MATTER HOW MUCH IT SANG, "CUCKOO?"

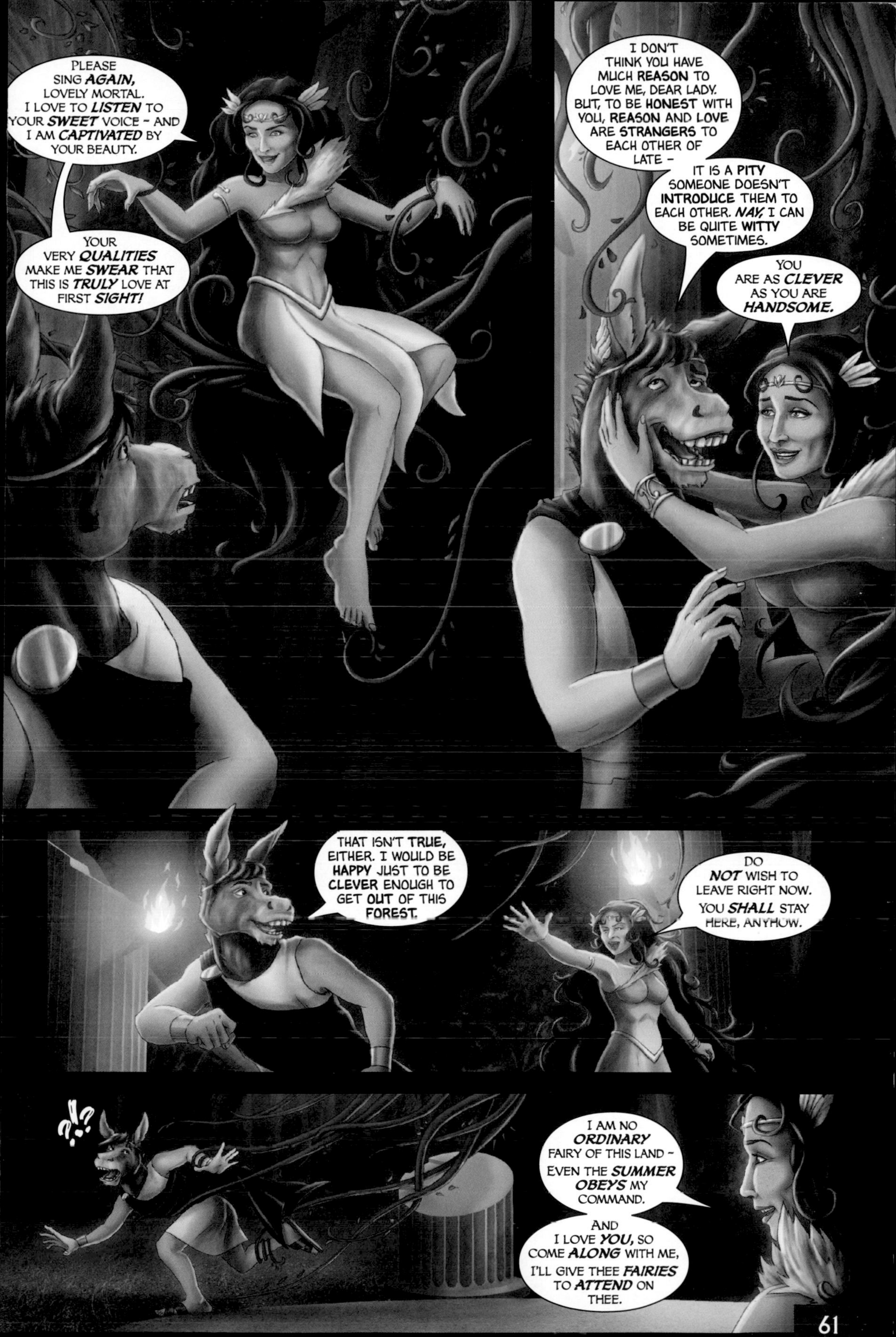
PLEASE SING AGAIN, LOVELY MORTAL. I LOVE TO LISTEN TO YOUR SWEET VOICE - AND I AM CAPTIVATED BY YOUR BEAUTY.
YOUR VERY QUALITIES MAKE ME SWEAR THAT THIS IS TRULY LOVE AT FIRST SIGHT!
I DON'T THINK YOU HAVE MUCH REASON TO LOVE ME, DEAR LADY. BUT, TO BE HONEST WITH YOU, REASON AND LOVE ARE STRANGERS TO EACH OTHER OF LATE -
IT IS A PITY SOMEONE DOESN'T INTRODUCE THEM TO EACH OTHER. NAY, I CAN BE QUITE WITTY SOMETIMES.
YOU ARE AS CLEVER AS YOU ARE HANDSOME.
THAT ISN'T TRUE, EITHER. I WOULD BE HAPPY JUST TO BE CLEVER ENOUGH TO GET OUT OF THIS FOREST.
DO NOT WISH TO LEAVE RIGHT NOW.
YOU SHALL STAY HERE, ANYHOW.
!?
I AM NO ORDINARY FAIRY OF THIS LAND -
EVEN THE SUMMER OBEYS MY COMMAND.
AND I LOVE YOU, SO COME ALONG WITH ME,
I'LL GIVE THEE FAIRIES TO ATTEND ON THEE.

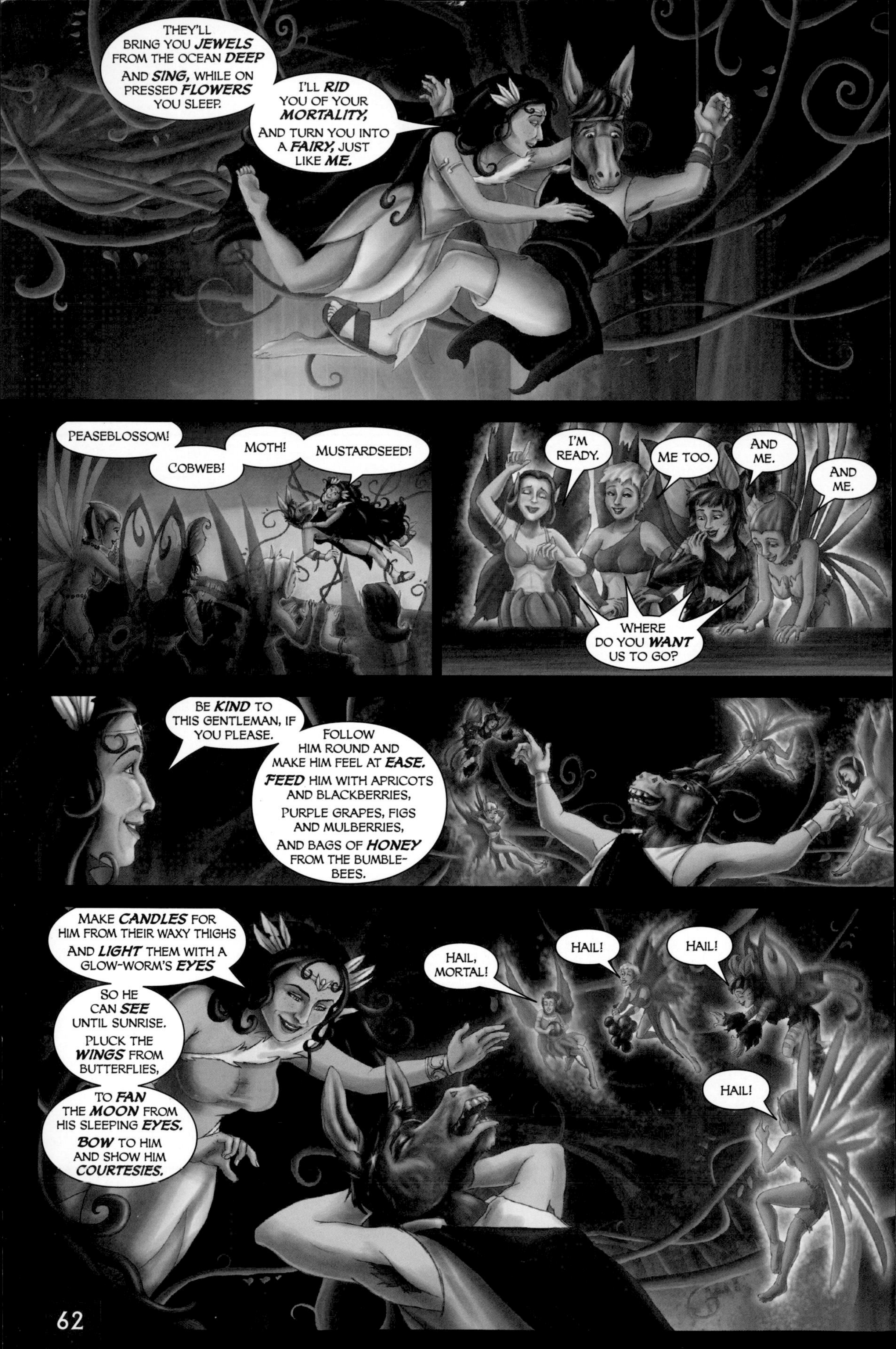
THEY'LL BRING YOU JEWELS FROM THE OCEAN DEEP
AND SING, WHILE ON PRESSED FLOWERS YOU SLEEP.
I'LL RID YOU OF YOUR MORTALITY,
AND TURN YOU INTO A FAIRY, JUST LIKE ME.
PEASEBLOSSOM!
COBWEB!
MOTH!
MUSTARDSEED!
I'M READY.
ME TOO.
AND ME.
AND ME.
WHERE DO YOU WANT US TO GO?
BE KIND TO THIS GENTLEMAN, IF YOU PLEASE.
FOLLOW HIM ROUND AND MAKE HIM FEEL AT EASE.
FEED HIM WITH APRICOTS AND BLACKBERRIES,
PURPLE GRAPES, FIGS AND MULBERRIES,
AND BAGS OF HONEY FROM THE BUMBLE-BEES.
MAKE CANDLES FOR HIM FROM THEIR WAXY THIGHS
AND LIGHT THEM WITH A GLOW-WORM'S EYES
SO HE CAN SEE UNTIL SUNRISE.
PLUCK THE WINGS FROM BUTTERFLIES,
TO FAN THE MOON FROM HIS SLEEPING EYES.
BOW TO HIM AND SHOW HIM COURTESIES.
HAIL, MORTAL!
HAIL!
HAIL!
HAIL!

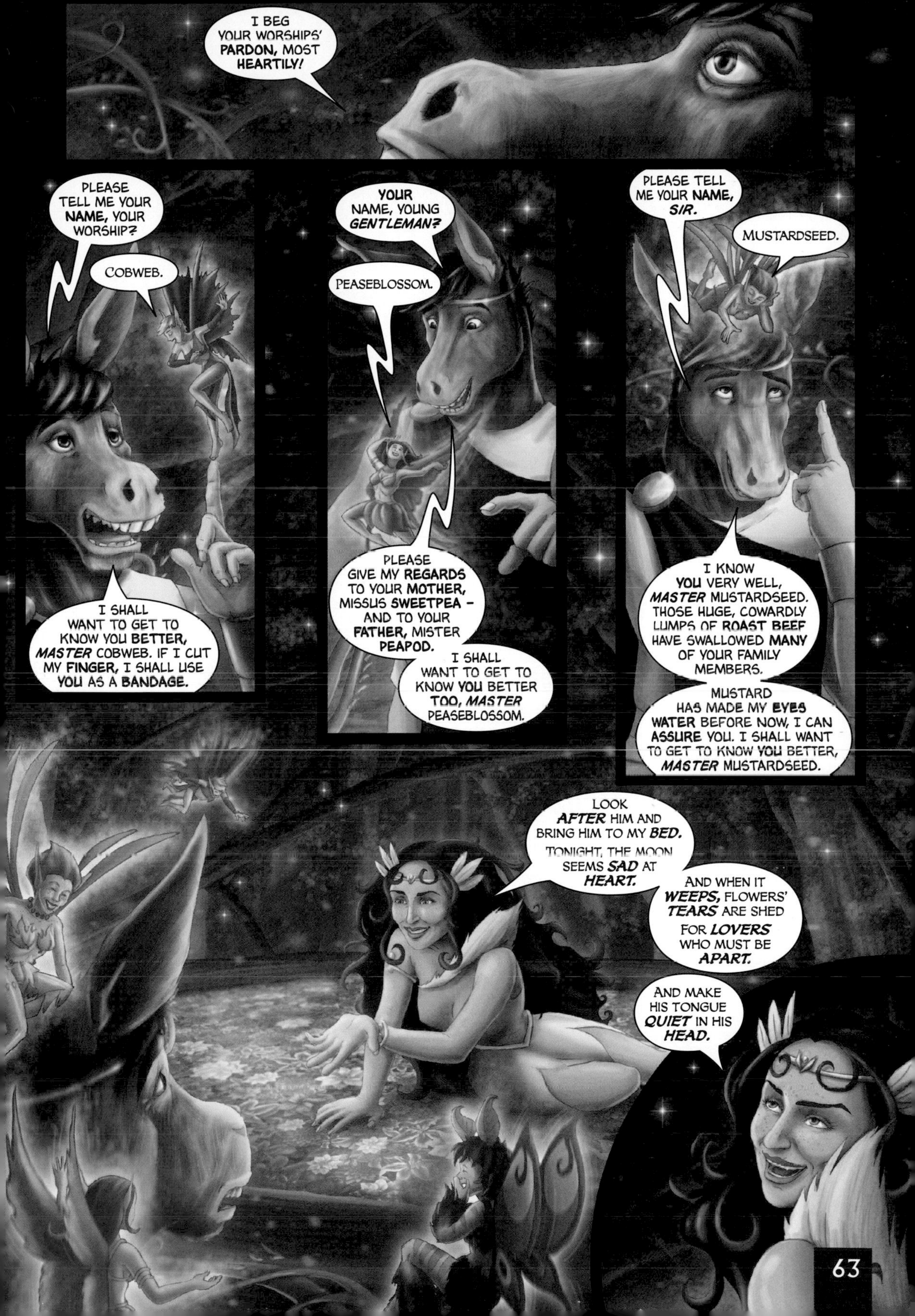
I BEG YOUR WORSHIPS' PARDON, MOST HEARTILY!
PLEASE TELL ME YOUR NAME, YOUR WORSHIP?
COBWEB.
I SHALL WANT TO GET TO KNOW YOU BETTER, MASTER COBWEB. IF I CUT MY FINGER, I SHALL USE YOU AS A BANDAGE.
YOUR NAME, YOUNG GENTLEMAN?
PEASEBLOSSOM.
PLEASE GIVE MY REGARDS TO YOUR MOTHER, MISSUS SWEETPEA - AND TO YOUR FATHER, MISTER PEAPOD.
I SHALL WANT TO GET TO KNOW YOU BETTER TOO, MASTER PEASEBLOSSOM.
PLEASE TELL ME YOUR NAME, SIR.
MUSTARDSEED.
I KNOW YOU VERY WELL, MASTER MUSTARDSEED. THOSE HUGE, COWARDLY LUMPS OF ROAST BEEF HAVE SWALLOWED MANY OF YOUR FAMILY MEMBERS.
MUSTARD HAS MADE MY EYES WATER BEFORE NOW, I CAN ASSURE YOU. I SHALL WANT TO GET TO KNOW YOU BETTER, MASTER MUSTARDSEED.
LOOK AFTER HIM AND BRING HIM TO MY BED.
TONIGHT, THE MOON SEEMS SAD AT HEART.
AND WHEN IT WEEPS, FLOWERS' TEARS ARE SHED FOR LOVERS WHO MUST BE APART.
AND MAKE HIS TONGUE QUIET IN HIS HEAD.

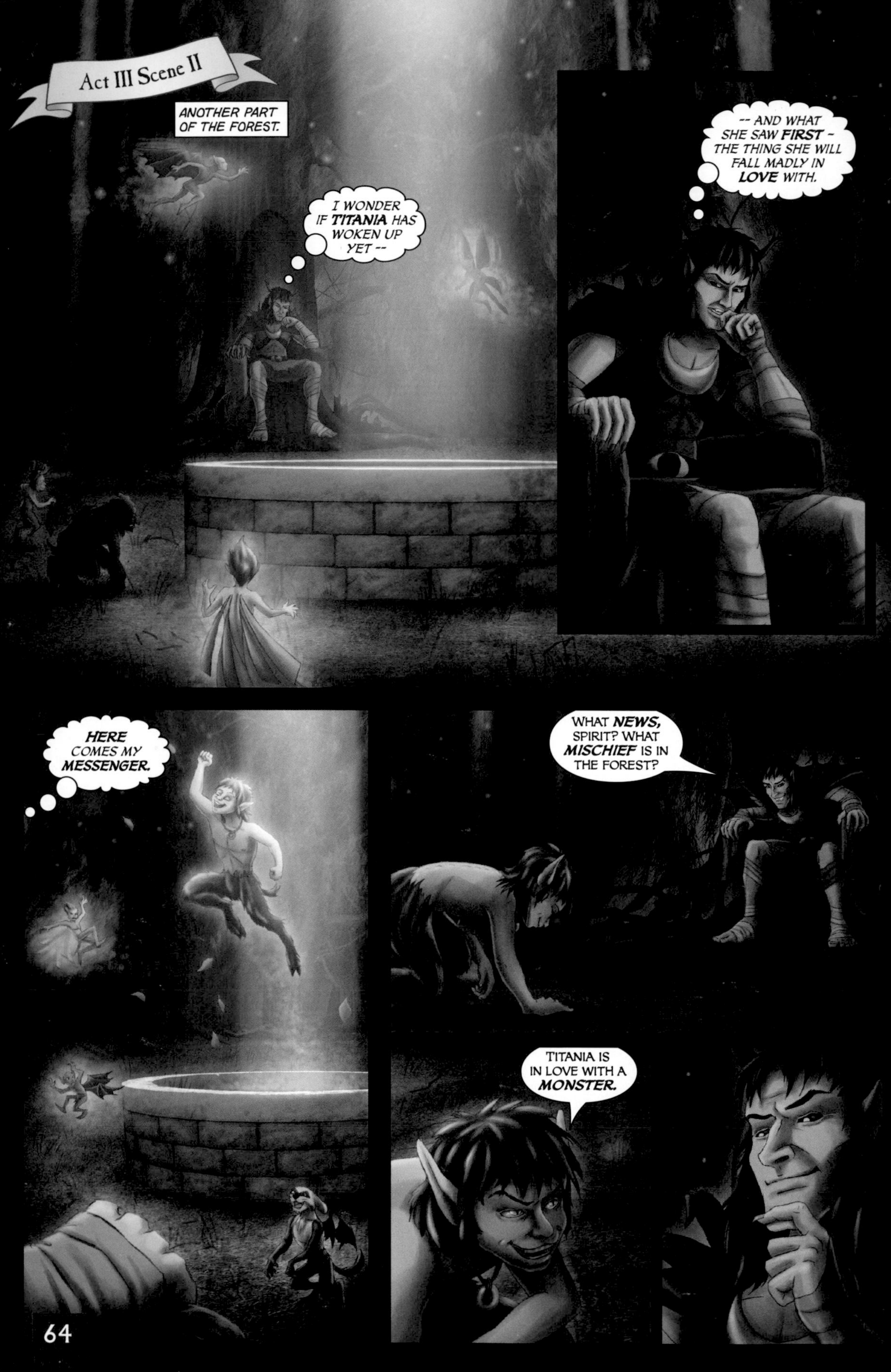
Act III Scene II
ANOTHER PART OF THE FOREST.
I WONDER IF TITANIA HAS WOKEN UP YET --
-- AND WHAT SHE SAW FIRST - THE THING SHE WILL FALL MADLY IN LOVE WITH.
HERE COMES MY MESSENGER.
WHAT NEWS, SPIRIT? WHAT MISCHIEF IS IN THE FOREST?
TITANIA IS IN LOVE WITH A MONSTER.

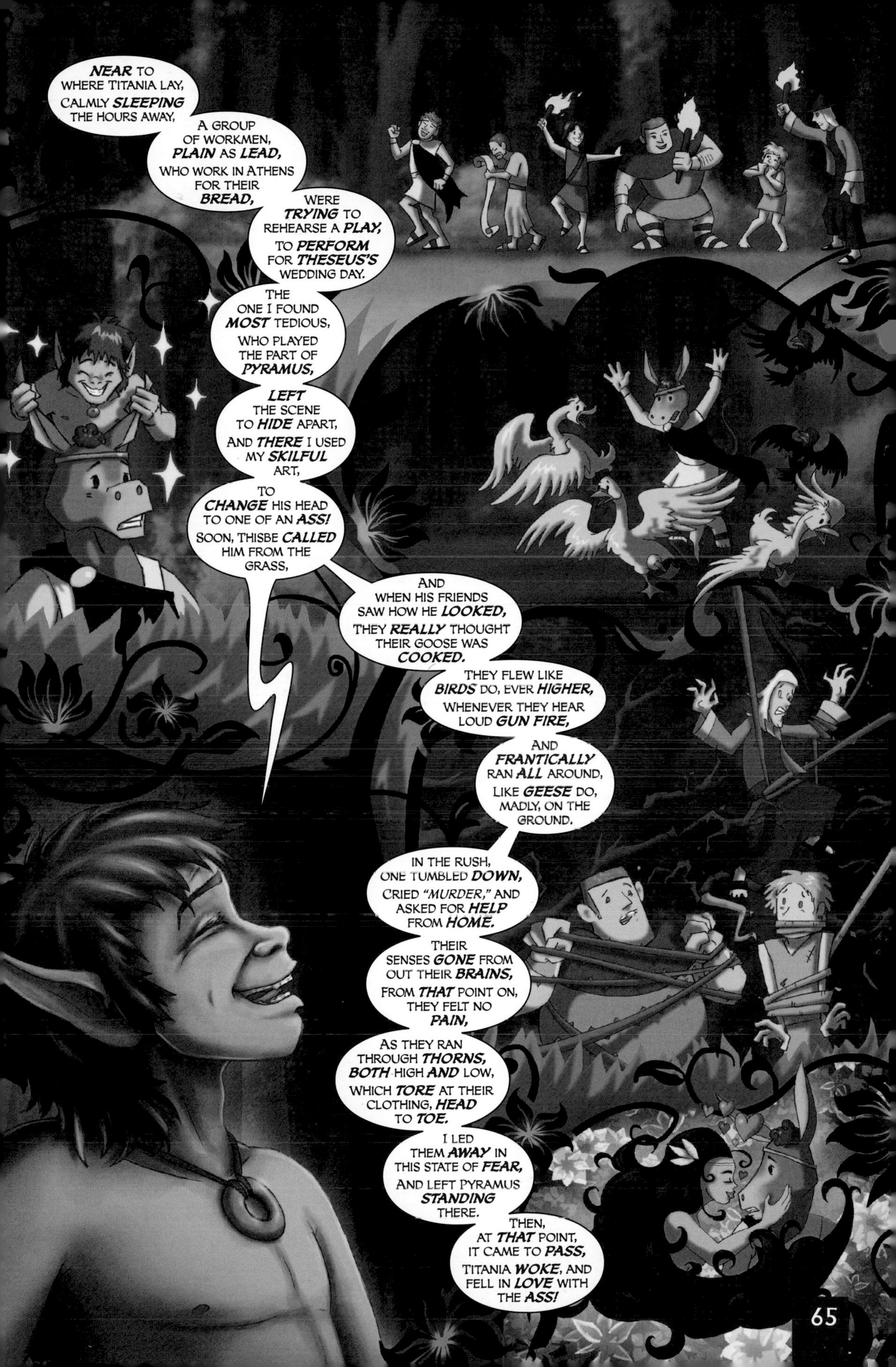
NEAR TO WHERE TITANIA LAY, CALMLY SLEEPING THE HOURS AWAY,
A GROUP OF WORKMEN, PLAIN AS LEAD, WHO WORK IN ATHENS FOR THEIR BREAD,
WERE TRYING TO REHEARSE A PLAY, TO PERFORM FOR THESEUS'S WEDDING DAY.
THE ONE I FOUND MOST TEDIOUS, WHO PLAYED THE PART OF PYRAMUS,
LEFT THE SCENE TO HIDE APART, AND THERE I USED MY SKILFUL ART,
TO CHANGE HIS HEAD TO ONE OF AN ASS! SOON, THISBE CALLED HIM FROM THE GRASS,
AND WHEN HIS FRIENDS SAW HOW HE LOOKED, THEY REALLY THOUGHT THEIR GOOSE WAS COOKED.
THEY FLEW LIKE BIRDS DO, EVER HIGHER, WHENEVER THEY HEAR LOUD GUN FIRE,
AND FRANTICALLY RAN ALL AROUND, LIKE GEESE DO, MADLY, ON THE GROUND.
IN THE RUSH, ONE TUMBLED DOWN, CRIED "MURDER," AND ASKED FOR HELP FROM HOME.
THEIR SENSES GONE FROM OUT THEIR BRAINS, FROM THAT POINT ON, THEY FELT NO PAIN,
AS THEY RAN THROUGH THORNS, BOTH HIGH AND LOW, WHICH TORE AT THEIR CLOTHING, HEAD TO TOE.
I LED THEM AWAY IN THIS STATE OF FEAR, AND LEFT PYRAMUS STANDING THERE.
THEN, AT THAT POINT, IT CAME TO PASS, TITANIA WOKE, AND FELL IN LOVE WITH THE ASS!

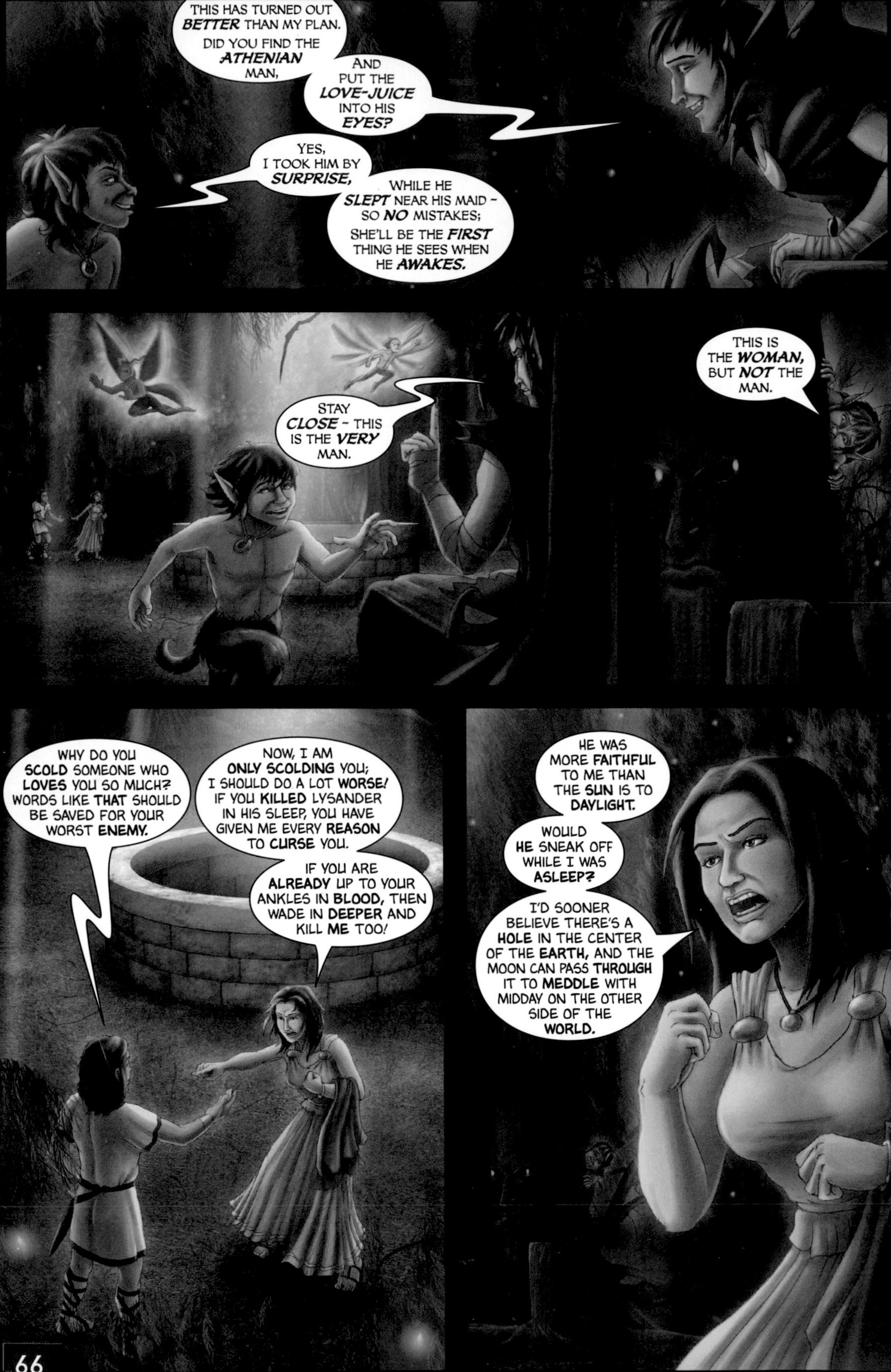
THIS HAS TURNED OUT BETTER THAN MY PLAN.
DID YOU FIND THE ATHENIAN MAN,
AND PUT THE LOVE-JUICE INTO HIS EYES?
YES, I TOOK HIM BY SURPRISE,
WHILE HE SLEPT NEAR HIS MAID - SO NO MISTAKES;
SHE'LL BE THE FIRST THING HE SEES WHEN HE AWAKES.
STAY CLOSE - THIS IS THE VERY MAN.
THIS IS THE WOMAN, BUT NOT THE MAN.
WHY DO YOU SCOLD SOMEONE WHO LOVES YOU SO MUCH? WORDS LIKE THAT SHOULD BE SAVED FOR YOUR WORST ENEMY.
NOW, I AM ONLY SCOLDING YOU; I SHOULD DO A LOT WORSE! IF YOU KILLED LYSANDER IN HIS SLEEP, YOU HAVE GIVEN ME EVERY REASON TO CURSE YOU.
IF YOU ARE ALREADY UP TO YOUR ANKLES IN BLOOD, THEN WADE IN DEEPER AND KILL ME TOO!
HE WAS MORE FAITHFUL TO ME THAN THE SUN IS TO DAYLIGHT.
WOULD HE SNEAK OFF WHILE I WAS ASLEEP?
I'D SOONER BELIEVE THERE'S A HOLE IN THE CENTER OF THE EARTH, AND THE MOON CAN PASS THROUGH IT TO MEDDLE WITH MIDDAY ON THE OTHER SIDE OF THE WORLD.

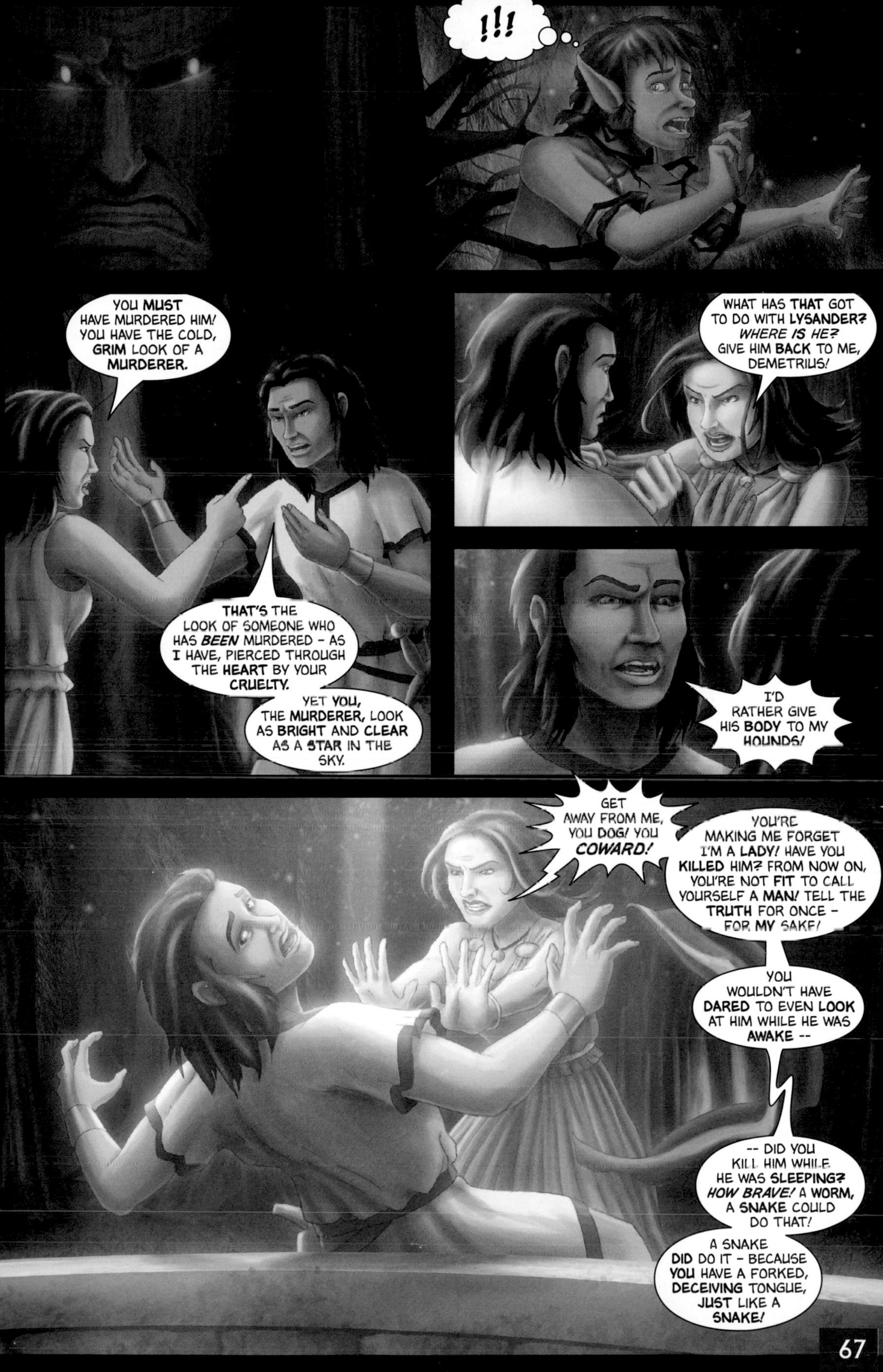
!!!
YOU MUST HAVE MURDERED HIM! YOU HAVE THE COLD, GRIM LOOK OF A MURDERER.
THAT'S THE LOOK OF SOMEONE WHO HAS BEEN MURDERED – AS I HAVE, PIERCED THROUGH THE HEART BY YOUR CRUELTY.
YET YOU, THE MURDERER, LOOK AS BRIGHT AND CLEAR AS A STAR IN THE SKY.
WHAT HAS THAT GOT TO DO WITH LYSANDER? WHERE IS HE? GIVE HIM BACK TO ME, DEMETRIUS!
I'D RATHER GIVE HIS BODY TO MY HOUNDS!
GET AWAY FROM ME, YOU DOG! YOU COWARD!
YOU'RE MAKING ME FORGET I'M A LADY! HAVE YOU KILLED HIM? FROM NOW ON, YOU'RE NOT FIT TO CALL YOURSELF A MAN! TELL THE TRUTH FOR ONCE – FOR MY SAKE!
YOU WOULDN'T HAVE DARED TO EVEN LOOK AT HIM WHILE HE WAS AWAKE --
-- DID YOU KILL HIM WHILE HE WAS SLEEPING? HOW BRAVE! A WORM, A SNAKE COULD DO THAT!
A SNAKE DID DO IT – BECAUSE YOU HAVE A FORKED, DECEIVING TONGUE, JUST LIKE A SNAKE!

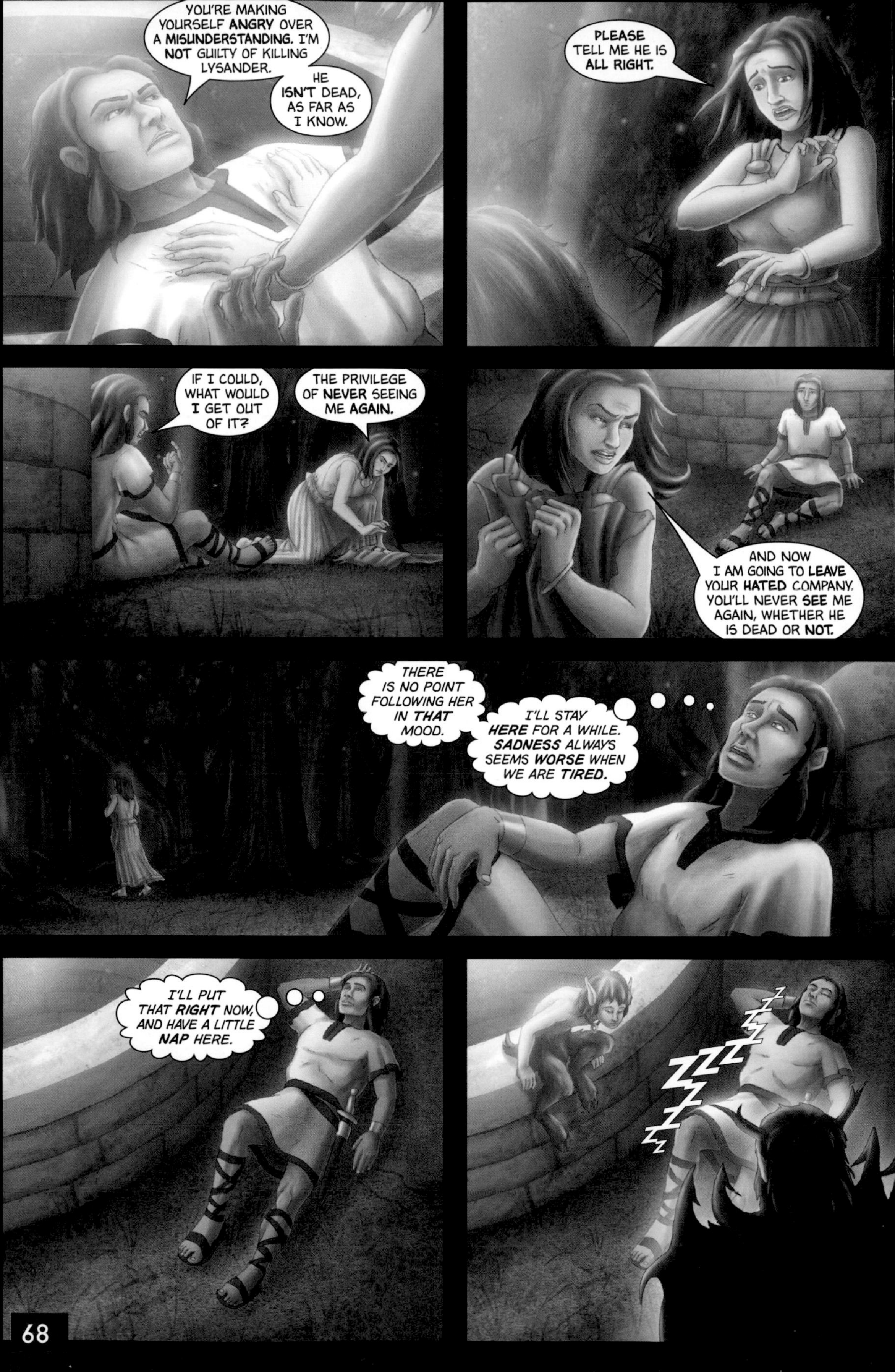
YOU'RE MAKING YOURSELF ANGRY OVER A MISUNDERSTANDING. I'M NOT GUILTY OF KILLING LYSANDER.
HE ISN'T DEAD, AS FAR AS I KNOW.
PLEASE TELL ME HE IS ALL RIGHT.
IF I COULD, WHAT WOULD I GET OUT OF IT?
THE PRIVILEGE OF NEVER SEEING ME AGAIN.
AND NOW I AM GOING TO LEAVE YOUR HATED COMPANY. YOU'LL NEVER SEE ME AGAIN, WHETHER HE IS DEAD OR NOT.
THERE IS NO POINT FOLLOWING HER IN THAT MOOD.
I'LL STAY HERE FOR A WHILE. SADNESS ALWAYS SEEMS WORSE WHEN WE ARE TIRED.
I'LL PUT THAT RIGHT NOW, AND HAVE A LITTLE NAP HERE.
ZZZZ

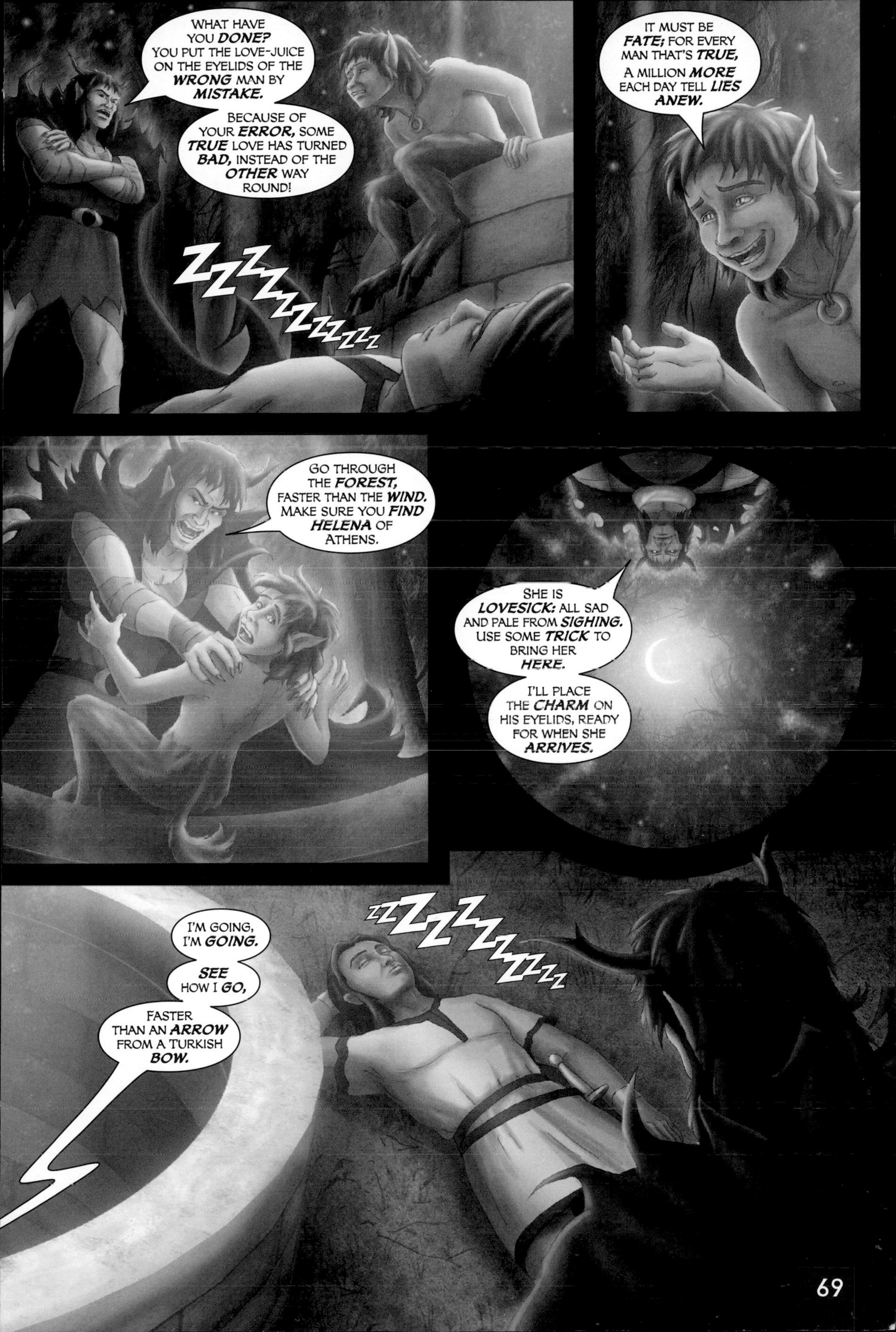
WHAT HAVE YOU DONE? YOU PUT THE LOVE-JUICE ON THE EYELIDS OF THE WRONG MAN BY MISTAKE.
BECAUSE OF YOUR ERROR, SOME TRUE LOVE HAS TURNED BAD, INSTEAD OF THE OTHER WAY ROUND!
ZZZZZZZZZZZZ
IT MUST BE FATE; FOR EVERY MAN THAT'S TRUE, A MILLION MORE EACH DAY TELL LIES ANEW.
GO THROUGH THE FOREST, FASTER THAN THE WIND. MAKE SURE YOU FIND HELENA OF ATHENS.
SHE IS LOVESICK: ALL SAD AND PALE FROM SIGHING. USE SOME TRICK TO BRING HER HERE.
I'LL PLACE THE CHARM ON HIS EYELIDS, READY FOR WHEN SHE ARRIVES.
I'M GOING, I'M GOING.
SEE HOW I GO,
FASTER THAN AN ARROW FROM A TURKISH BOW.
ZZZZZZZZZZZ

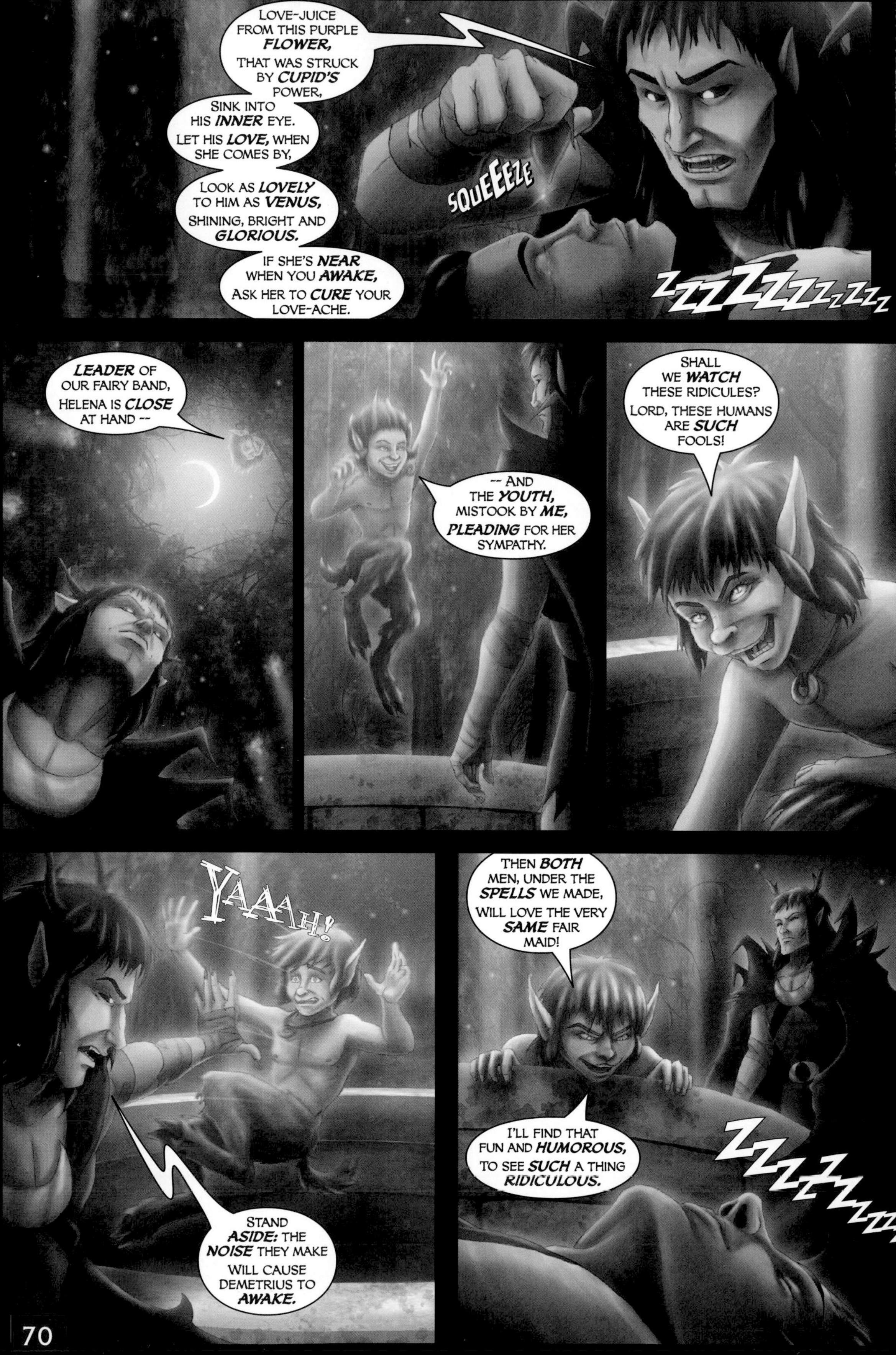
LOVE-JUICE FROM THIS PURPLE FLOWER,
THAT WAS STRUCK BY CUPID'S POWER,
SINK INTO HIS INNER EYE.
LET HIS LOVE, WHEN SHE COMES BY,
LOOK AS LOVELY TO HIM AS VENUS,
SHINING, BRIGHT AND GLORIOUS.
IF SHE'S NEAR WHEN YOU AWAKE,
ASK HER TO CURE YOUR LOVE-ACHE.
SQUEEEZE
ZZZZZZZZZZZZ
LEADER OF OUR FAIRY BAND, HELENA IS CLOSE AT HAND --
-- AND THE YOUTH, MISTOOK BY ME, PLEADING FOR HER SYMPATHY.
SHALL WE WATCH THESE RIDICULES?
LORD, THESE HUMANS ARE SUCH FOOLS!
YAAAH!
STAND ASIDE: THE NOISE THEY MAKE
WILL CAUSE DEMETRIUS TO AWAKE.
THEN BOTH MEN, UNDER THE SPELLS WE MADE,
WILL LOVE THE VERY SAME FAIR MAID!
I'LL FIND THAT FUN AND HUMOROUS,
TO SEE SUCH A THING RIDICULOUS.
ZZZZZZ

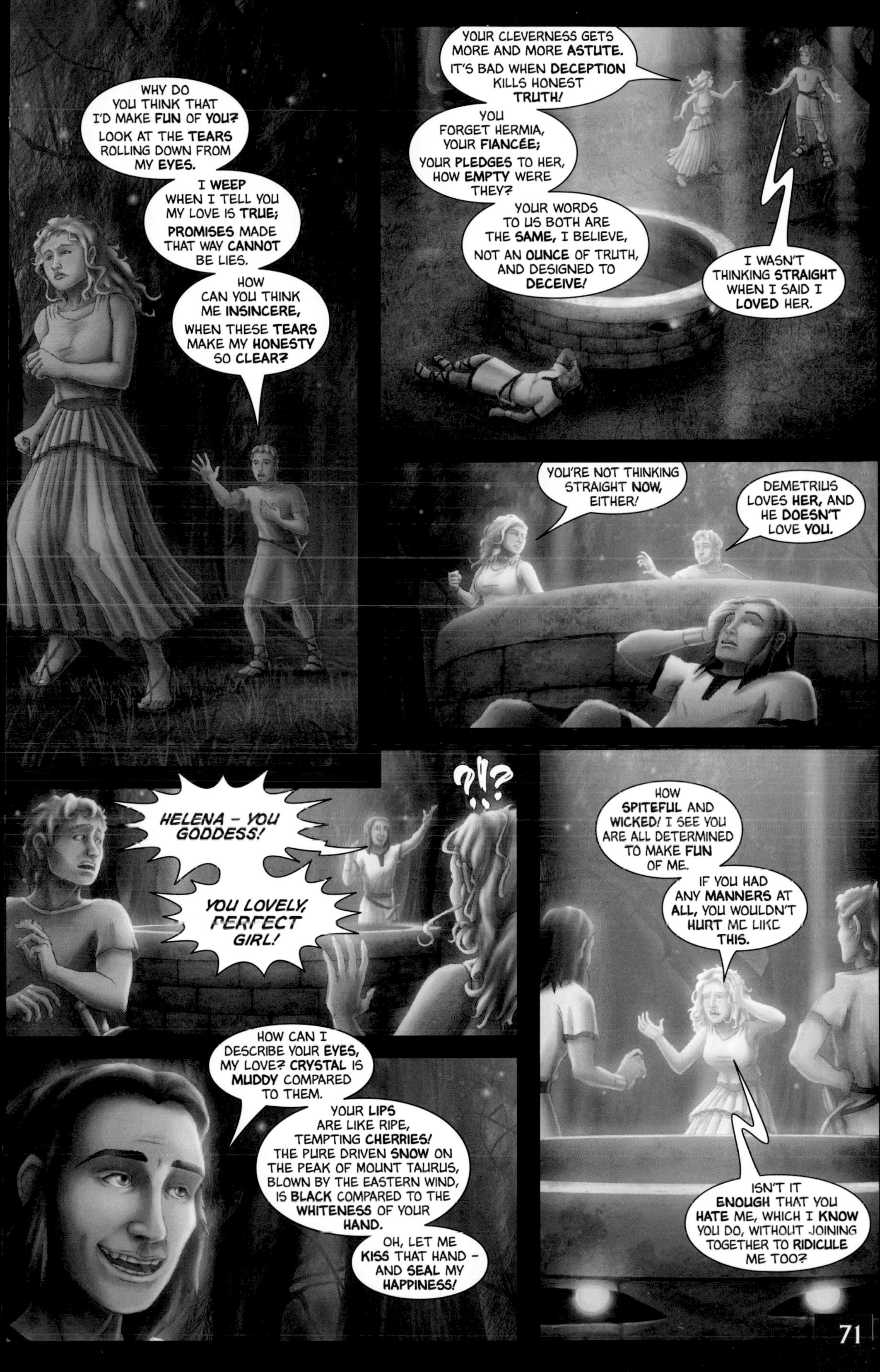
WHY DO YOU THINK THAT I'D MAKE FUN OF YOU? LOOK AT THE TEARS ROLLING DOWN FROM MY EYES.
I WEEP WHEN I TELL YOU MY LOVE IS TRUE; PROMISES MADE THAT WAY CANNOT BE LIES.
HOW CAN YOU THINK ME INSINCERE, WHEN THESE TEARS MAKE MY HONESTY SO CLEAR?
YOUR CLEVERNESS GETS MORE AND MORE ASTUTE. IT'S BAD WHEN DECEPTION KILLS HONEST TRUTH!
YOU FORGET HERMIA, YOUR FIANCÉE; YOUR PLEDGES TO HER, HOW EMPTY WERE THEY?
YOUR WORDS TO US BOTH ARE THE SAME, I BELIEVE, NOT AN OUNCE OF TRUTH, AND DESIGNED TO DECEIVE!
I WASN'T THINKING STRAIGHT WHEN I SAID I LOVED HER.
YOU'RE NOT THINKING STRAIGHT NOW, EITHER!
DEMETRIUS LOVES HER, AND HE DOESN'T LOVE YOU.
HELENA – YOU GODDESS!
?!?
YOU LOVELY, PERFECT GIRL!
HOW CAN I DESCRIBE YOUR EYES, MY LOVE? CRYSTAL IS MUDDY COMPARED TO THEM.
YOUR LIPS ARE LIKE RIPE, TEMPTING CHERRIES! THE PURE DRIVEN SNOW ON THE PEAK OF MOUNT TAURUS, BLOWN BY THE EASTERN WIND, IS BLACK COMPARED TO THE WHITENESS OF YOUR HAND.
OH, LET ME KISS THAT HAND – AND SEAL MY HAPPINESS!
HOW SPITEFUL AND WICKED! I SEE YOU ARE ALL DETERMINED TO MAKE FUN OF ME.
IF YOU HAD ANY MANNERS AT ALL, YOU WOULDN'T HURT ME LIKE THIS.
ISN'T IT ENOUGH THAT YOU HATE ME, WHICH I KNOW YOU DO, WITHOUT JOINING TOGETHER TO RIDICULE ME TOO?

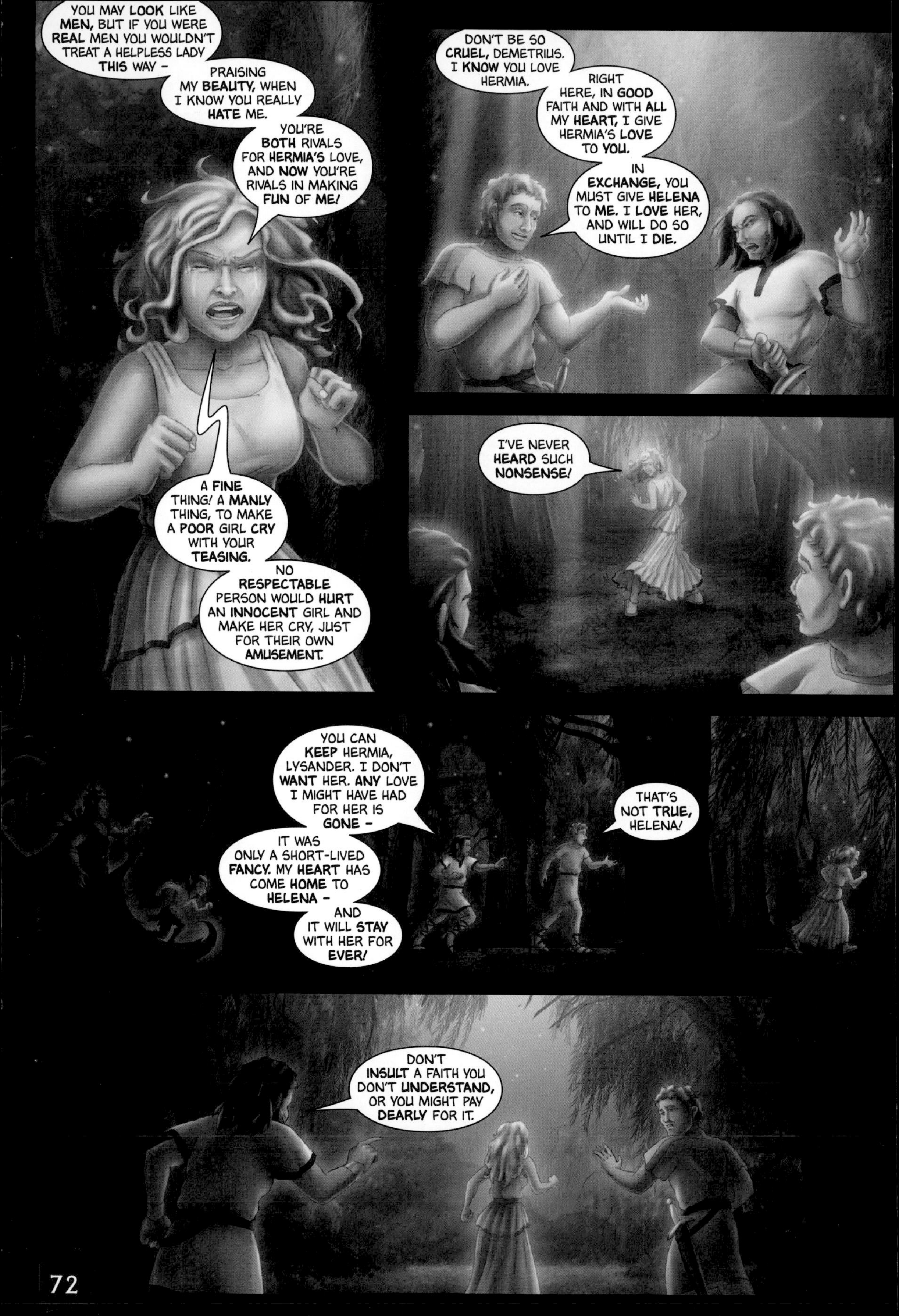
YOU MAY LOOK LIKE MEN, BUT IF YOU WERE REAL MEN YOU WOULDN'T TREAT A HELPLESS LADY THIS WAY –
PRAISING MY BEAUTY, WHEN I KNOW YOU REALLY HATE ME.
YOU'RE BOTH RIVALS FOR HERMIA'S LOVE, AND NOW YOU'RE RIVALS IN MAKING FUN OF ME!
A FINE THING! A MANLY THING, TO MAKE A POOR GIRL CRY WITH YOUR TEASING.
NO RESPECTABLE PERSON WOULD HURT AN INNOCENT GIRL AND MAKE HER CRY, JUST FOR THEIR OWN AMUSEMENT.
DON'T BE SO CRUEL, DEMETRIUS. I KNOW YOU LOVE HERMIA.
RIGHT HERE, IN GOOD FAITH AND WITH ALL MY HEART, I GIVE HERMIA'S LOVE TO YOU.
IN EXCHANGE, YOU MUST GIVE HELENA TO ME. I LOVE HER, AND WILL DO SO UNTIL I DIE.
I'VE NEVER HEARD SUCH NONSENSE!
YOU CAN KEEP HERMIA, LYSANDER. I DON'T WANT HER. ANY LOVE I MIGHT HAVE HAD FOR HER IS GONE –
IT WAS ONLY A SHORT-LIVED FANCY. MY HEART HAS COME HOME TO HELENA –
AND IT WILL STAY WITH HER FOR EVER!
THAT'S NOT TRUE, HELENA!
DON'T INSULT A FAITH YOU DON'T UNDERSTAND, OR YOU MIGHT PAY DEARLY FOR IT.

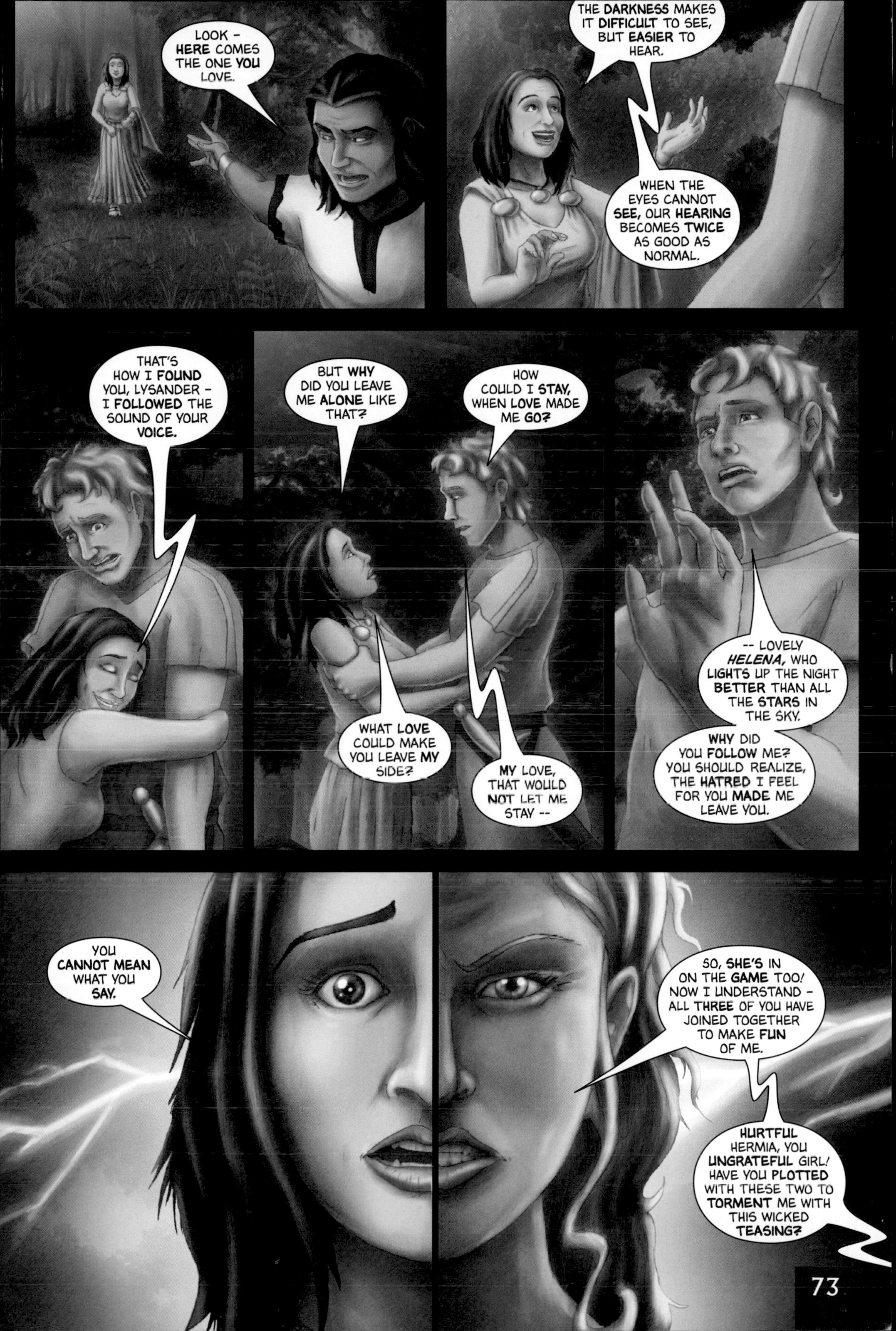
LOOK – HERE COMES THE ONE YOU LOVE.
THE DARKNESS MAKES IT DIFFICULT TO SEE, BUT EASIER TO HEAR.
WHEN THE EYES CANNOT SEE, OUR HEARING BECOMES TWICE AS GOOD AS NORMAL.
THAT'S HOW I FOUND YOU, LYSANDER – I FOLLOWED THE SOUND OF YOUR VOICE.
BUT WHY DID YOU LEAVE ME ALONE LIKE THAT?
HOW COULD I STAY, WHEN LOVE MADE ME GO?
WHAT LOVE COULD MAKE YOU LEAVE MY SIDE?
MY LOVE, THAT WOULD NOT LET ME STAY --
-- LOVELY HELENA, WHO LIGHTS UP THE NIGHT BETTER THAN ALL THE STARS IN THE SKY.
WHY DID YOU FOLLOW ME? YOU SHOULD REALIZE, THE HATRED I FEEL FOR YOU MADE ME LEAVE YOU.
YOU CANNOT MEAN WHAT YOU SAY.
SO, SHE'S IN ON THE GAME TOO! NOW I UNDERSTAND – ALL THREE OF YOU HAVE JOINED TOGETHER TO MAKE FUN OF ME.
HURTFUL HERMIA, YOU UNGRATEFUL GIRL! HAVE YOU PLOTTED WITH THESE TWO TO TORMENT ME WITH THIS WICKED TEASING?

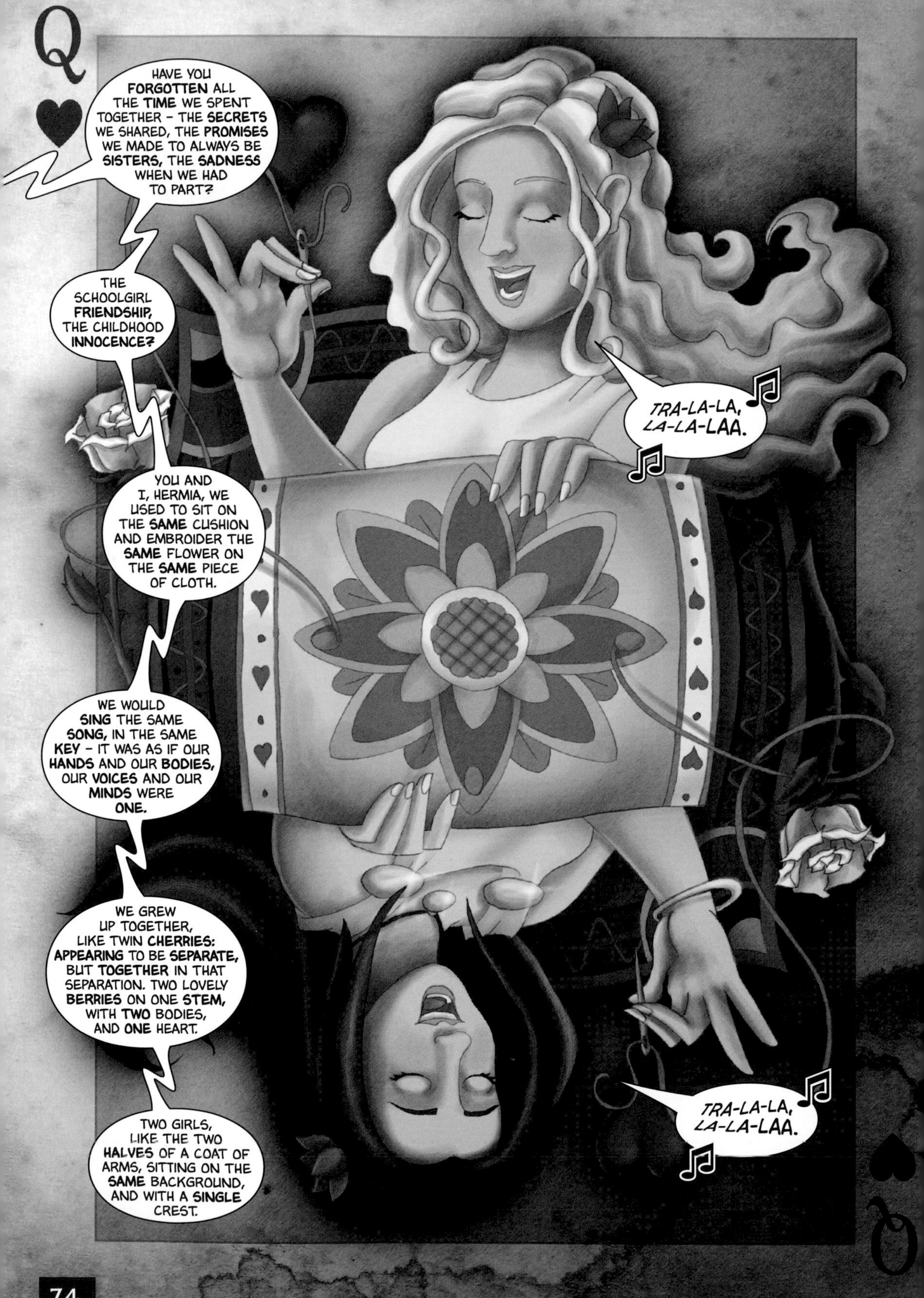
Q
HAVE YOU FORGOTTEN ALL THE TIME WE SPENT TOGETHER - THE SECRETS WE SHARED, THE PROMISES WE MADE TO ALWAYS BE SISTERS, THE SADNESS WHEN WE HAD TO PART?
THE SCHOOLGIRL FRIENDSHIP, THE CHILDHOOD INNOCENCE?
TRA-LA-LA, LA-LA-LAA.
YOU AND I, HERMIA, WE USED TO SIT ON THE SAME CUSHION AND EMBROIDER THE SAME FLOWER ON THE SAME PIECE OF CLOTH.
WE WOULD SING THE SAME SONG, IN THE SAME KEY - IT WAS AS IF OUR HANDS AND OUR BODIES, OUR VOICES AND OUR MINDS WERE ONE.
WE GREW UP TOGETHER, LIKE TWIN CHERRIES: APPEARING TO BE SEPARATE, BUT TOGETHER IN THAT SEPARATION. TWO LOVELY BERRIES ON ONE STEM, WITH TWO BODIES, AND ONE HEART.
TWO GIRLS, LIKE THE TWO HALVES OF A COAT OF ARMS, SITTING ON THE SAME BACKGROUND, AND WITH A SINGLE CREST.
TRA-LA-LA, LA-LA-LAA.

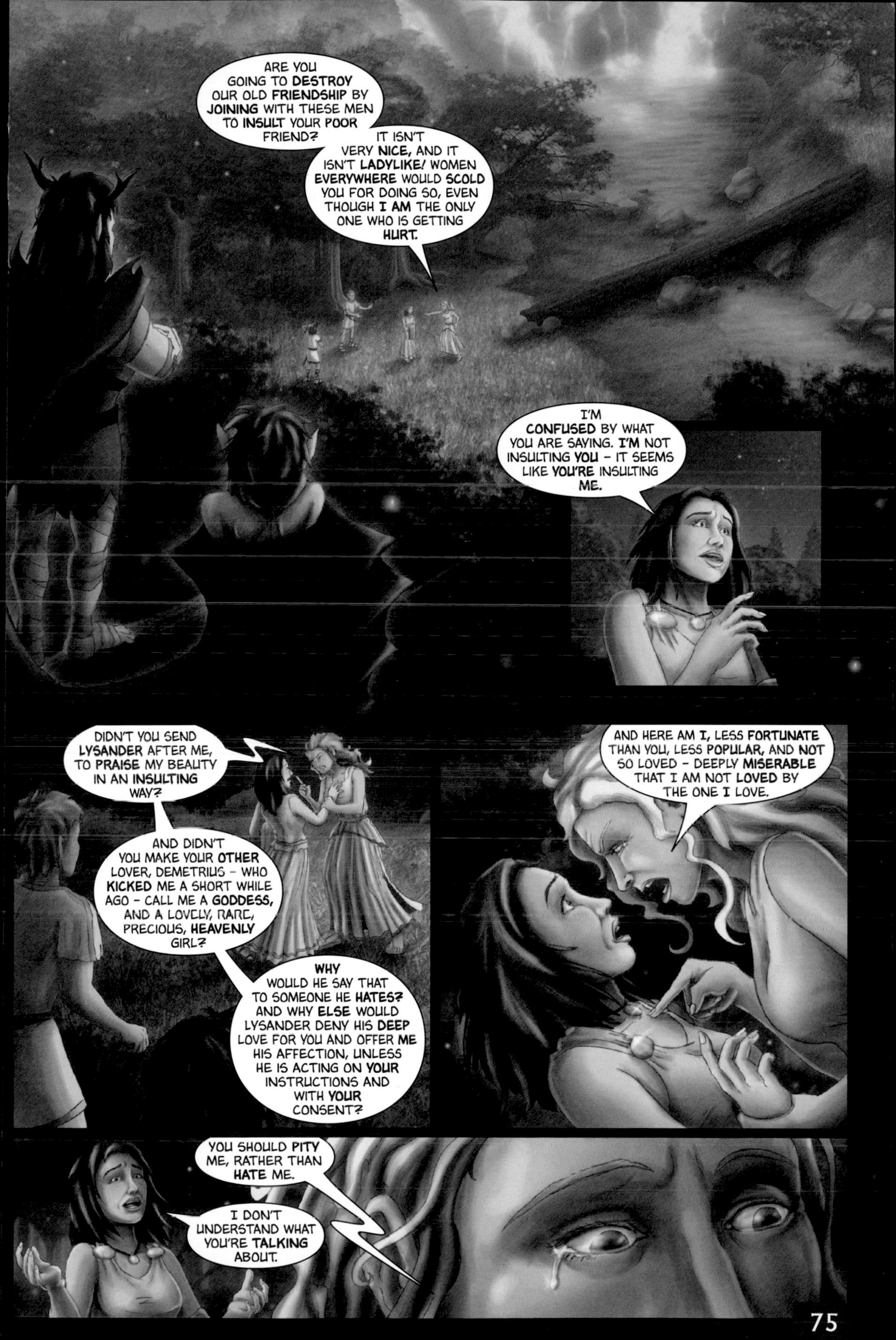

ARE YOU GOING TO DESTROY OUR OLD FRIENDSHIP BY JOINING WITH THESE MEN TO INSULT YOUR POOR FRIEND?
IT ISN'T VERY NICE, AND IT ISN'T LADYLIKE! WOMEN EVERYWHERE WOULD SCOLD YOU FOR DOING SO, EVEN THOUGH I AM THE ONLY ONE WHO IS GETTING HURT.
I'M CONFUSED BY WHAT YOU ARE SAYING. I'M NOT INSULTING YOU - IT SEEMS LIKE YOU'RE INSULTING ME.
DIDN'T YOU SEND LYSANDER AFTER ME, TO PRAISE MY BEAUTY IN AN INSULTING WAY?
AND DIDN'T YOU MAKE YOUR OTHER LOVER, DEMETRIUS - WHO KICKED ME A SHORT WHILE AGO - CALL ME A GODDESS, AND A LOVELY, RARE, PRECIOUS, HEAVENLY GIRL?
WHY WOULD HE SAY THAT TO SOMEONE HE HATES? AND WHY ELSE WOULD LYSANDER DENY HIS DEEP LOVE FOR YOU AND OFFER ME HIS AFFECTION, UNLESS HE IS ACTING ON YOUR INSTRUCTIONS AND WITH YOUR CONSENT?
AND HERE AM I, LESS FORTUNATE THAN YOU, LESS POPULAR, AND NOT SO LOVED - DEEPLY MISERABLE THAT I AM NOT LOVED BY THE ONE I LOVE.
YOU SHOULD PITY ME, RATHER THAN HATE ME.
I DON'T UNDERSTAND WHAT YOU'RE TALKING ABOUT.

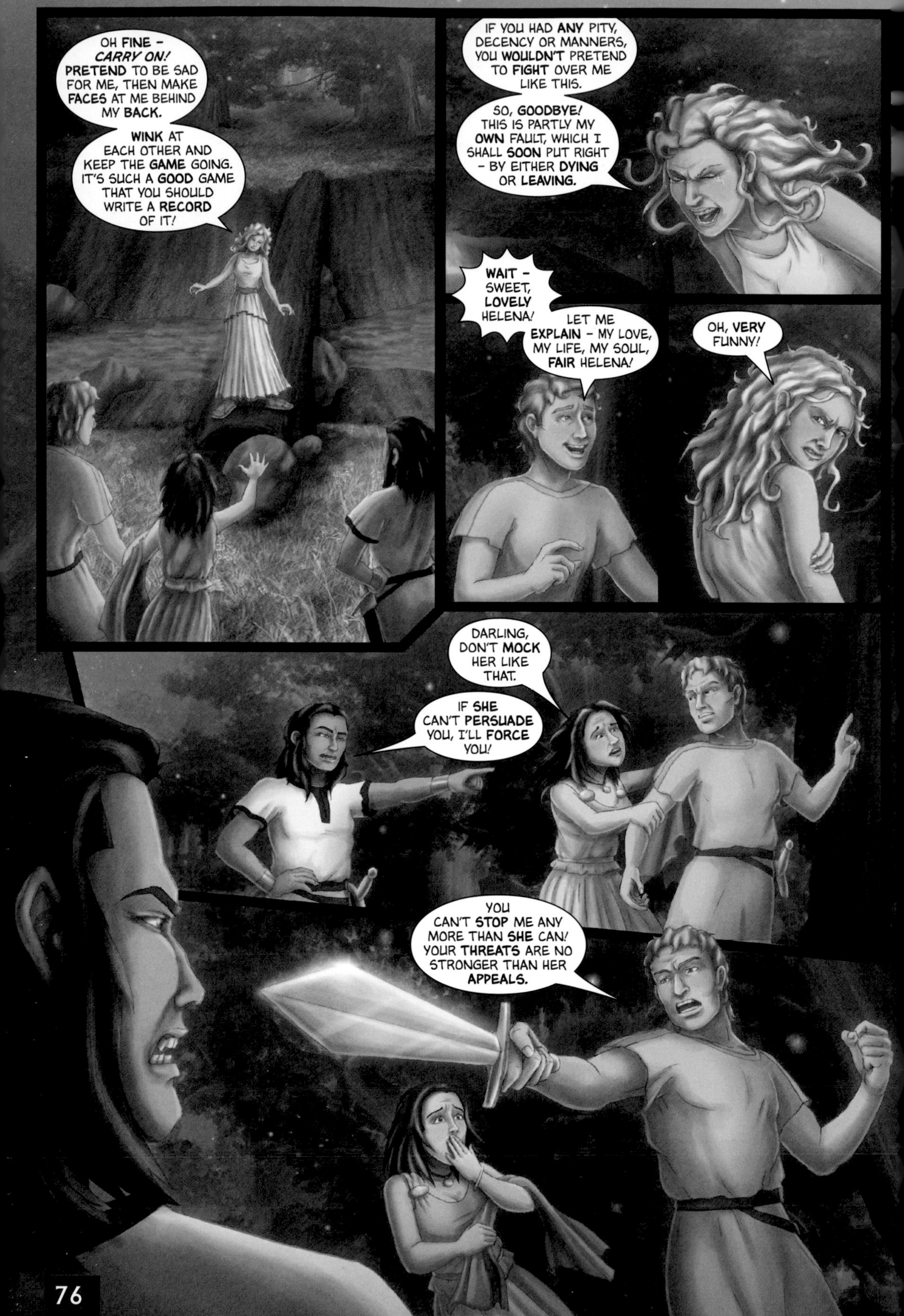
OH FINE - CARRY ON! PRETEND TO BE SAD FOR ME, THEN MAKE FACES AT ME BEHIND MY BACK.
WINK AT EACH OTHER AND KEEP THE GAME GOING. IT'S SUCH A GOOD GAME THAT YOU SHOULD WRITE A RECORD OF IT!
IF YOU HAD ANY PITY, DECENCY OR MANNERS, YOU WOULDN'T PRETEND TO FIGHT OVER ME LIKE THIS.
SO, GOODBYE! THIS IS PARTLY MY OWN FAULT, WHICH I SHALL SOON PUT RIGHT - BY EITHER DYING OR LEAVING.
WAIT - SWEET, LOVELY HELENA!
LET ME EXPLAIN - MY LOVE, MY LIFE, MY SOUL, FAIR HELENA!
OH, VERY FUNNY!
DARLING, DON'T MOCK HER LIKE THAT.
IF SHE CAN'T PERSUADE YOU, I'LL FORCE YOU!
YOU CAN'T STOP ME ANY MORE THAN SHE CAN! YOUR THREATS ARE NO STRONGER THAN HER APPEALS.

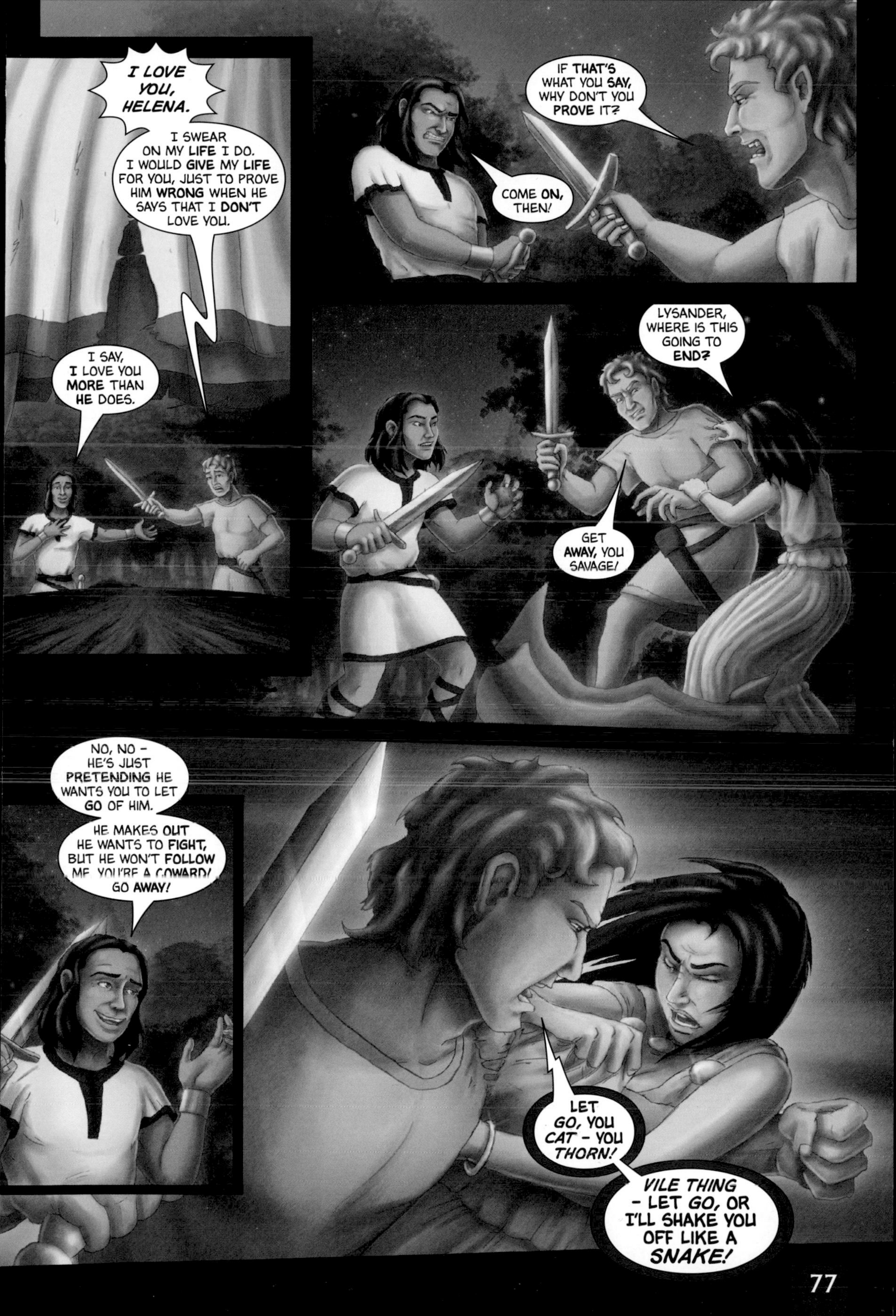
I LOVE YOU, HELENA.
I SWEAR ON MY LIFE I DO. I WOULD GIVE MY LIFE FOR YOU, JUST TO PROVE HIM WRONG WHEN HE SAYS THAT I DON'T LOVE YOU.
IF THAT'S WHAT YOU SAY, WHY DON'T YOU PROVE IT?
COME ON, THEN!
I SAY, I LOVE YOU MORE THAN HE DOES.
LYSANDER, WHERE IS THIS GOING TO END?
GET AWAY, YOU SAVAGE!
NO, NO – HE'S JUST PRETENDING HE WANTS YOU TO LET GO OF HIM.
HE MAKES OUT HE WANTS TO FIGHT, BUT HE WON'T FOLLOW ME. YOU'RE A COWARD! GO AWAY!
LET GO, YOU CAT – YOU THORN!
VILE THING – LET GO, OR I'LL SHAKE YOU OFF LIKE A SNAKE!

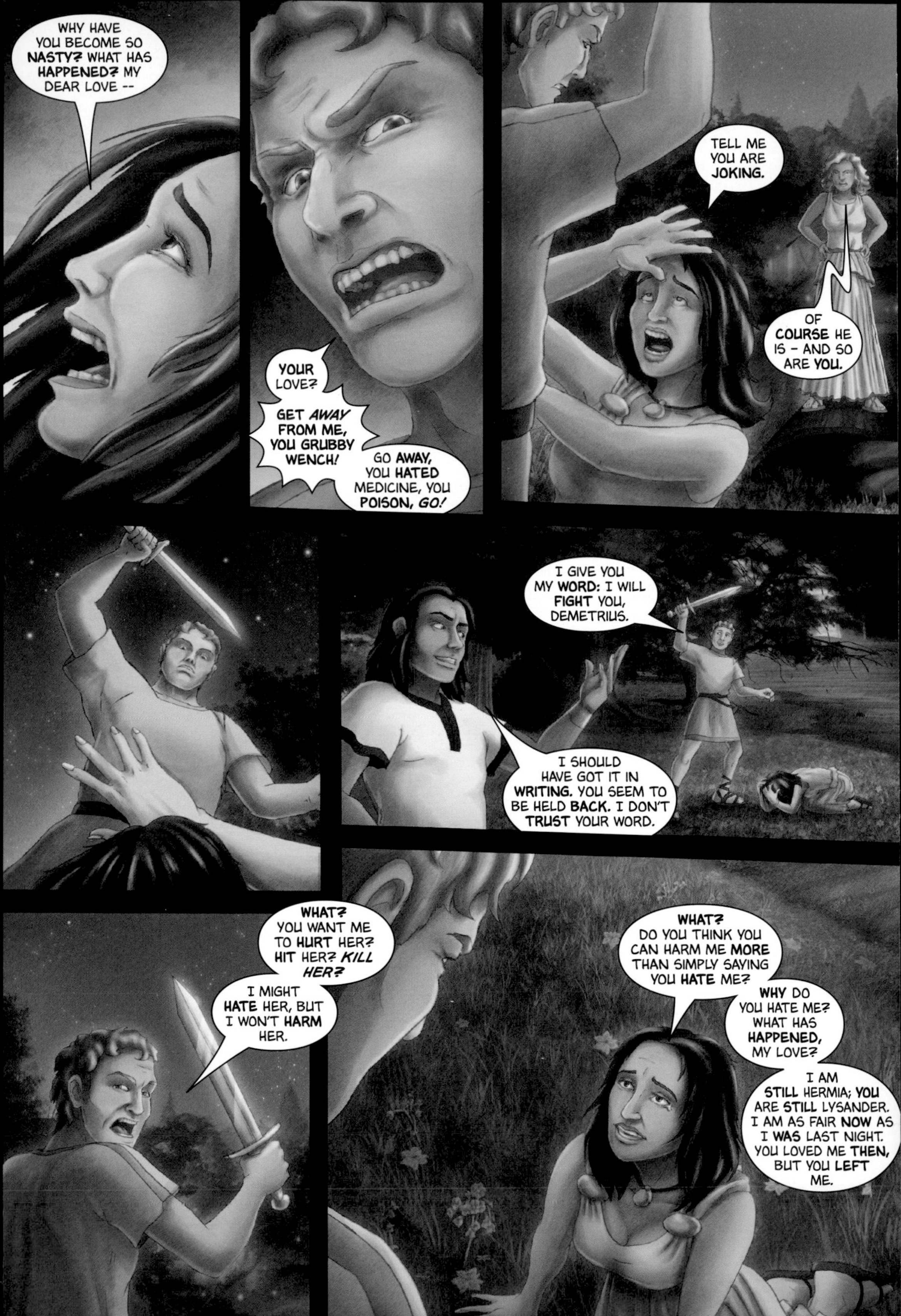
WHY HAVE YOU BECOME SO NASTY? WHAT HAS HAPPENED? MY DEAR LOVE --
YOUR LOVE?
GET AWAY FROM ME, YOU GRUBBY WENCH!
GO AWAY, YOU HATED MEDICINE, YOU POISON, GO!
TELL ME YOU ARE JOKING.
OF COURSE HE IS - AND SO ARE YOU.
I GIVE YOU MY WORD: I WILL FIGHT YOU, DEMETRIUS.
I SHOULD HAVE GOT IT IN WRITING. YOU SEEM TO BE HELD BACK. I DON'T TRUST YOUR WORD.
WHAT? YOU WANT ME TO HURT HER? HIT HER? KILL HER?
I MIGHT HATE HER, BUT I WON'T HARM HER.
WHAT? DO YOU THINK YOU CAN HARM ME MORE THAN SIMPLY SAYING YOU HATE ME?
WHY DO YOU HATE ME? WHAT HAS HAPPENED, MY LOVE?
I AM STILL HERMIA; YOU ARE STILL LYSANDER. I AM AS FAIR NOW AS I WAS LAST NIGHT. YOU LOVED ME THEN, BUT YOU LEFT ME.

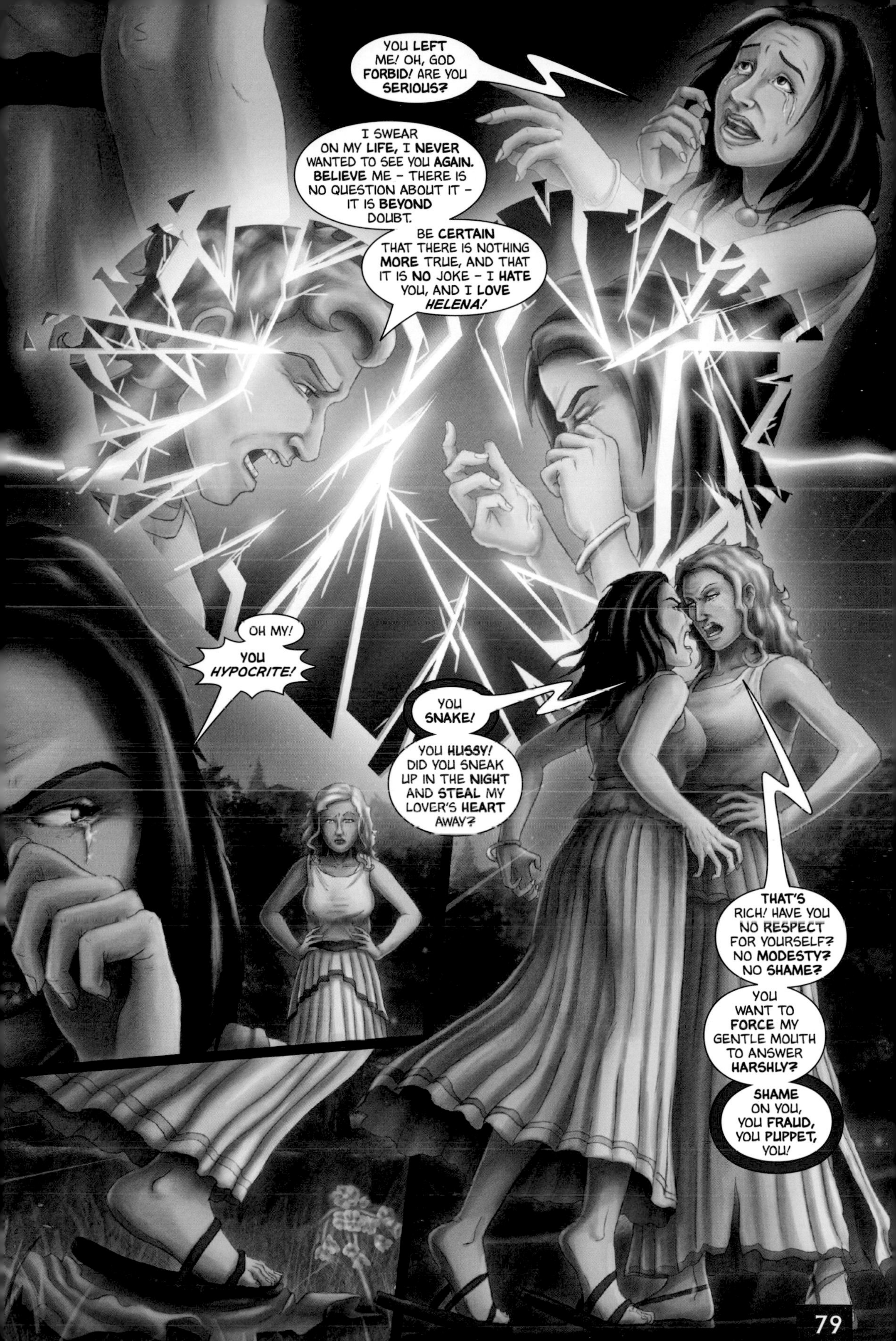
YOU LEFT ME! OH, GOD FORBID! ARE YOU SERIOUS?
I SWEAR ON MY LIFE, I NEVER WANTED TO SEE YOU AGAIN. BELIEVE ME – THERE IS NO QUESTION ABOUT IT – IT IS BEYOND DOUBT.
BE CERTAIN THAT THERE IS NOTHING MORE TRUE, AND THAT IT IS NO JOKE – I HATE YOU, AND I LOVE HELENA!
OH MY!
YOU HYPOCRITE!
YOU SNAKE!
YOU HUSSY! DID YOU SNEAK UP IN THE NIGHT AND STEAL MY LOVER'S HEART AWAY?
THAT'S RICH! HAVE YOU NO RESPECT FOR YOURSELF? NO MODESTY? NO SHAME?
YOU WANT TO FORCE MY GENTLE MOUTH TO ANSWER HARSHLY?
SHAME ON YOU, YOU FRAUD, YOU PUPPET, YOU!

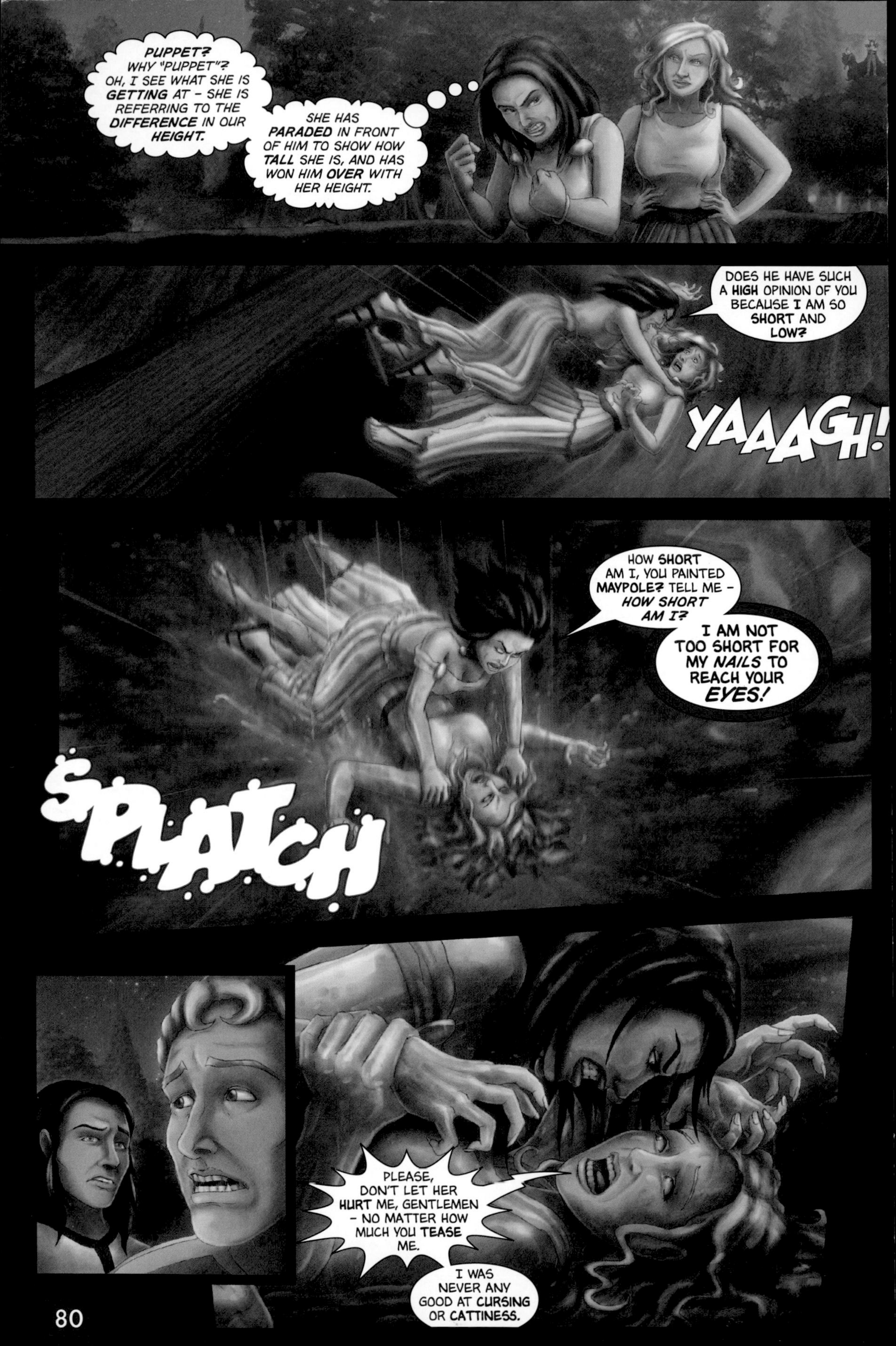
PUPPET? WHY "PUPPET"? OH, I SEE WHAT SHE IS GETTING AT – SHE IS REFERRING TO THE DIFFERENCE IN OUR HEIGHT.
SHE HAS PARADED IN FRONT OF HIM TO SHOW HOW TALL SHE IS, AND HAS WON HIM OVER WITH HER HEIGHT.
DOES HE HAVE SUCH A HIGH OPINION OF YOU BECAUSE I AM SO SHORT AND LOW?
YAAAGH!
HOW SHORT AM I, YOU PAINTED MAYPOLE? TELL ME – HOW SHORT AM I?
I AM NOT TOO SHORT FOR MY NAILS TO REACH YOUR EYES!
SPLATCH
PLEASE, DON'T LET HER HURT ME, GENTLEMEN – NO MATTER HOW MUCH YOU TEASE ME.
I WAS NEVER ANY GOOD AT CURSING OR CATTINESS.

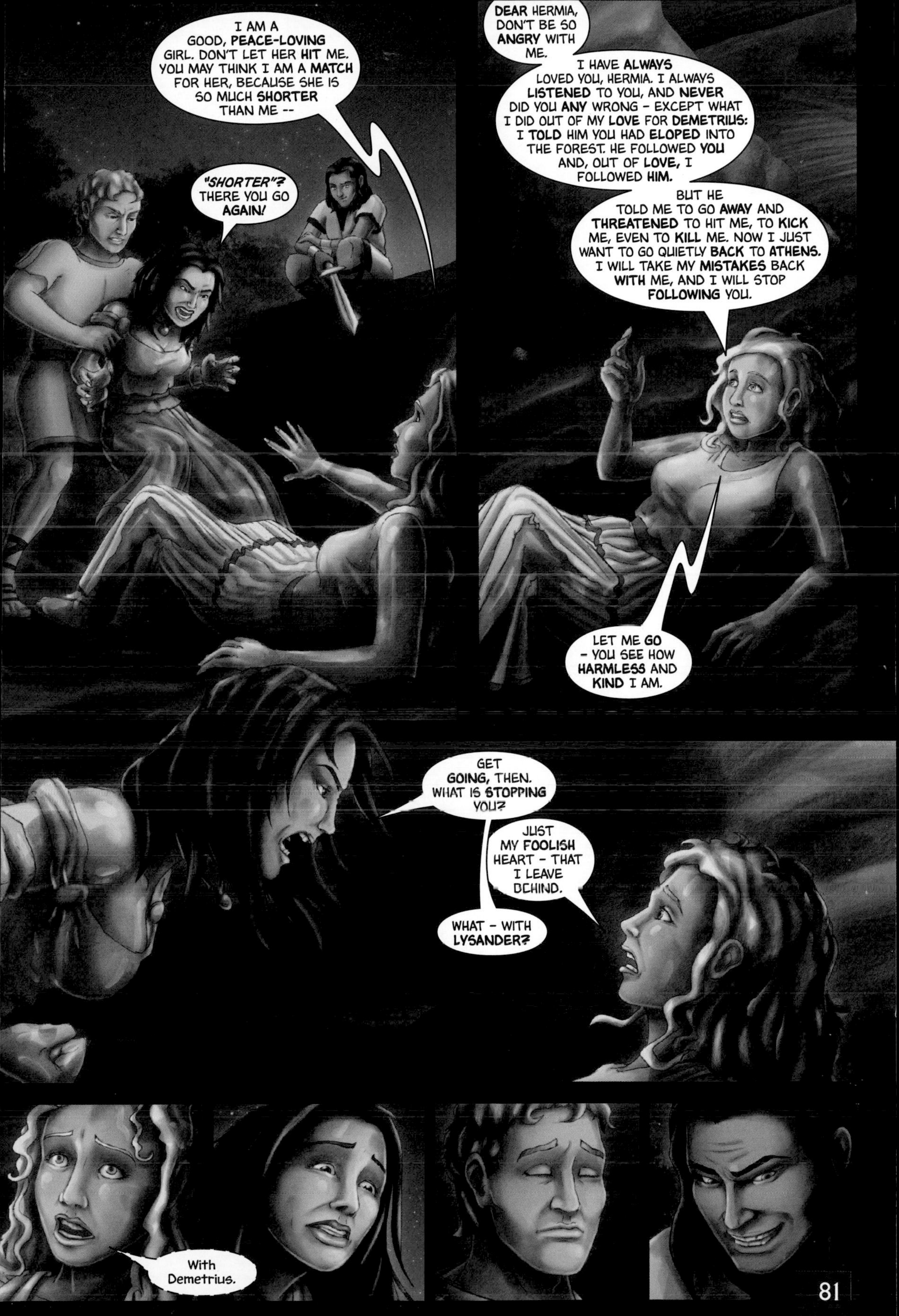
I AM A GOOD, PEACE-LOVING GIRL. DON'T LET HER HIT ME. YOU MAY THINK I AM A MATCH FOR HER, BECAUSE SHE IS SO MUCH SHORTER THAN ME --
"SHORTER"? THERE YOU GO AGAIN!
DEAR HERMIA, DON'T BE SO ANGRY WITH ME.
I HAVE ALWAYS LOVED YOU, HERMIA. I ALWAYS LISTENED TO YOU, AND NEVER DID YOU ANY WRONG - EXCEPT WHAT I DID OUT OF MY LOVE FOR DEMETRIUS: I TOLD HIM YOU HAD ELOPED INTO THE FOREST. HE FOLLOWED YOU AND, OUT OF LOVE, I FOLLOWED HIM.
BUT HE TOLD ME TO GO AWAY AND THREATENED TO HIT ME, TO KICK ME, EVEN TO KILL ME. NOW I JUST WANT TO GO QUIETLY BACK TO ATHENS. I WILL TAKE MY MISTAKES BACK WITH ME, AND I WILL STOP FOLLOWING YOU.
LET ME GO - YOU SEE HOW HARMLESS AND KIND I AM.
GET GOING, THEN. WHAT IS STOPPING YOU?
JUST MY FOOLISH HEART - THAT I LEAVE BEHIND.
WHAT - WITH LYSANDER?
With Demetrius.

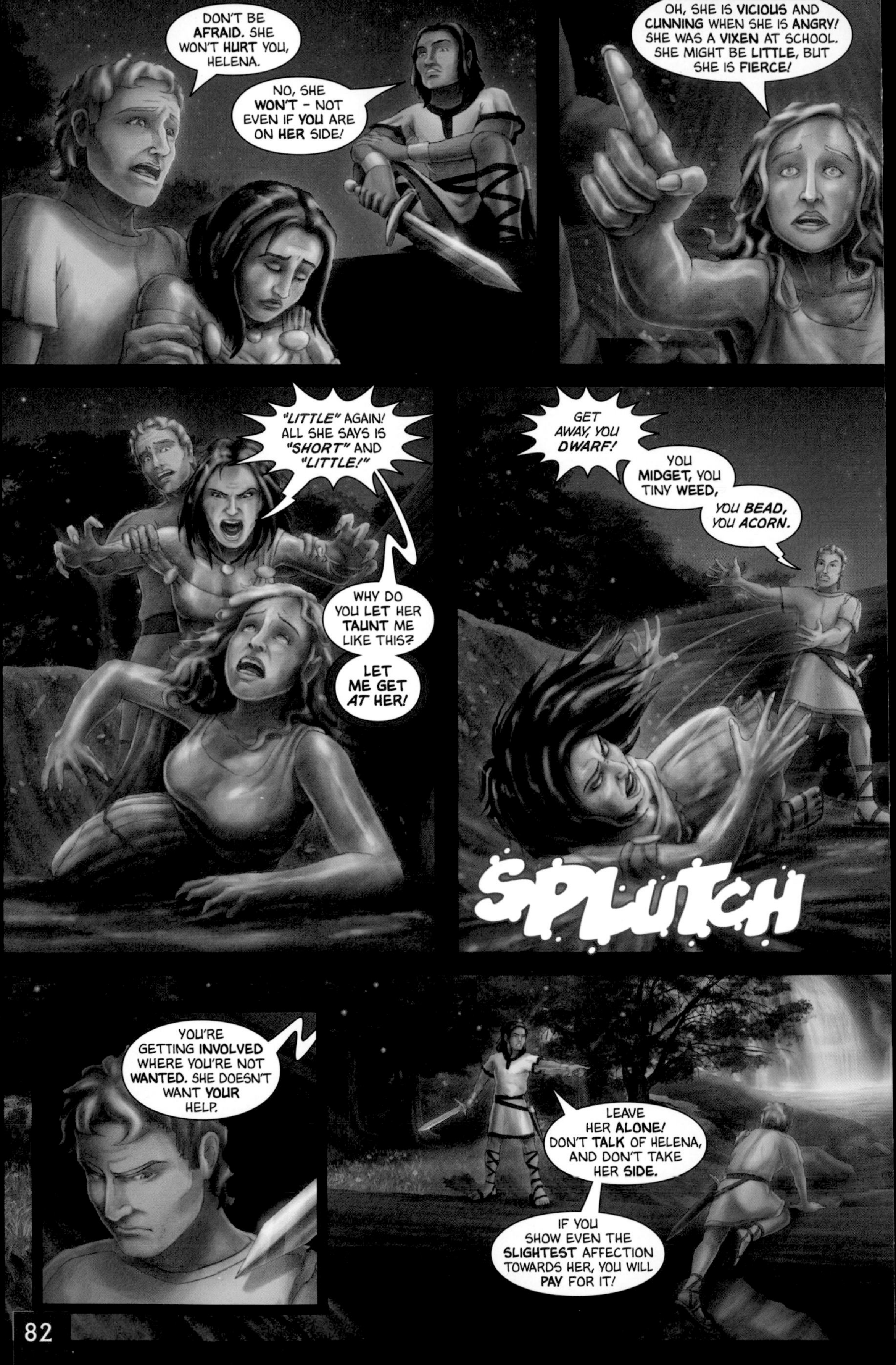

DON'T BE AFRAID. SHE WON'T HURT YOU, HELENA.
NO, SHE WON'T – NOT EVEN IF YOU ARE ON HER SIDE!
OH, SHE IS VICIOUS AND CUNNING WHEN SHE IS ANGRY! SHE WAS A VIXEN AT SCHOOL. SHE MIGHT BE LITTLE, BUT SHE IS FIERCE!
"LITTLE" AGAIN! ALL SHE SAYS IS "SHORT" AND "LITTLE!"
WHY DO YOU LET HER TAUNT ME LIKE THIS?
LET ME GET AT HER!
GET AWAY, YOU DWARF!
YOU MIDGET, YOU TINY WEED,
YOU BEAD, YOU ACORN.
SPLUTCH
YOU'RE GETTING INVOLVED WHERE YOU'RE NOT WANTED. SHE DOESN'T WANT YOUR HELP.
LEAVE HER ALONE! DON'T TALK OF HELENA, AND DON'T TAKE HER SIDE.
IF YOU SHOW EVEN THE SLIGHTEST AFFECTION TOWARDS HER, YOU WILL PAY FOR IT!

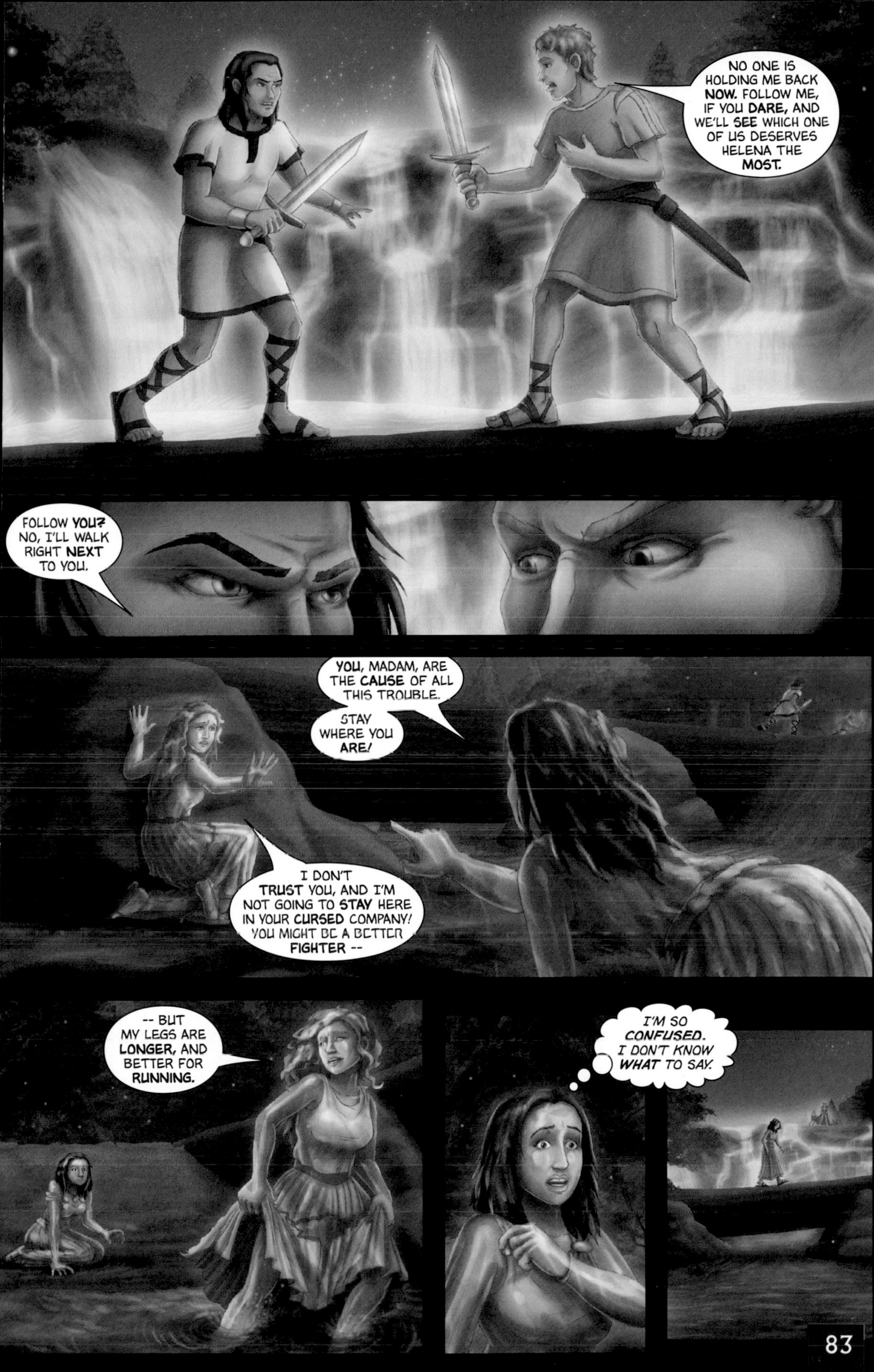
NO ONE IS HOLDING ME BACK NOW. FOLLOW ME, IF YOU DARE, AND WE'LL SEE WHICH ONE OF US DESERVES HELENA THE MOST.
FOLLOW YOU? NO, I'LL WALK RIGHT NEXT TO YOU.
YOU, MADAM, ARE THE CAUSE OF ALL THIS TROUBLE.
STAY WHERE YOU ARE!
I DON'T TRUST YOU, AND I'M NOT GOING TO STAY HERE IN YOUR CURSED COMPANY! YOU MIGHT BE A BETTER FIGHTER --
-- BUT MY LEGS ARE LONGER, AND BETTER FOR RUNNING.
I'M SO CONFUSED. I DON'T KNOW WHAT TO SAY.

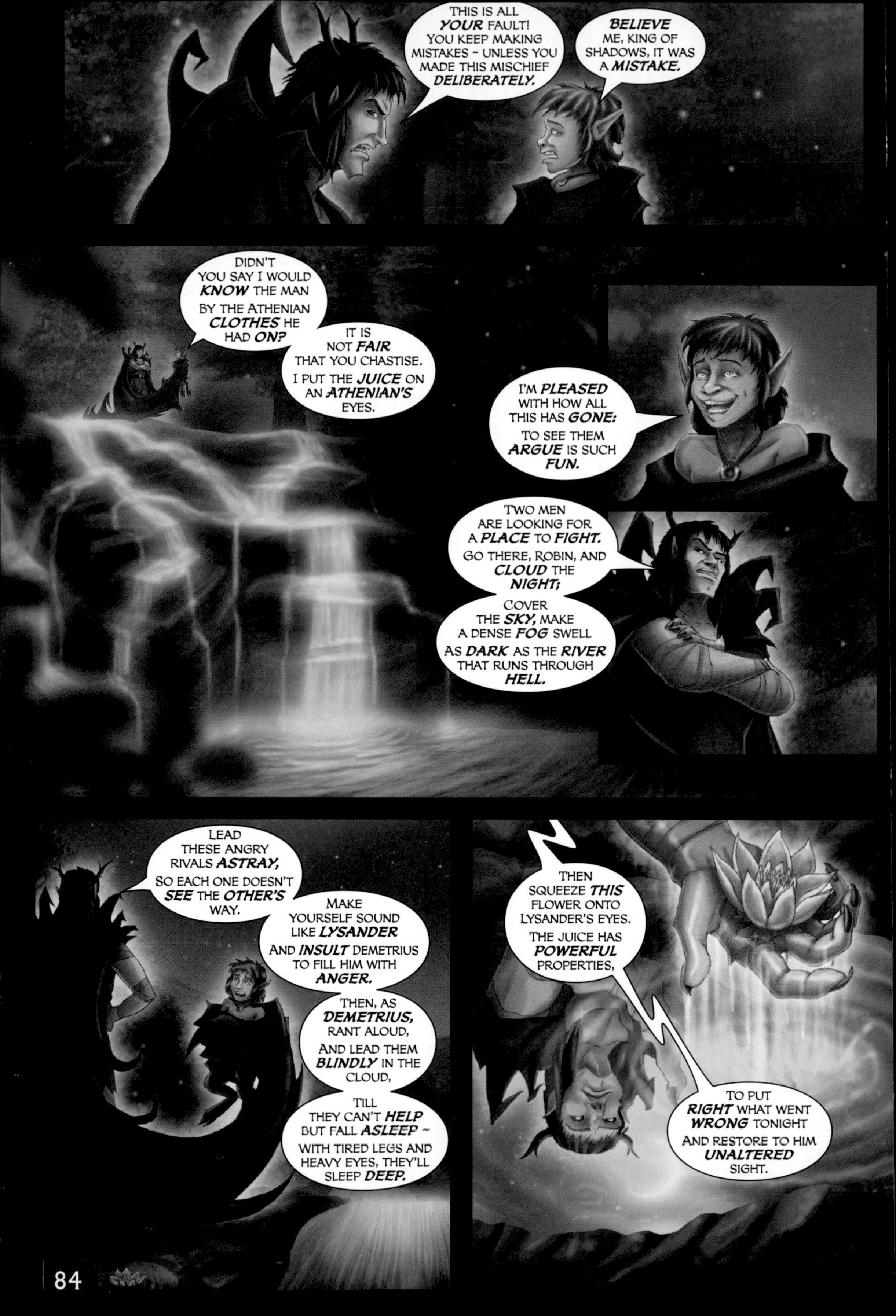
THIS IS ALL YOUR FAULT! YOU KEEP MAKING MISTAKES – UNLESS YOU MADE THIS MISCHIEF DELIBERATELY.
BELIEVE ME, KING OF SHADOWS, IT WAS A MISTAKE.
DIDN'T YOU SAY I WOULD KNOW THE MAN BY THE ATHENIAN CLOTHES HE HAD ON?
IT IS NOT FAIR THAT YOU CHASTISE. I PUT THE JUICE ON AN ATHENIAN'S EYES.
I'M PLEASED WITH HOW ALL THIS HAS GONE: TO SEE THEM ARGUE IS SUCH FUN.
TWO MEN ARE LOOKING FOR A PLACE TO FIGHT. GO THERE, ROBIN, AND CLOUD THE NIGHT;
COVER THE SKY, MAKE A DENSE FOG SWELL AS DARK AS THE RIVER THAT RUNS THROUGH HELL.
LEAD THESE ANGRY RIVALS ASTRAY, SO EACH ONE DOESN'T SEE THE OTHER'S WAY.
MAKE YOURSELF SOUND LIKE LYSANDER AND INSULT DEMETRIUS TO FILL HIM WITH ANGER.
THEN, AS DEMETRIUS, RANT ALOUD, AND LEAD THEM BLINDLY IN THE CLOUD,
TILL THEY CAN'T HELP BUT FALL ASLEEP – WITH TIRED LEGS AND HEAVY EYES, THEY'LL SLEEP DEEP.
THEN SQUEEZE THIS FLOWER ONTO LYSANDER'S EYES. THE JUICE HAS POWERFUL PROPERTIES,
TO PUT RIGHT WHAT WENT WRONG TONIGHT AND RESTORE TO HIM UNALTERED SIGHT.

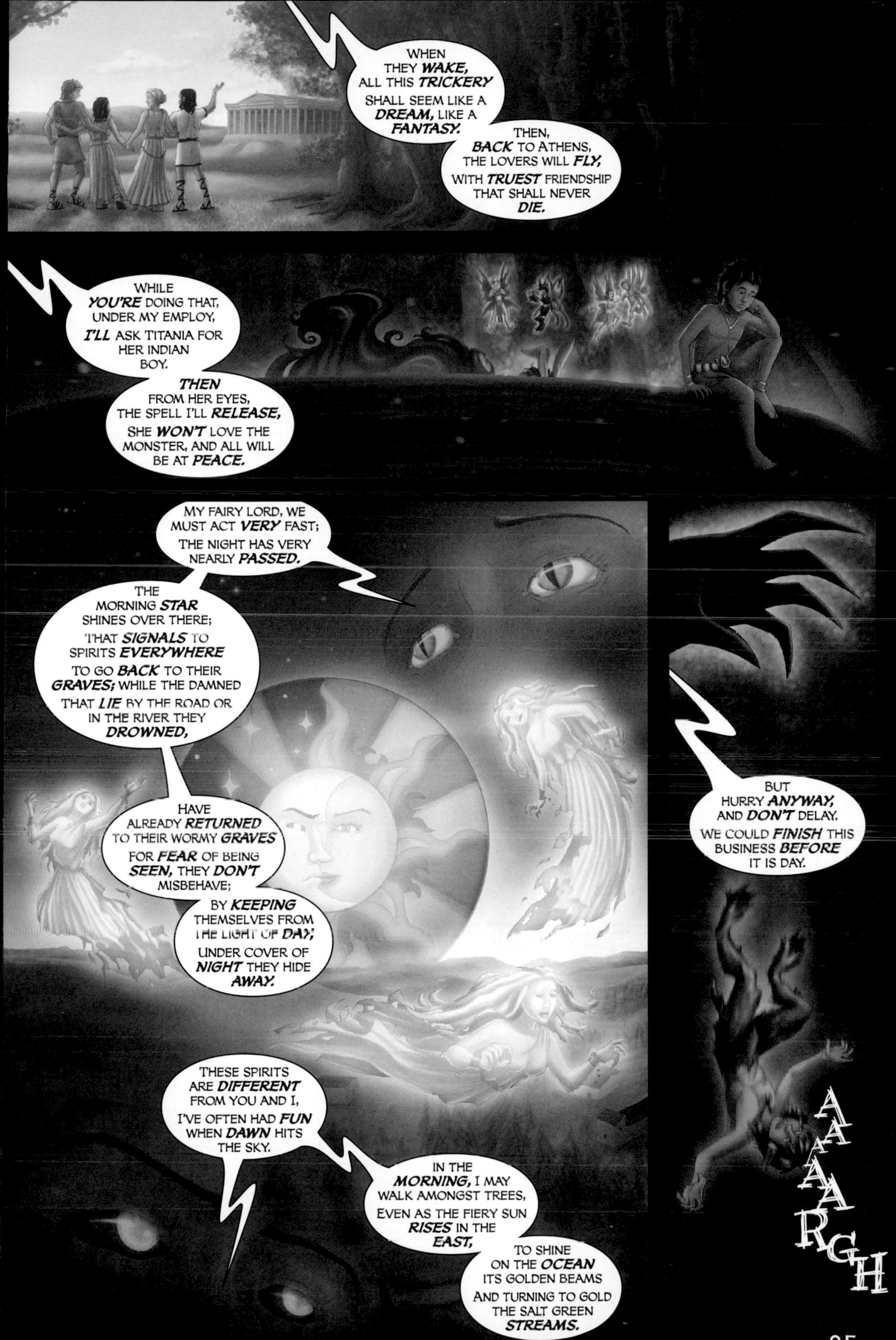

WHEN THEY WAKE, ALL THIS TRICKERY SHALL SEEM LIKE A DREAM, LIKE A FANTASY.
THEN, BACK TO ATHENS, THE LOVERS WILL FLY, WITH TRUEST FRIENDSHIP THAT SHALL NEVER DIE.
WHILE YOU'RE DOING THAT, UNDER MY EMPLOY, I'LL ASK TITANIA FOR HER INDIAN BOY.
THEN FROM HER EYES, THE SPELL I'LL RELEASE, SHE WON'T LOVE THE MONSTER, AND ALL WILL BE AT PEACE.
MY FAIRY LORD, WE MUST ACT VERY FAST; THE NIGHT HAS VERY NEARLY PASSED.
THE MORNING STAR SHINES OVER THERE; THAT SIGNALS TO SPIRITS EVERYWHERE TO GO BACK TO THEIR GRAVES; WHILE THE DAMNED THAT LIE BY THE ROAD OR IN THE RIVER THEY DROWNED,
HAVE ALREADY RETURNED TO THEIR WORMY GRAVES FOR FEAR OF BEING SEEN, THEY DON'T MISBEHAVE;
BY KEEPING THEMSELVES FROM THE LIGHT OF DAY; UNDER COVER OF NIGHT THEY HIDE AWAY.
THESE SPIRITS ARE DIFFERENT FROM YOU AND I, I'VE OFTEN HAD FUN WHEN DAWN HITS THE SKY.
IN THE MORNING, I MAY WALK AMONGST TREES, EVEN AS THE FIERY SUN RISES IN THE EAST,
TO SHINE ON THE OCEAN ITS GOLDEN BEAMS AND TURNING TO GOLD THE SALT GREEN STREAMS.
BUT HURRY ANYWAY, AND DON'T DELAY. WE COULD FINISH THIS BUSINESS BEFORE IT IS DAY.
AAAAARGH

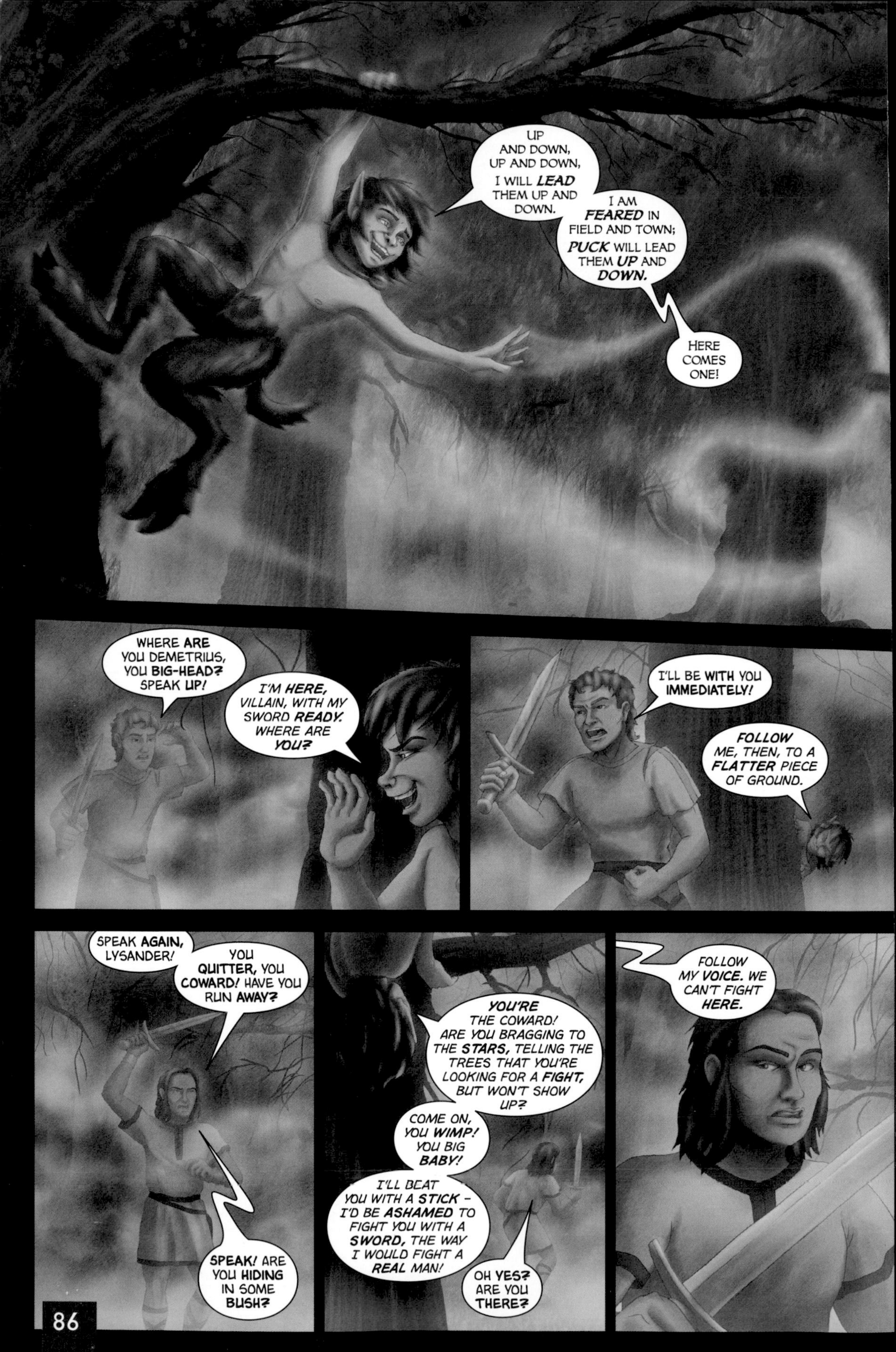
UP AND DOWN, UP AND DOWN, I WILL LEAD THEM UP AND DOWN.
I AM FEARED IN FIELD AND TOWN; PUCK WILL LEAD THEM UP AND DOWN.
HERE COMES ONE!
WHERE ARE YOU DEMETRIUS, YOU BIG-HEAD? SPEAK UP!
I'M HERE, VILLAIN, WITH MY SWORD READY. WHERE ARE YOU?
I'LL BE WITH YOU IMMEDIATELY!
FOLLOW ME, THEN, TO A FLATTER PIECE OF GROUND.
SPEAK AGAIN, LYSANDER!
YOU QUITTER, YOU COWARD! HAVE YOU RUN AWAY?
SPEAK! ARE YOU HIDING IN SOME BUSH?
YOU'RE THE COWARD! ARE YOU BRAGGING TO THE STARS, TELLING THE TREES THAT YOU'RE LOOKING FOR A FIGHT, BUT WON'T SHOW UP?
COME ON, YOU WIMP! YOU BIG BABY!
I'LL BEAT YOU WITH A STICK – I'D BE ASHAMED TO FIGHT YOU WITH A SWORD, THE WAY I WOULD FIGHT A REAL MAN!
OH YES? ARE YOU THERE?
FOLLOW MY VOICE. WE CAN'T FIGHT HERE.

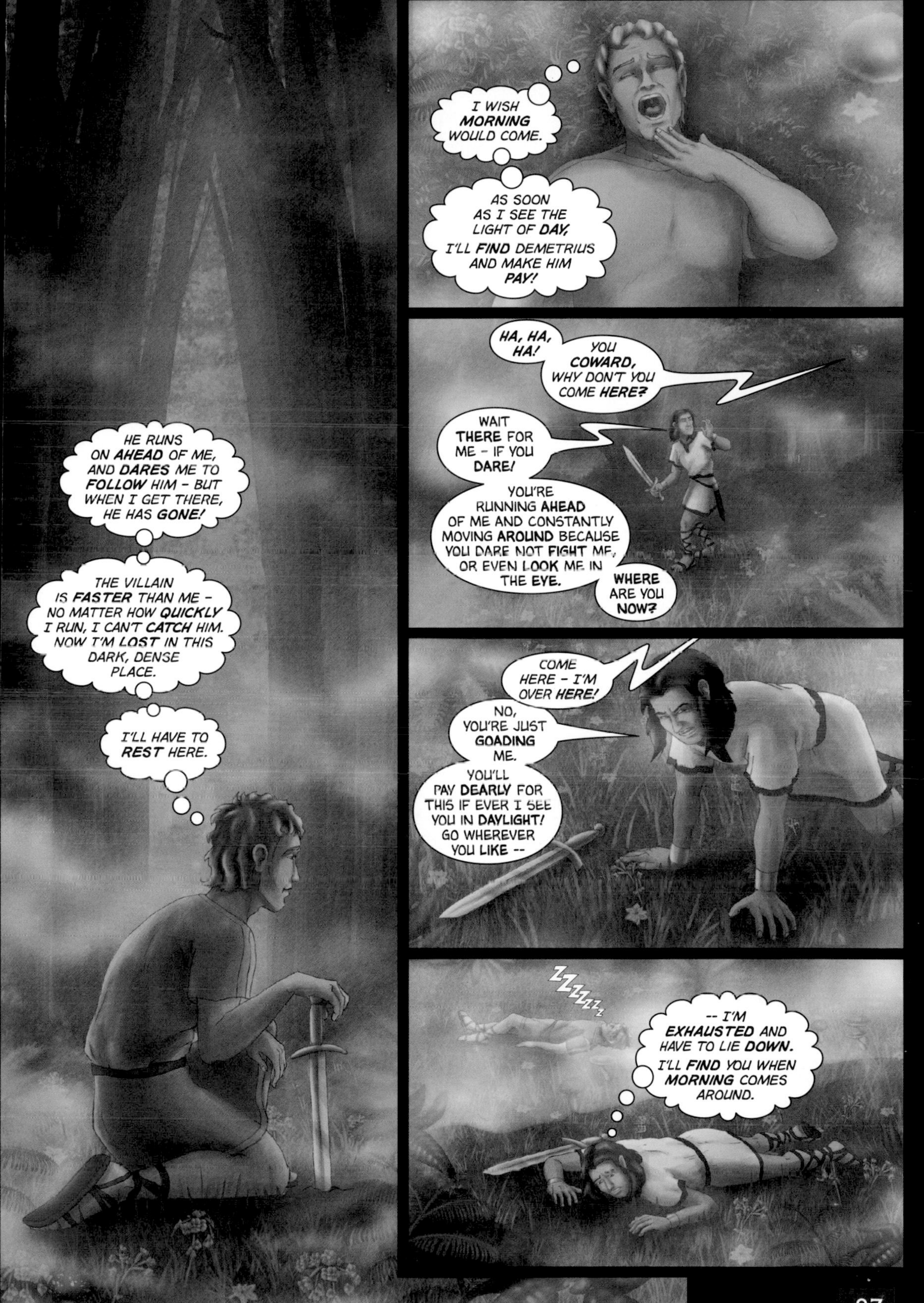
HE RUNS ON AHEAD OF ME, AND DARES ME TO FOLLOW HIM - BUT WHEN I GET THERE, HE HAS GONE!
THE VILLAIN IS FASTER THAN ME - NO MATTER HOW QUICKLY I RUN, I CAN'T CATCH HIM. NOW I'M LOST IN THIS DARK, DENSE PLACE.
I'LL HAVE TO REST HERE.
I WISH MORNING WOULD COME.
AS SOON AS I SEE THE LIGHT OF DAY, I'LL FIND DEMETRIUS AND MAKE HIM PAY!
HA, HA, HA!
YOU COWARD, WHY DON'T YOU COME HERE?
WAIT THERE FOR ME - IF YOU DARE!
YOU'RE RUNNING AHEAD OF ME AND CONSTANTLY MOVING AROUND BECAUSE YOU DARE NOT FIGHT ME, OR EVEN LOOK ME IN THE EYE.
WHERE ARE YOU NOW?
COME HERE - I'M OVER HERE!
NO, YOU'RE JUST GOADING ME.
YOU'LL PAY DEARLY FOR THIS IF EVER I SEE YOU IN DAYLIGHT! GO WHEREVER YOU LIKE --
ZZZZZZZ
-- I'M EXHAUSTED AND HAVE TO LIE DOWN.
I'LL FIND YOU WHEN MORNING COMES AROUND.

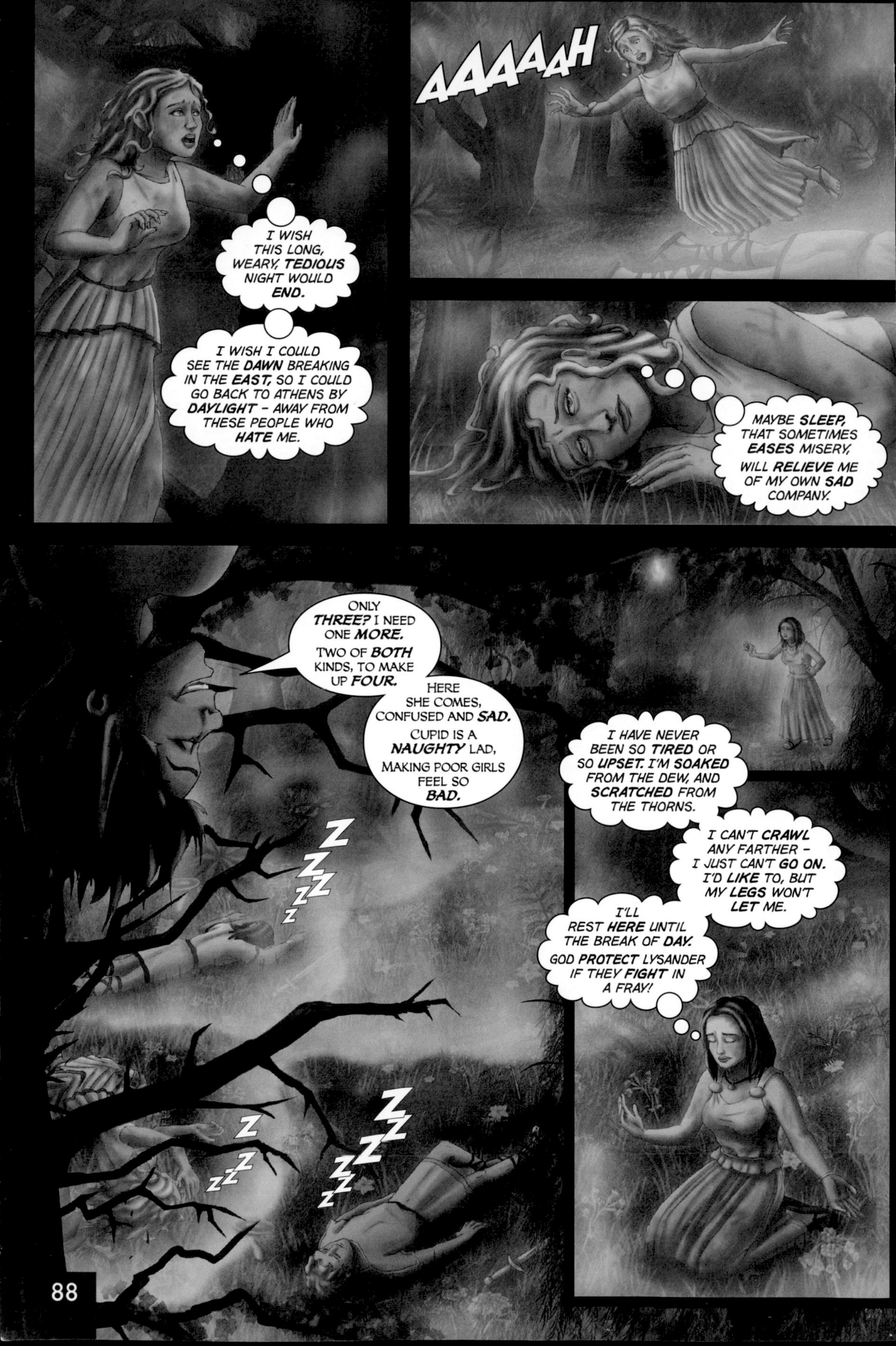
I WISH THIS LONG, WEARY, TEDIOUS NIGHT WOULD END.
I WISH I COULD SEE THE DAWN BREAKING IN THE EAST, SO I COULD GO BACK TO ATHENS BY DAYLIGHT - AWAY FROM THESE PEOPLE WHO HATE ME.
AAAAAH
MAYBE SLEEP, THAT SOMETIMES EASES MISERY, WILL RELIEVE ME OF MY OWN SAD COMPANY.
ONLY THREE? I NEED ONE MORE. TWO OF BOTH KINDS, TO MAKE UP FOUR.
HERE SHE COMES, CONFUSED AND SAD. CUPID IS A NAUGHTY LAD, MAKING POOR GIRLS FEEL SO BAD.
ZZZZZ
I HAVE NEVER BEEN SO TIRED OR SO UPSET. I'M SOAKED FROM THE DEW, AND SCRATCHED FROM THE THORNS.
I CAN'T CRAWL ANY FARTHER - I JUST CAN'T GO ON. I'D LIKE TO, BUT MY LEGS WON'T LET ME.
I'LL REST HERE UNTIL THE BREAK OF DAY. GOD PROTECT LYSANDER IF THEY FIGHT IN A FRAY!
ZZZZ
ZZZZZZ

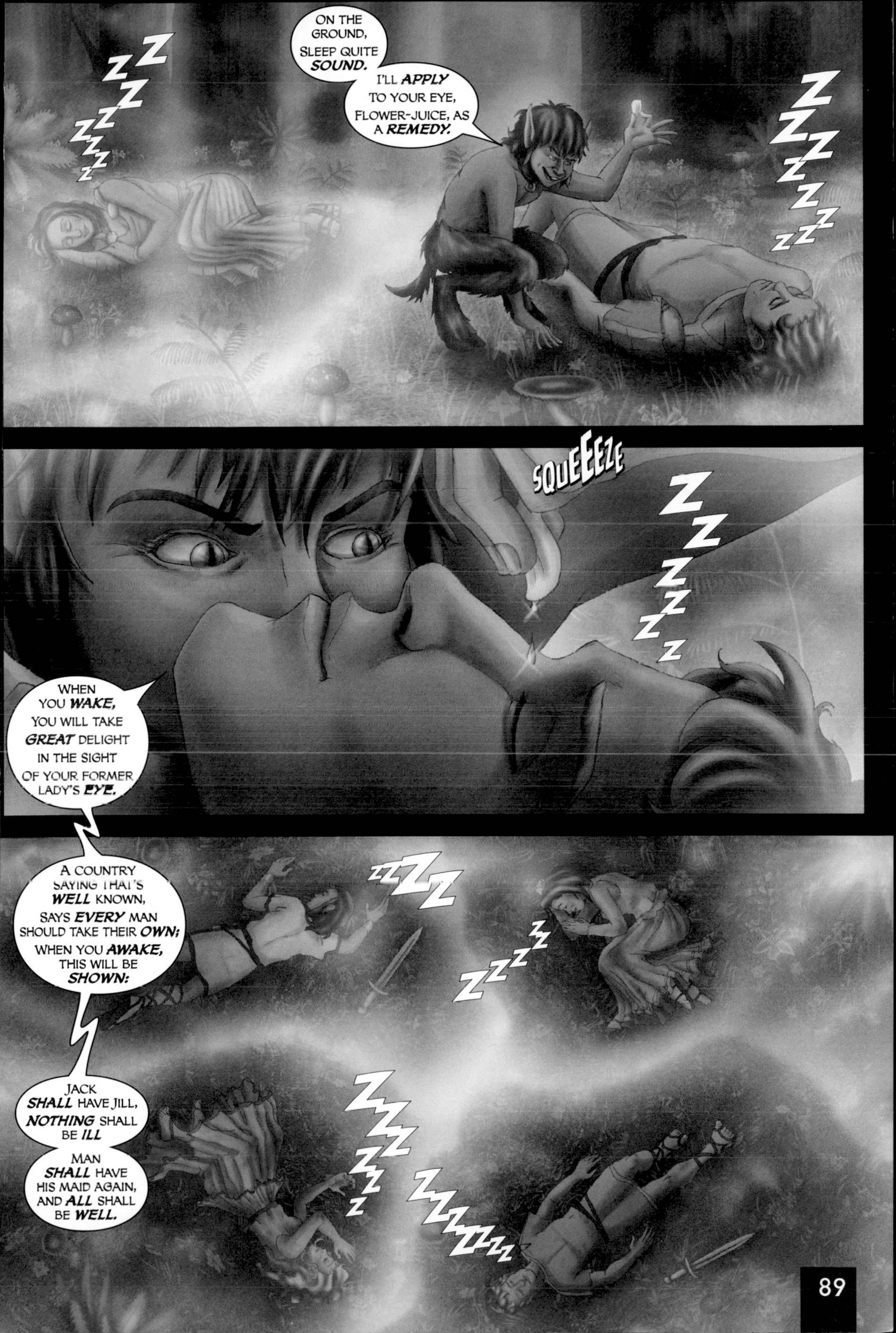
ZZZZZZZ
ON THE GROUND, SLEEP QUITE SOUND.
I'LL APPLY TO YOUR EYE, FLOWER-JUICE, AS A REMEDY.
ZZZZZZZ
SQUEEEZE
ZZZZZZ
WHEN YOU WAKE, YOU WILL TAKE GREAT DELIGHT IN THE SIGHT OF YOUR FORMER LADY'S EYE.
A COUNTRY SAYING THAT'S WELL KNOWN, SAYS EVERY MAN SHOULD TAKE THEIR OWN; WHEN YOU AWAKE, THIS WILL BE SHOWN:
ZZZZ
ZZZZZZ
JACK SHALL HAVE JILL, NOTHING SHALL BE ILL
MAN SHALL HAVE HIS MAID AGAIN, AND ALL SHALL BE WELL.
ZZZZZZ
ZZZZZZZZ

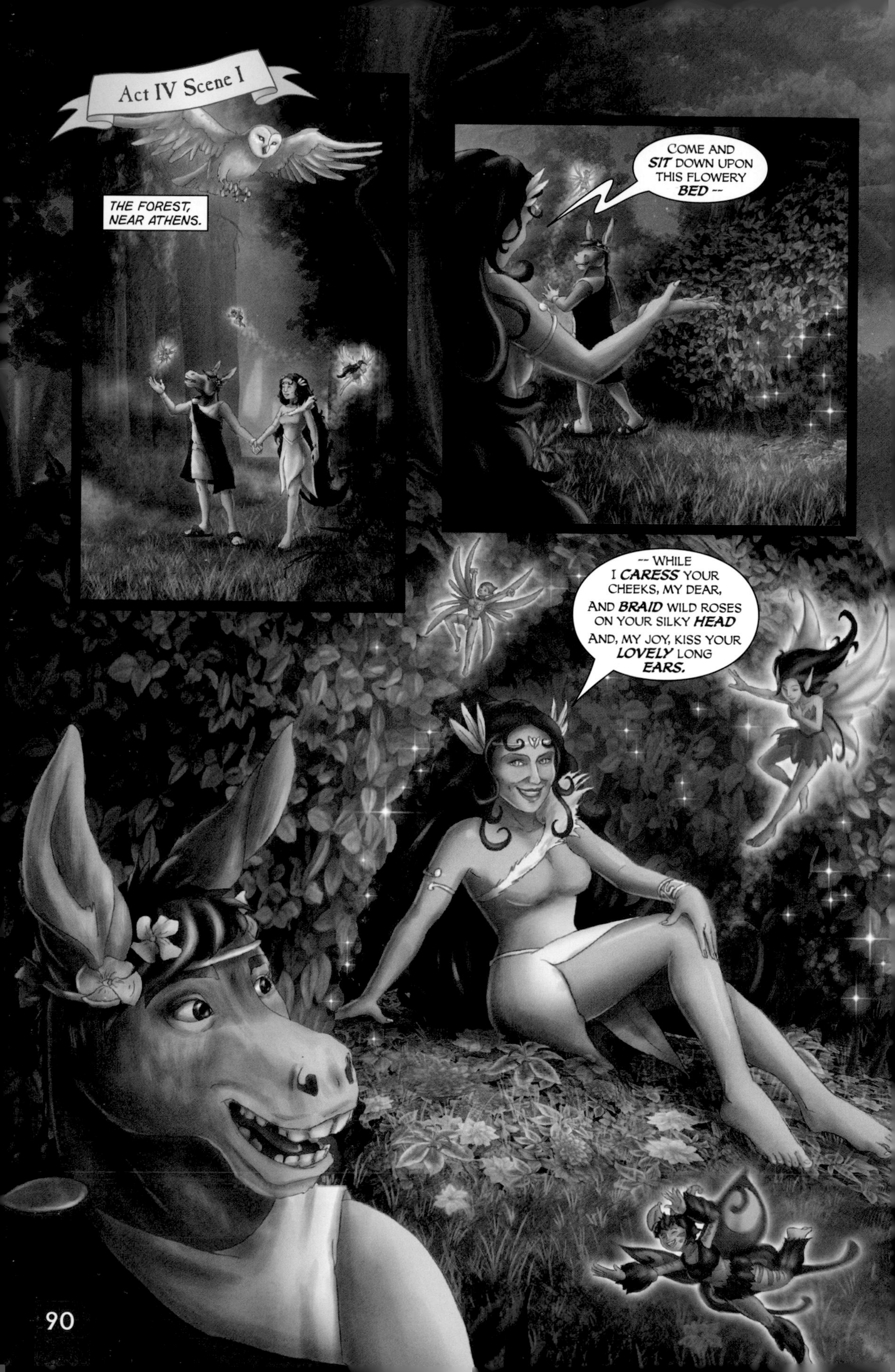
Act IV Scene I
THE FOREST, NEAR ATHENS.
COME AND SIT DOWN UPON THIS FLOWERY BED --
-- WHILE I CARESS YOUR CHEEKS, MY DEAR, AND BRAID WILD ROSES ON YOUR SILKY HEAD AND, MY JOY, KISS YOUR LOVELY LONG EARS.

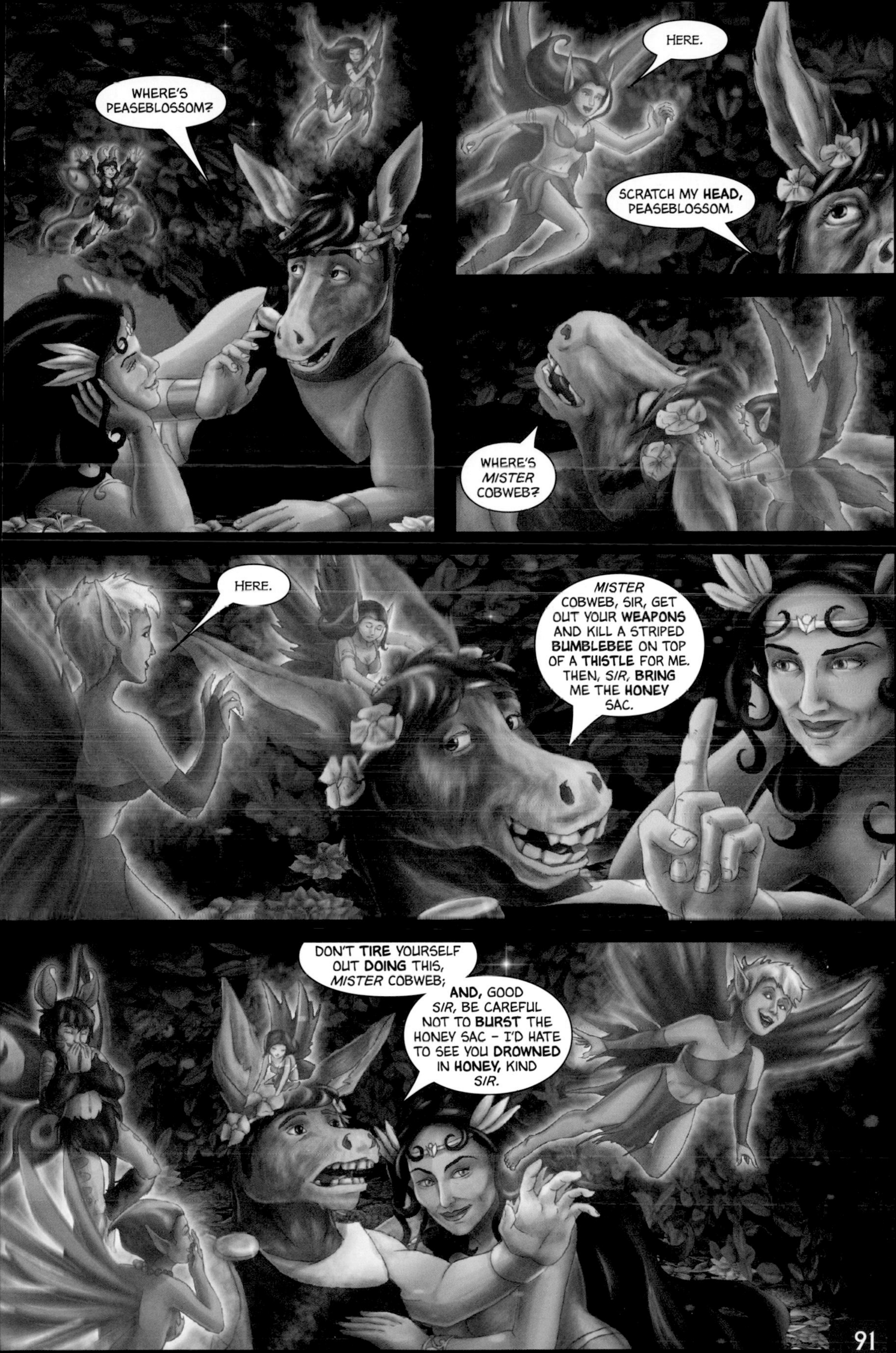
WHERE'S PEASEBLOSSOM?
HERE.
SCRATCH MY HEAD, PEASEBLOSSOM.
WHERE'S MISTER COBWEB?
HERE.
MISTER COBWEB, SIR, GET OUT YOUR WEAPONS AND KILL A STRIPED BUMBLEBEE ON TOP OF A THISTLE FOR ME. THEN, SIR, BRING ME THE HONEY SAC.
DON'T TIRE YOURSELF OUT DOING THIS, MISTER COBWEB;
AND, GOOD SIR, BE CAREFUL NOT TO BURST THE HONEY SAC – I'D HATE TO SEE YOU DROWNED IN HONEY, KIND SIR.

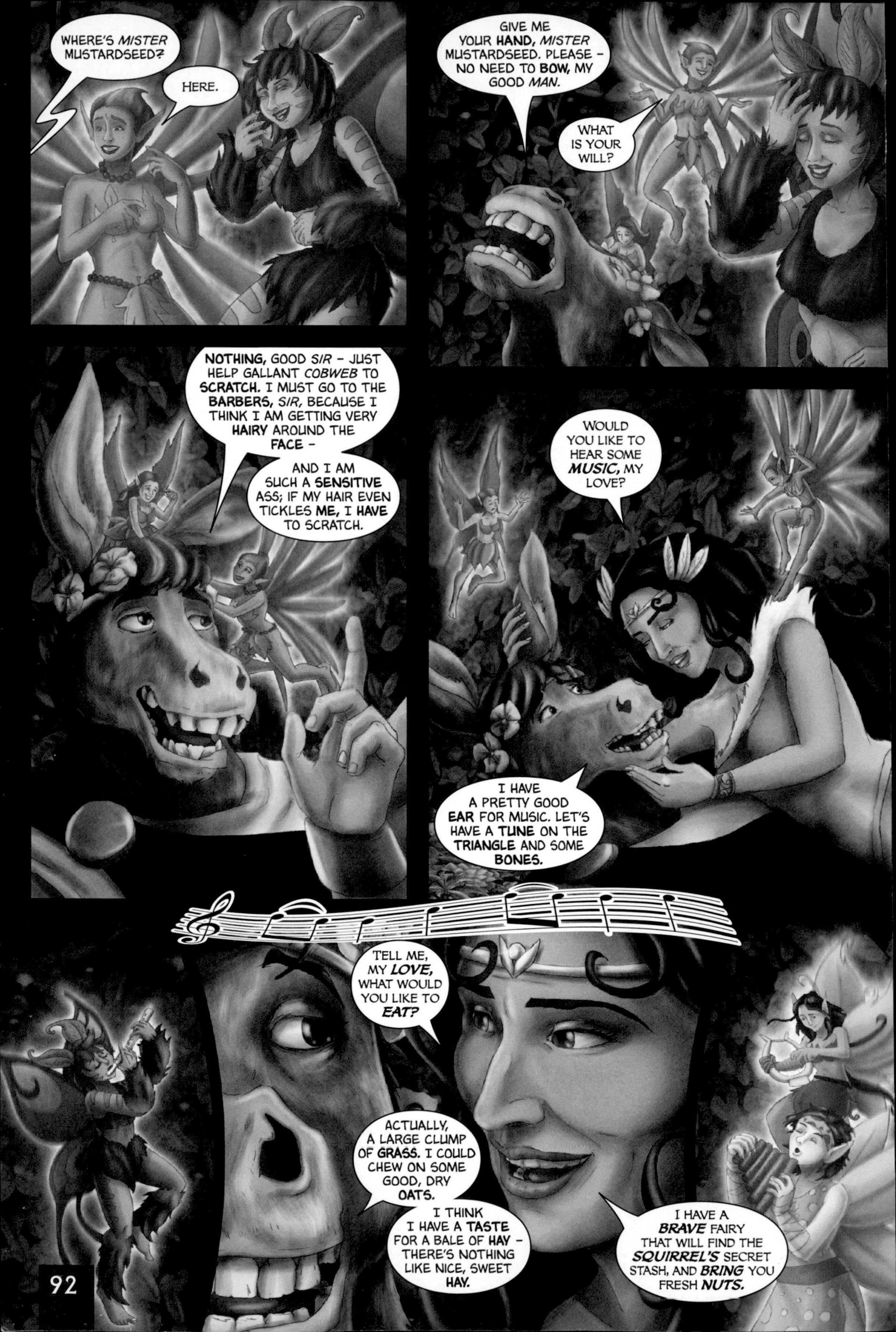

WHERE'S *MISTER* MUSTARDSEED?
HERE.
GIVE ME YOUR **HAND**, *MISTER* MUSTARDSEED. PLEASE – NO NEED TO **BOW**, MY GOOD *MAN*.
WHAT IS YOUR WILL?
NOTHING, GOOD *SIR* – JUST HELP GALLANT *COBWEB* TO **SCRATCH.** I MUST GO TO THE **BARBERS,** *SIR,* BECAUSE I THINK I AM GETTING VERY **HAIRY** AROUND THE **FACE** –
AND I AM SUCH A **SENSITIVE** ASS; IF MY HAIR EVEN TICKLES **ME,** I **HAVE** TO SCRATCH.
WOULD YOU LIKE TO HEAR SOME ***MUSIC,*** MY LOVE?
I HAVE A PRETTY GOOD **EAR** FOR MUSIC. LET'S HAVE A **TUNE** ON THE **TRIANGLE** AND SOME **BONES.**
TELL ME, MY ***LOVE,*** WHAT WOULD YOU LIKE TO ***EAT?***
ACTUALLY, A LARGE CLUMP OF **GRASS.** I COULD CHEW ON SOME GOOD, DRY **OATS.**
I THINK I HAVE A **TASTE** FOR A BALE OF **HAY** – THERE'S NOTHING LIKE NICE, SWEET **HAY.**
I HAVE A ***BRAVE*** FAIRY THAT WILL FIND THE ***SQUIRREL'S*** SECRET STASH, AND ***BRING*** YOU FRESH ***NUTS.***

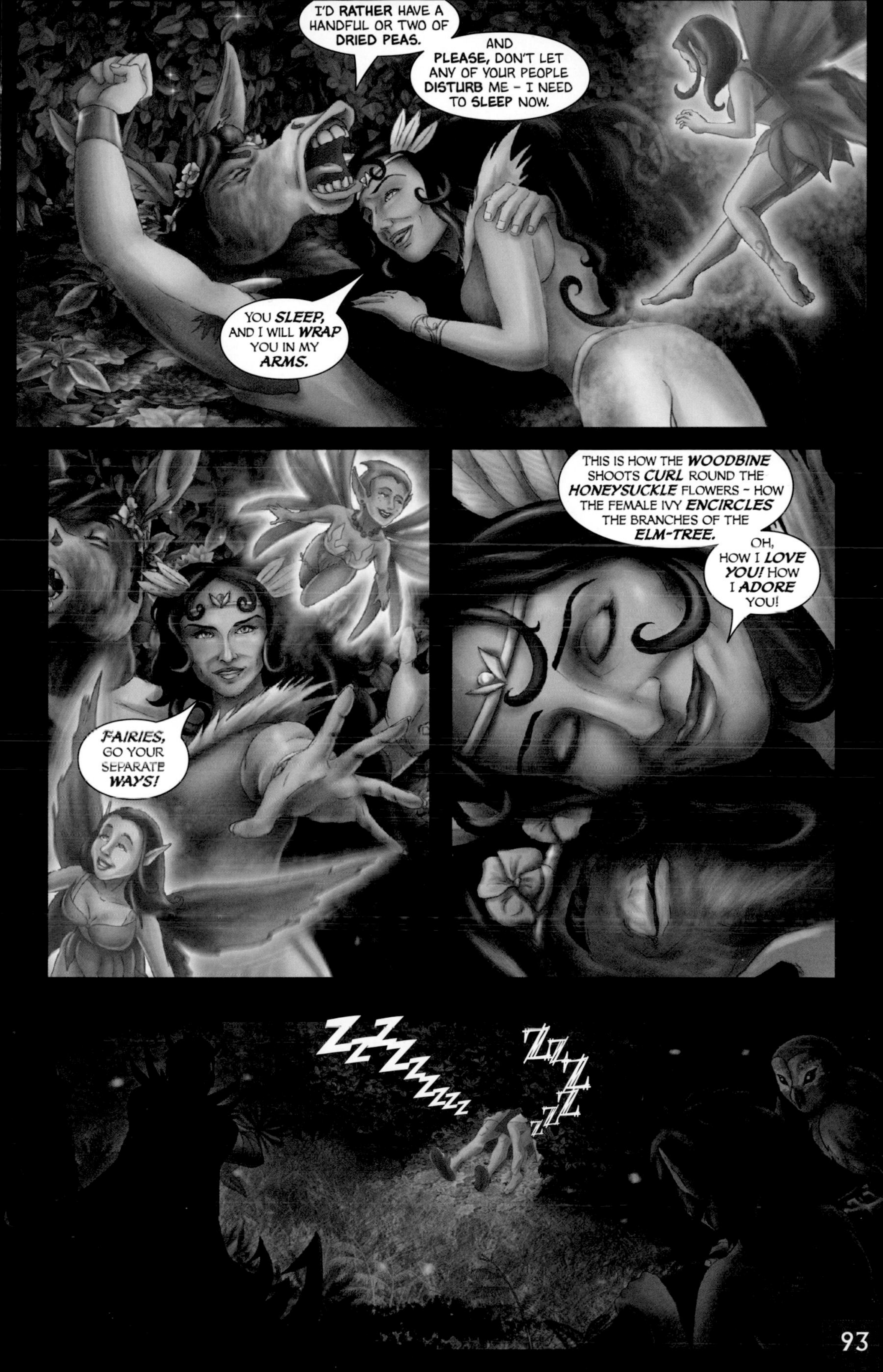
I'D RATHER HAVE A HANDFUL OR TWO OF DRIED PEAS.
AND PLEASE, DON'T LET ANY OF YOUR PEOPLE DISTURB ME – I NEED TO SLEEP NOW.
YOU SLEEP, AND I WILL WRAP YOU IN MY ARMS.
FAIRIES, GO YOUR SEPARATE WAYS!
THIS IS HOW THE WOODBINE SHOOTS CURL ROUND THE HONEYSUCKLE FLOWERS – HOW THE FEMALE IVY ENCIRCLES THE BRANCHES OF THE ELM-TREE.
OH, HOW I LOVE YOU! HOW I ADORE YOU!
ZZZZZZZZZ
ZZZZZZ

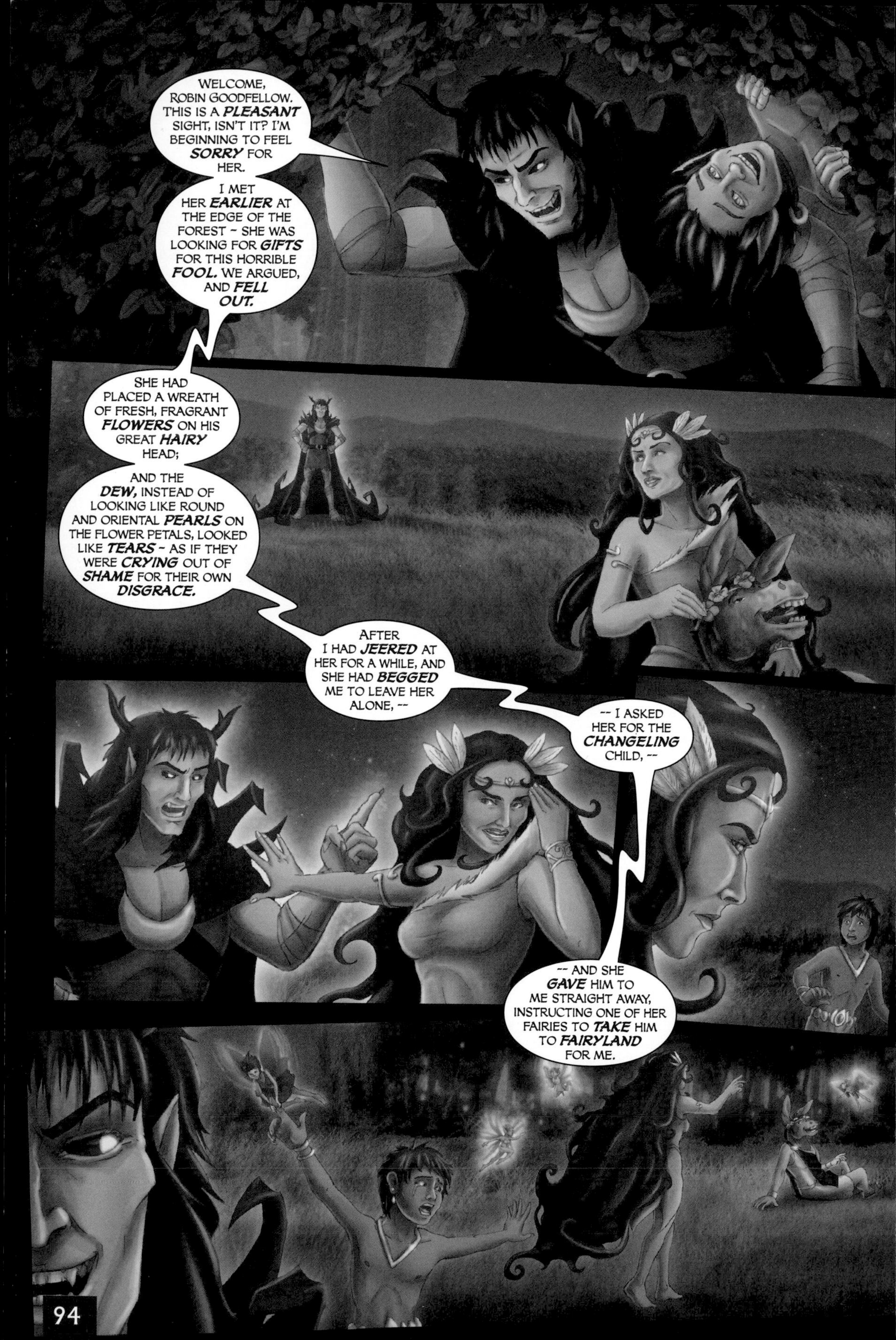
WELCOME, ROBIN GOODFELLOW. THIS IS A PLEASANT SIGHT, ISN'T IT? I'M BEGINNING TO FEEL SORRY FOR HER.
I MET HER EARLIER AT THE EDGE OF THE FOREST - SHE WAS LOOKING FOR GIFTS FOR THIS HORRIBLE FOOL. WE ARGUED, AND FELL OUT.
SHE HAD PLACED A WREATH OF FRESH, FRAGRANT FLOWERS ON HIS GREAT HAIRY HEAD;
AND THE DEW, INSTEAD OF LOOKING LIKE ROUND AND ORIENTAL PEARLS ON THE FLOWER PETALS, LOOKED LIKE TEARS - AS IF THEY WERE CRYING OUT OF SHAME FOR THEIR OWN DISGRACE.
AFTER I HAD JEERED AT HER FOR A WHILE, AND SHE HAD BEGGED ME TO LEAVE HER ALONE, --
-- I ASKED HER FOR THE CHANGELING CHILD, --
-- AND SHE GAVE HIM TO ME STRAIGHT AWAY, INSTRUCTING ONE OF HER FAIRIES TO TAKE HIM TO FAIRYLAND FOR ME.

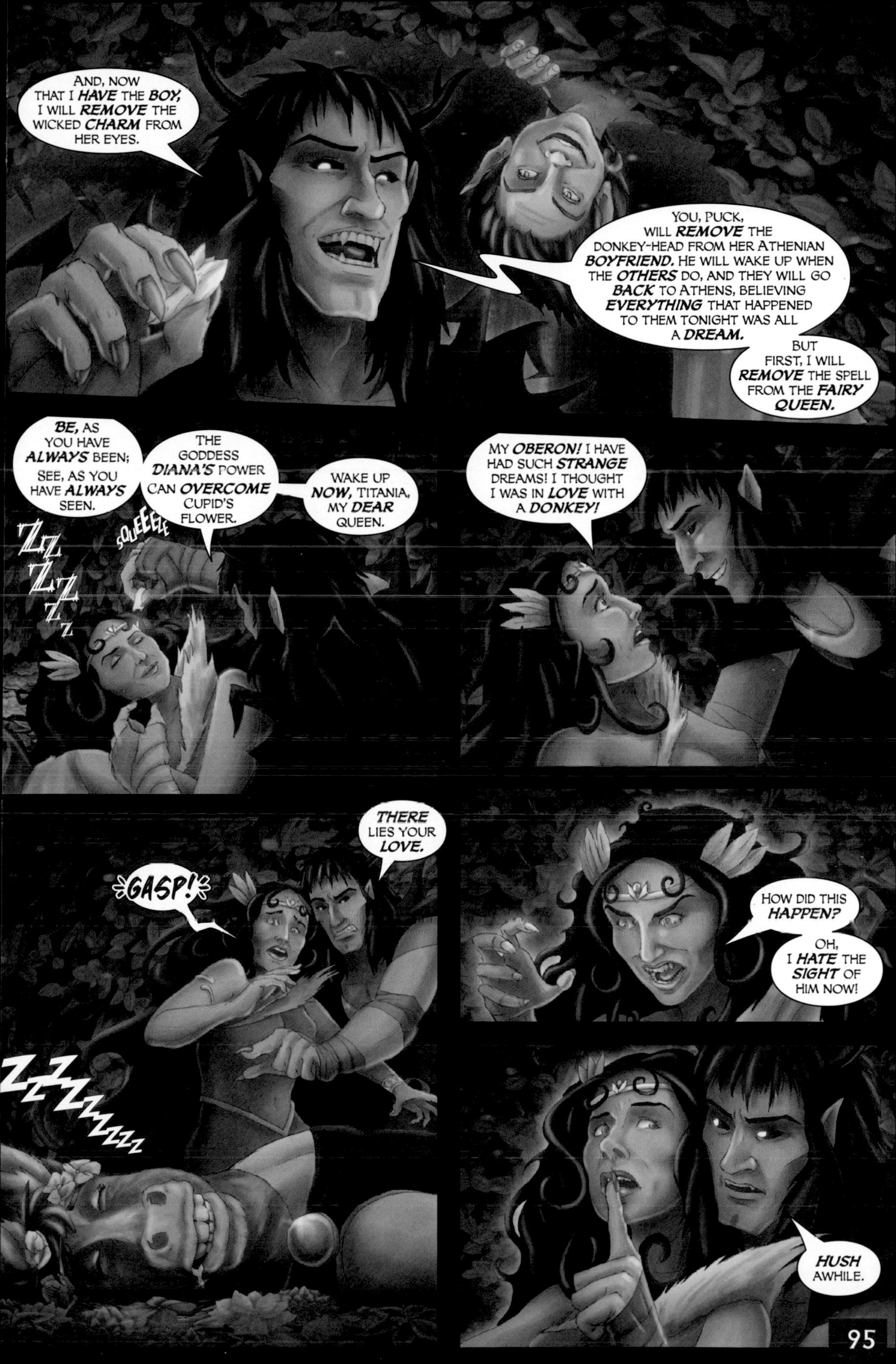
AND, NOW THAT I HAVE THE BOY, I WILL REMOVE THE WICKED CHARM FROM HER EYES.
YOU, PUCK, WILL REMOVE THE DONKEY-HEAD FROM HER ATHENIAN BOYFRIEND. HE WILL WAKE UP WHEN THE OTHERS DO, AND THEY WILL GO BACK TO ATHENS, BELIEVING EVERYTHING THAT HAPPENED TO THEM TONIGHT WAS ALL A DREAM.
BUT FIRST, I WILL REMOVE THE SPELL FROM THE FAIRY QUEEN.
BE, AS YOU HAVE ALWAYS BEEN; SEE, AS YOU HAVE ALWAYS SEEN.
THE GODDESS DIANA'S POWER CAN OVERCOME CUPID'S FLOWER.
WAKE UP NOW, TITANIA, MY DEAR QUEEN.
SQUEEEZE
ZZZZZ
MY OBERON! I HAVE HAD SUCH STRANGE DREAMS! I THOUGHT I WAS IN LOVE WITH A DONKEY!
THERE LIES YOUR LOVE.
GASP!
ZZZZZZZZZ
HOW DID THIS HAPPEN?
OH, I HATE THE SIGHT OF HIM NOW!
HUSH AWHILE.

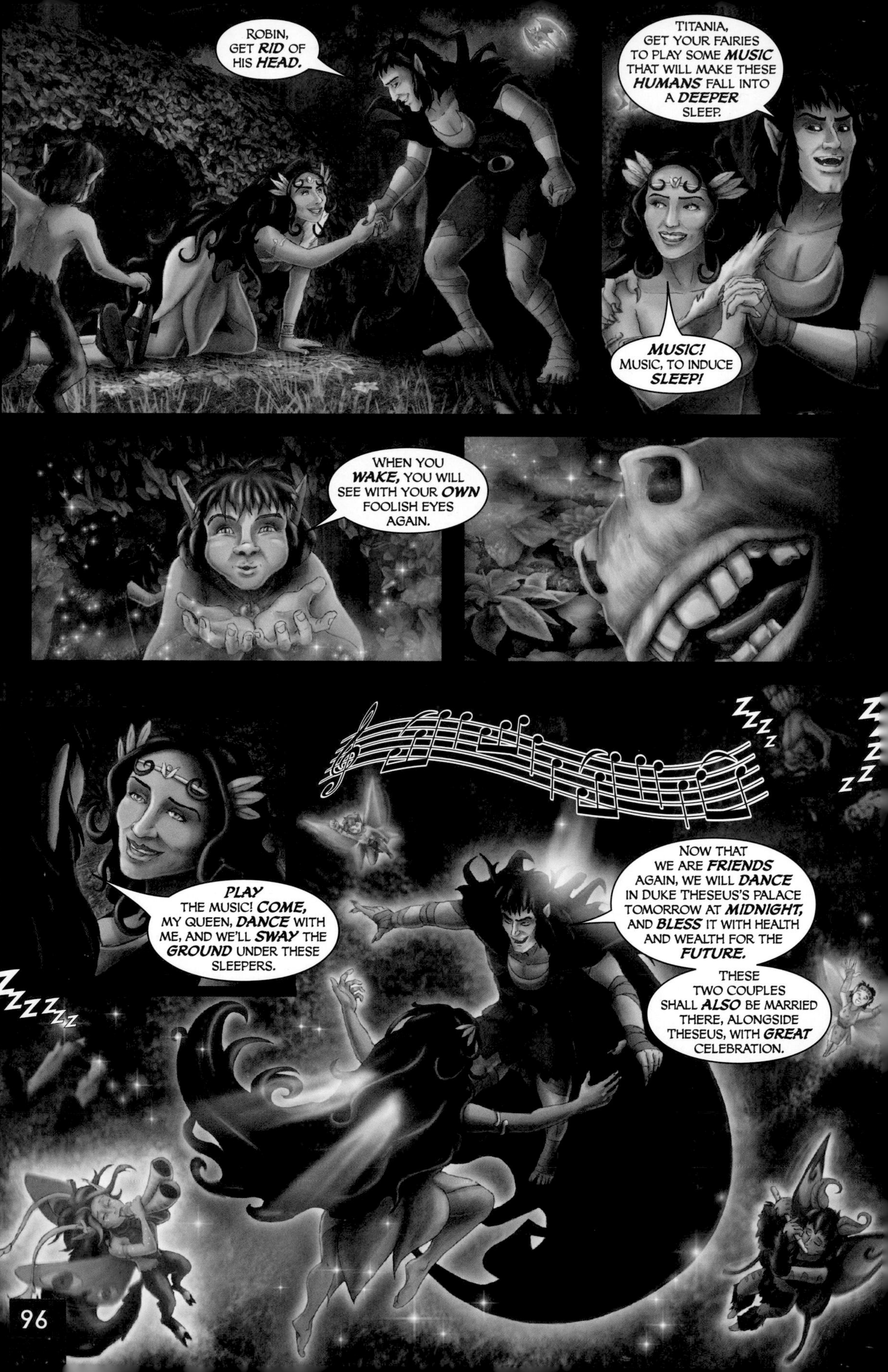
ROBIN, GET RID OF HIS HEAD.
TITANIA, GET YOUR FAIRIES TO PLAY SOME MUSIC THAT WILL MAKE THESE HUMANS FALL INTO A DEEPER SLEEP.
MUSIC! MUSIC, TO INDUCE SLEEP!
WHEN YOU WAKE, YOU WILL SEE WITH YOUR OWN FOOLISH EYES AGAIN.
ZZZ
ZZZZ
PLAY THE MUSIC! COME, MY QUEEN, DANCE WITH ME, AND WE'LL SWAY THE GROUND UNDER THESE SLEEPERS.
NOW THAT WE ARE FRIENDS AGAIN, WE WILL DANCE IN DUKE THESEUS'S PALACE TOMORROW AT MIDNIGHT, AND BLESS IT WITH HEALTH AND WEALTH FOR THE FUTURE.
THESE TWO COUPLES SHALL ALSO BE MARRIED THERE, ALONGSIDE THESEUS, WITH GREAT CELEBRATION.
ZZZZZZ

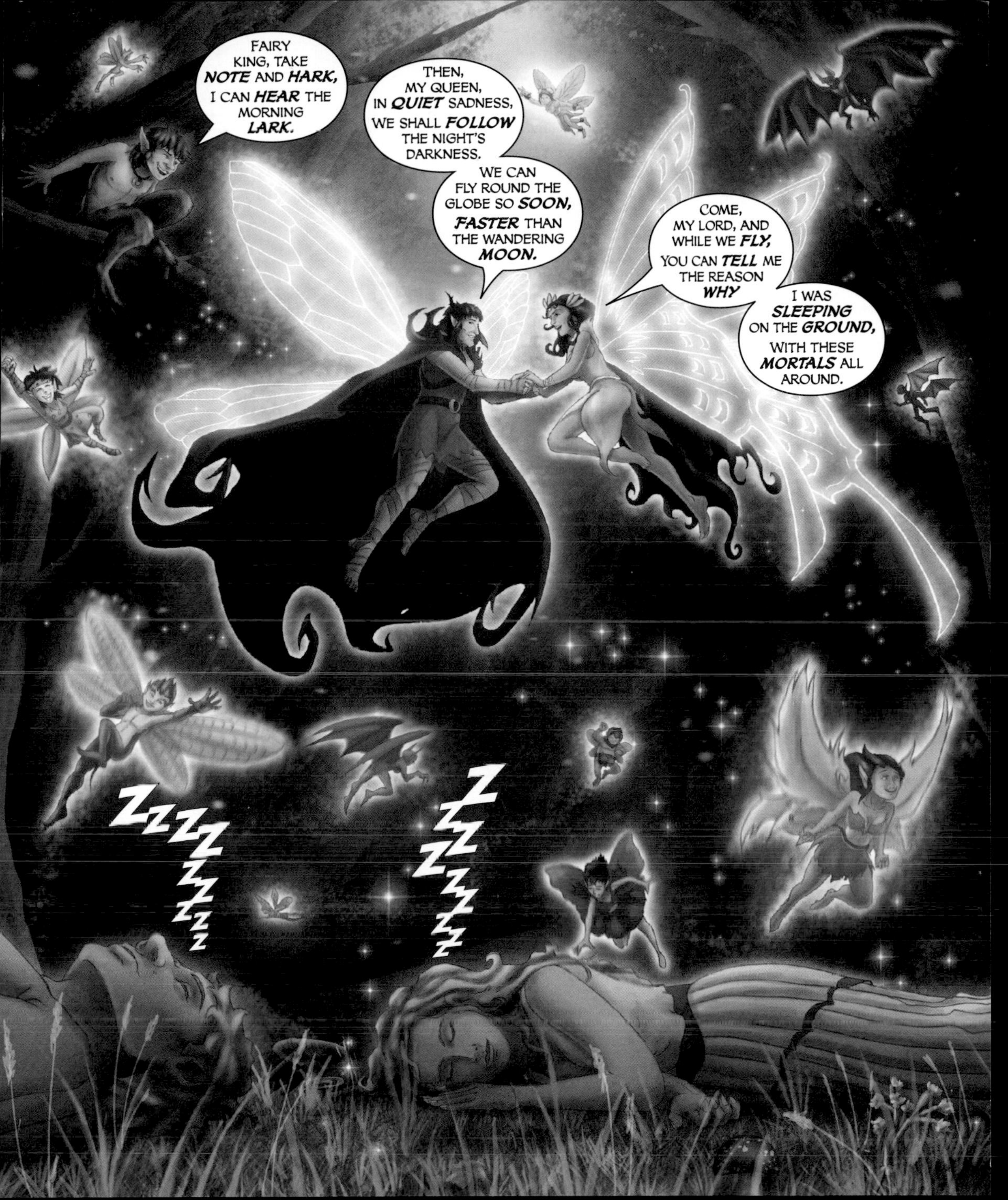
FAIRY KING, TAKE NOTE AND HARK, I CAN HEAR THE MORNING LARK.
THEN, MY QUEEN, IN QUIET SADNESS, WE SHALL FOLLOW THE NIGHT'S DARKNESS.
WE CAN FLY ROUND THE GLOBE SO SOON, FASTER THAN THE WANDERING MOON.
COME, MY LORD, AND WHILE WE FLY, YOU CAN TELL ME THE REASON WHY
I WAS SLEEPING ON THE GROUND, WITH THESE MORTALS ALL AROUND.

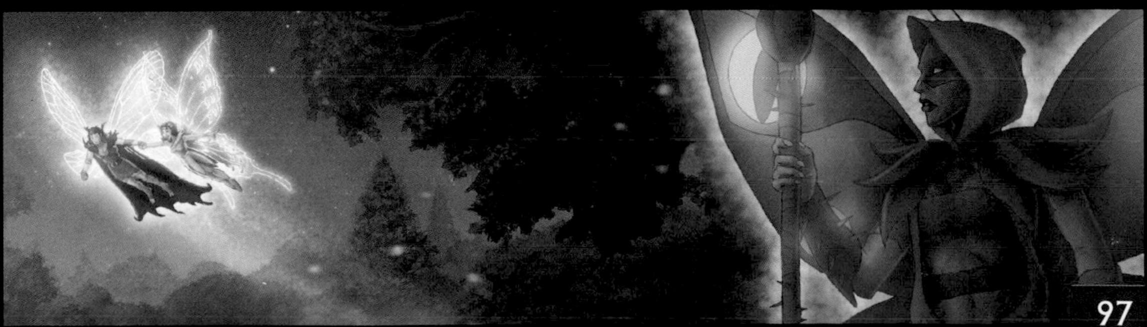

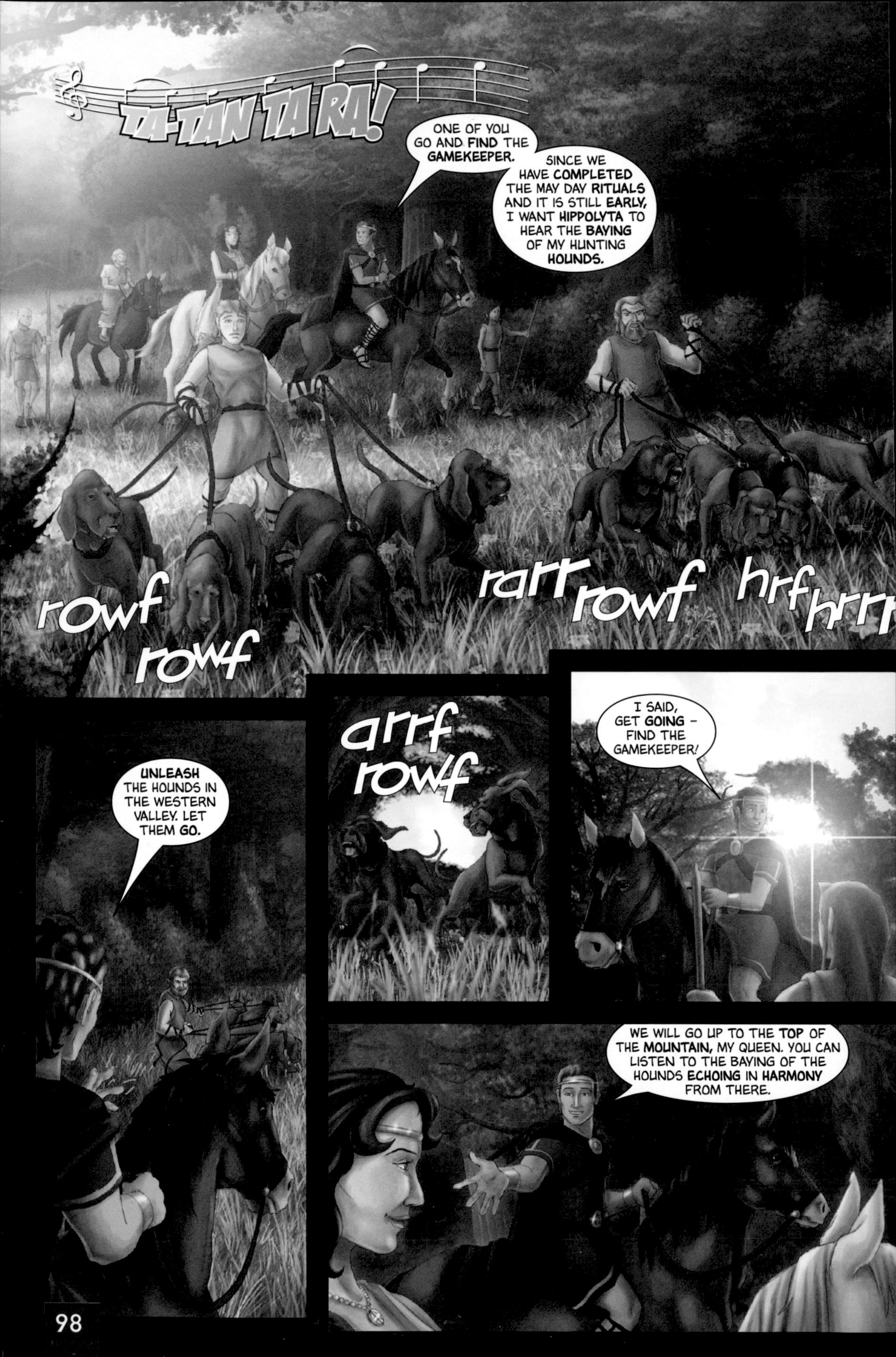
TA-TAN TA RA!
ONE OF YOU GO AND FIND THE GAMEKEEPER.
SINCE WE HAVE COMPLETED THE MAY DAY RITUALS AND IT IS STILL EARLY, I WANT HIPPOLYTA TO HEAR THE BAYING OF MY HUNTING HOUNDS.
rowf rowf
rarr rowf hrf hrrr
UNLEASH THE HOUNDS IN THE WESTERN VALLEY. LET THEM GO.
arrf rowf
I SAID, GET GOING – FIND THE GAMEKEEPER!
WE WILL GO UP TO THE TOP OF THE MOUNTAIN, MY QUEEN. YOU CAN LISTEN TO THE BAYING OF THE HOUNDS ECHOING IN HARMONY FROM THERE.

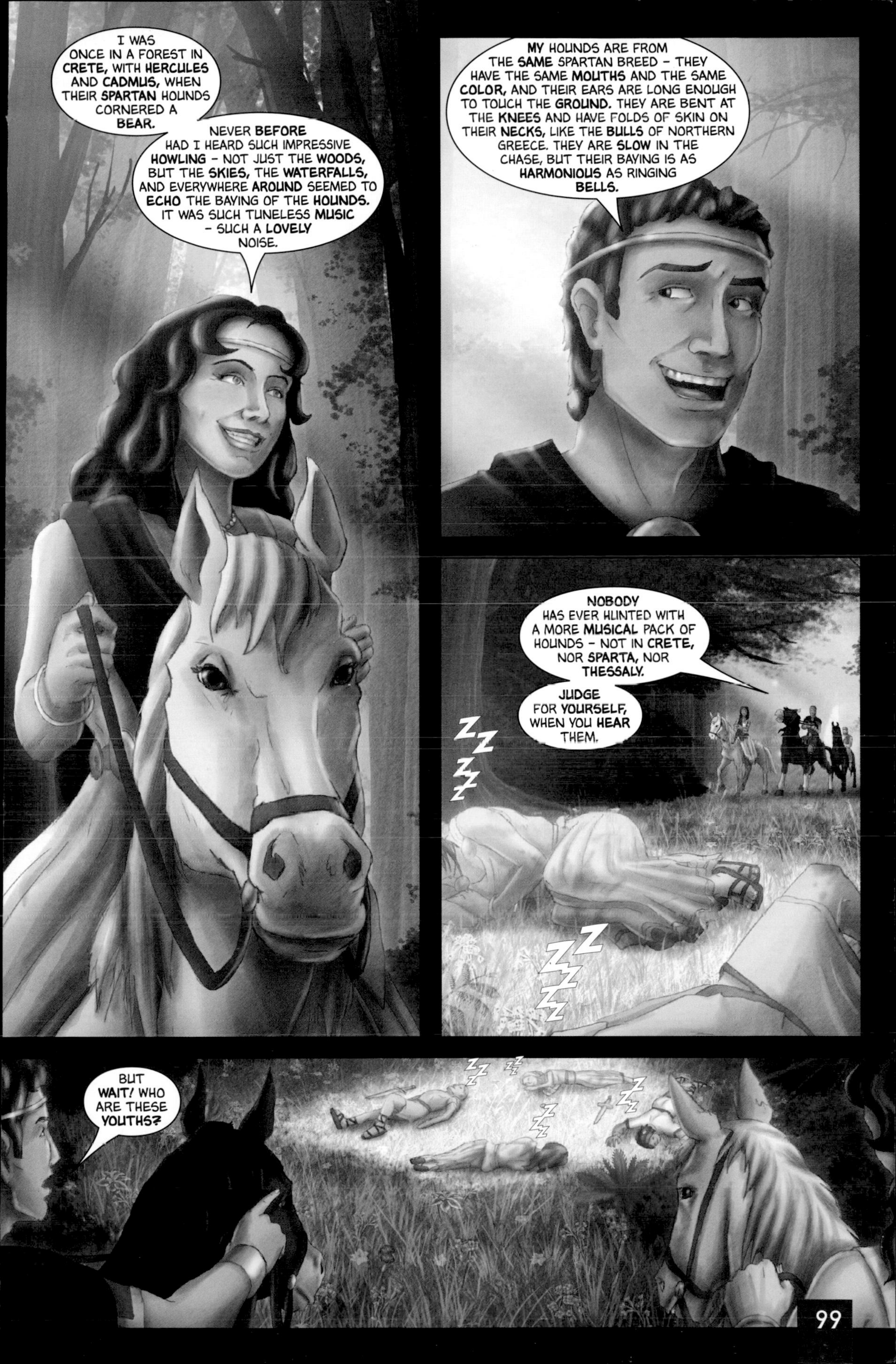
I WAS ONCE IN A FOREST IN CRETE, WITH HERCULES AND CADMUS, WHEN THEIR SPARTAN HOUNDS CORNERED A BEAR.
NEVER BEFORE HAD I HEARD SUCH IMPRESSIVE HOWLING – NOT JUST THE WOODS, BUT THE SKIES, THE WATERFALLS, AND EVERYWHERE AROUND SEEMED TO ECHO THE BAYING OF THE HOUNDS. IT WAS SUCH TUNELESS MUSIC – SUCH A LOVELY NOISE.
MY HOUNDS ARE FROM THE SAME SPARTAN BREED – THEY HAVE THE SAME MOUTHS AND THE SAME COLOR, AND THEIR EARS ARE LONG ENOUGH TO TOUCH THE GROUND. THEY ARE BENT AT THE KNEES AND HAVE FOLDS OF SKIN ON THEIR NECKS, LIKE THE BULLS OF NORTHERN GREECE. THEY ARE SLOW IN THE CHASE, BUT THEIR BAYING IS AS HARMONIOUS AS RINGING BELLS.
NOBODY HAS EVER HUNTED WITH A MORE MUSICAL PACK OF HOUNDS – NOT IN CRETE, NOR SPARTA, NOR THESSALY.
JUDGE FOR YOURSELF, WHEN YOU HEAR THEM.
ZZZZ
ZZZZ
BUT WAIT! WHO ARE THESE YOUTHS?

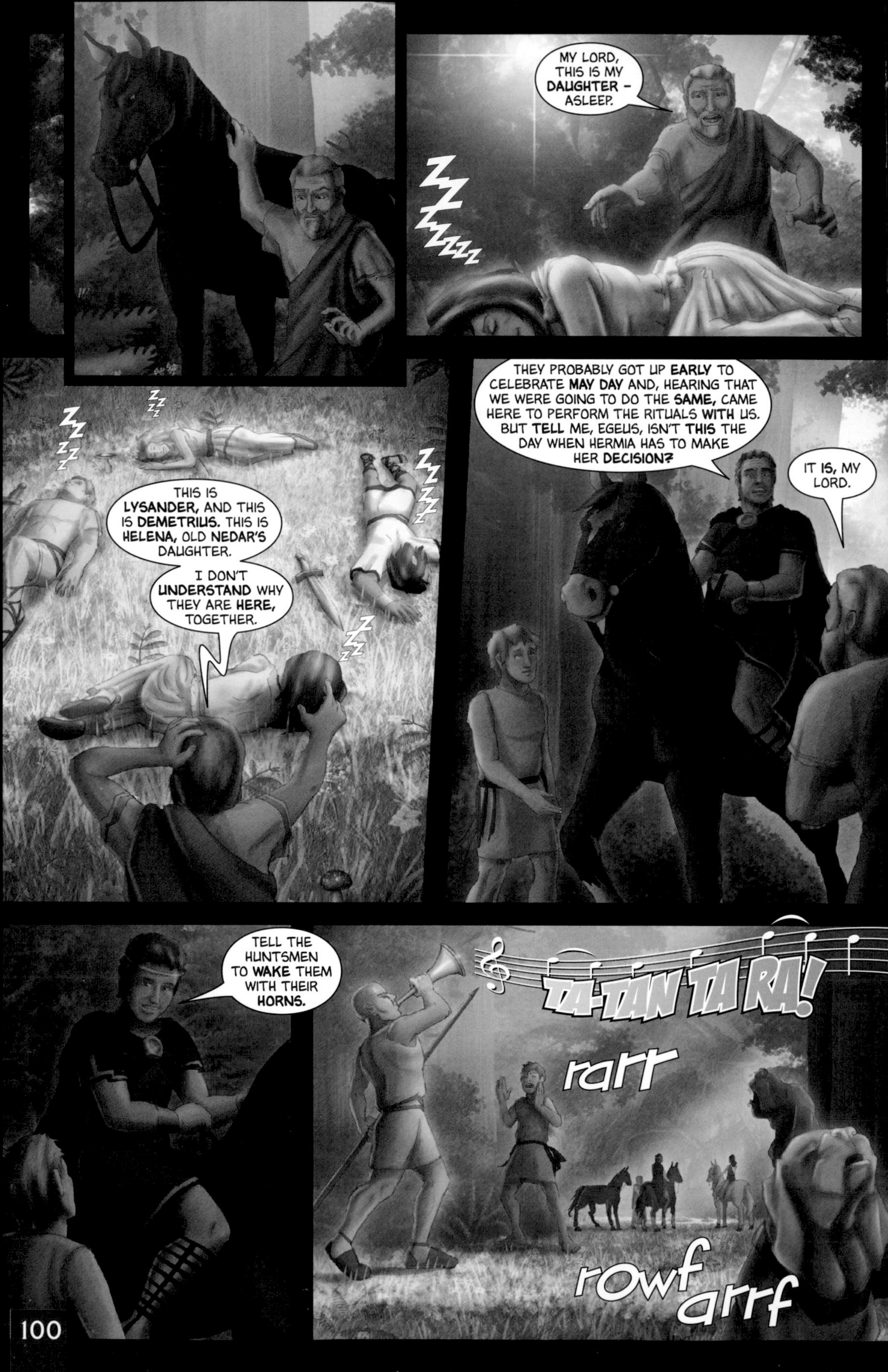

MY LORD, THIS IS MY DAUGHTER – ASLEEP.
ZZZZZZ
ZZZ
ZZZ
THIS IS LYSANDER, AND THIS IS DEMETRIUS. THIS IS HELENA, OLD NEDAR'S DAUGHTER.
I DON'T UNDERSTAND WHY THEY ARE HERE, TOGETHER.
ZZZ
ZZZZ
THEY PROBABLY GOT UP EARLY TO CELEBRATE MAY DAY AND, HEARING THAT WE WERE GOING TO DO THE SAME, CAME HERE TO PERFORM THE RITUALS WITH US. BUT TELL ME, EGEUS, ISN'T THIS THE DAY WHEN HERMIA HAS TO MAKE HER DECISION?
IT IS, MY LORD.
TELL THE HUNTSMEN TO WAKE THEM WITH THEIR HORNS.
TA-TAN TA RA!
rarr
rowf
arrf

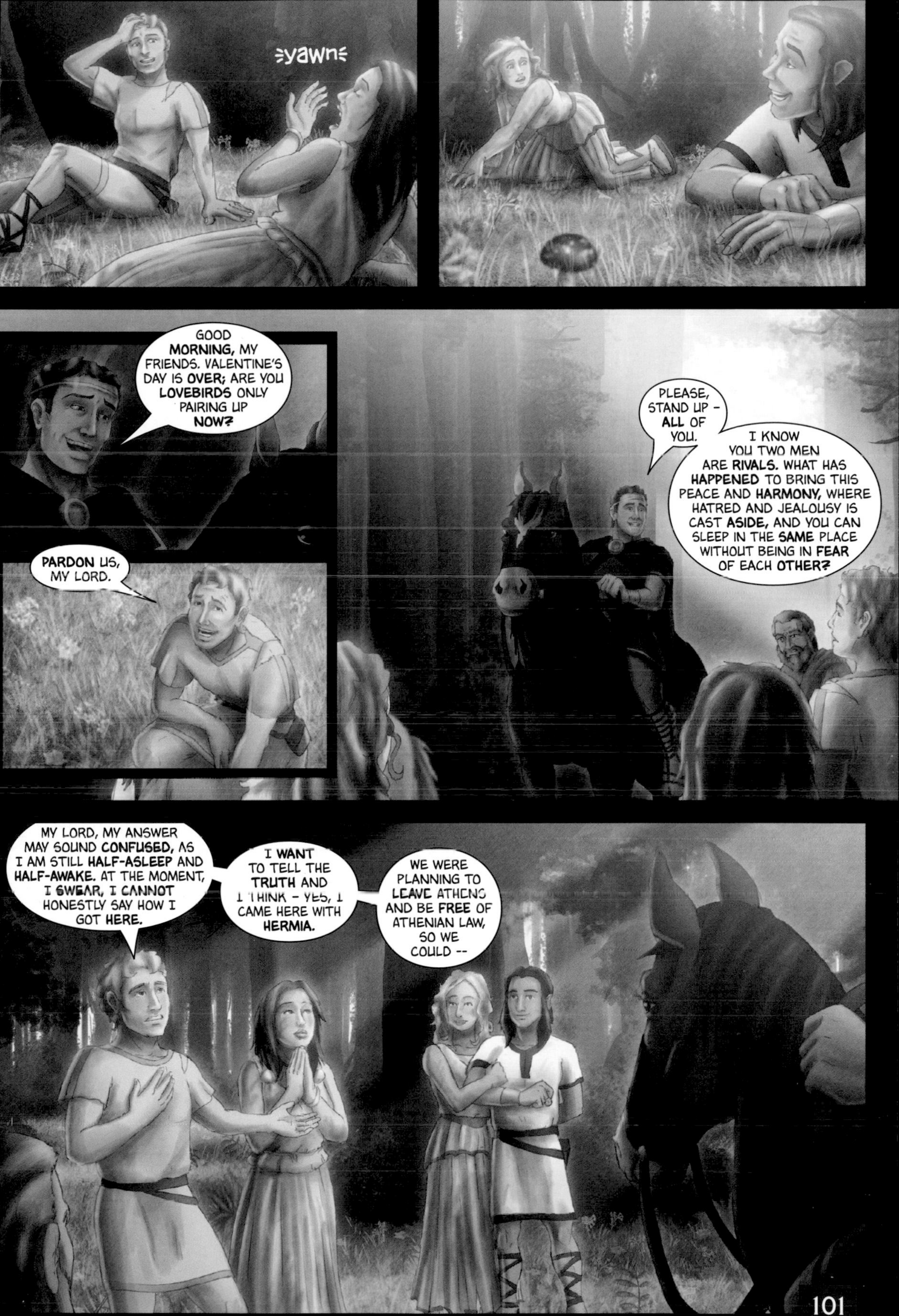
yawn
GOOD MORNING, MY FRIENDS. VALENTINE'S DAY IS OVER; ARE YOU LOVEBIRDS ONLY PAIRING UP NOW?
PARDON US, MY LORD.
PLEASE, STAND UP - ALL OF YOU.
I KNOW YOU TWO MEN ARE RIVALS. WHAT HAS HAPPENED TO BRING THIS PEACE AND HARMONY, WHERE HATRED AND JEALOUSY IS CAST ASIDE, AND YOU CAN SLEEP IN THE SAME PLACE WITHOUT BEING IN FEAR OF EACH OTHER?
MY LORD, MY ANSWER MAY SOUND CONFUSED, AS I AM STILL HALF-ASLEEP AND HALF-AWAKE. AT THE MOMENT, I SWEAR, I CANNOT HONESTLY SAY HOW I GOT HERE.
I WANT TO TELL THE TRUTH AND I THINK - YES, I CAME HERE WITH HERMIA.
WE WERE PLANNING TO LEAVE ATHENS AND BE FREE OF ATHENIAN LAW, SO WE COULD --

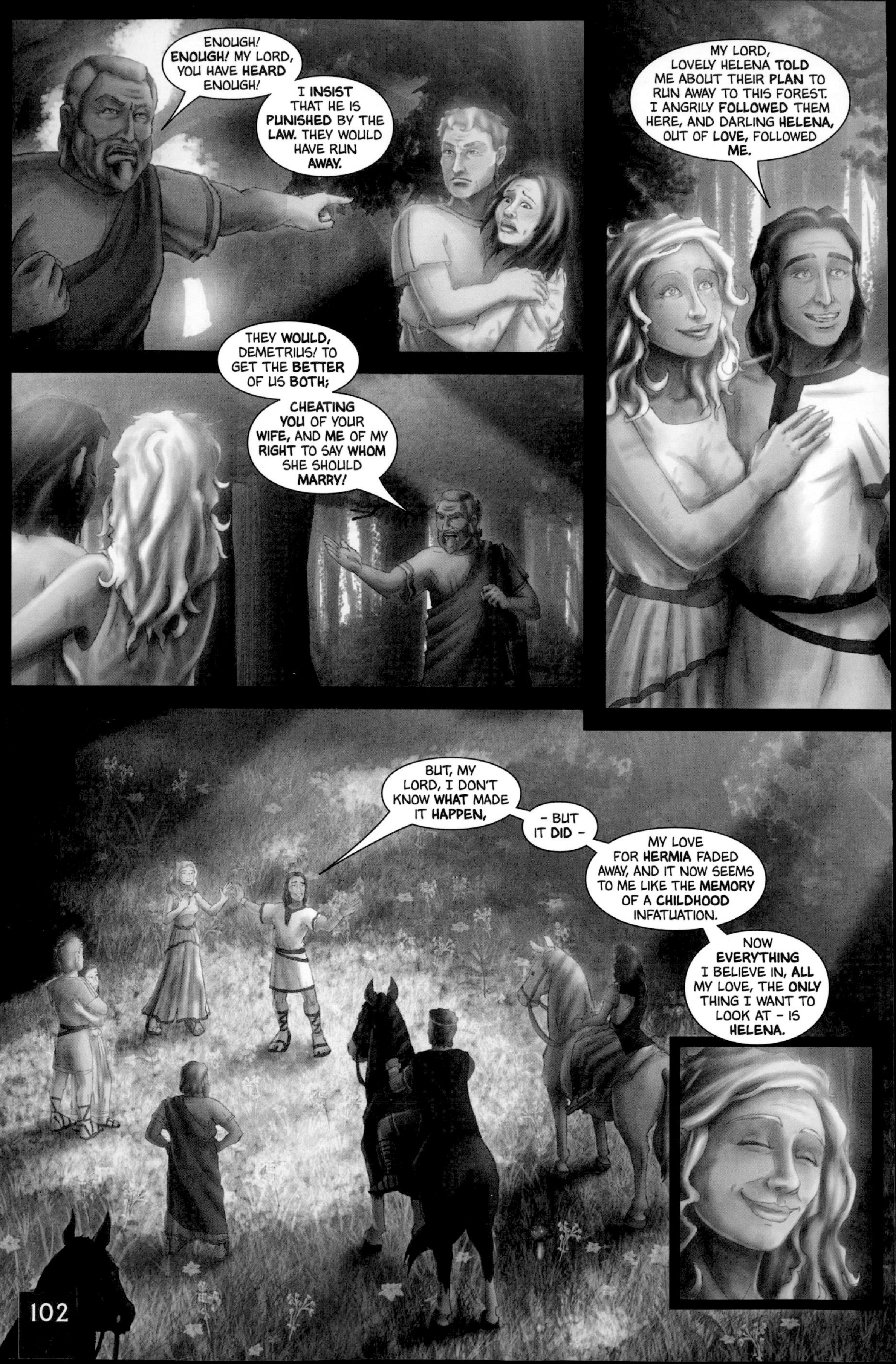

ENOUGH! ENOUGH! MY LORD, YOU HAVE HEARD ENOUGH!
I INSIST THAT HE IS PUNISHED BY THE LAW. THEY WOULD HAVE RUN AWAY.
MY LORD, LOVELY HELENA TOLD ME ABOUT THEIR PLAN TO RUN AWAY TO THIS FOREST. I ANGRILY FOLLOWED THEM HERE, AND DARLING HELENA, OUT OF LOVE, FOLLOWED ME.
THEY WOULD, DEMETRIUS! TO GET THE BETTER OF US BOTH;
CHEATING YOU OF YOUR WIFE, AND ME OF MY RIGHT TO SAY WHOM SHE SHOULD MARRY!
BUT, MY LORD, I DON'T KNOW WHAT MADE IT HAPPEN,
- BUT IT DID -
MY LOVE FOR HERMIA FADED AWAY, AND IT NOW SEEMS TO ME LIKE THE MEMORY OF A CHILDHOOD INFATUATION.
NOW EVERYTHING I BELIEVE IN, ALL MY LOVE, THE ONLY THING I WANT TO LOOK AT - IS HELENA.

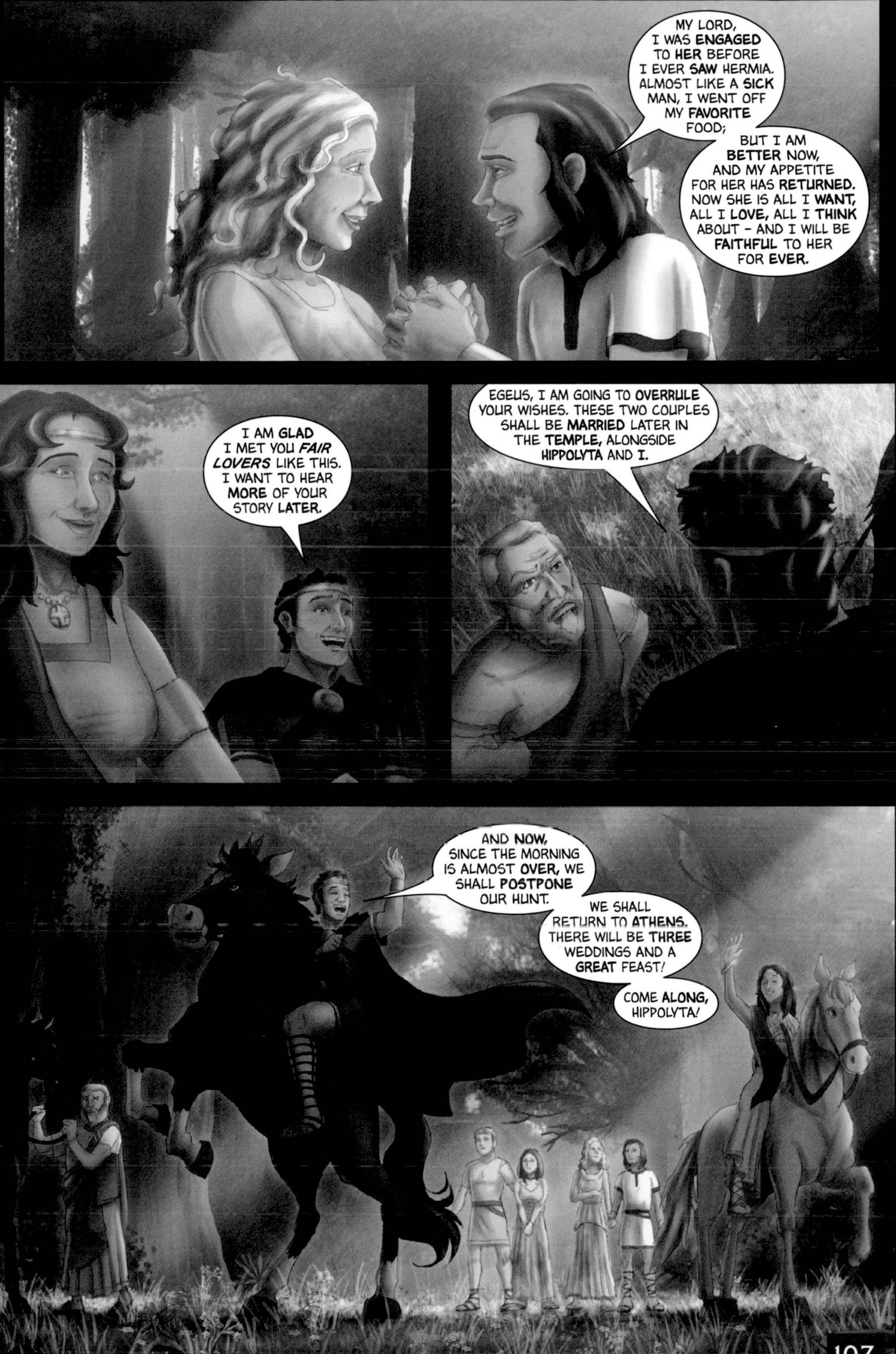
MY LORD, I WAS ENGAGED TO HER BEFORE I EVER SAW HERMIA. ALMOST LIKE A SICK MAN, I WENT OFF MY FAVORITE FOOD;
BUT I AM BETTER NOW, AND MY APPETITE FOR HER HAS RETURNED. NOW SHE IS ALL I WANT, ALL I LOVE, ALL I THINK ABOUT - AND I WILL BE FAITHFUL TO HER FOR EVER.
I AM GLAD I MET YOU FAIR LOVERS LIKE THIS. I WANT TO HEAR MORE OF YOUR STORY LATER.
EGEUS, I AM GOING TO OVERRULE YOUR WISHES. THESE TWO COUPLES SHALL BE MARRIED LATER IN THE TEMPLE, ALONGSIDE HIPPOLYTA AND I.
AND NOW, SINCE THE MORNING IS ALMOST OVER, WE SHALL POSTPONE OUR HUNT.
WE SHALL RETURN TO ATHENS. THERE WILL BE THREE WEDDINGS AND A GREAT FEAST!
COME ALONG, HIPPOLYTA!

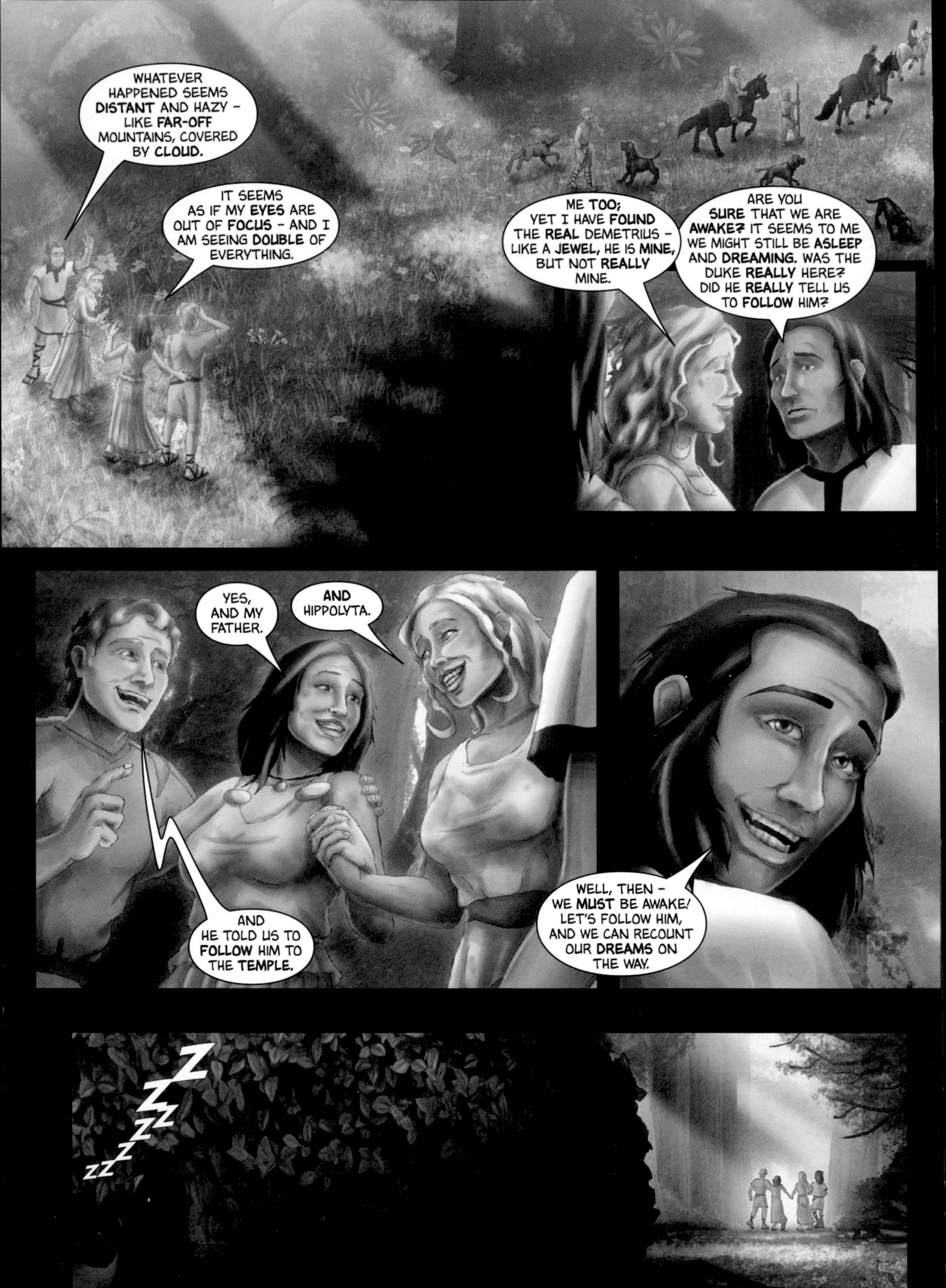
WHATEVER HAPPENED SEEMS DISTANT AND HAZY – LIKE FAR-OFF MOUNTAINS, COVERED BY CLOUD.
IT SEEMS AS IF MY EYES ARE OUT OF FOCUS – AND I AM SEEING DOUBLE OF EVERYTHING.
ME TOO; YET I HAVE FOUND THE REAL DEMETRIUS – LIKE A JEWEL, HE IS MINE, BUT NOT REALLY MINE.
ARE YOU SURE THAT WE ARE AWAKE? IT SEEMS TO ME WE MIGHT STILL BE ASLEEP AND DREAMING. WAS THE DUKE REALLY HERE? DID HE REALLY TELL US TO FOLLOW HIM?
YES, AND MY FATHER.
AND HIPPOLYTA.
AND HE TOLD US TO FOLLOW HIM TO THE TEMPLE.
WELL, THEN – WE MUST BE AWAKE! LET'S FOLLOW HIM, AND WE CAN RECOUNT OUR DREAMS ON THE WAY.
ZZZZZZZ

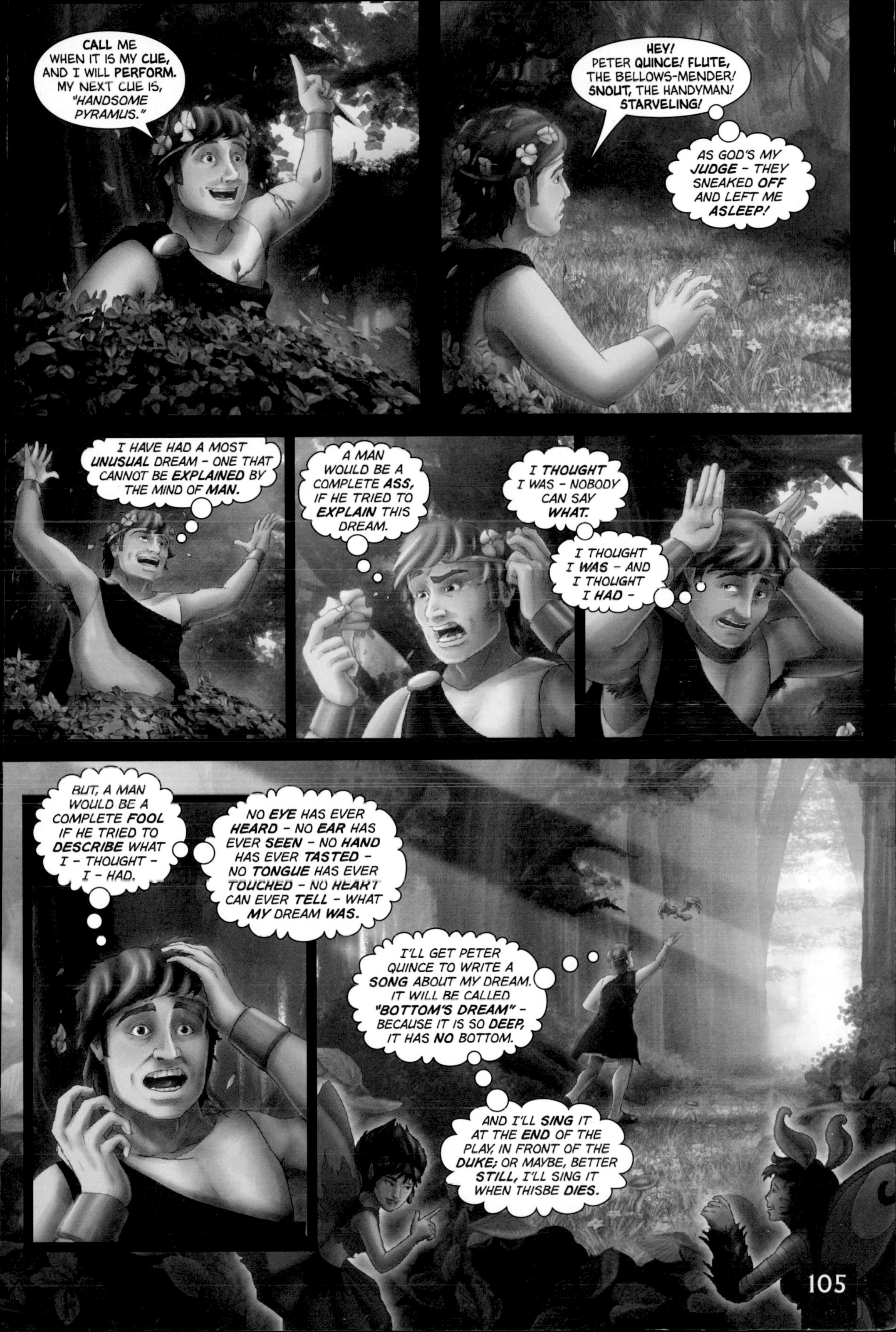
CALL ME WHEN IT IS MY CUE, AND I WILL PERFORM. MY NEXT CUE IS, "HANDSOME PYRAMUS."
HEY! PETER QUINCE! FLUTE, THE BELLOWS-MENDER! SNOUT, THE HANDYMAN! STARVELING!
AS GOD'S MY JUDGE – THEY SNEAKED OFF AND LEFT ME ASLEEP!
I HAVE HAD A MOST UNUSUAL DREAM – ONE THAT CANNOT BE EXPLAINED BY THE MIND OF MAN.
A MAN WOULD BE A COMPLETE ASS, IF HE TRIED TO EXPLAIN THIS DREAM.
I THOUGHT I WAS – NOBODY CAN SAY WHAT.
I THOUGHT I WAS – AND I THOUGHT I HAD –
BUT, A MAN WOULD BE A COMPLETE FOOL IF HE TRIED TO DESCRIBE WHAT I – THOUGHT – I – HAD.
NO EYE HAS EVER HEARD – NO EAR HAS EVER SEEN – NO HAND HAS EVER TASTED – NO TONGUE HAS EVER TOUCHED – NO HEART CAN EVER TELL – WHAT MY DREAM WAS.
I'LL GET PETER QUINCE TO WRITE A SONG ABOUT MY DREAM. IT WILL BE CALLED "BOTTOM'S DREAM" – BECAUSE IT IS SO DEEP, IT HAS NO BOTTOM.
AND I'LL SING IT AT THE END OF THE PLAY, IN FRONT OF THE DUKE; OR MAYBE, BETTER STILL, I'LL SING IT WHEN THISBE DIES.

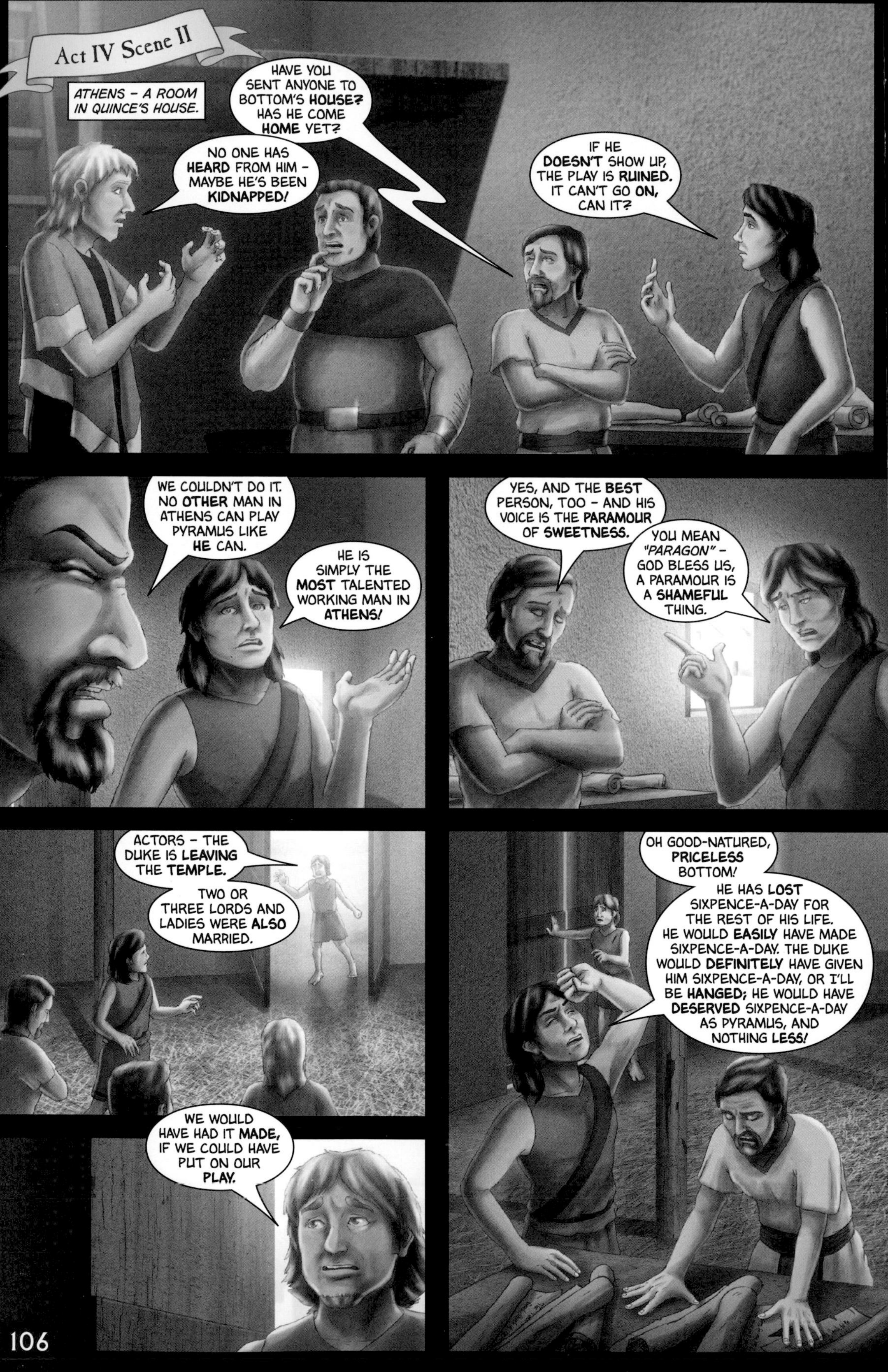
Act IV Scene II
ATHENS – A ROOM IN QUINCE'S HOUSE.
HAVE YOU SENT ANYONE TO BOTTOM'S HOUSE? HAS HE COME HOME YET?
NO ONE HAS HEARD FROM HIM – MAYBE HE'S BEEN KIDNAPPED!
IF HE DOESN'T SHOW UP, THE PLAY IS RUINED. IT CAN'T GO ON, CAN IT?
WE COULDN'T DO IT. NO OTHER MAN IN ATHENS CAN PLAY PYRAMUS LIKE HE CAN.
HE IS SIMPLY THE MOST TALENTED WORKING MAN IN ATHENS!
YES, AND THE BEST PERSON, TOO – AND HIS VOICE IS THE PARAMOUR OF SWEETNESS.
YOU MEAN "PARAGON" – GOD BLESS US, A PARAMOUR IS A SHAMEFUL THING.
ACTORS – THE DUKE IS LEAVING THE TEMPLE.
TWO OR THREE LORDS AND LADIES WERE ALSO MARRIED.
WE WOULD HAVE HAD IT MADE, IF WE COULD HAVE PUT ON OUR PLAY.
OH GOOD-NATURED, PRICELESS BOTTOM!
HE HAS LOST SIXPENCE-A-DAY FOR THE REST OF HIS LIFE. HE WOULD EASILY HAVE MADE SIXPENCE-A-DAY. THE DUKE WOULD DEFINITELY HAVE GIVEN HIM SIXPENCE-A-DAY, OR I'LL BE HANGED; HE WOULD HAVE DESERVED SIXPENCE-A-DAY AS PYRAMUS, AND NOTHING LESS!

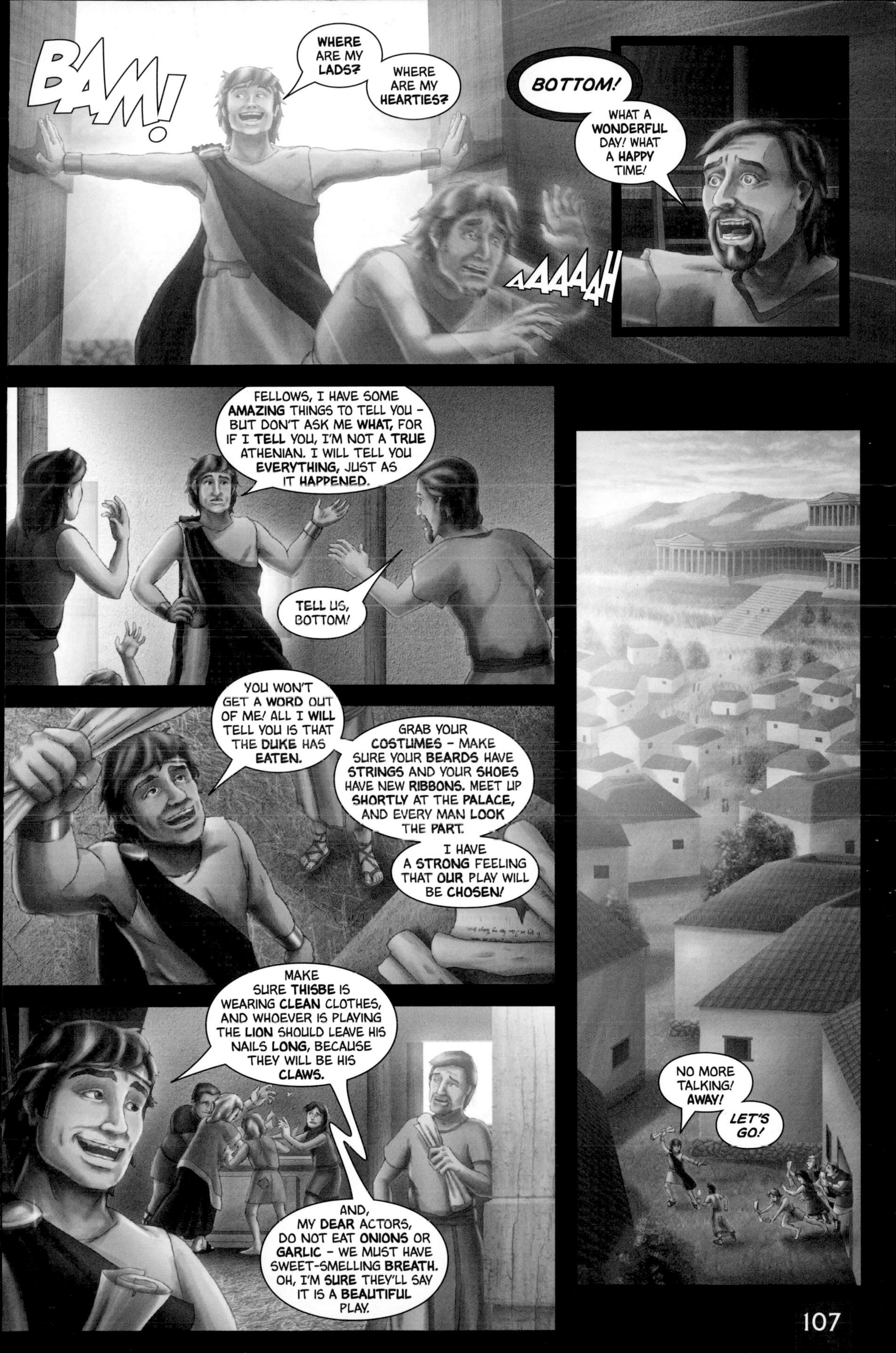
BAM!
WHERE ARE MY LADS?
WHERE ARE MY HEARTIES?
BOTTOM!
WHAT A WONDERFUL DAY! WHAT A HAPPY TIME!
AAAAAH
FELLOWS, I HAVE SOME AMAZING THINGS TO TELL YOU - BUT DON'T ASK ME WHAT, FOR IF I TELL YOU, I'M NOT A TRUE ATHENIAN. I WILL TELL YOU EVERYTHING, JUST AS IT HAPPENED.
TELL US, BOTTOM!
YOU WON'T GET A WORD OUT OF ME! ALL I WILL TELL YOU IS THAT THE DUKE HAS EATEN.
GRAB YOUR COSTUMES - MAKE SURE YOUR BEARDS HAVE STRINGS AND YOUR SHOES HAVE NEW RIBBONS. MEET UP SHORTLY AT THE PALACE, AND EVERY MAN LOOK THE PART.
I HAVE A STRONG FEELING THAT OUR PLAY WILL BE CHOSEN!
MAKE SURE THISBE IS WEARING CLEAN CLOTHES, AND WHOEVER IS PLAYING THE LION SHOULD LEAVE HIS NAILS LONG, BECAUSE THEY WILL BE HIS CLAWS.
AND, MY DEAR ACTORS, DO NOT EAT ONIONS OR GARLIC - WE MUST HAVE SWEET-SMELLING BREATH. OH, I'M SURE THEY'LL SAY IT IS A BEAUTIFUL PLAY.
NO MORE TALKING! AWAY!
LET'S GO!

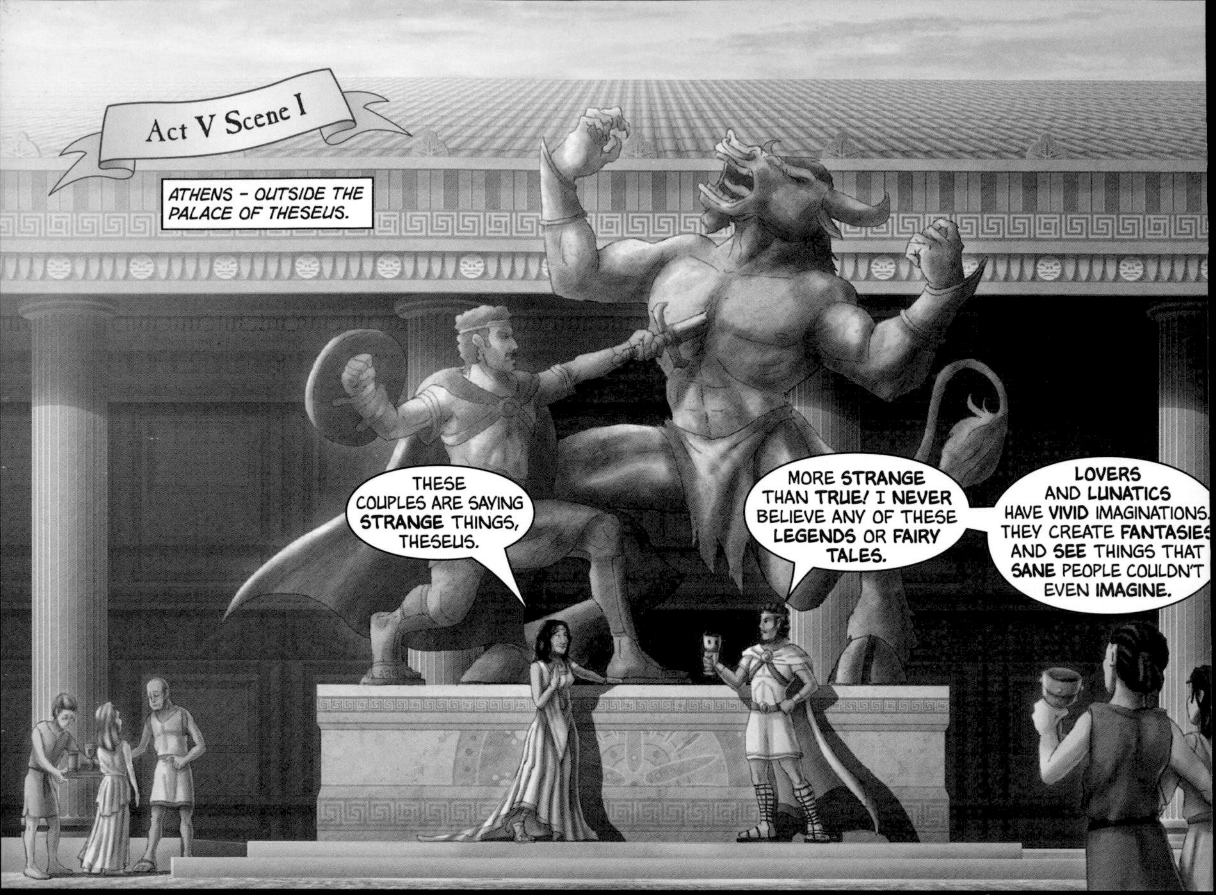
Act V Scene I
ATHENS – OUTSIDE THE PALACE OF THESEUS.
THESE COUPLES ARE SAYING STRANGE THINGS, THESEUS.
MORE STRANGE THAN TRUE! I NEVER BELIEVE ANY OF THESE LEGENDS OR FAIRY TALES.
LOVERS AND LUNATICS HAVE VIVID IMAGINATIONS. THEY CREATE FANTASIES AND SEE THINGS THAT SANE PEOPLE COULDN'T EVEN IMAGINE.

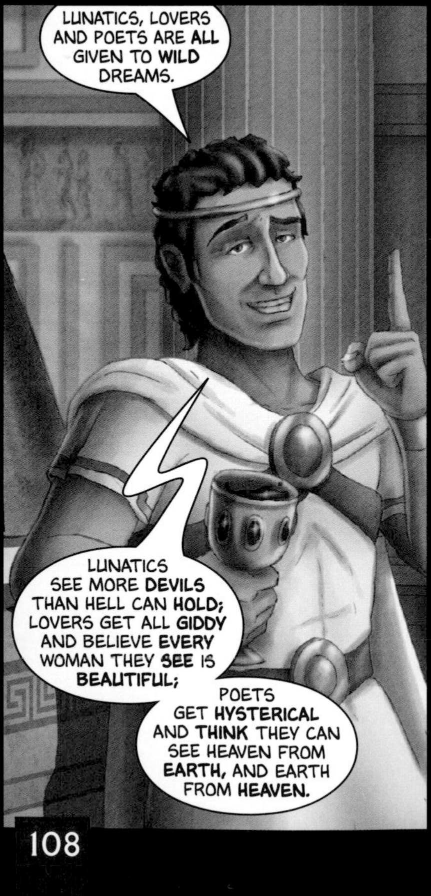
LUNATICS, LOVERS AND POETS ARE ALL GIVEN TO WILD DREAMS.
LUNATICS SEE MORE DEVILS THAN HELL CAN HOLD; LOVERS GET ALL GIDDY AND BELIEVE EVERY WOMAN THEY SEE IS BEAUTIFUL;
POETS GET HYSTERICAL AND THINK THEY CAN SEE HEAVEN FROM EARTH, AND EARTH FROM HEAVEN.

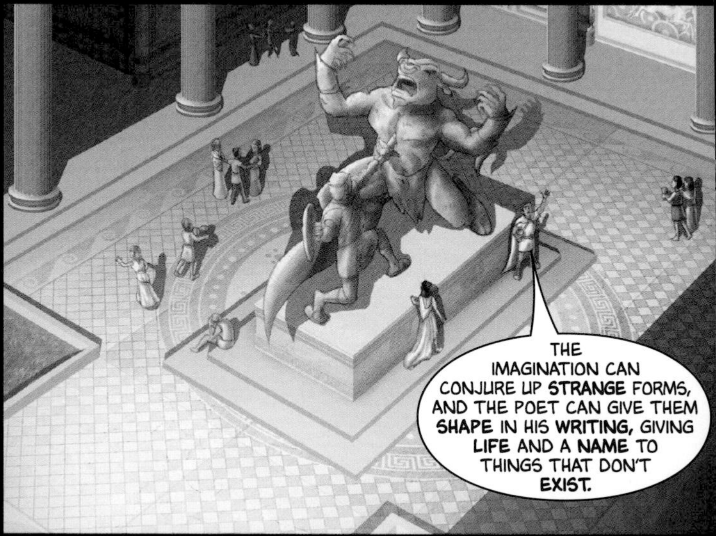
THE IMAGINATION CAN CONJURE UP STRANGE FORMS, AND THE POET CAN GIVE THEM SHAPE IN HIS WRITING, GIVING LIFE AND A NAME TO THINGS THAT DON'T EXIST.

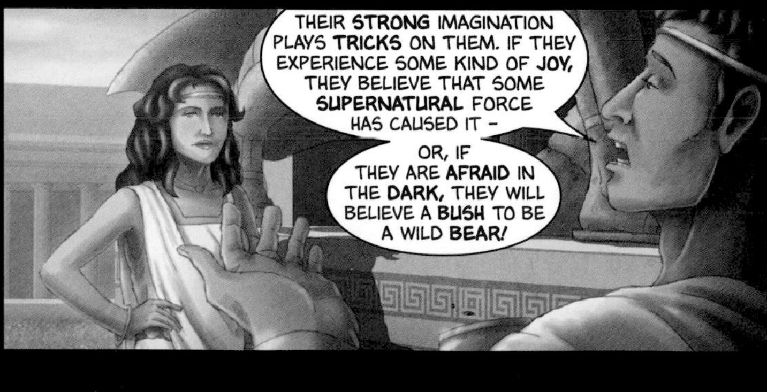
THEIR STRONG IMAGINATION PLAYS TRICKS ON THEM. IF THEY EXPERIENCE SOME KIND OF JOY, THEY BELIEVE THAT SOME SUPERNATURAL FORCE HAS CAUSED IT –
OR, IF THEY ARE AFRAID IN THE DARK, THEY WILL BELIEVE A BUSH TO BE A WILD BEAR!

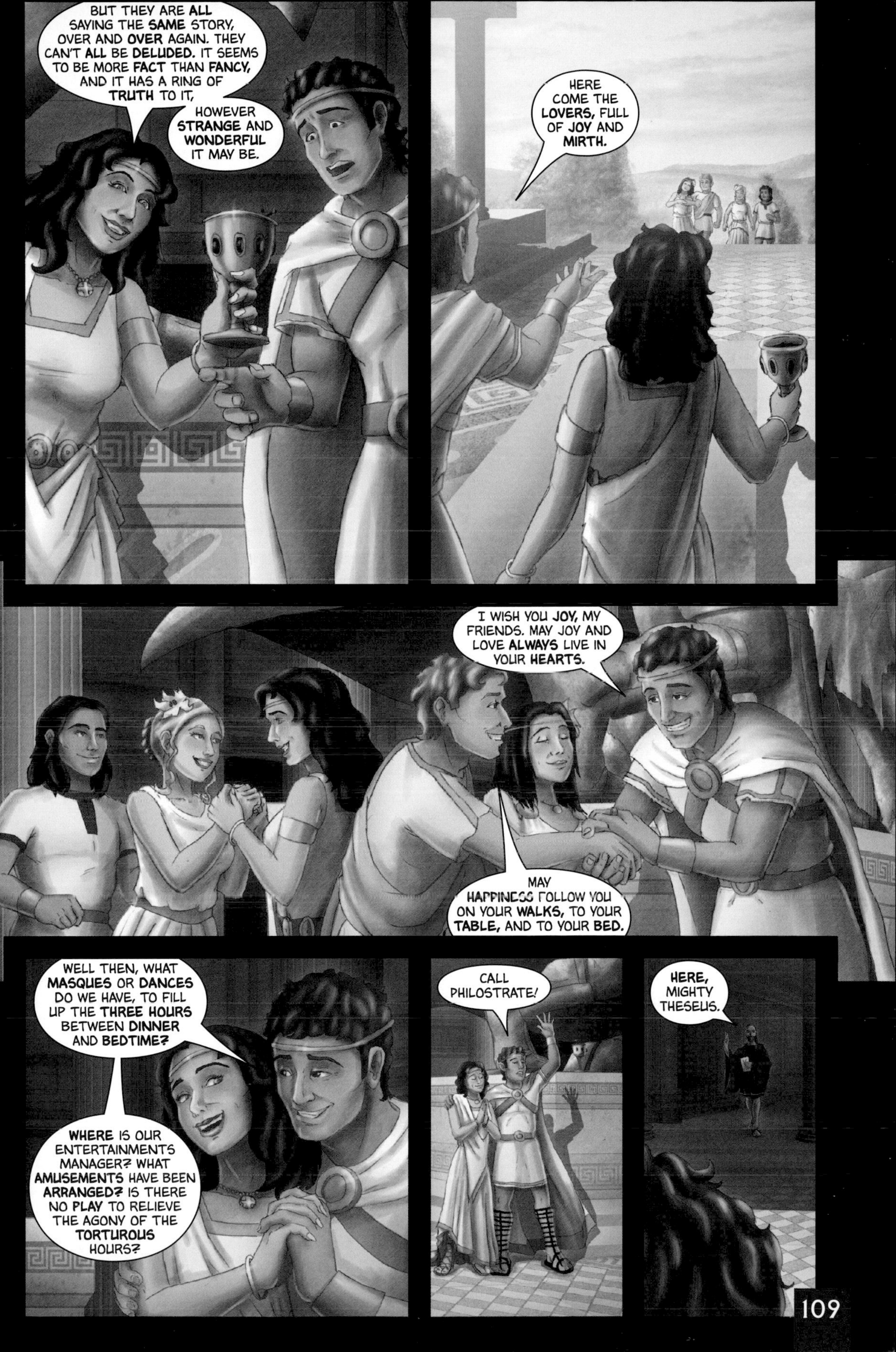

BUT THEY ARE ALL SAYING THE SAME STORY, OVER AND OVER AGAIN. THEY CAN'T ALL BE DELUDED. IT SEEMS TO BE MORE FACT THAN FANCY, AND IT HAS A RING OF TRUTH TO IT,
HOWEVER STRANGE AND WONDERFUL IT MAY BE.
HERE COME THE LOVERS, FULL OF JOY AND MIRTH.
I WISH YOU JOY, MY FRIENDS. MAY JOY AND LOVE ALWAYS LIVE IN YOUR HEARTS.
MAY HAPPINESS FOLLOW YOU ON YOUR WALKS, TO YOUR TABLE, AND TO YOUR BED.
WELL THEN, WHAT MASQUES OR DANCES DO WE HAVE, TO FILL UP THE THREE HOURS BETWEEN DINNER AND BEDTIME?
WHERE IS OUR ENTERTAINMENTS MANAGER? WHAT AMUSEMENTS HAVE BEEN ARRANGED? IS THERE NO PLAY TO RELIEVE THE AGONY OF THE TORTUROUS HOURS?
CALL PHILOSTRATE!
HERE, MIGHTY THESEUS.

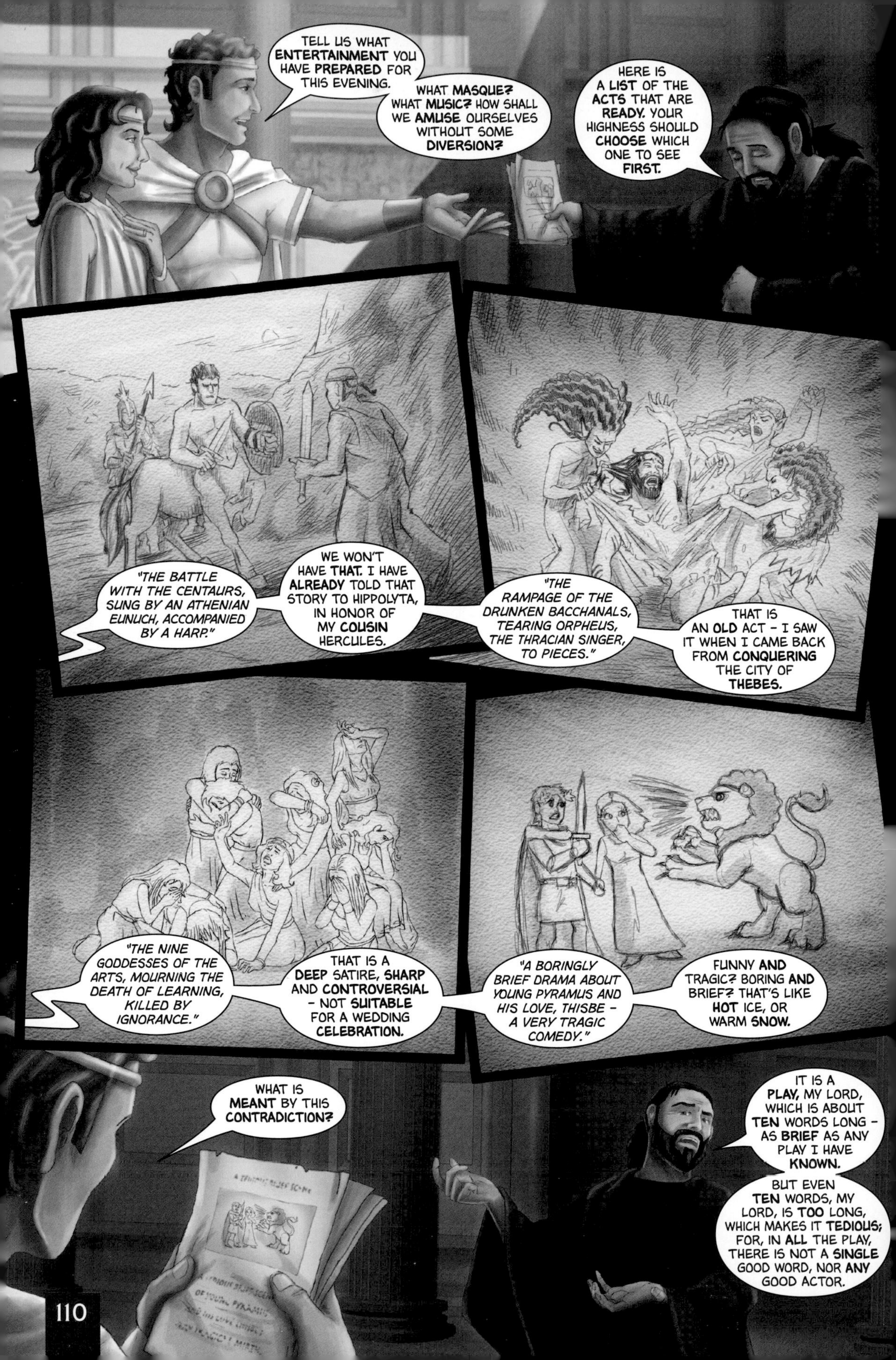
TELL US WHAT ENTERTAINMENT YOU HAVE PREPARED FOR THIS EVENING.
WHAT MASQUE? WHAT MUSIC? HOW SHALL WE AMUSE OURSELVES WITHOUT SOME DIVERSION?
HERE IS A LIST OF THE ACTS THAT ARE READY. YOUR HIGHNESS SHOULD CHOOSE WHICH ONE TO SEE FIRST.
"THE BATTLE WITH THE CENTAURS, SUNG BY AN ATHENIAN EUNUCH, ACCOMPANIED BY A HARP."
WE WON'T HAVE THAT. I HAVE ALREADY TOLD THAT STORY TO HIPPOLYTA, IN HONOR OF MY COUSIN HERCULES.
"THE RAMPAGE OF THE DRUNKEN BACCHANALS, TEARING ORPHEUS, THE THRACIAN SINGER, TO PIECES."
THAT IS AN OLD ACT - I SAW IT WHEN I CAME BACK FROM CONQUERING THE CITY OF THEBES.
"THE NINE GODDESSES OF THE ARTS, MOURNING THE DEATH OF LEARNING, KILLED BY IGNORANCE."
THAT IS A DEEP SATIRE, SHARP AND CONTROVERSIAL - NOT SUITABLE FOR A WEDDING CELEBRATION.
"A BORINGLY BRIEF DRAMA ABOUT YOUNG PYRAMUS AND HIS LOVE, THISBE - A VERY TRAGIC COMEDY."
FUNNY AND TRAGIC? BORING AND BRIEF? THAT'S LIKE HOT ICE, OR WARM SNOW.
WHAT IS MEANT BY THIS CONTRADICTION?
IT IS A PLAY, MY LORD, WHICH IS ABOUT TEN WORDS LONG - AS BRIEF AS ANY PLAY I HAVE KNOWN.
BUT EVEN TEN WORDS, MY LORD, IS TOO LONG, WHICH MAKES IT TEDIOUS; FOR, IN ALL THE PLAY, THERE IS NOT A SINGLE GOOD WORD, NOR ANY GOOD ACTOR.

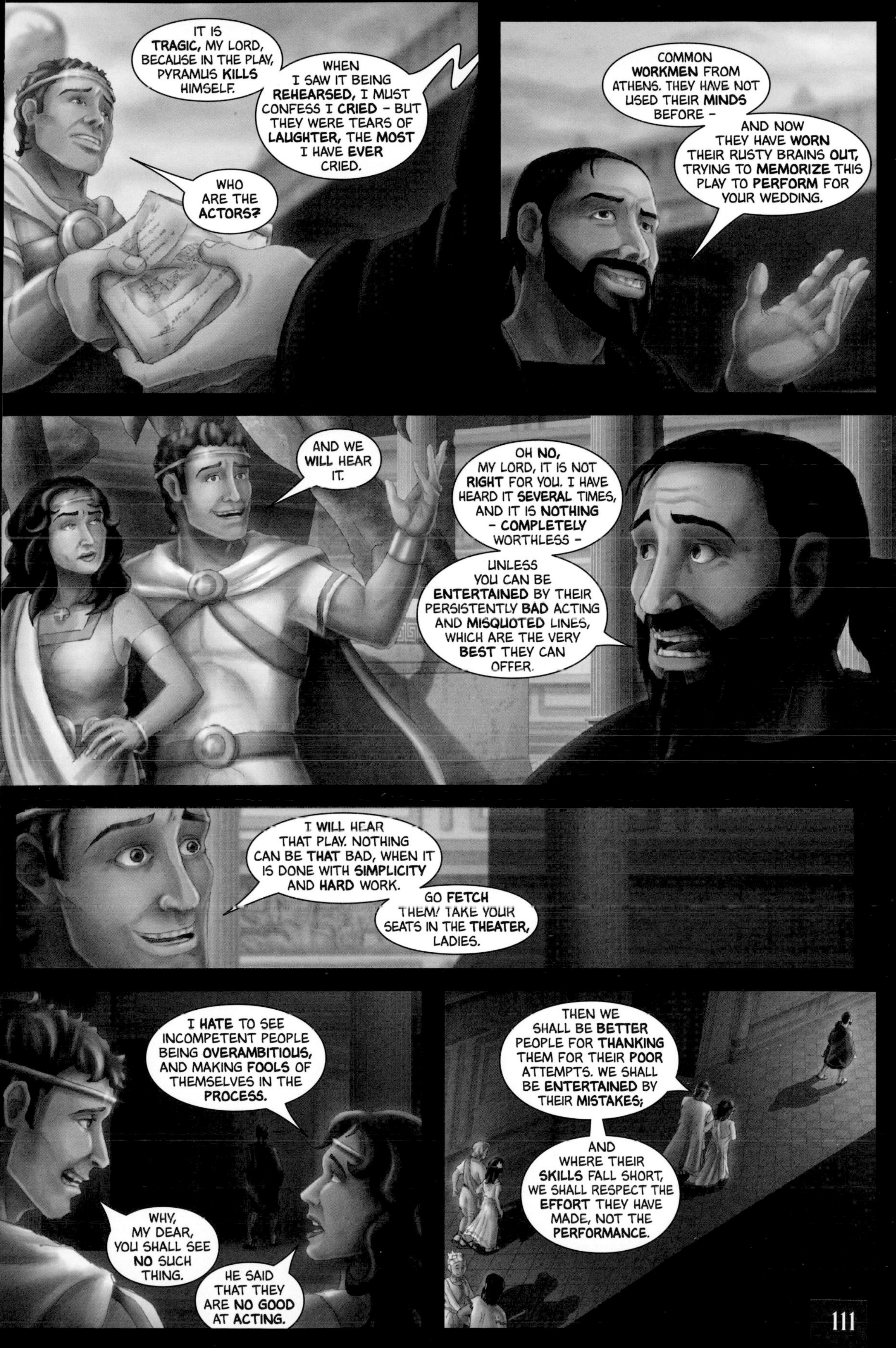
IT IS TRAGIC, MY LORD, BECAUSE IN THE PLAY, PYRAMUS KILLS HIMSELF.
WHEN I SAW IT BEING REHEARSED, I MUST CONFESS I CRIED – BUT THEY WERE TEARS OF LAUGHTER, THE MOST I HAVE EVER CRIED.
WHO ARE THE ACTORS?
COMMON WORKMEN FROM ATHENS. THEY HAVE NOT USED THEIR MINDS BEFORE –
AND NOW THEY HAVE WORN THEIR RUSTY BRAINS OUT, TRYING TO MEMORIZE THIS PLAY TO PERFORM FOR YOUR WEDDING.
AND WE WILL HEAR IT.
OH NO, MY LORD, IT IS NOT RIGHT FOR YOU. I HAVE HEARD IT SEVERAL TIMES, AND IT IS NOTHING – COMPLETELY WORTHLESS –
UNLESS YOU CAN BE ENTERTAINED BY THEIR PERSISTENTLY BAD ACTING AND MISQUOTED LINES, WHICH ARE THE VERY BEST THEY CAN OFFER.
I WILL HEAR THAT PLAY. NOTHING CAN BE THAT BAD, WHEN IT IS DONE WITH SIMPLICITY AND HARD WORK.
GO FETCH THEM! TAKE YOUR SEATS IN THE THEATER, LADIES.
I HATE TO SEE INCOMPETENT PEOPLE BEING OVERAMBITIOUS, AND MAKING FOOLS OF THEMSELVES IN THE PROCESS.
WHY, MY DEAR, YOU SHALL SEE NO SUCH THING.
HE SAID THAT THEY ARE NO GOOD AT ACTING.
THEN WE SHALL BE BETTER PEOPLE FOR THANKING THEM FOR THEIR POOR ATTEMPTS. WE SHALL BE ENTERTAINED BY THEIR MISTAKES;
AND WHERE THEIR SKILLS FALL SHORT, WE SHALL RESPECT THE EFFORT THEY HAVE MADE, NOT THE PERFORMANCE.

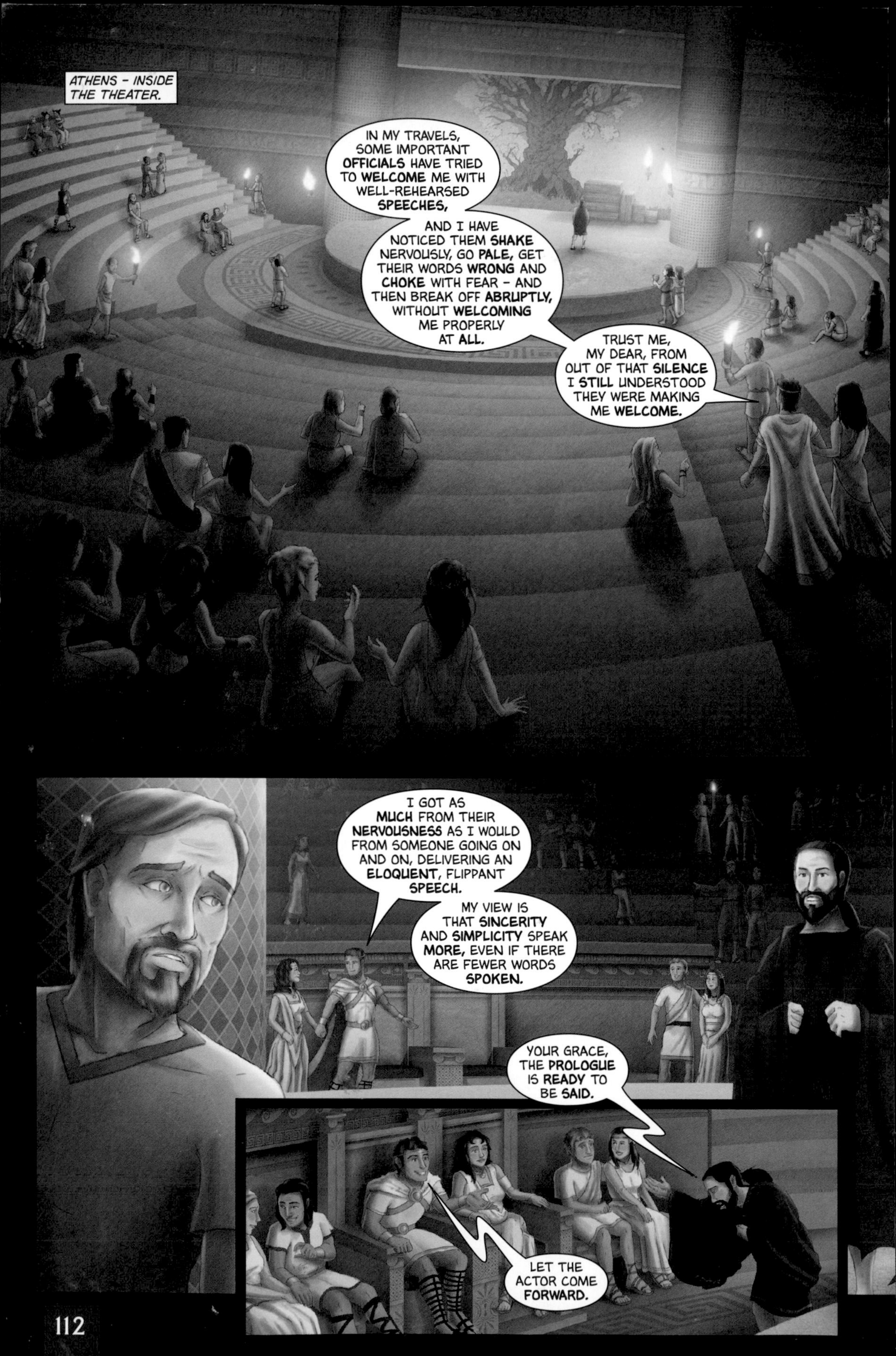
ATHENS - INSIDE THE THEATER.
IN MY TRAVELS, SOME IMPORTANT OFFICIALS HAVE TRIED TO WELCOME ME WITH WELL-REHEARSED SPEECHES,
AND I HAVE NOTICED THEM SHAKE NERVOUSLY, GO PALE, GET THEIR WORDS WRONG AND CHOKE WITH FEAR - AND THEN BREAK OFF ABRUPTLY, WITHOUT WELCOMING ME PROPERLY AT ALL.
TRUST ME, MY DEAR, FROM OUT OF THAT SILENCE I STILL UNDERSTOOD THEY WERE MAKING ME WELCOME.
I GOT AS MUCH FROM THEIR NERVOUSNESS AS I WOULD FROM SOMEONE GOING ON AND ON, DELIVERING AN ELOQUENT, FLIPPANT SPEECH.
MY VIEW IS THAT SINCERITY AND SIMPLICITY SPEAK MORE, EVEN IF THERE ARE FEWER WORDS SPOKEN.
YOUR GRACE, THE PROLOGUE IS READY TO BE SAID.
LET THE ACTOR COME FORWARD.

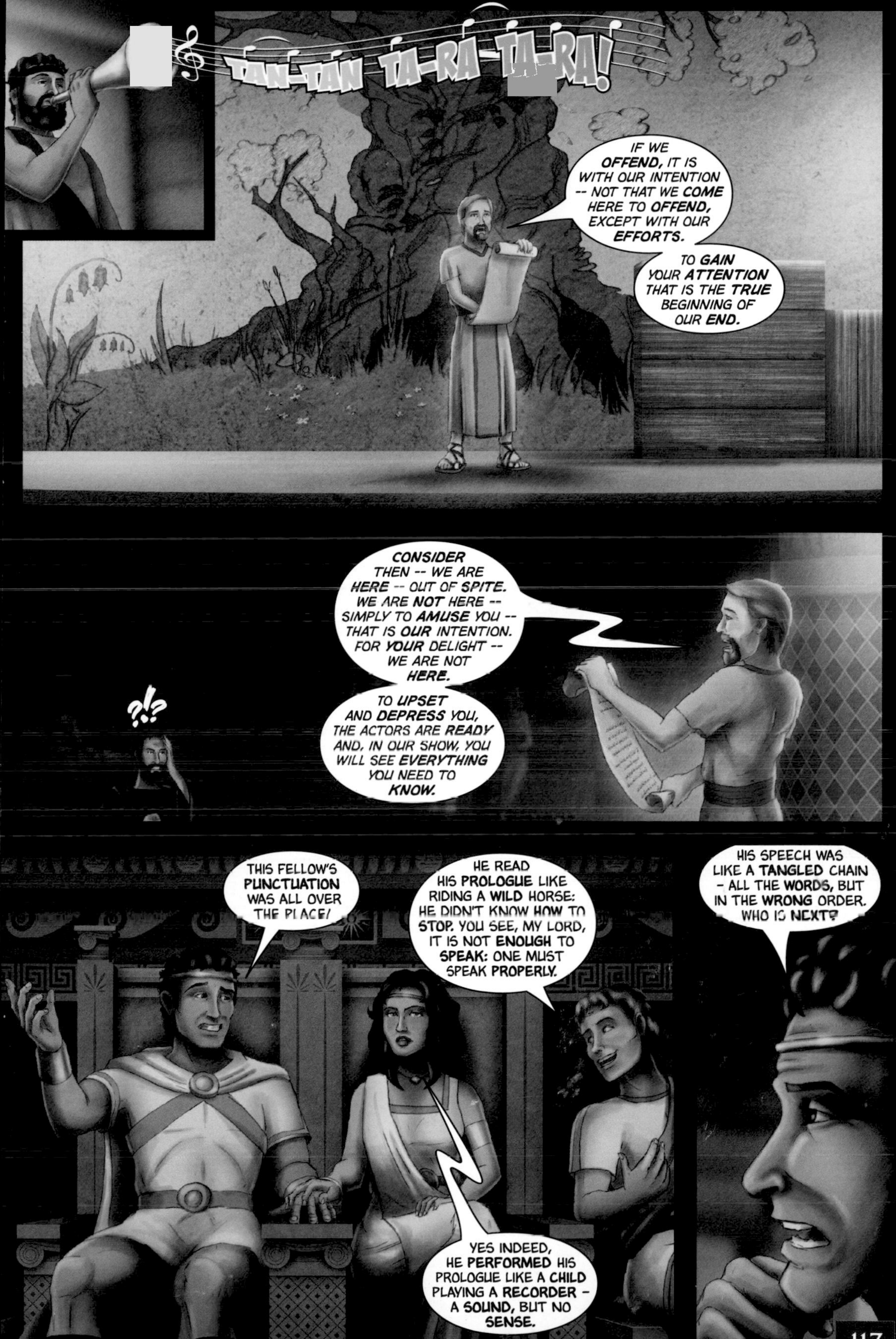
TAN-TAN TA-RA-TA-RA!
IF WE OFFEND, IT IS WITH OUR INTENTION -- NOT THAT WE COME HERE TO OFFEND, EXCEPT WITH OUR EFFORTS.
TO GAIN YOUR ATTENTION THAT IS THE TRUE BEGINNING OF OUR END.
CONSIDER THEN -- WE ARE HERE -- OUT OF SPITE. WE ARE NOT HERE -- SIMPLY TO AMUSE YOU -- THAT IS OUR INTENTION. FOR YOUR DELIGHT -- WE ARE NOT HERE.
TO UPSET AND DEPRESS YOU, THE ACTORS ARE READY AND, IN OUR SHOW, YOU WILL SEE EVERYTHING YOU NEED TO KNOW.
?!?
THIS FELLOW'S PUNCTUATION WAS ALL OVER THE PLACE!
HE READ HIS PROLOGUE LIKE RIDING A WILD HORSE: HE DIDN'T KNOW HOW TO STOP. YOU SEE, MY LORD, IT IS NOT ENOUGH TO SPEAK: ONE MUST SPEAK PROPERLY.
YES INDEED, HE PERFORMED HIS PROLOGUE LIKE A CHILD PLAYING A RECORDER - A SOUND, BUT NO SENSE.
HIS SPEECH WAS LIKE A TANGLED CHAIN - ALL THE WORDS, BUT IN THE WRONG ORDER. WHO IS NEXT?

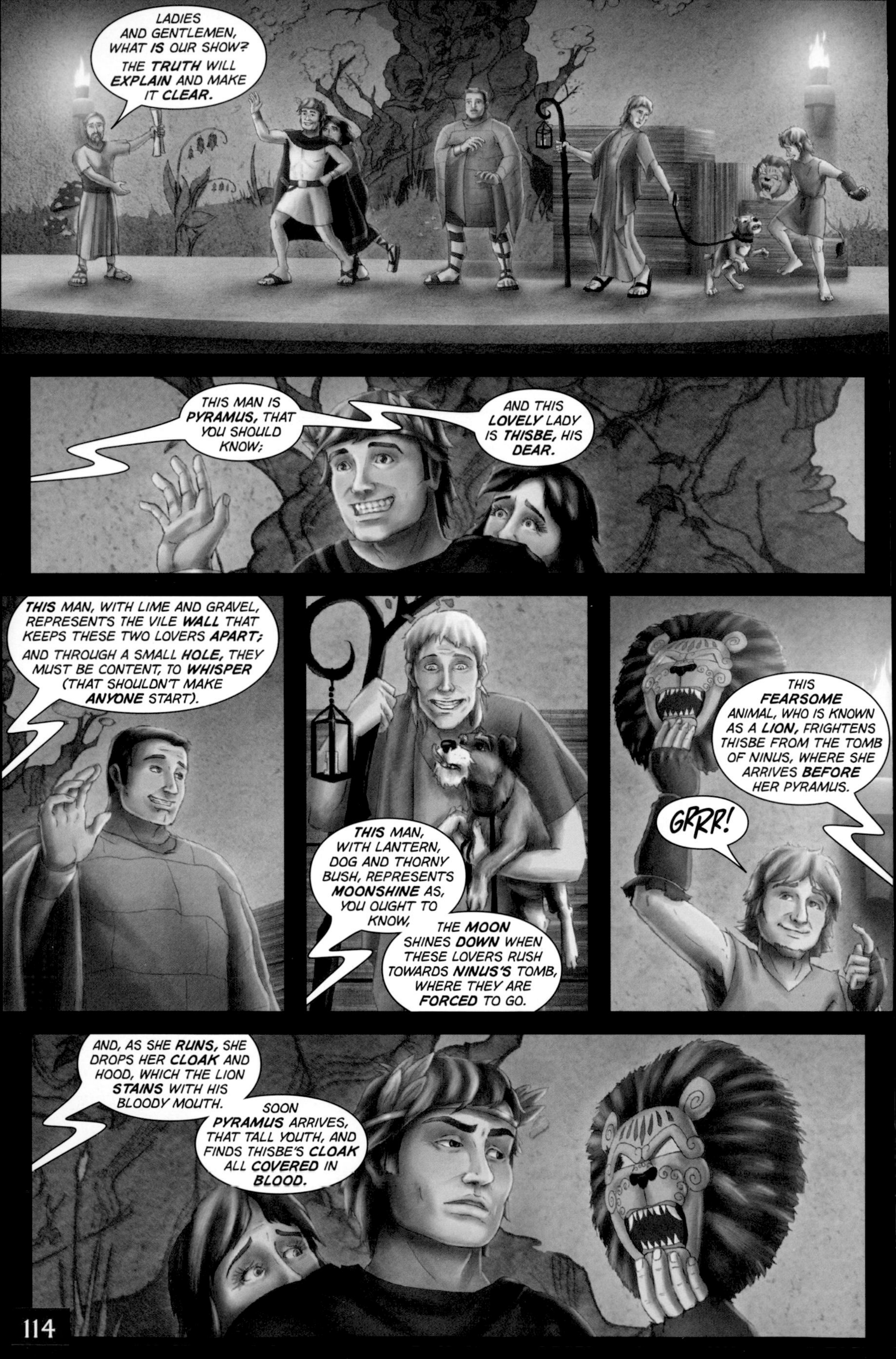
LADIES AND GENTLEMEN, WHAT IS OUR SHOW? THE TRUTH WILL EXPLAIN AND MAKE IT CLEAR.
THIS MAN IS PYRAMUS, THAT YOU SHOULD KNOW;
AND THIS LOVELY LADY IS THISBE, HIS DEAR.
THIS MAN, WITH LIME AND GRAVEL, REPRESENTS THE VILE WALL THAT KEEPS THESE TWO LOVERS APART; AND THROUGH A SMALL HOLE, THEY MUST BE CONTENT, TO WHISPER (THAT SHOULDN'T MAKE ANYONE START).
THIS MAN, WITH LANTERN, DOG AND THORNY BUSH, REPRESENTS MOONSHINE AS, YOU OUGHT TO KNOW,
THE MOON SHINES DOWN WHEN THESE LOVERS RUSH TOWARDS NINUS'S TOMB, WHERE THEY ARE FORCED TO GO.
THIS FEARSOME ANIMAL, WHO IS KNOWN AS A LION, FRIGHTENS THISBE FROM THE TOMB OF NINUS, WHERE SHE ARRIVES BEFORE HER PYRAMUS.
GRRR!
AND, AS SHE RUNS, SHE DROPS HER CLOAK AND HOOD, WHICH THE LION STAINS WITH HIS BLOODY MOUTH.
SOON PYRAMUS ARRIVES, THAT TALL YOUTH, AND FINDS THISBE'S CLOAK ALL COVERED IN BLOOD.

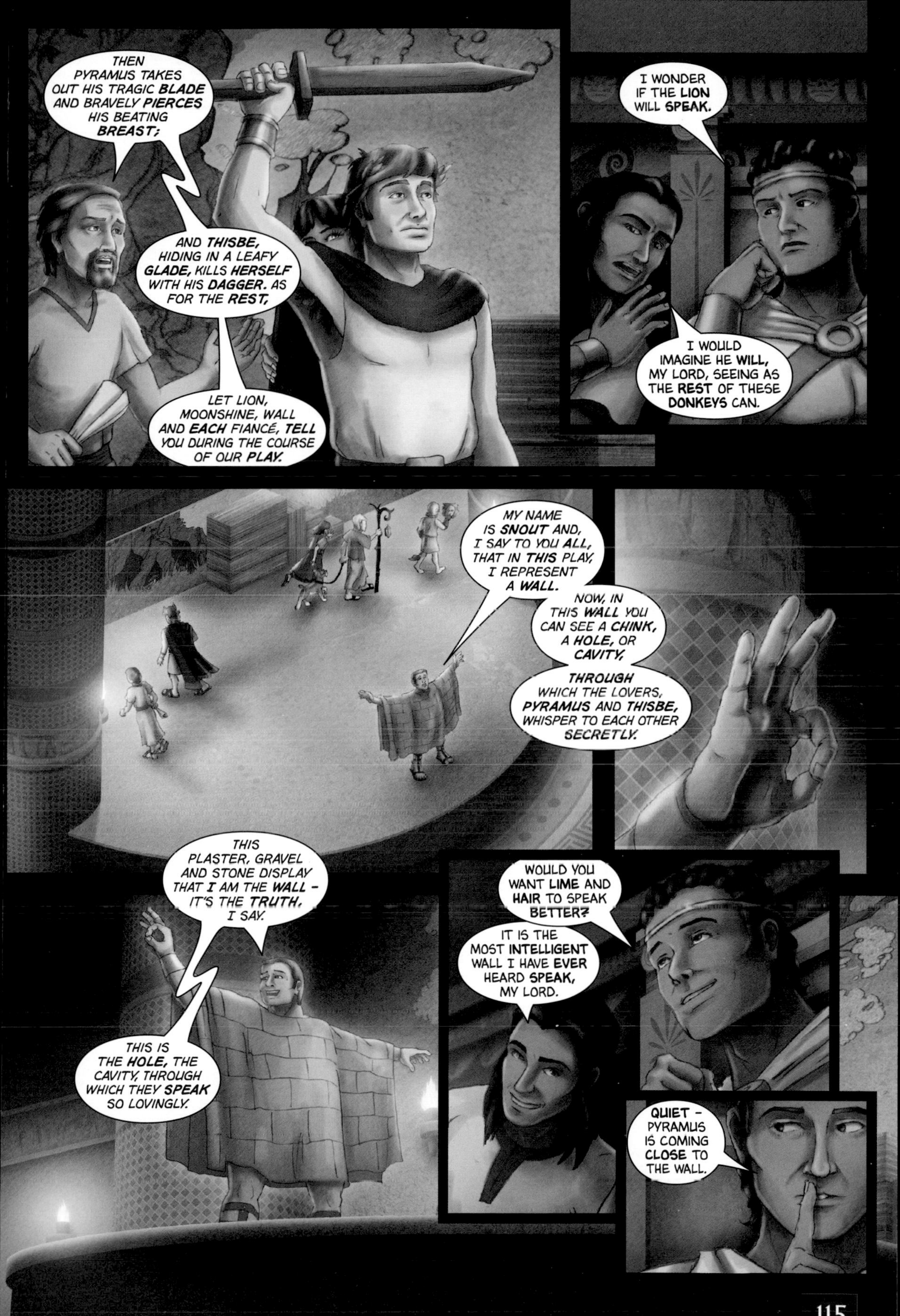
THEN PYRAMUS TAKES OUT HIS TRAGIC BLADE AND BRAVELY PIERCES HIS BEATING BREAST;
AND THISBE, HIDING IN A LEAFY GLADE, KILLS HERSELF WITH HIS DAGGER. AS FOR THE REST,
LET LION, MOONSHINE, WALL AND EACH FIANCÉ, TELL YOU DURING THE COURSE OF OUR PLAY.
I WONDER IF THE LION WILL SPEAK.
I WOULD IMAGINE HE WILL, MY LORD, SEEING AS THE REST OF THESE DONKEYS CAN.
MY NAME IS SNOUT AND, I SAY TO YOU ALL, THAT IN THIS PLAY, I REPRESENT A WALL.
NOW, IN THIS WALL YOU CAN SEE A CHINK, A HOLE, OR CAVITY,
THROUGH WHICH THE LOVERS, PYRAMUS AND THISBE, WHISPER TO EACH OTHER SECRETLY.
THIS PLASTER, GRAVEL AND STONE DISPLAY THAT I AM THE WALL - IT'S THE TRUTH, I SAY.
THIS IS THE HOLE, THE CAVITY, THROUGH WHICH THEY SPEAK SO LOVINGLY.
WOULD YOU WANT LIME AND HAIR TO SPEAK BETTER?
IT IS THE MOST INTELLIGENT WALL I HAVE EVER HEARD SPEAK, MY LORD.
QUIET - PYRAMUS IS COMING CLOSE TO THE WALL.

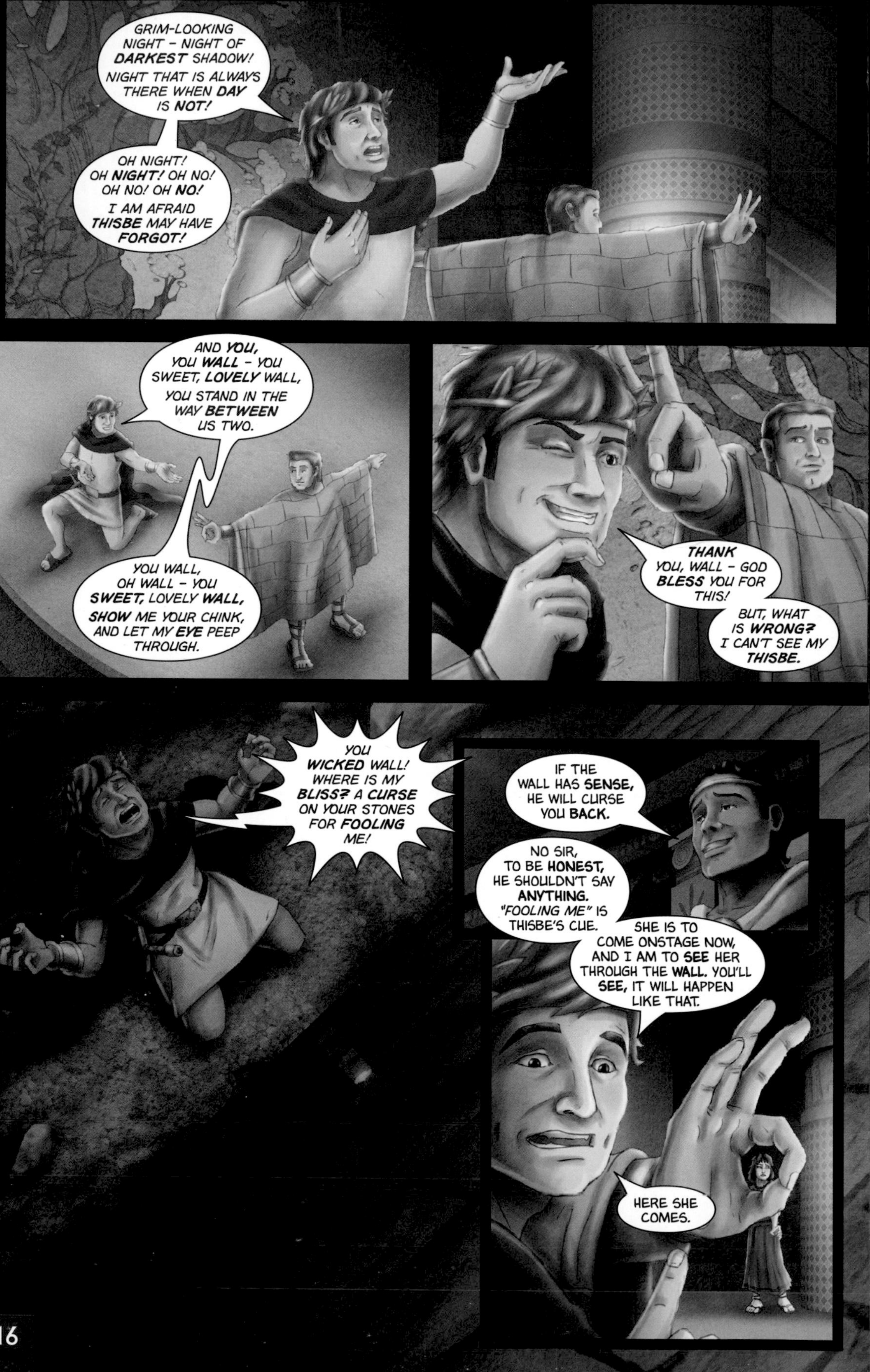
GRIM-LOOKING NIGHT – NIGHT OF DARKEST SHADOW! NIGHT THAT IS ALWAYS THERE WHEN DAY IS NOT!
OH NIGHT! OH NIGHT! OH NO! OH NO! OH NO! I AM AFRAID THISBE MAY HAVE FORGOT!
AND YOU, YOU WALL – YOU SWEET, LOVELY WALL, YOU STAND IN THE WAY BETWEEN US TWO.
YOU WALL, OH WALL – YOU SWEET, LOVELY WALL, SHOW ME YOUR CHINK, AND LET MY EYE PEEP THROUGH.
THANK YOU, WALL – GOD BLESS YOU FOR THIS!
BUT, WHAT IS WRONG? I CAN'T SEE MY THISBE.
YOU WICKED WALL! WHERE IS MY BLISS? A CURSE ON YOUR STONES FOR FOOLING ME!
IF THE WALL HAS SENSE, HE WILL CURSE YOU BACK.
NO SIR, TO BE HONEST, HE SHOULDN'T SAY ANYTHING. "FOOLING ME" IS THISBE'S CUE.
SHE IS TO COME ONSTAGE NOW, AND I AM TO SEE HER THROUGH THE WALL. YOU'LL SEE, IT WILL HAPPEN LIKE THAT.
HERE SHE COMES.

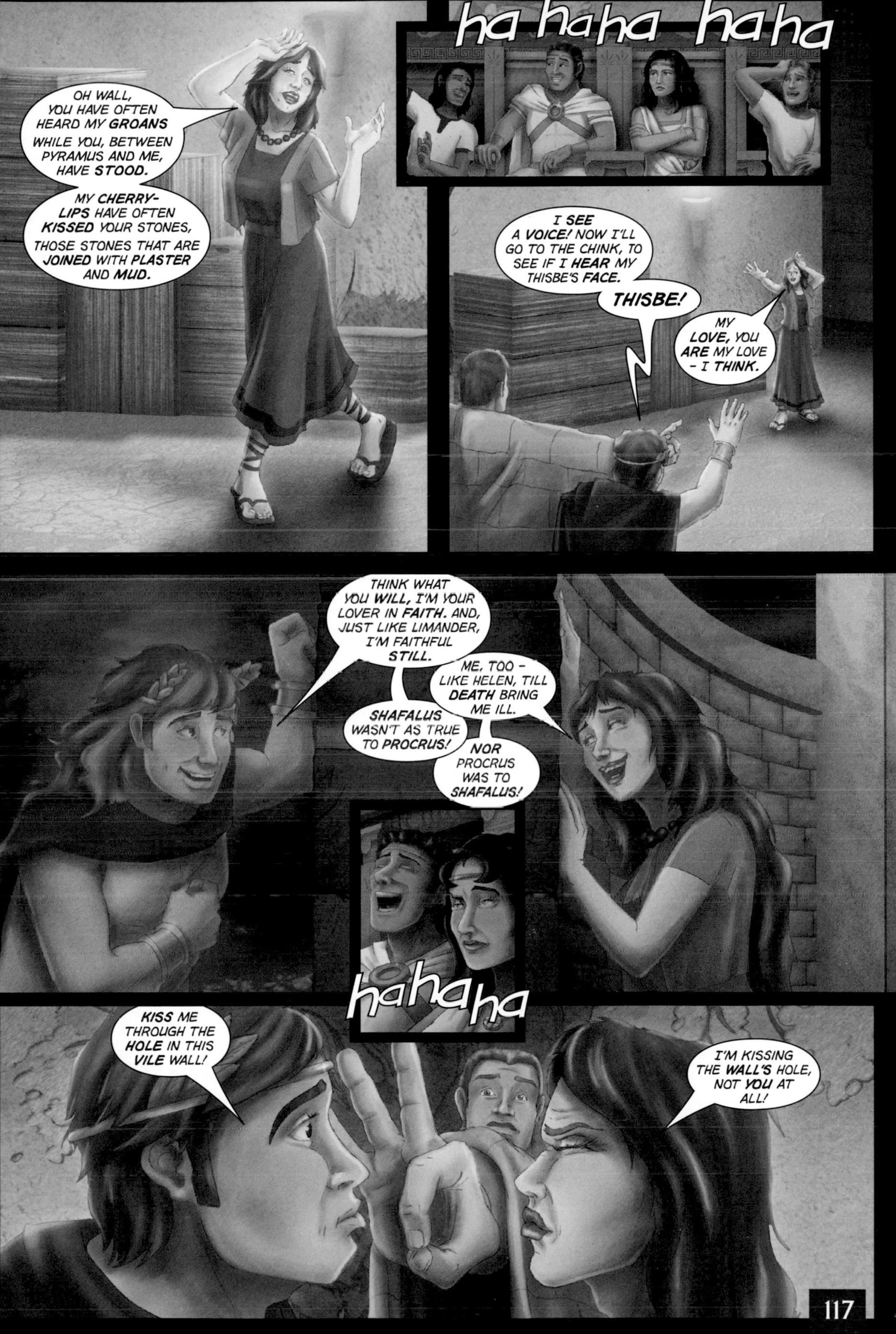
OH WALL, YOU HAVE OFTEN HEARD MY GROANS WHILE YOU, BETWEEN PYRAMUS AND ME, HAVE STOOD.
MY CHERRY-LIPS HAVE OFTEN KISSED YOUR STONES, THOSE STONES THAT ARE JOINED WITH PLASTER AND MUD.
ha ha ha ha ha ha ha
I SEE A VOICE! NOW I'LL GO TO THE CHINK, TO SEE IF I HEAR MY THISBE'S FACE.
THISBE!
MY LOVE, YOU ARE MY LOVE - I THINK.
THINK WHAT YOU WILL, I'M YOUR LOVER IN FAITH. AND, JUST LIKE LIMANDER, I'M FAITHFUL STILL.
ME, TOO - LIKE HELEN, TILL DEATH BRING ME ILL.
SHAFALUS WASN'T AS TRUE TO PROCRUS!
NOR PROCRUS WAS TO SHAFALUS!
ha ha ha ha
KISS ME THROUGH THE HOLE IN THIS VILE WALL!
I'M KISSING THE WALL'S HOLE, NOT YOU AT ALL!

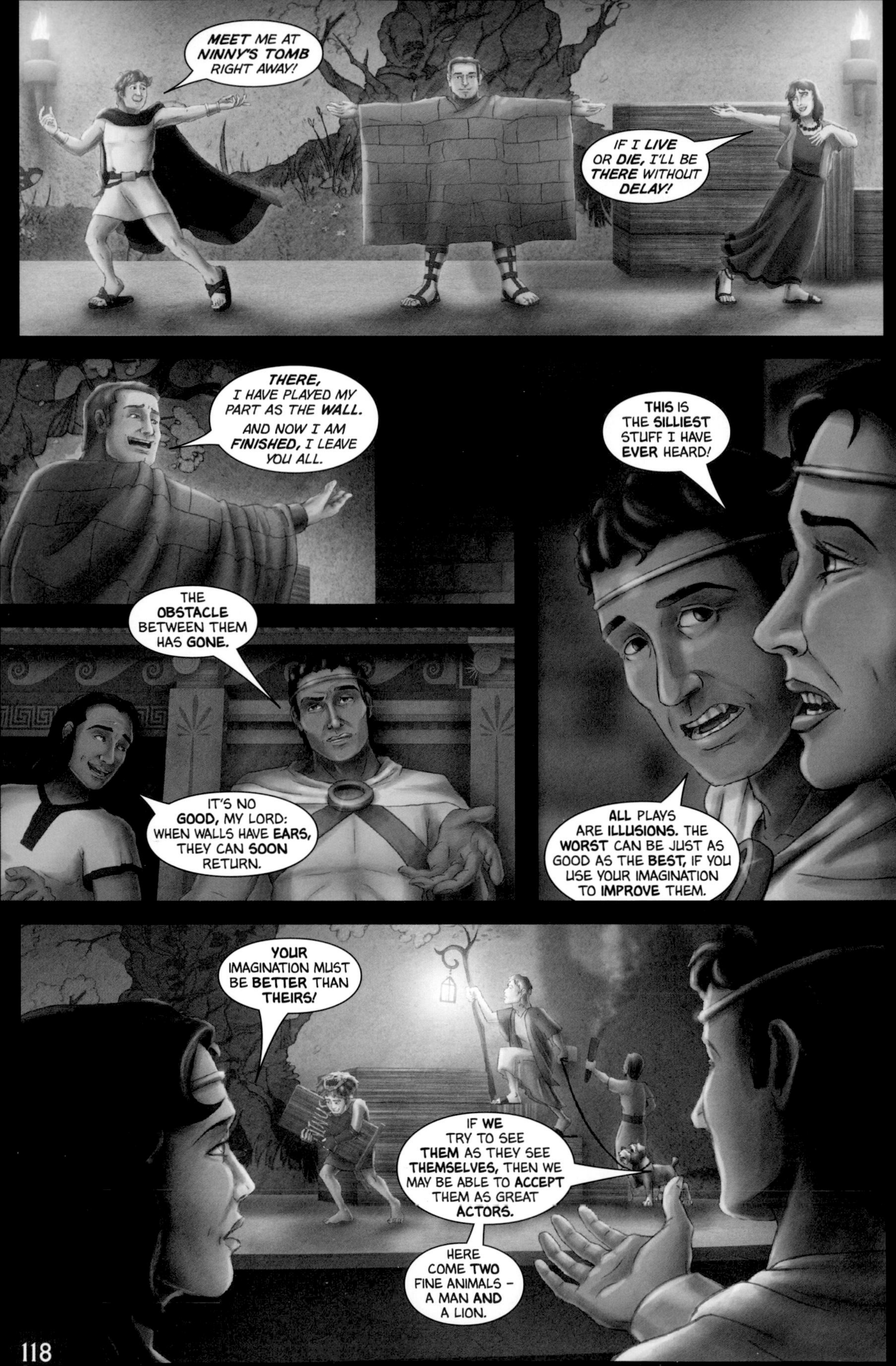
MEET ME AT NINNY'S TOMB RIGHT AWAY!
IF I LIVE OR DIE, I'LL BE THERE WITHOUT DELAY!
THERE, I HAVE PLAYED MY PART AS THE WALL. AND NOW I AM FINISHED, I LEAVE YOU ALL.
THE OBSTACLE BETWEEN THEM HAS GONE.
IT'S NO GOOD, MY LORD: WHEN WALLS HAVE EARS, THEY CAN SOON RETURN.
THIS IS THE SILLIEST STUFF I HAVE EVER HEARD!
ALL PLAYS ARE ILLUSIONS. THE WORST CAN BE JUST AS GOOD AS THE BEST, IF YOU USE YOUR IMAGINATION TO IMPROVE THEM.
YOUR IMAGINATION MUST BE BETTER THAN THEIRS!
IF WE TRY TO SEE THEM AS THEY SEE THEMSELVES, THEN WE MAY BE ABLE TO ACCEPT THEM AS GREAT ACTORS.
HERE COME TWO FINE ANIMALS – A MAN AND A LION.

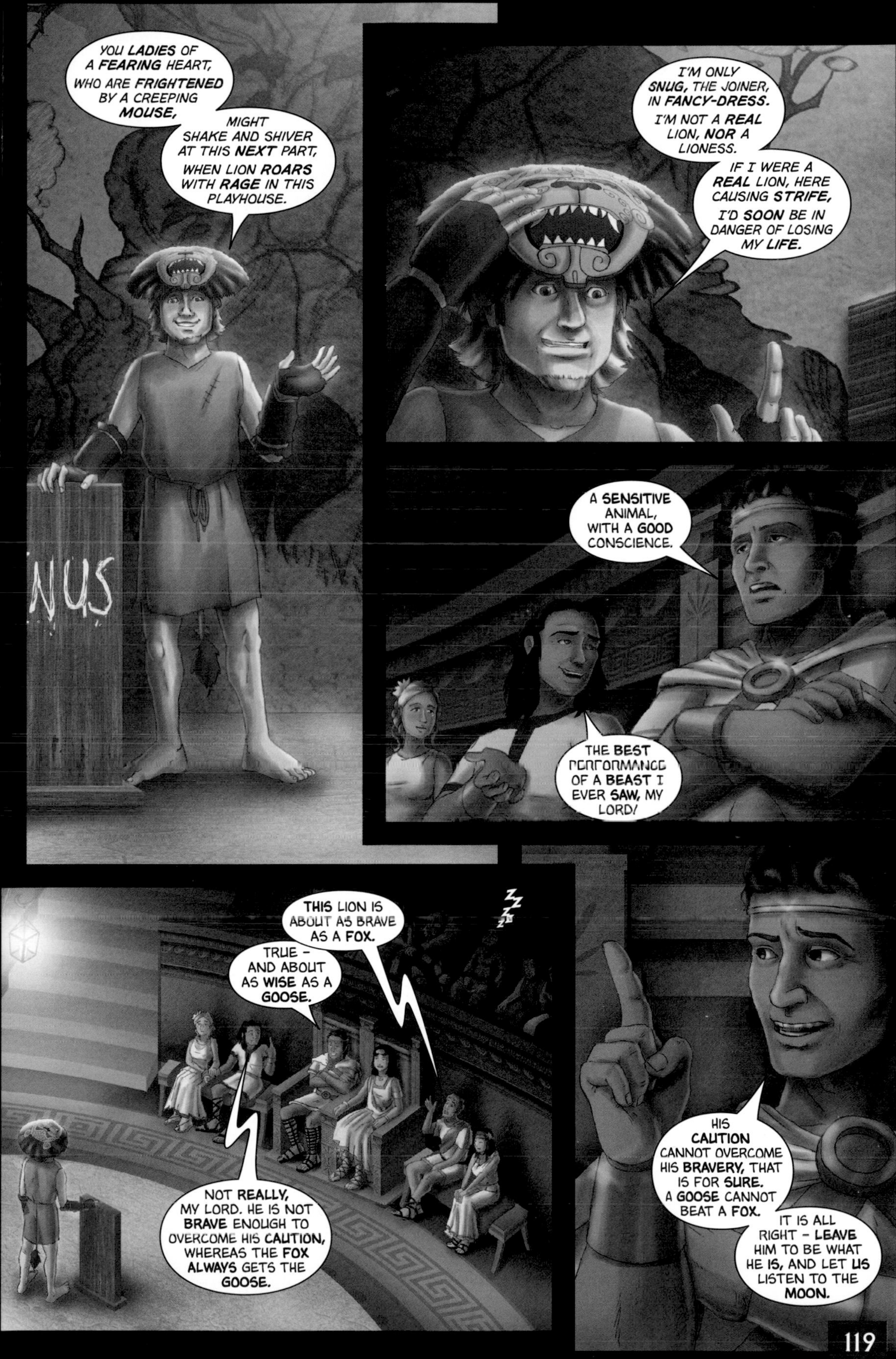
YOU LADIES OF A FEARING HEART, WHO ARE FRIGHTENED BY A CREEPING MOUSE,
MIGHT SHAKE AND SHIVER AT THIS NEXT PART, WHEN LION ROARS WITH RAGE IN THIS PLAYHOUSE.
I'M ONLY SNUG, THE JOINER, IN FANCY-DRESS. I'M NOT A REAL LION, NOR A LIONESS.
IF I WERE A REAL LION, HERE CAUSING STRIFE, I'D SOON BE IN DANGER OF LOSING MY LIFE.
A SENSITIVE ANIMAL, WITH A GOOD CONSCIENCE.
THE BEST PERFORMANCE OF A BEAST I EVER SAW, MY LORD!
THIS LION IS ABOUT AS BRAVE AS A FOX.
TRUE – AND ABOUT AS WISE AS A GOOSE.
ZZZ
NOT REALLY, MY LORD. HE IS NOT BRAVE ENOUGH TO OVERCOME HIS CAUTION, WHEREAS THE FOX ALWAYS GETS THE GOOSE.
HIS CAUTION CANNOT OVERCOME HIS BRAVERY, THAT IS FOR SURE. A GOOSE CANNOT BEAT A FOX.
IT IS ALL RIGHT – LEAVE HIM TO BE WHAT HE IS, AND LET US LISTEN TO THE MOON.

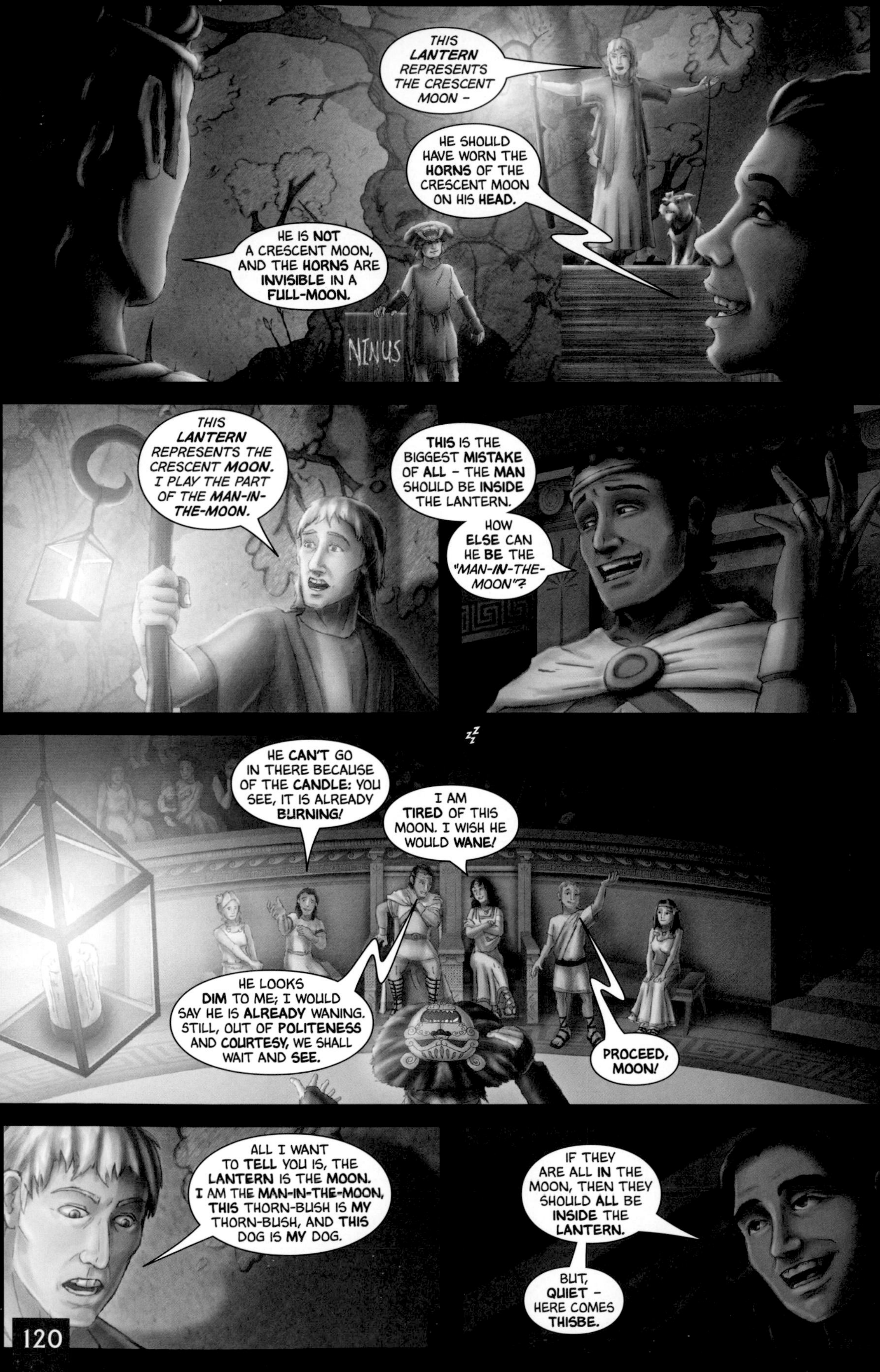
THIS LANTERN REPRESENTS THE CRESCENT MOON –
HE SHOULD HAVE WORN THE HORNS OF THE CRESCENT MOON ON HIS HEAD.
HE IS NOT A CRESCENT MOON, AND THE HORNS ARE INVISIBLE IN A FULL-MOON.
NINUS
THIS LANTERN REPRESENTS THE CRESCENT MOON. I PLAY THE PART OF THE MAN-IN-THE-MOON.
THIS IS THE BIGGEST MISTAKE OF ALL – THE MAN SHOULD BE INSIDE THE LANTERN.
HOW ELSE CAN HE BE THE "MAN-IN-THE-MOON"?
ZZZ
HE CAN'T GO IN THERE BECAUSE OF THE CANDLE: YOU SEE, IT IS ALREADY BURNING!
I AM TIRED OF THIS MOON. I WISH HE WOULD WANE!
HE LOOKS DIM TO ME; I WOULD SAY HE IS ALREADY WANING. STILL, OUT OF POLITENESS AND COURTESY, WE SHALL WAIT AND SEE.
PROCEED, MOON!
ALL I WANT TO TELL YOU IS, THE LANTERN IS THE MOON. I AM THE MAN-IN-THE-MOON, THIS THORN-BUSH IS MY THORN-BUSH, AND THIS DOG IS MY DOG.
IF THEY ARE ALL IN THE MOON, THEN THEY SHOULD ALL BE INSIDE THE LANTERN.
BUT, QUIET – HERE COMES THISBE.

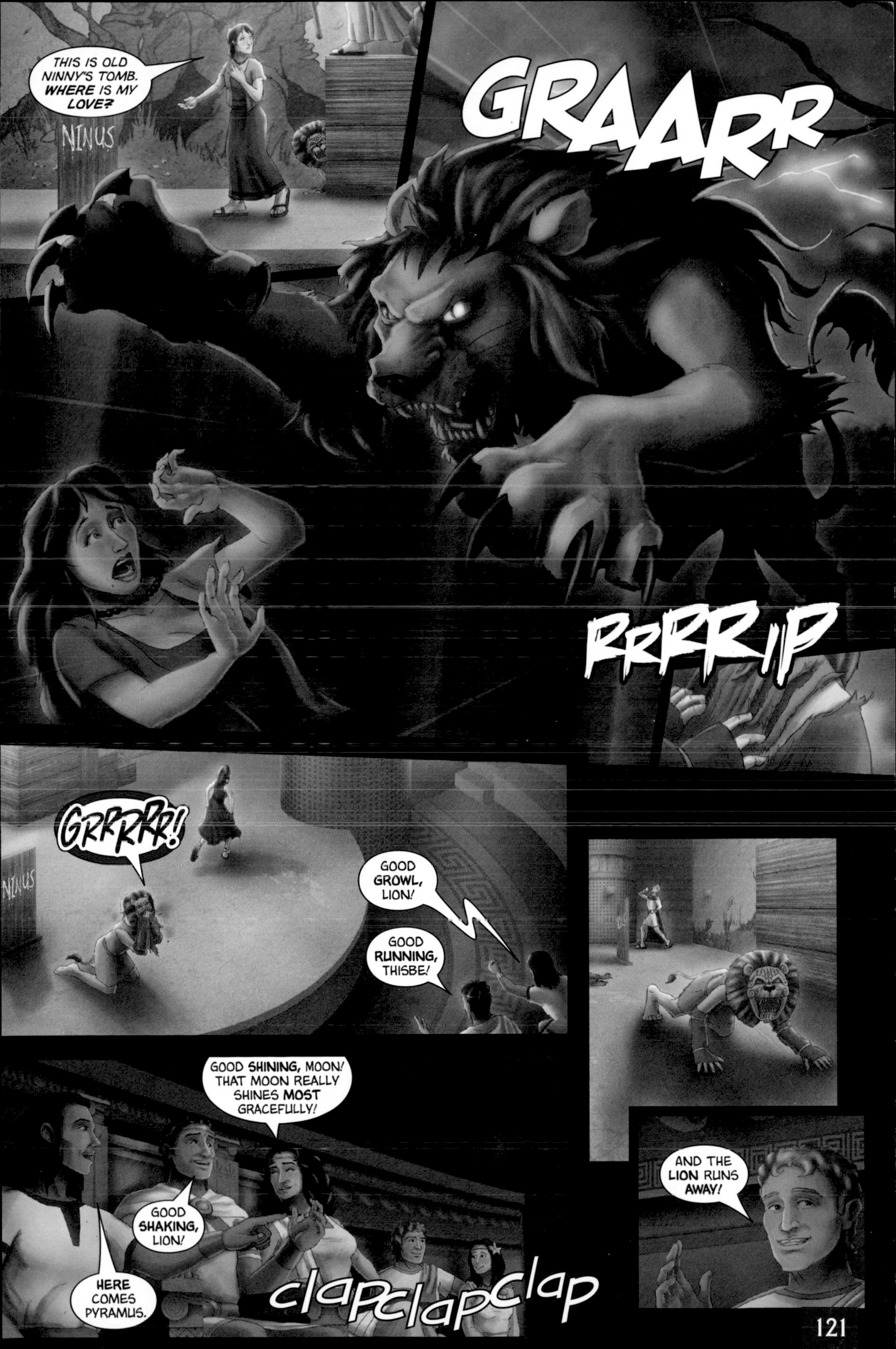
THIS IS OLD NINNY'S TOMB. WHERE IS MY LOVE?
NINUS
GRAARR
RRRRIP
GRRRRR!
NINUS
GOOD GROWL, LION!
GOOD RUNNING, THISBE!
GOOD SHINING, MOON! THAT MOON REALLY SHINES MOST GRACEFULLY!
GOOD SHAKING, LION!
HERE COMES PYRAMUS.
clapclapclap
AND THE LION RUNS AWAY!

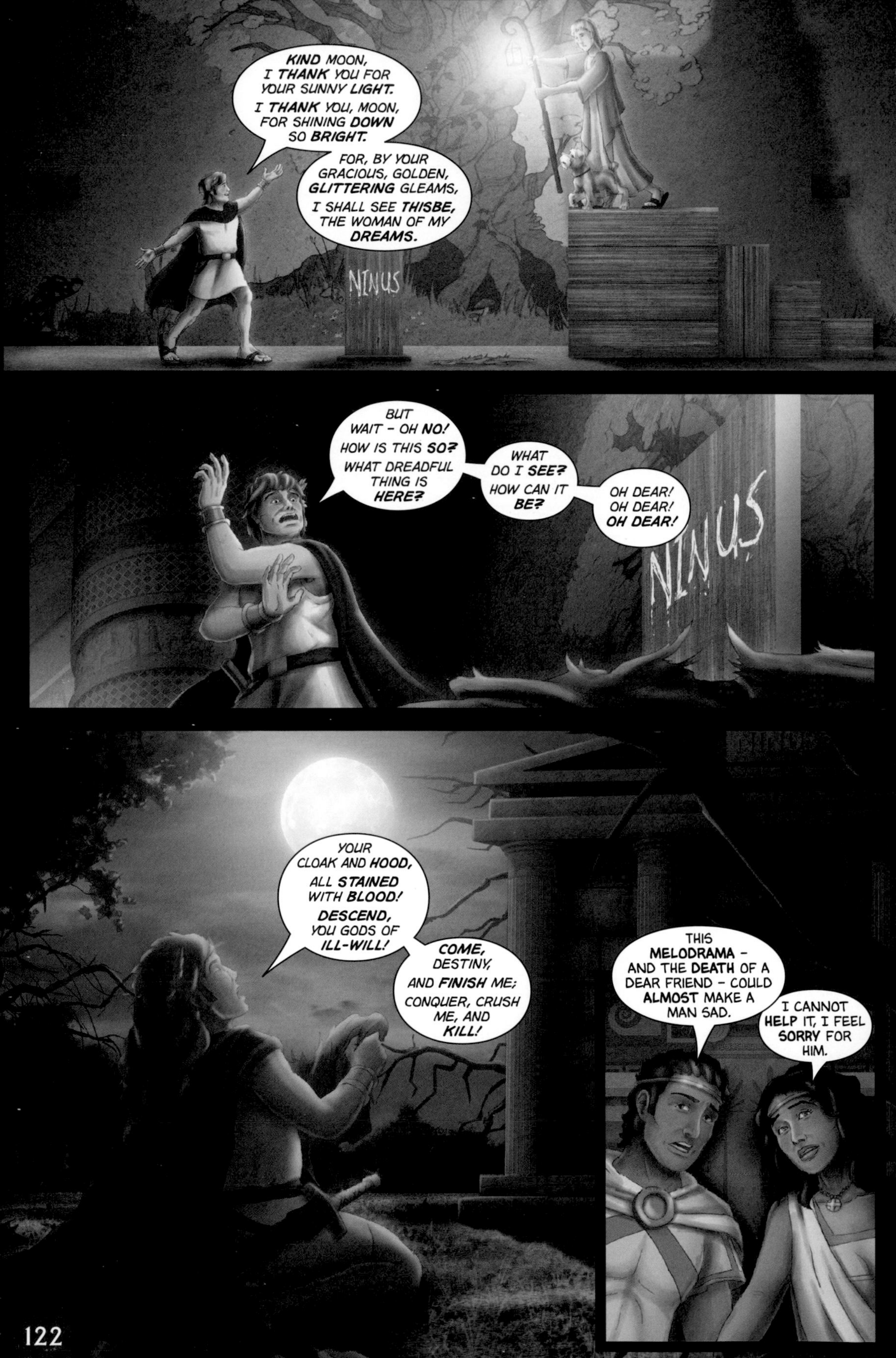
KIND MOON, I THANK YOU FOR YOUR SUNNY LIGHT. I THANK YOU, MOON, FOR SHINING DOWN SO BRIGHT.
FOR, BY YOUR GRACIOUS, GOLDEN, GLITTERING GLEAMS, I SHALL SEE THISBE, THE WOMAN OF MY DREAMS.
NINUS
BUT WAIT - OH NO! HOW IS THIS SO? WHAT DREADFUL THING IS HERE?
WHAT DO I SEE? HOW CAN IT BE?
OH DEAR! OH DEAR! OH DEAR!
NINUS
YOUR CLOAK AND HOOD, ALL STAINED WITH BLOOD! DESCEND, YOU GODS OF ILL-WILL!
COME, DESTINY, AND FINISH ME; CONQUER, CRUSH ME, AND KILL!
THIS MELODRAMA - AND THE DEATH OF A DEAR FRIEND - COULD ALMOST MAKE A MAN SAD.
I CANNOT HELP IT, I FEEL SORRY FOR HIM.

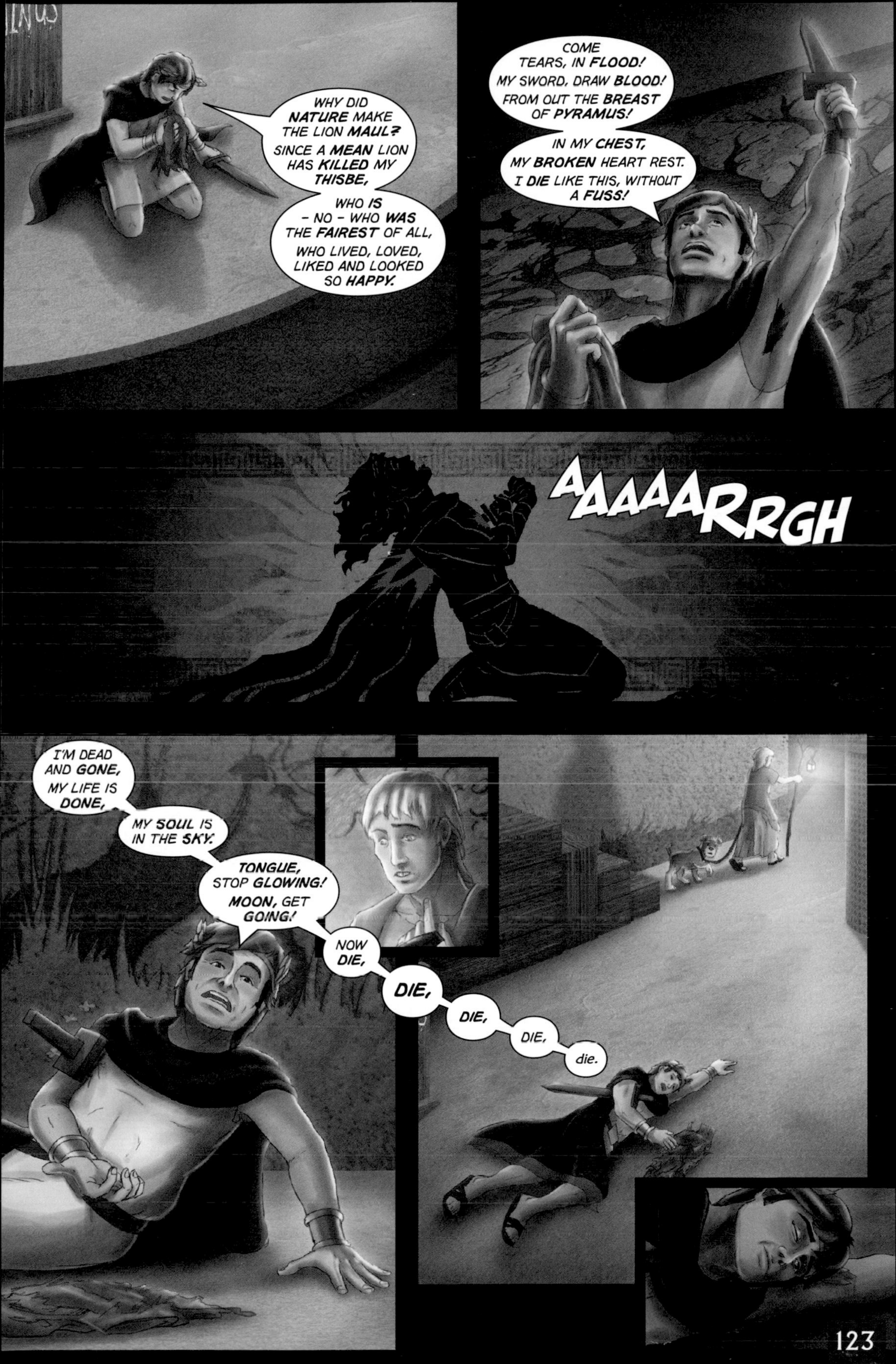

WHY DID NATURE MAKE THE LION MAUL? SINCE A MEAN LION HAS KILLED MY THISBE,
WHO IS – NO – WHO WAS THE FAIREST OF ALL, WHO LIVED, LOVED, LIKED AND LOOKED SO HAPPY.
COME TEARS, IN FLOOD! MY SWORD, DRAW BLOOD! FROM OUT THE BREAST OF PYRAMUS!
IN MY CHEST, MY BROKEN HEART REST. I DIE LIKE THIS, WITHOUT A FUSS!
AAAAARRGH
I'M DEAD AND GONE, MY LIFE IS DONE,
MY SOUL IS IN THE SKY.
TONGUE, STOP GLOWING! MOON, GET GOING!
NOW DIE,
DIE,
DIE,
DIE,
die.

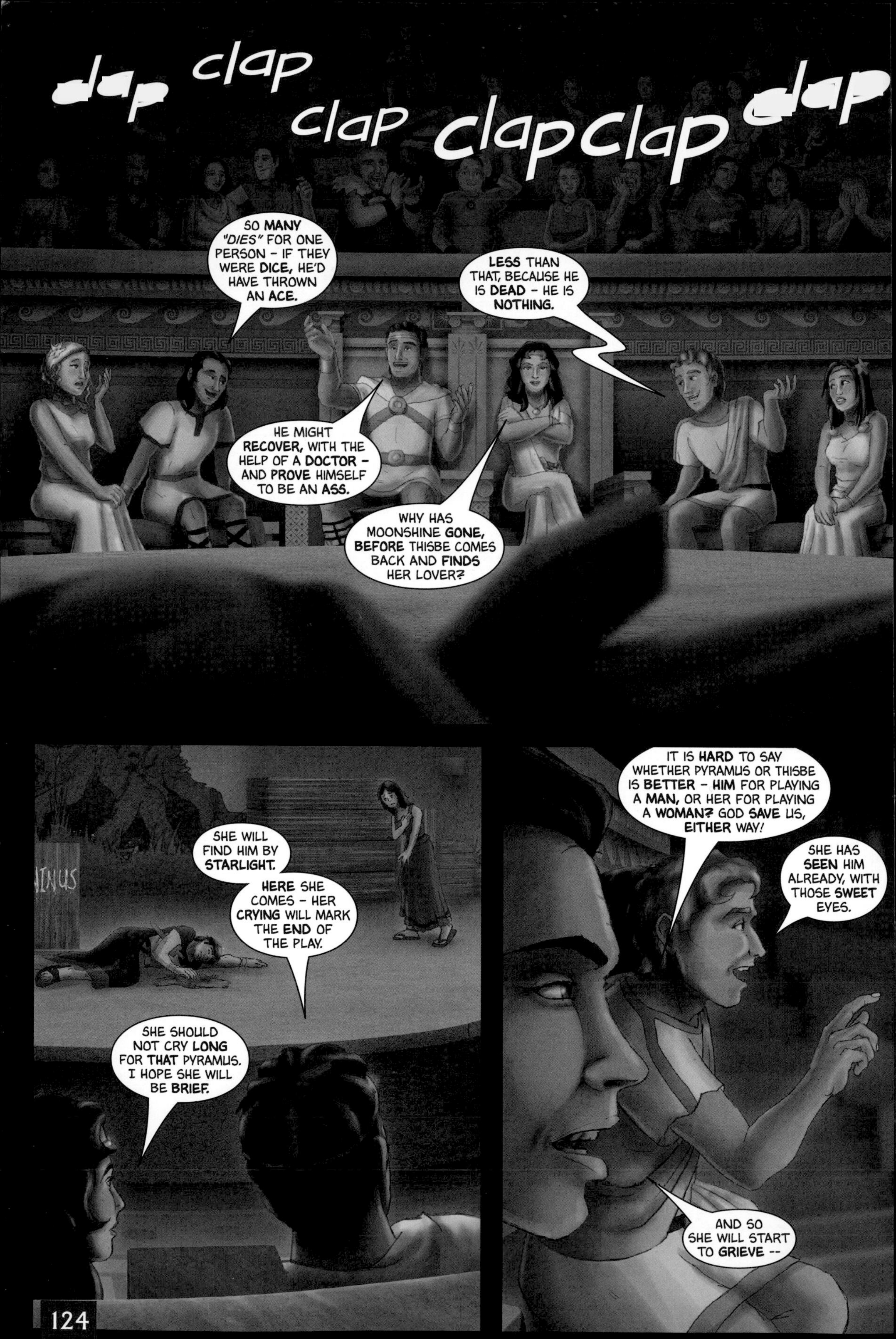
clap
clap
clap clap
SO MANY "DIES" FOR ONE PERSON – IF THEY WERE DICE, HE'D HAVE THROWN AN ACE.
LESS THAN THAT, BECAUSE HE IS DEAD – HE IS NOTHING.
HE MIGHT RECOVER, WITH THE HELP OF A DOCTOR – AND PROVE HIMSELF TO BE AN ASS.
WHY HAS MOONSHINE GONE, BEFORE THISBE COMES BACK AND FINDS HER LOVER?
SHE WILL FIND HIM BY STARLIGHT.
HERE SHE COMES – HER CRYING WILL MARK THE END OF THE PLAY.
SHE SHOULD NOT CRY LONG FOR THAT PYRAMUS. I HOPE SHE WILL BE BRIEF.
IT IS HARD TO SAY WHETHER PYRAMUS OR THISBE IS BETTER – HIM FOR PLAYING A MAN, OR HER FOR PLAYING A WOMAN? GOD SAVE US, EITHER WAY!
SHE HAS SEEN HIM ALREADY, WITH THOSE SWEET EYES.
AND SO SHE WILL START TO GRIEVE --

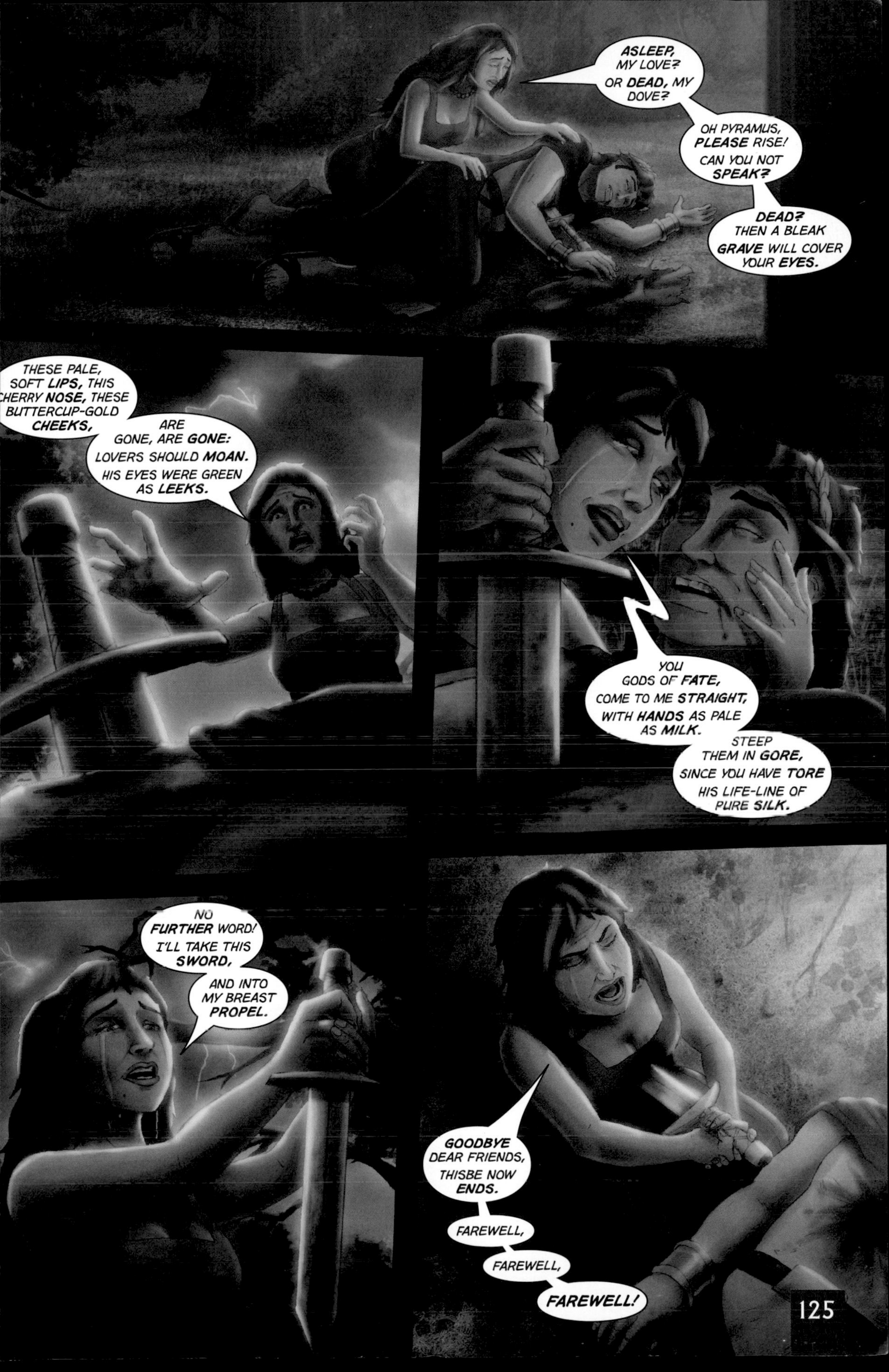
ASLEEP, MY LOVE? OR DEAD, MY DOVE?
OH PYRAMUS, PLEASE RISE! CAN YOU NOT SPEAK?
DEAD? THEN A BLEAK GRAVE WILL COVER YOUR EYES.
THESE PALE, SOFT LIPS, THIS CHERRY NOSE, THESE BUTTERCUP-GOLD CHEEKS,
ARE GONE, ARE GONE: LOVERS SHOULD MOAN. HIS EYES WERE GREEN AS LEEKS.
YOU GODS OF FATE, COME TO ME STRAIGHT, WITH HANDS AS PALE AS MILK.
STEEP THEM IN GORE, SINCE YOU HAVE TORE HIS LIFE-LINE OF PURE SILK.
NO FURTHER WORD! I'LL TAKE THIS SWORD,
AND INTO MY BREAST PROPEL.
GOODBYE DEAR FRIENDS, THISBE NOW ENDS.
FAREWELL,
FAREWELL,
FAREWELL!

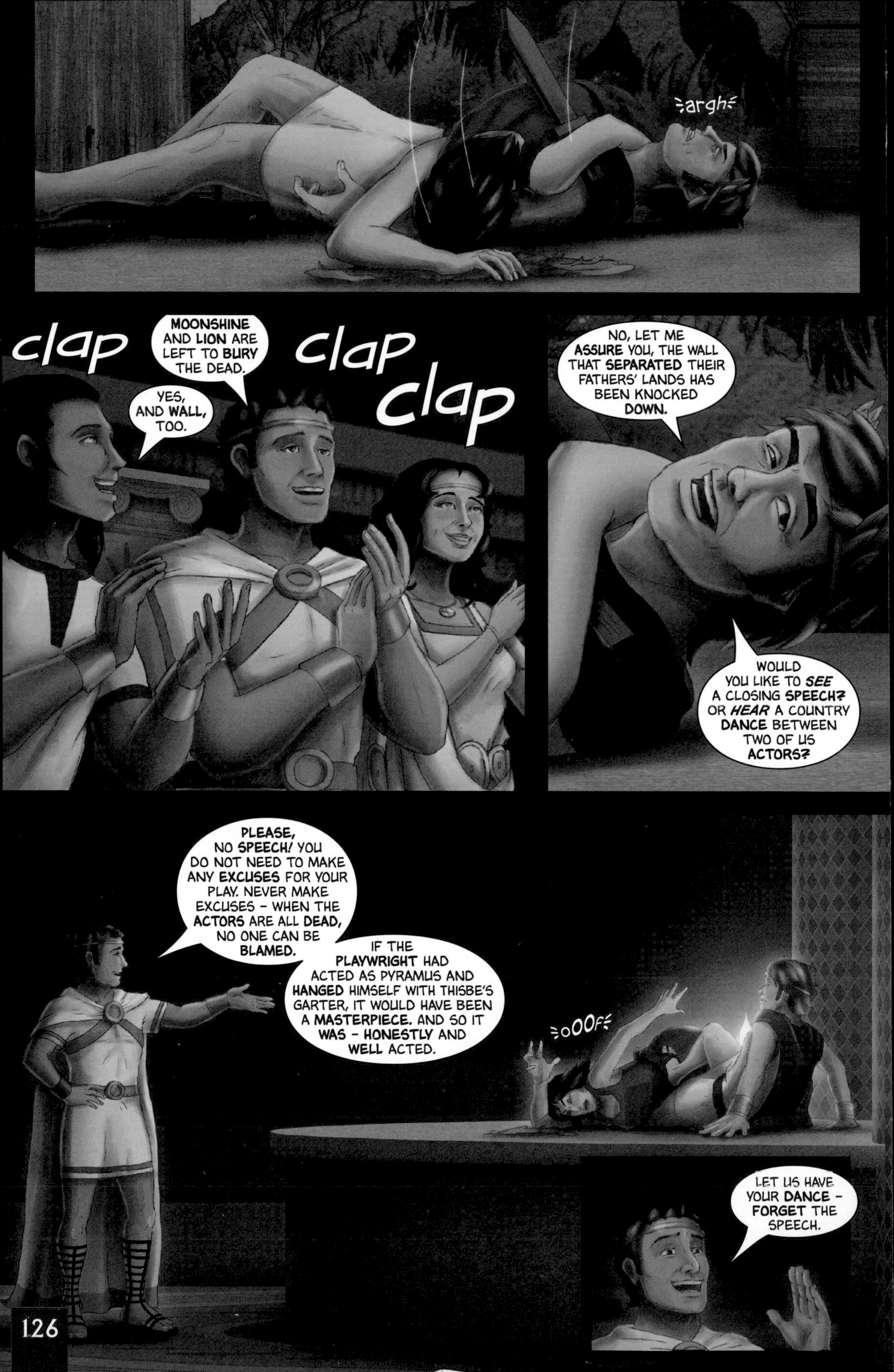
argh
clap
MOONSHINE AND LION ARE LEFT TO BURY THE DEAD.
YES, AND WALL, TOO.
clap
clap
NO, LET ME ASSURE YOU, THE WALL THAT SEPARATED THEIR FATHERS' LANDS HAS BEEN KNOCKED DOWN.
WOULD YOU LIKE TO SEE A CLOSING SPEECH? OR HEAR A COUNTRY DANCE BETWEEN TWO OF US ACTORS?
PLEASE, NO SPEECH! YOU DO NOT NEED TO MAKE ANY EXCUSES FOR YOUR PLAY. NEVER MAKE EXCUSES - WHEN THE ACTORS ARE ALL DEAD, NO ONE CAN BE BLAMED.
IF THE PLAYWRIGHT HAD ACTED AS PYRAMUS AND HANGED HIMSELF WITH THISBE'S GARTER, IT WOULD HAVE BEEN A MASTERPIECE. AND SO IT WAS - HONESTLY AND WELL ACTED.
oOOF
LET US HAVE YOUR DANCE - FORGET THE SPEECH.

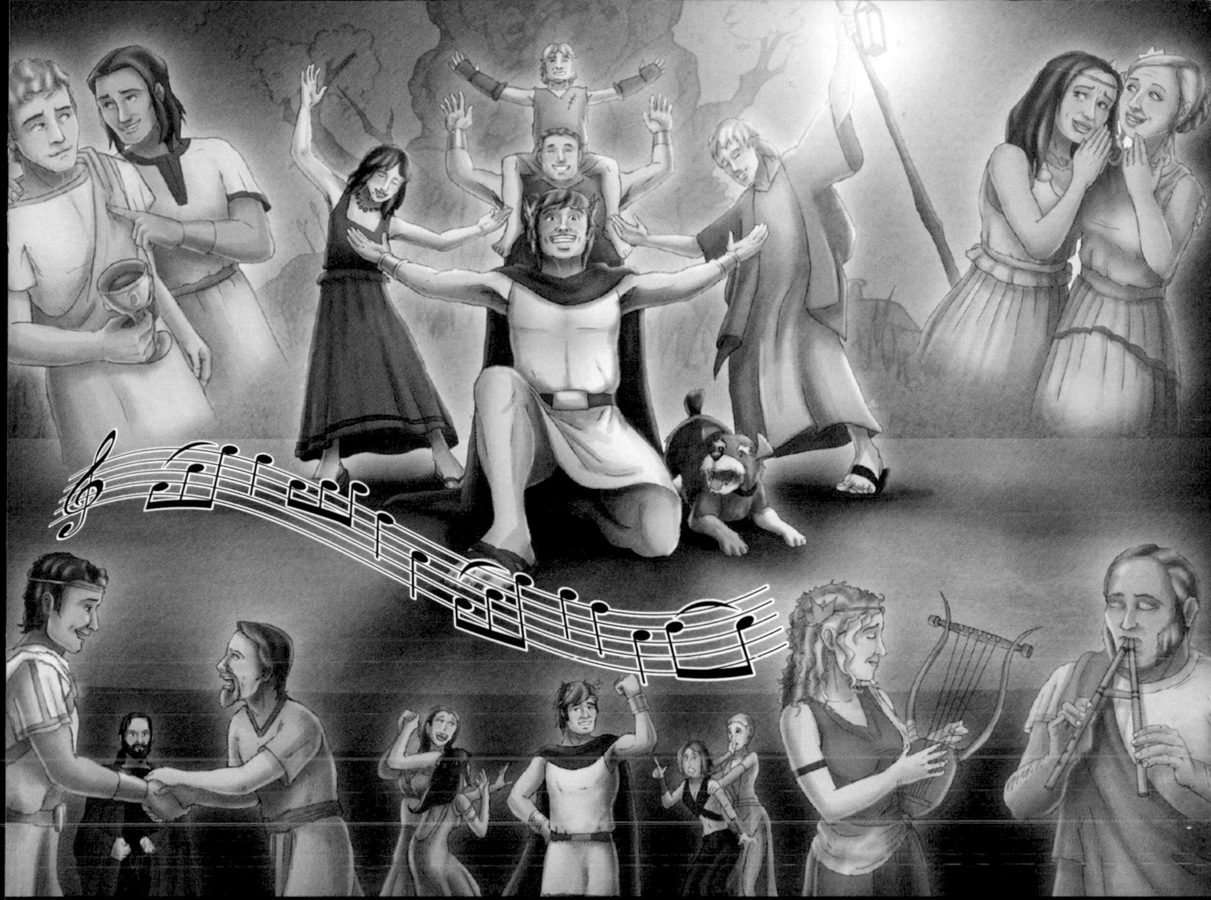

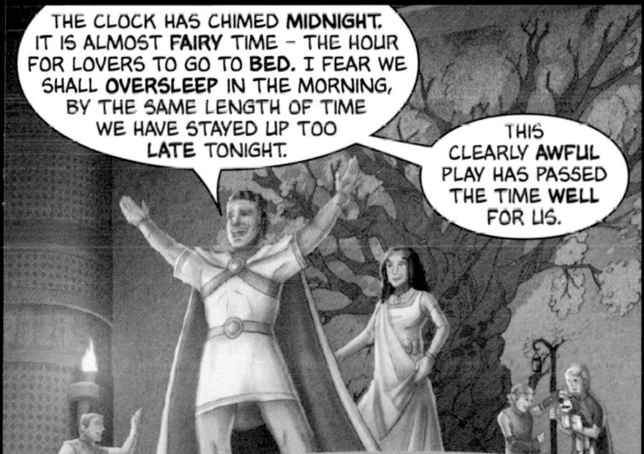
THE CLOCK HAS CHIMED MIDNIGHT. IT IS ALMOST FAIRY TIME – THE HOUR FOR LOVERS TO GO TO BED. I FEAR WE SHALL OVERSLEEP IN THE MORNING, BY THE SAME LENGTH OF TIME WE HAVE STAYED UP TOO LATE TONIGHT.
THIS CLEARLY AWFUL PLAY HAS PASSED THE TIME WELL FOR US.

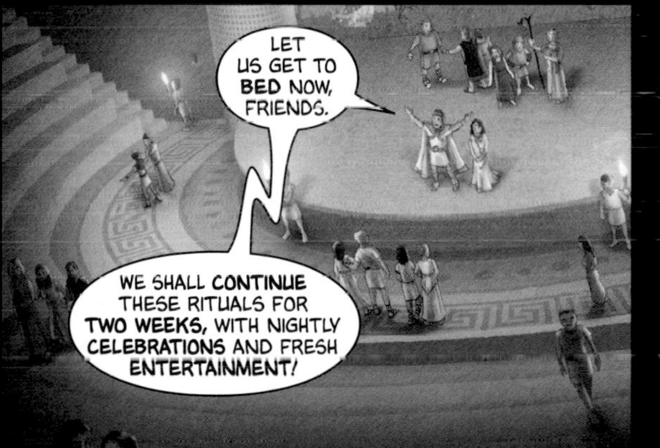
LET US GET TO BED NOW, FRIENDS.
WE SHALL CONTINUE THESE RITUALS FOR TWO WEEKS, WITH NIGHTLY CELEBRATIONS AND FRESH ENTERTAINMENT!

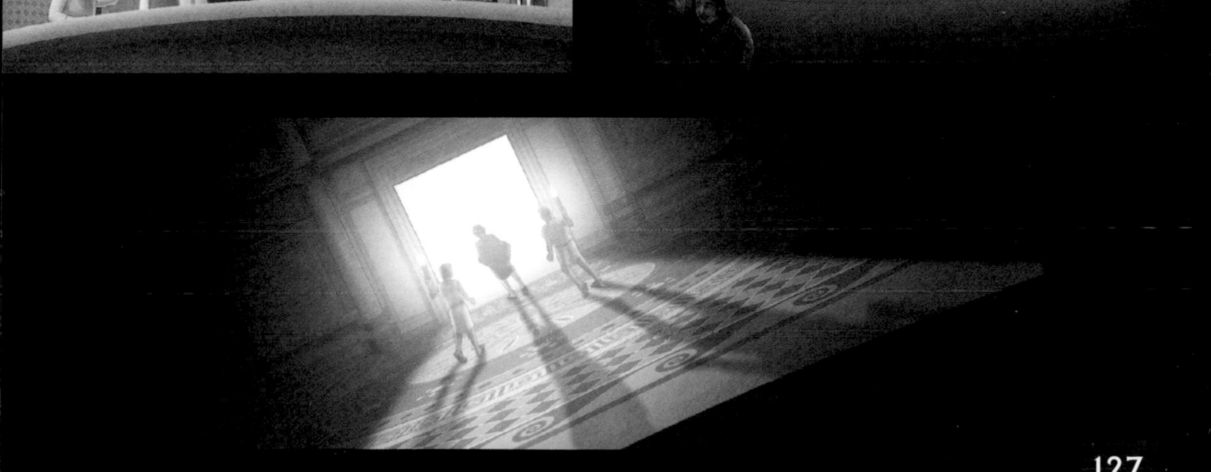

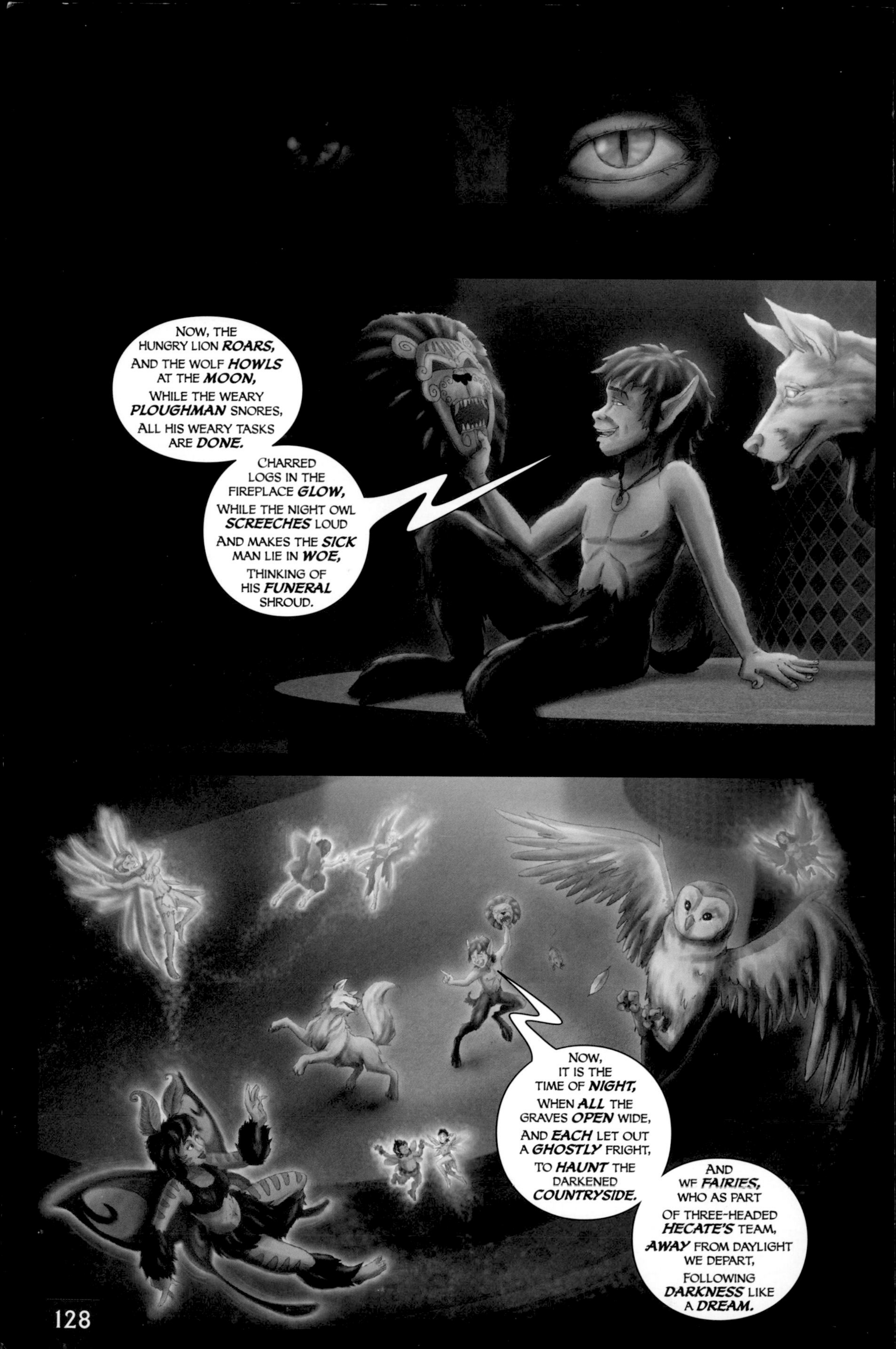
NOW, THE HUNGRY LION ROARS, AND THE WOLF HOWLS AT THE MOON, WHILE THE WEARY PLOUGHMAN SNORES, ALL HIS WEARY TASKS ARE DONE.
CHARRED LOGS IN THE FIREPLACE GLOW, WHILE THE NIGHT OWL SCREECHES LOUD AND MAKES THE SICK MAN LIE IN WOE, THINKING OF HIS FUNERAL SHROUD.
NOW, IT IS THE TIME OF NIGHT, WHEN ALL THE GRAVES OPEN WIDE, AND EACH LET OUT A GHOSTLY FRIGHT, TO HAUNT THE DARKENED COUNTRYSIDE.
AND WF FAIRIES, WHO AS PART OF THREE-HEADED HECATE'S TEAM, AWAY FROM DAYLIGHT WE DEPART, FOLLOWING DARKNESS LIKE A DREAM.

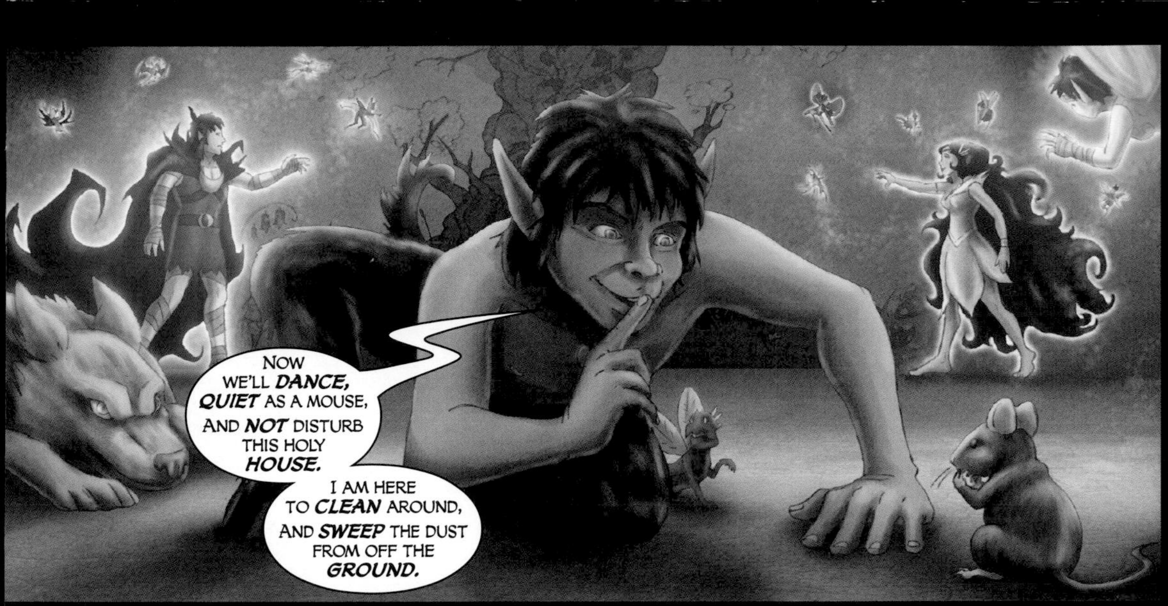
NOW WE'LL DANCE, QUIET AS A MOUSE, AND NOT DISTURB THIS HOLY HOUSE.
I AM HERE TO CLEAN AROUND, AND SWEEP THE DUST FROM OFF THE GROUND.

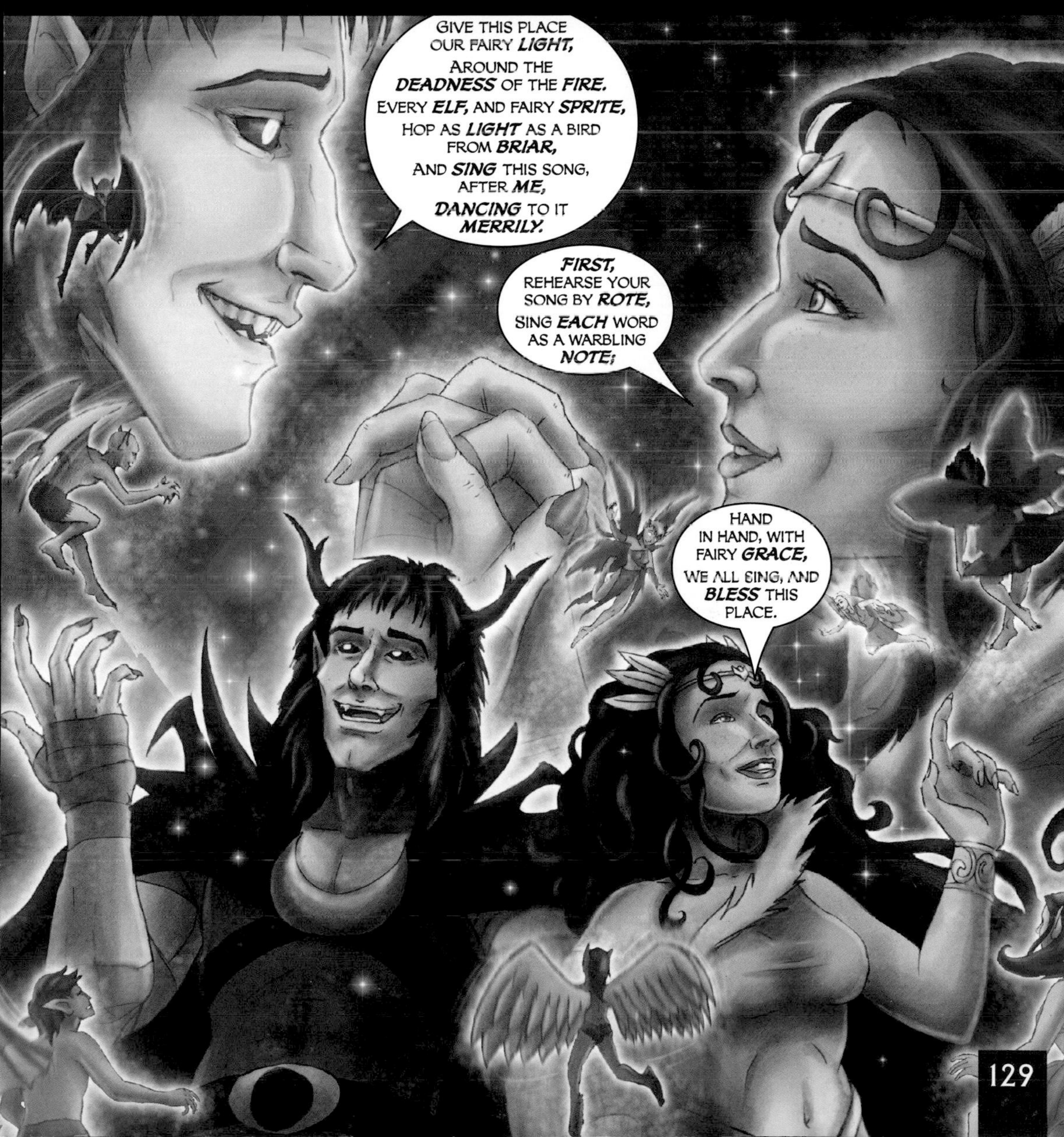
GIVE THIS PLACE OUR FAIRY LIGHT, AROUND THE DEADNESS OF THE FIRE. EVERY ELF, AND FAIRY SPRITE, HOP AS LIGHT AS A BIRD FROM BRIAR, AND SING THIS SONG, AFTER ME, DANCING TO IT MERRILY.
FIRST, REHEARSE YOUR SONG BY ROTE, SING EACH WORD AS A WARBLING NOTE;
HAND IN HAND, WITH FAIRY GRACE, WE ALL SING, AND BLESS THIS PLACE.

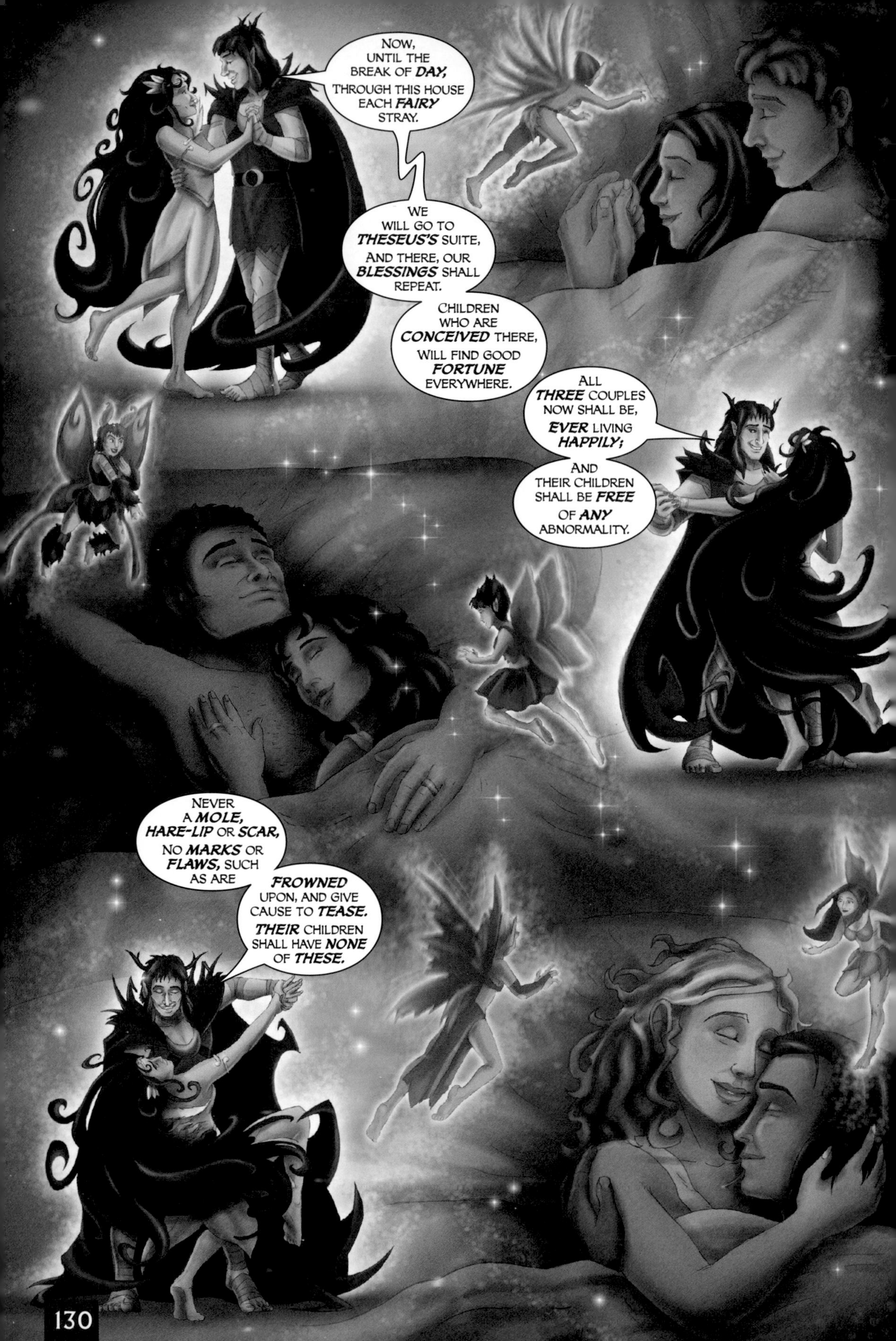
Now, until the break of DAY, through this house each FAIRY stray.
We will go to THESEUS'S suite, And there, our BLESSINGS shall repeat.
Children who are CONCEIVED there, Will find good FORTUNE everywhere.
All THREE couples now shall be, EVER living HAPPILY;
And their children shall be FREE of ANY abnormality.
Never a MOLE, HARE-LIP or SCAR, No MARKS or FLAWS, such as are
FROWNED upon, and give cause to TEASE.
THEIR children shall have NONE of THESE.

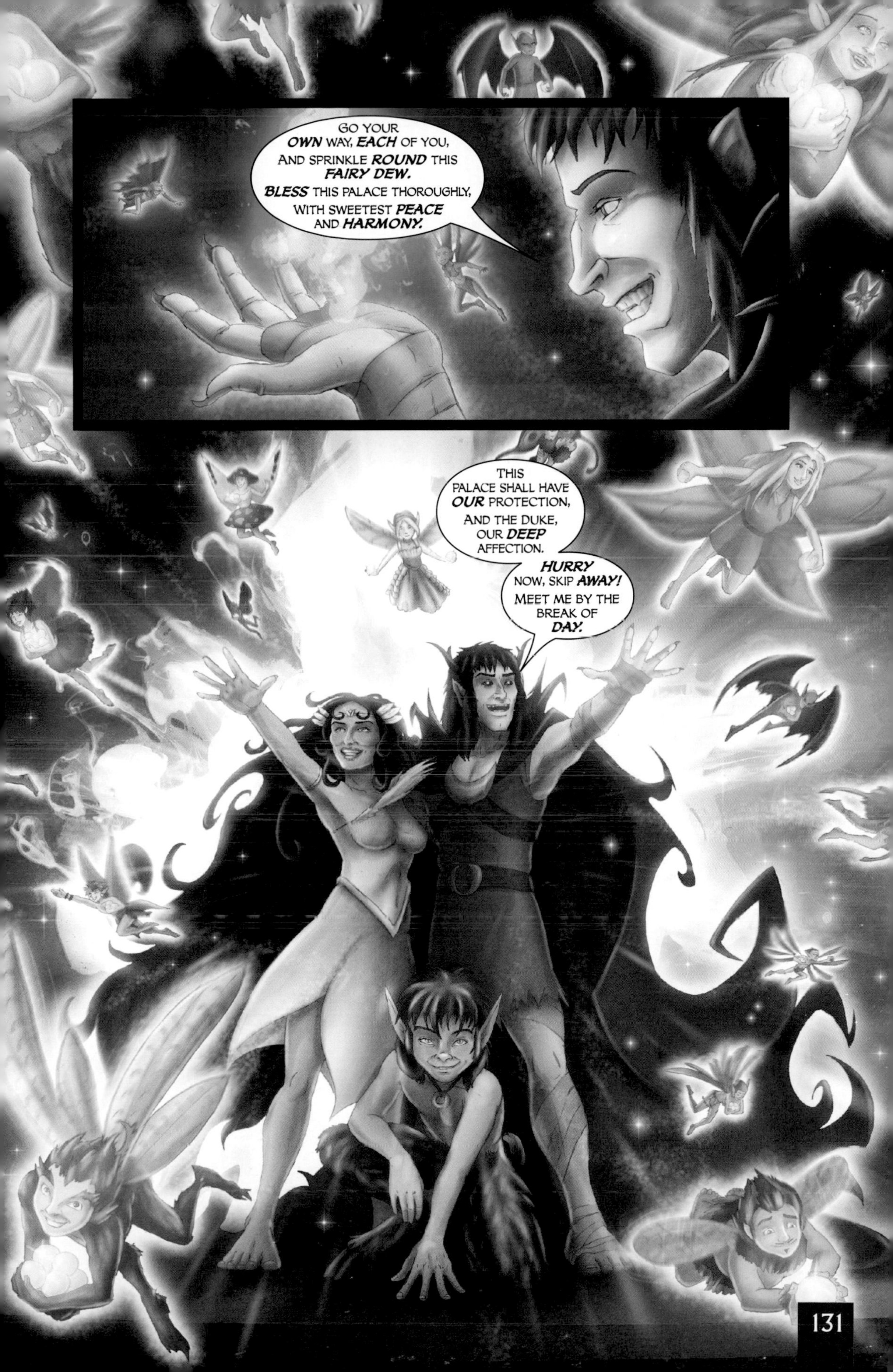

GO YOUR OWN WAY, EACH OF YOU, AND SPRINKLE ROUND THIS FAIRY DEW. BLESS THIS PALACE THOROUGHLY, WITH SWEETEST PEACE AND HARMONY.
THIS PALACE SHALL HAVE OUR PROTECTION, AND THE DUKE, OUR DEEP AFFECTION.
HURRY NOW, SKIP AWAY! MEET ME BY THE BREAK OF DAY.

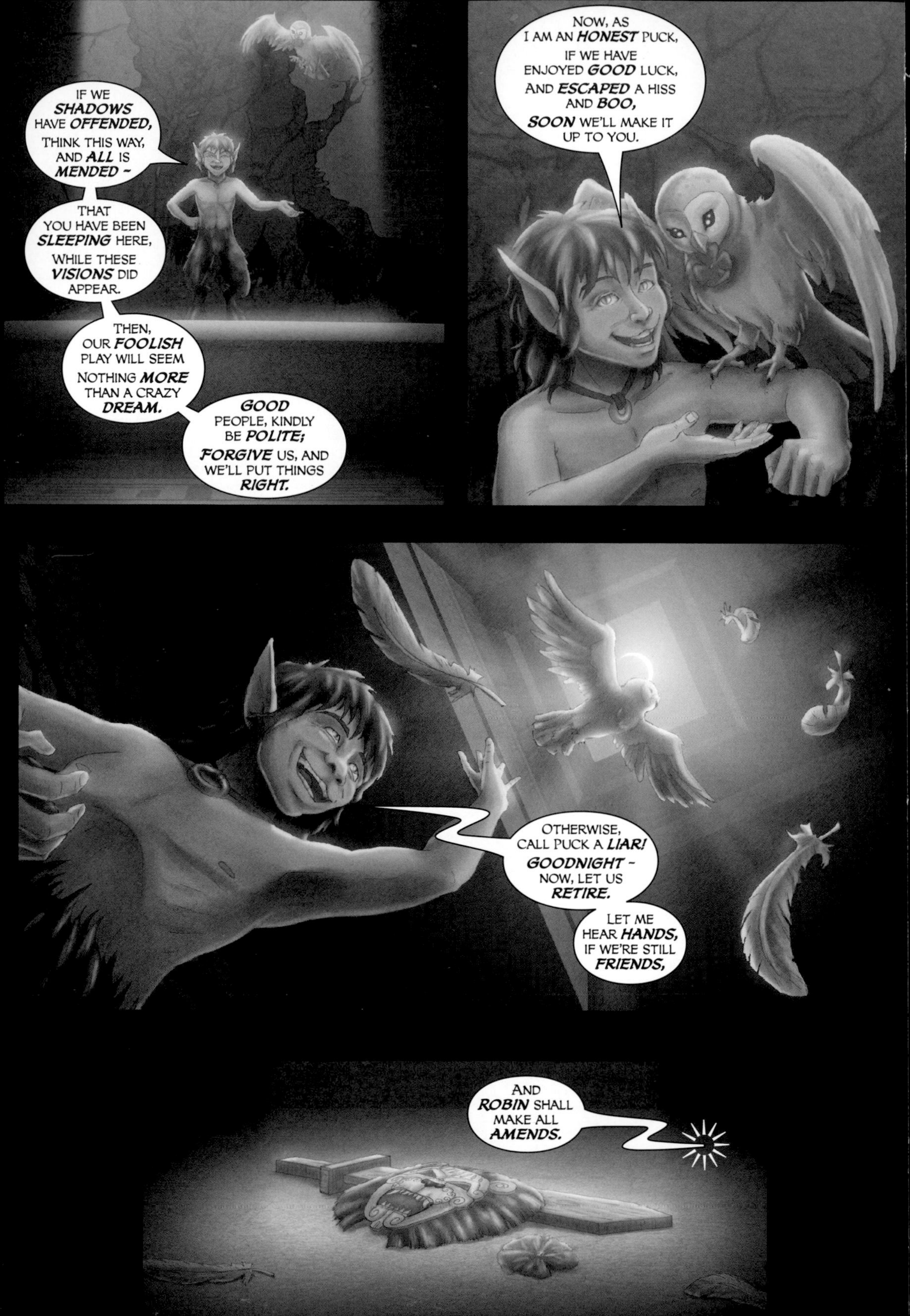
IF WE SHADOWS HAVE OFFENDED, THINK THIS WAY, AND ALL IS MENDED –
THAT YOU HAVE BEEN SLEEPING HERE, WHILE THESE VISIONS DID APPEAR.
THEN, OUR FOOLISH PLAY WILL SEEM NOTHING MORE THAN A CRAZY DREAM.
GOOD PEOPLE, KINDLY BE POLITE; FORGIVE US, AND WE'LL PUT THINGS RIGHT.
NOW, AS I AM AN HONEST PUCK, IF WE HAVE ENJOYED GOOD LUCK, AND ESCAPED A HISS AND BOO, SOON WE'LL MAKE IT UP TO YOU.
OTHERWISE, CALL PUCK A LIAR! GOODNIGHT – NOW, LET US RETIRE.
LET ME HEAR HANDS, IF WE'RE STILL FRIENDS,
AND ROBIN SHALL MAKE ALL AMENDS.

A Midsummer Night's Dream

The End

William Shakespeare

(c.1564 - 1616 AD)

National Portrait Gallery, London

Shakespeare is, without question, the world's most famous playwright. Yet, despite his fame, very few records and artifacts exist for him — we don't even know the exact date of his birth! April 23, 1564 (St George's Day) is taken to be his birthday, as this was three days before his baptism (for which we do have a record). Records also tell us that he died on the same date in 1616, aged fifty-two.

The life of William Shakespeare can be divided into three acts.

Act One – Stratford-upon-Avon

William was the eldest son of tradesman John Shakespeare and Mary Arden, and the third of eight children (he had two older sisters). The Shakespeares were a respectable family. The year after William was born, John (who made gloves and traded leather) became an alderman of Stratford-upon-Avon, and four years later he became High Bailiff (or mayor) of the town.

Little is known of William's childhood. He learned to read and write at the local primary school, and later is believed to have attended the local grammar school, where he studied Latin and English Literature. In 1582, aged eighteen, William married a local farmer's daughter, Anne Hathaway. Anne was eight years his senior and three months pregnant. During their marriage they had three children: Susanna, born on

May 26, 1583, and twins, Hamnet and Judith, born on February 2, 1585. Hamnet (William's only son) died in 1596, aged eleven, from Bubonic Plague.

Act Two – London

Five years into his marriage, in 1587, William's wife and children stayed in Stratford, while he moved to London. He appeared as an actor at *The Theatre* (England's first permanent theater) and gave public recitals of his own poems; but it was his playwriting that created the most interest. His fame soon spread far and wide. When Queen Elizabeth I died in 1603, the new King James I (who was already King James VI of Scotland) gave royal consent for Shakespeare's acting company, *The Lord Chamberlain's Men* to be called *The King's Men* in return for entertaining the court. This association was to shape a

number of plays, such as *Macbeth*, which was written to please the Scottish King.

William Shakespeare is attributed with writing and collaborating on 38 plays, 154 sonnets and 5 poems, in just twenty-three years between 1590 and 1613. No original manuscript exists for any of his plays, making it hard to accurately date any of them. Printing was still in its infancy, and plays tended to change as they were performed. Shakespeare would write manuscript for the actors and continue to refine them over a number of performances. The plays we know today have survived from written copies taken at various stages of each play and usually written by the actors from memory. This has given rise to variations in texts of what is now known as "quarto" versions of the plays, until we reach the first official printing of each play in the 1623 *"folio" Mr William Shakespeare's Comedies, Histories, & Tragedies*. His last solo-authored work was *The Tempest* in 1611, which was only followed by collaborative work on two plays (*Henry VIII* and *Two Noble Kinsmen*) with John Fletcher. Shakespeare is strongly associated with the famous *Globe Theatre*. Built by his troupe in 1599, it became his "spiritual home", with thousands of people crammed into the small space for each performance. There were 3,000 people in the building in 1613 when a cannon-shot during a performance of *Henry VIII* set fire to the thatched roof and the entire theater was burned to the ground. Although it was rebuilt a year later, it marked an end to Shakespeare's writing and to his time in London.

Act Three - Retirement

Shortly after the 1613 accident at *The Globe*, Shakespeare left the capital and returned to live once more with his family in Stratford-upon-Avon. He died on April 23, 1616 and was buried two days later at the Church of the Holy Trinity (the same church where he had been baptized fifty-two years earlier). The cause of his death remains unknown.

Epilogue

At the time of his death, Shakespeare had substantial properties, which he bestowed on his family and associates from the theater. He had no son to inherit his wealth, and he left the majority of his possessions to his eldest daughter Susanna. Curiously, the only thing that he left to his wife Anne was his second-best bed! (although she continued to live in the family home after his death). William Shakespeare's last direct descendant died in 1670. She was his granddaughter, Elizabeth.

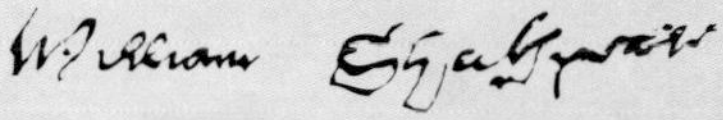

Shakespeare Birthplace Trust

As so few relics survive from Shakespeare's life, it is amazing that the house where he was born and raised remains intact. It is owned and cared for by the Shakespeare Birthplace Trust, which looks after a number of houses in the area:

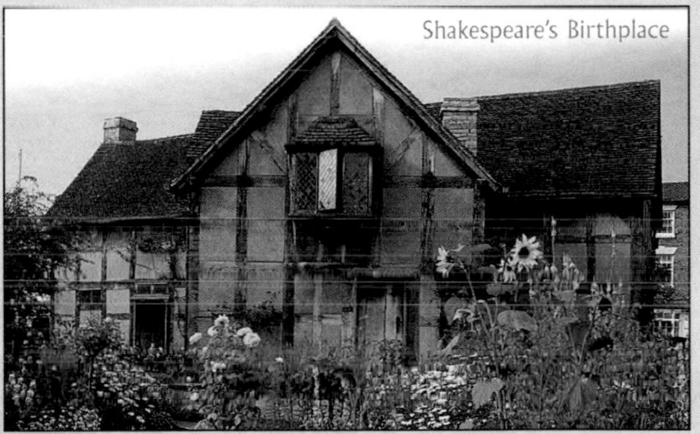

Shakespeare's Birthplace

- Shakespeare's Birthplace.
- Mary Arden's Farm: The childhood home of Shakespeare's mother.
- Anne Hathaway's Cottage: The childhood home of Shakespeare's wife.
- Hall's Croft: The home of Shakespeare's eldest daughter, Susanna.
- New Place: Only the grounds exist of the house where Shakespeare died in 1616.
- Nash's House: The home of Shakespeare's granddaughter.

www.shakespeare.org.uk

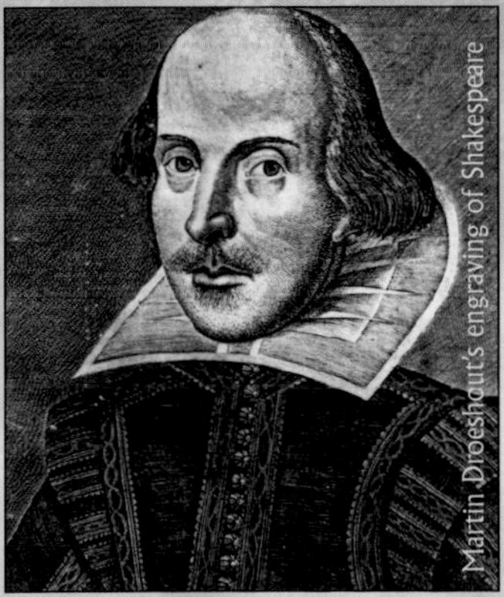

Martin Droeshout's engraving of Shakespeare

Formed in 1847, the Trust also works to promote Shakespeare around the world. In early 2009, it announced that it had found a new Shakespeare portrait, believed to have been painted within his lifetime, with a trail of provenance that links it to Shakespeare himself.

It is accepted that Martin Droeshout's engraving (left) that appears on the First Folio of 1623 is an authentic likeness of Shakespeare because the people involved in its publication would have personally known him. This new portrait (once owned by Henry Wriothesley, 3rd Earl of Southampton, one of Shakespeare's most loyal supporters) is so similar in all facial aspects that it is now suspected to have been the source that Droeshout used for his famous engraving.

www.shakespearefound.org.uk

History of A Midsummer Night's Dream

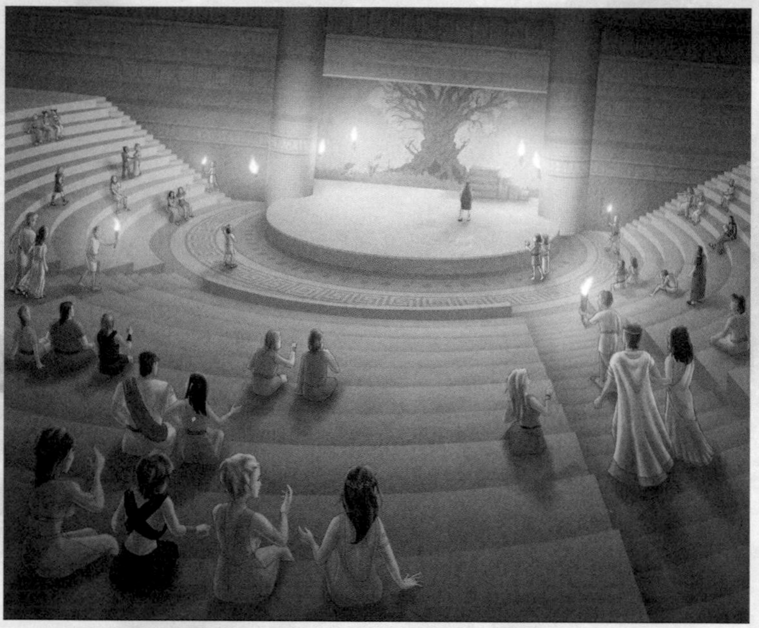

A *Midsummer Night's Dream* was an early success for Shakespeare. The first printed edition of 1600 says it was "sundry times publickely acted," although there is little evidence to support the belief that it was written for, or ever performed as part of, any wedding celebration.

While it is hard to date Shakespeare's plays with absolute precision, certain references within *A Midsummer Night's Dream* lead us to believe it was written in 1595-6, just before he completed *Romeo and Juliet* (both plays have a domineering father trying to force his daughter to marry someone she doesn't love). It was most definitely written in the reign of Elizabeth I (1533-1603), and there is a cryptic reference made to her in Act II Scene I (page 35), where Oberon recounts Cupid taking aim at her with his bow, but the arrow missing its target, allowing the "Virgin Queen" to continue in her worthy meditation. Shakespeare's association with the monarchy strengthened when James I came to the throne, and there is a record of the play being performed in court in 1604 – almost ten years after it was written.

As much as the play is loved today, and as often as it has been performed to rapturous crowds since its creation, the play has also had its share of detractors through the years. The great diarist, Samuel Pepys, wrote of a production in 1662 (46 years after Shakespeare's death) describing it as ***"the most insipid, ridiculous play that I ever saw in my life."*** Pepys was similarly scathing about *Romeo and Juliet* that same year, so he either attended poor performances of both these masterpieces of the stage, or he wasn't the biggest fan of Shakespeare's plays!

Time and Place

The title of *A Midsummer Night's Dream* is a little misleading. Midsummer is another name for the summer solstice, when the sun is as its highest due to the angle of the earth's axis to the sun. Today this is recognized as occurring on June 21 in the northern hemisphere (December 21 in the southern hemisphere), but in Shakespeare's day, this was thought to occur on June 24. The only mention of a date occurs in Act IV Scene I (page 100), when Theseus suspects the youths were in the forest to "observe the rite of May," making it "May Day" (May 1). For this to be consistent, the term "Midsummer" must refer to "Midsummer Madness" (crazy behavior that can happen at any time), setting Act IV on May 1.

As for the era, legend has it that Theseus lived before the times of the Trojan Wars, setting it around 1250 BC, although the play feels as if it takes place much later than that, in a time almost current to Shakespeare's day.

The location is also strange, with the characters being from Athens in Greece, but the woodland setting much more representative of the English countryside where Shakespeare was raised. This is poetic licence on Shakespeare's part, to place grand subjects such as Theseus and Hippolyta in a setting that would be familiar to the audience he was trying to entertain. These anomalies somehow seem to add to the intrigue and magic of the play.

made by Arthur Golding in 1567.

Theseus and Hippolyta appear in that other iconic work of the Middle Ages, Chaucer's *Canterbury Tales.* "The Knight's Tale" describes how Theseus, the Duke of Athens, conquers and captures the heart of "Ipolita" the Queen of the Amazons, as mentioned in Act I Scene I (page 8). The names of Philostrate and Egeus are also both taken from the same verse.

(donkey/fool) and the comedy of the beautiful Titania falling in love with this man-creature. Shakespeare took this idea from a 1566 translation of a second-century Latin story, *Transformations of Lucius or The Golden Ass*, in which a man is temporarily turned into an ass, whom a respectable woman falls in love with. Interestingly, though, there is an intriguing passage in Scot's *The Discoverie of Witchcraft* which must have inspired the play:

Sources

Unlike many of Shakespeare's other plays, *A Midsummer Night's Dream* is not a straight adaptation of any prior work, and the sources he drew upon reveal what a learned man he was.

A major influence was Ovid's *Metamorphoses* — a book of Latin verse that he would have studied at school. *Metamorphoses* tries to explain aspects of nature as the outcome of mythical events. In a similar vein, Titania explains how bad weather is the result of the disagreement between herself and Oberon in Act II Scene I (page 32). Although the name of Titania is taken from the book, it is Shakespeare who first gives that name to the Fairy Queen (references for Oberon being the name of the Fairy King predate the play).

The story of Pyramus and Thisbe also comes from *Metamorphoses,* in which Pyramus's blood is given as the reason for mulberry trees being dark red. The amateur production of this tale in Act V Scene I (pp 113-126) could be the Bard poking fun at a poor adaptation of the work,

In Act II Scene I, the mischievous spirit Puck is introduced to the audience also as Robin Goodfellow and Hobgoblin (page 28). Both these names appear in a 1584 publication, *The Discoverie of Witchcraft* by Reginald Scot. In that book, Scot details how people would leave clothes, milk and bread out for this spirit, to stop him from playing tricks on them. Like a Bogeyman, the character was used as a threat to children in order to get them to behave. He was also thought to sweep up at night for those mortals who left things out for him, as mentioned in Act V Scene I (page 129).

Of course, the most notable event of the play is Bottom's head becoming that of a donkey. This sets up wordplays of "ass"

If I affirme, that with certeine charmes and popish praiers I can set an horsse or an asses head upon a mans shoulders, I shall not be believed; or if I doo it, I shall be thought a witch.

Regardless of what Pepys said in 1662, *A Midsummer Night's Dream* remains one of the Bard's best-loved plays, and is the one most often performed in open air theatres across the world — the perfect magical entertainment for a warm evening.

Page Creation

Page 35

105. Close on Oberon speaking to Puck. We see him recalling sitting with Puck on a cliff.

OBERON	Thou remember'st Since once I sat upon a promontory, And heard a mermaid, on a dolphin's back Uttering such dulcet and harmonious breath, That the rude sea grew civil at her song, And certain stars shot madly from their spheres, To hear the sea-maid's music.	Do you remember the time I sat on a cliff and listened to a mermaid singing as she rode on a dolphin's back? It was such a beautiful song that it calmed the rough sea – and some stars fell crazily from their orbits to hear the sea-maiden's music.	Do you remember the time when I sat on a cliff and listened to a mermaid singing?
PUCK	I remember.	I remember.	I remember.

106. Away in the distance, close to the moon, a silhouette of Cupid is letting fly his arrow of love. **Note:** [*"a fair vestal throned by the west" is believed to be a reference to Queen Elizabeth I and how she never married*].

OBERON	That very time I saw (but thou couldst not), Flying between the cold moon and the earth, Cupid all arm'd: a certain aim he took At a fair vestal throned by the west, And loos'd his love-shaft smartly from his bow, As it should pierce a hundred thousand hearts.	That same night I saw – but you could not – Cupid, flying between the moon and the earth. He was armed with his arrows, and he took aim at a fair virgin queen in the west. He shot an arrow from his bow so fast, it could have pierced a hundred-thousand hearts.	That night, I saw Cupid shoot an arrow towards a lovely virgin queen –

107. High view above the Forest clearing. Moonbeams have turned Cupid's arrow downwards, towards the ground. Oberon is speaking to Puck, below. **Note:** [*"imperial votaress" is also believed to be a reference to queen Elizabeth I*].

OBERON	But I might see young Cupid's fiery shaft Quench'd in the chaste beams of the wat'ry moon, And the imperial votaress passed on, In maiden meditation, fancy-free.	But I saw Cupid's fiery arrow extinguished by the purity of the moon's watery beams – and the virgin queen went on her way, in innocent prayer, without being hit.	-- but the arrow was deflected by moonbeams, and it missed its target.

108. Oberon is speaking to Puck in distant **bg**. In Oberon's thoughts, close up in **fg**, a white flower has been pierced by Cupid's arrow. The flower is turning from white to purple (over three panels)

OBERON	Yet mark'd I where the bolt of Cupid fell: It fell upon a little western flower, Before milk-white, now purple with love's wound, And maidens call it love-in-idleness.	Still, I noted where his arrow fell. It landed on a little western flower, which was milk-white, but soon turned purple from the love-arrow's wound. Young maidens call it "love-in-idleness".	It fell upon a little white flower and turned it purple.

Page 35 from the script of *A Midsummer Night's Dream* showing the three text versions.

1. Script

The first stage in creating a graphic novel adaptation of a Shakespeare play is to split the original script into comic book panels, describing the images to be drawn as well as the dialogue, captions and sound effects. To do this, not only does the scriptwriter (John McDonald) need to know the play well, but he also needs to visualize the layout of each panel and page in his head in order to write the art descriptions (there are over 450 panels in *A Midsummer Night's Dream*). Once this is created, the dialogue is adapted into Plain Text and Quick Text to create the three versions of the book, which all use the same artwork.

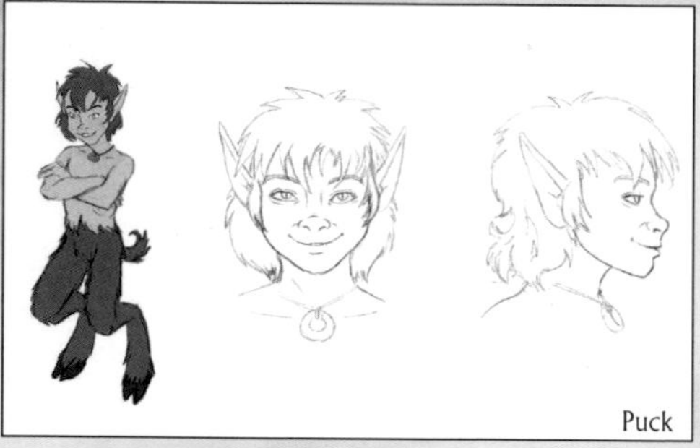

Puck

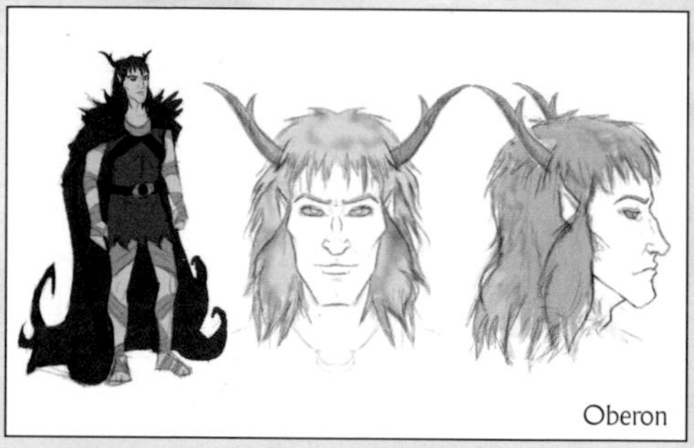

Oberon

2. Character Sheets

As well as creating the script, the scriptwriter also writes descriptions of how he imagines each character to look. The artists (Kat Nicholson and Jason Cardy) couple these with their own ideas to create a number of character sheets. These sheets provide a point of reference when drawing the pages, but more importantly they allow the artists to familiarize themselves with the characters – to the point where they almost take on a life of their own.

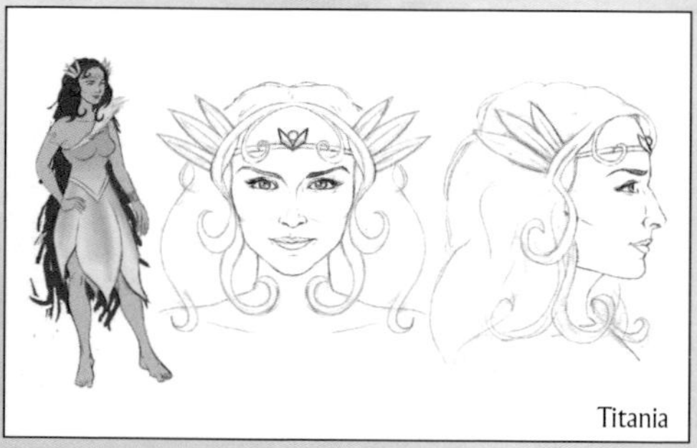

Titania

3. Rough Layout

There is a wealth of detail in each panel of this book, making it critically important to solve any problems in the layouts before undertaking the finished drawing. Here is Kat and Jason's initial layout of page 35. Comparing it to the finished page, you can see how a number of alterations were made. Kat and Jason created the rough layouts digitally, which made it easier to resize and amend panels, and work on the page as a whole. For instance, to show who is speaking, Oberon and Puck were added to the left-hand edge of the page. A sequence was also added to show the flower changing color from white to purple, and the images of Cupid and Oberon's eye have moved to accommodate these amendments.

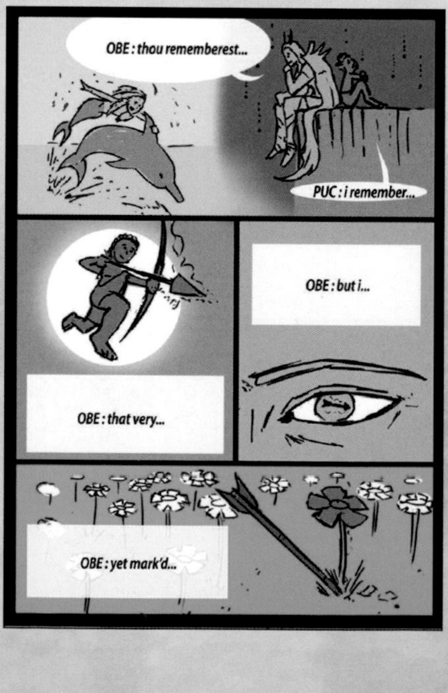
OBE : thou rememberest...
PUC : i remember...
OBE : but i...
OBE : that very...
OBE : yet mark'd...

The rough layout created from the script.

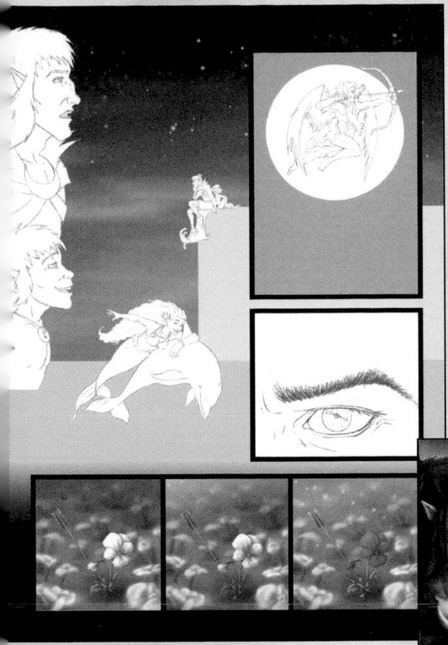

Linework image with gray backgrounds, ready for coloring.

4. Linework

The characters for each panel were first drawn in pencil. These images were then scanned into the computer and positioned over digitally prepared backgrounds. Kat and Jason were always thinking in terms of the finished colored page, and backgrounds were created in isolation to the linework. Creating the artwork in this way meant that the usually distinct stages of fully pencilled and inked linework became one single stage of light, open linework. Here you can see linework for the characters set against grayscale backgrounds that were already finished at this point. It is still possible to make alterations to the page at this level of completion, and the decision was made to zoom closer into Oberon's eye to make the arrow more prominent.

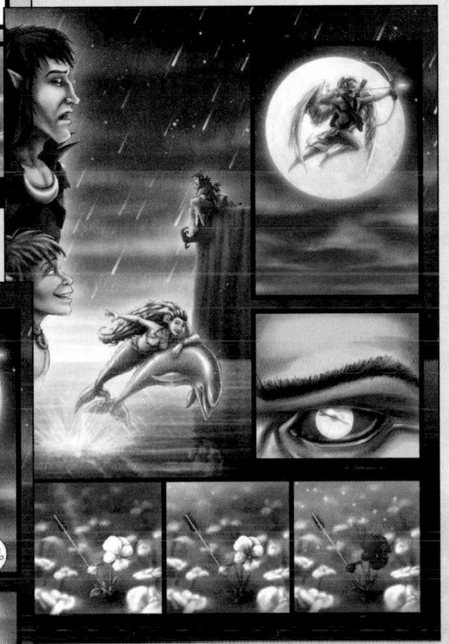

The final colored artwork.

5. Coloring

Kat and Jason are wonderful colorists and have worked on a number of books for Classical Comics. They had a particular "look" in mind for ***A Midsummer Night's Dream,*** to create a fine art, paint-like image using digital art techniques. You can see this in the detail of Oberon's eye, which looks like it could have been painted with acrylics, while there are wonderful digital effects on this page, such as the glow around the moon and the soft focus on the flowers.

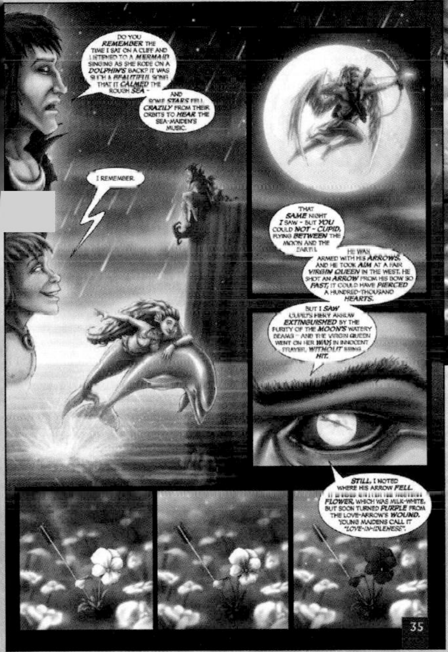
DO YOU REMEMBER THE TIME I SAT ON A CLIFF AND LISTENED TO A MERMAID SINGING AS SHE RODE ON A DOLPHIN'S BACK? IT WAS SUCH A BEAUTIFUL SONG THAT IT CALMED THE ROUGH SEA -
AND SOME STARS FELL CRAZILY FROM THEIR ORBITS TO HEAR THE SEA-MAIDEN'S MUSIC.
I REMEMBER.
THAT SAME NIGHT I SAW - BUT YOU COULD NOT - CUPID, FLYING BETWEEN THE MOON AND THE EARTH.
HE WAS ARMED WITH HIS ARROWS, AND HE TOOK AIM AT A FAIR VIRGIN QUEEN IN THE WEST. HE SHOT AN ARROW FROM HIS BOW SO FAST, IT COULD HAVE PIERCED A HUNDRED-THOUSAND HEARTS.
BUT I SAW CUPID'S FIERY ARROW EXTINGUISHED BY THE PURITY OF THE MOON'S WATERY BEAMS - AND THE VIRGIN QUEEN WENT ON HER WAY IN INNOCENT PRAYER, WITHOUT BEING HIT.
STILL, I NOTED WHERE HIS ARROW FELL. FLOWER, WHICH WAS MILK-WHITE, BUT SOON TURNED PURPLE FROM THE LOVE-ARROW'S WOUND. YOUNG MAIDENS CALL IT "LOVE-IN-IDLENESS".
35

The finished page 35 with Plain Text lettering.

6. Lettering

The final stage is to add the captions, sound effects, and speech bubbles from the script. These are placed on top of the finished colored pages, and the positioning of the speech balloons is designed to lead the eye around the page to give a natural reading flow. Three versions of each page are lettered, one for each of the three versions of the book (Original Text, Plain Text and Quick Text).

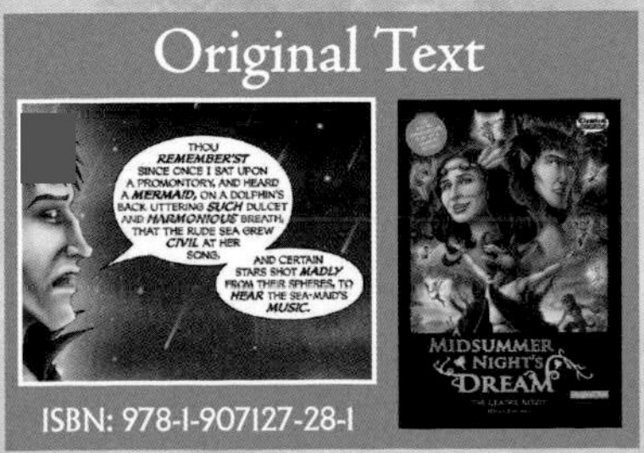
Original Text
THOU REMEMBER'ST SINCE ONCE I SAT UPON A PROMONTORY, AND HEARD A MERMAID, ON A DOLPHIN'S BACK UTTERING SUCH DULCET AND HARMONIOUS BREATH, THAT THE RUDE SEA GREW CIVIL AT HER SONG,
AND CERTAIN STARS SHOT MADLY FROM THEIR SPHERES, TO HEAR THE SEA-MAID'S MUSIC.
MIDSUMMER NIGHT'S DREAM
ISBN: 978-1-907127-28-1

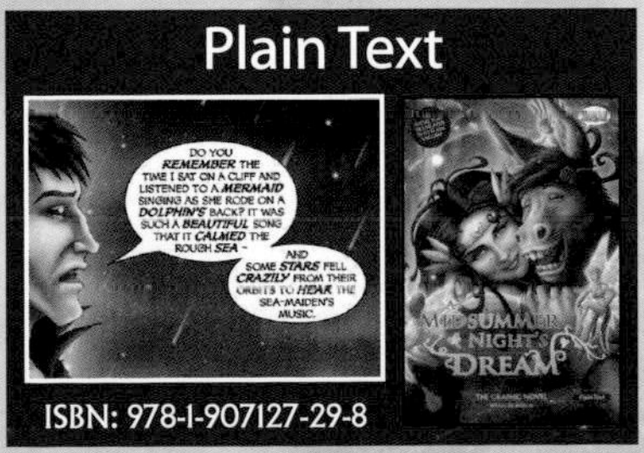
Plain Text
DO YOU REMEMBER THE TIME I SAT ON A CLIFF AND LISTENED TO A MERMAID SINGING AS SHE RODE ON A DOLPHIN'S BACK? IT WAS SUCH A BEAUTIFUL SONG THAT IT CALMED THE ROUGH SEA -
AND SOME STARS FELL CRAZILY FROM THEIR ORBITS TO HEAR THE SEA-MAIDEN'S MUSIC.
MIDSUMMER NIGHT'S DREAM
ISBN: 978-1-907127-29-8

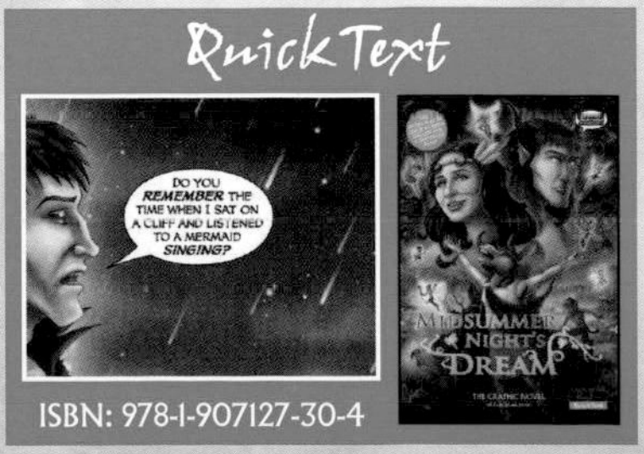
Quick Text
DO YOU REMEMBER THE TIME WHEN I SAT ON A CLIFF AND LISTENED TO A MERMAID SINGING?
MIDSUMMER NIGHT'S DREAM
ISBN: 978-1-907127-30-4

Shakespeare's Globe

The Globe Theatre and Shakespeare

It is hard to appreciate today how theaters were actually a new idea in William Shakespeare's time. The very first theater in Elizabethan London to only show plays, aptly called *The Theatre*, was introduced by an entrepreneur by the name of James Burbage. In fact, *The Globe Theatre*, possibly the most famous theater of that era, was built from the timbers of *The Theatre*. The landlord of *The Theatre* was Giles Allen, a Puritan who disapproved of theatrical entertainment. When he decided to enforce a huge rent increase in the winter of 1598, the theater members dismantled the building piece by piece and shipped it across the Thames to Southwark for reassembly. Allen was powerless to do anything, as the company owned the wood - although he spent three years in court trying to sue the perpetrators!

The report of the dismantling party (written by Schoenbaum)

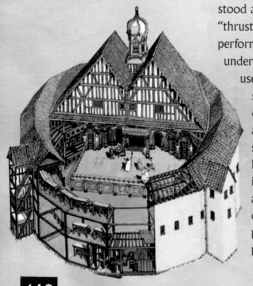

says: *"ryotous... armed... with divers and manye unlawfull and offensive weapons... in verye ryotous outragious and forcyble manner and contrarye to the lawes of your highnes Realme... and there pulling breaking and throwing downe the sayd Theater in verye outragious violent and riotous sort to the great disturbance and terrefyeing not onlye of your subjectes... but of divers others of your majesties loving subjectes there neere inhabitinge."*

William Shakespeare became a part owner of this new *Globe Theatre* in 1599. It was one of four major theaters in the area, along with the *Swan*, the *Rose*, and the *Hope*. The exact physical structure of the *Globe* is unknown, although scholars are fairly sure of some details through drawings from the period. The theater itself was a closed structure with an open courtyard where the stage stood. Tiered galleries around the open area accommodated the wealthier patrons who could afford seats, and those of the lower classes - the "groundlings" - stood around the platform or "thrust" stage during the performance of a play. The space under and behind the stage was used for special effects, storage and costume changes. Surprisingly, although the entire structure was not very big by modern standards, it is known to have accommodated fairly large crowds - as many as 3,000 people - during a single performance.

The Globe II

In 1613, the original *Globe Theatre* burned to the ground when a cannon shot during a performance of *Henry VIII* set fire to the thatched roof of the gallery. Undeterred, the company completed a new *Globe* (this time with a tiled roof) on the foundations of its predecessor. Shakespeare didn't write any new plays for this theater, which opened in 1614. He retired to Stratford-upon-Avon that year, and died two years later. Despite that, performances continued until 1642, when the Puritans closed down all theaters and places of entertainment. Two years later, the Puritans razed the building to the ground in order to build tenements upon the site. No more was to be seen of the *Globe* for 352 years.

Shakespeare's Globe

Led by the vision of the late Sam Wanamaker, work began on the construction of a new *Globe* in 1993, close to the site of the original theater. It was completed three years later, and Queen Elizabeth II officially opened the *New Globe Theatre* on June 12, 1997 with a production of *Henry V*.

The *New Globe Theatre* is as faithful a reproduction as possible to the Elizabethan theater, given that the details of the original are only known from sketches of the time. The building can accommodate 1,500 people in all, across the galleries and the "groundlings."

www.shakespeares-globe.org

A Midsummer Night's Dream Teaching Resource Pack

Helping you prepare motivating and stimulating lessons

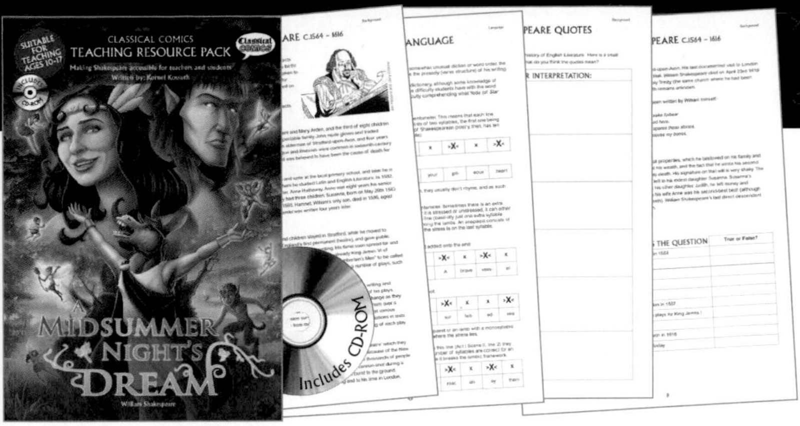
CLASSICAL COMICS
TEACHING RESOURCE PACK
A MIDSUMMER NIGHT'S DREAM
Includes CD-ROM

ISBN: 978-1-907127-75-5

- *Over 100 spiral-bound, photocopiable pages.*
- *Cross-curricular topics and activities.*
- *Ideal for differentiated teaching.*
- *CD includes an electronic version of the teaching book for whiteboards, laptops and digital printing.*
- *Only $22.95*

To accompany each title in our series of graphic novels and to help with their application in the classroom, we also publish teaching resource packs. These widely acclaimed 100+ page books are spiral-bound, making the pages easy to photocopy. They also include a CD-ROM with the pages in PDF format, ideal for whole-class teaching on whiteboards, laptops, etc or for direct digital printing. These books are written by teachers, for teachers, helping students to engage in the play or novel. Suitable for teaching ages 10-17, each book provides exercises that cover structure, listening, understanding, motivation and character as well as key words, themes and literary techniques. Devised to encompass a broad range of skill levels, they provide many opportunities for differentiated teaching and the tailoring of lessons to meet individual needs.

"Thank you! These will be fantastic for all our students. It is a brilliant resource and to have the lesson ideas too are great. Thanks again to all your team who have created these."

"...this is a fantastic way to teach and progress English literature and language!"

"As to the resource, I can't wait to start using it! Well done on a fantastic service."

OUR RANGE OF TEACHING RESOURCE PACKS AVAILABLE

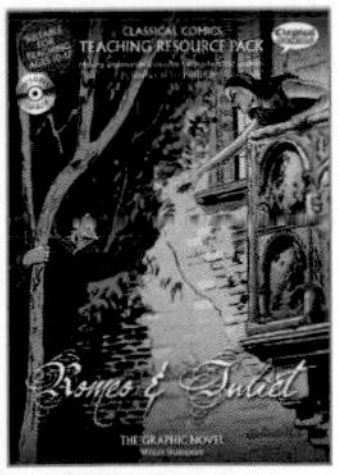
Romeo & Juliet

Romeo & Juliet
978-1-906332-74-7

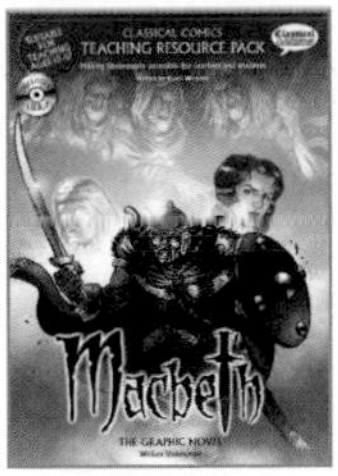
Macbeth

Macbeth
978-1-906332-54-9

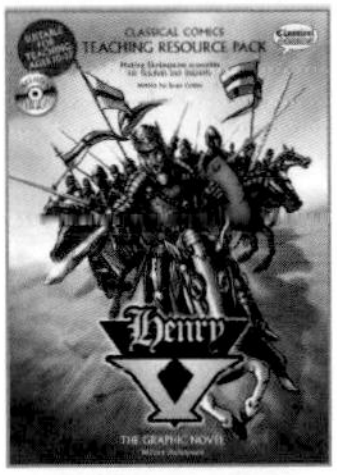
Henry V

Henry V
978-1-906332-53-2

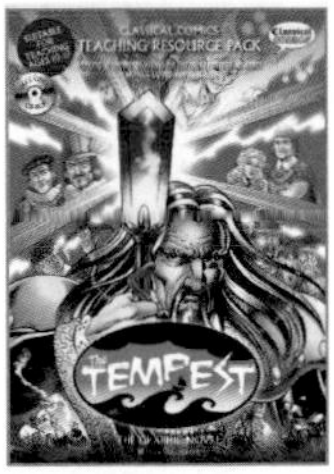
TEMPEST

The Tempest
978-1-906332-77-8

- Only $22.95 each
- 100+ spiral-bound, photocopiable pages.
- Electronic version included for whole-class teaching and digital printing.
- Cross-curricular topics and activities.
- Ideal for differentiated teaching.

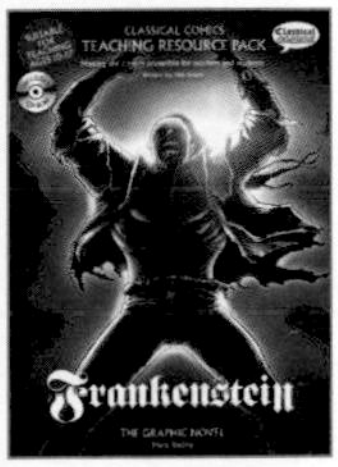
Frankenstein

Frankenstein
978-1-906332-56-3

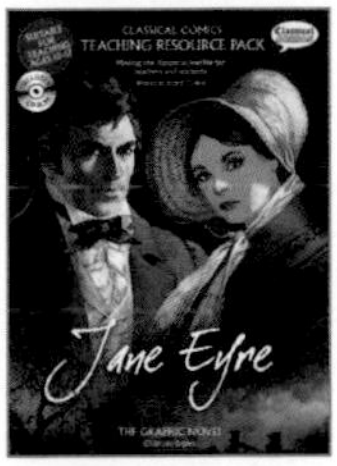
Jane Eyre

Jane Eyre
978-1-906332-55-6

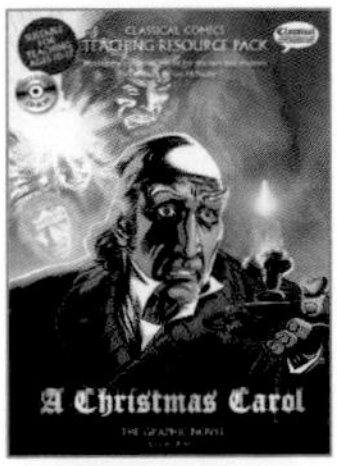
A Christmas Carol

A Christmas Carol
978-1-906332-57-0

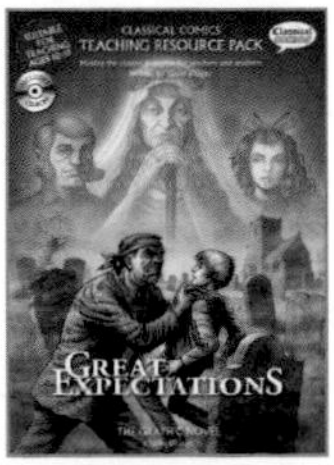
GREAT EXPECTATIONS

Great Expectations
978-1-906332-58-7

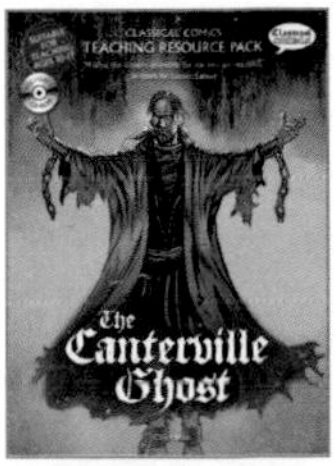
The Canterville Ghost

The Canterville Ghost
978-1-906332-78-5

MORE TITLES AVAILABLE FROM

Shakespeare's plays in a choice of 3 text versions. Simply choose the text version to match your reading level.

Original Text	SHAKESPEARE'S ENTIRE PLAY AS A FULL-COLOR GRAPHIC NOVEL!
Plain Text	THE ENTIRE PLAY TRANSLATED INTO PLAIN ENGLISH!
Quick Text	THE ENTIRE PLAY IN QUICK MODERN ENGLISH FOR A FAST-PACED READ!

Macbeth: The Graphic Novel (William Shakespeare)

• Script Adaptation: John McDonald • Pencils: & Inks: Jon Haward
• Inking Assistant: Gary Erskine • Colors & Letters: Nigel Dobbyn

144 Pages • $16.95

I HAVE THEE NOT, AND YET I SEE THEE STILL. ART THOU NOT, FATAL VISION, SENSIBLE TO FEELING AS TO SIGHT? OR ART THOU BUT A DAGGER OF THE MIND, A FALSE CREATION, PROCEEDING FROM THE HEAT-OPPRESSED BRAIN?
ISBN: 978-1-906332-44-0

I CAN'T CATCH YOU, BUT I CAN STILL SEE YOU. AREN'T YOU AS RESPONSIVE TO TOUCH AS YOU ARE TO SIGHT? OR ARE YOU JUST A DAGGER OF THE MIND... A MIRAGE, COMING FROM AN OVERHEATED BRAIN?
ISBN: 978-1-906332-45-7

I CAN'T HOLD YOU! -- ARE YOU JUST A DAGGER OF THE MIND?
ISBN: 978-1-906332-46-4

Romeo & Juliet: The Graphic Novel (William Shakespeare)

• Script Adaptation: John McDonald • Linework: Will Volley
• Colors: Jim Devlin • Letters: Jim Campbell

168 Pages • $16.95

HE JESTS AT SCARS THAT NEVER FELT A WOUND.
BUT SOFT! WHAT LIGHT THROUGH YONDER WINDOW BREAKS?
IT IS THE EAST, AND JULIET IS THE SUN. ARISE, FAIR SUN, AND KILL THE ENVIOUS MOON, WHO IS ALREADY SICK AND PALE WITH GRIEF THAT THOU HER MAID ARE FAR MORE FAIR THAN SHE.
ISBN: 978-1-906332-61-7

ONLY THOSE WHO HAVE NEVER BEEN IN LOVE MAKE JOKES ABOUT A BROKEN HEART.
- BUT, SOFT! WHAT LIGHT THROUGH YONDER WINDOW BREAKS?
IT IS THE EAST, AND JULIET IS THE SUN. RISE, LOVELY SUN, AND KILL THAT OLD JEALOUS MOON! IT IS PALE AND SAD BECAUSE JULIET IS MORE BEAUTIFUL.
ISBN: 978-1-906332-62-4

LET THEM MAKE THEIR JOKES --
WHAT LIGHT THROUGH YONDER WINDOW BREAKS?
IT MUST BE THE EAST, AND JULIET IS THE RISING SUN.
ISBN: 978-1-906332-63-1

The Tempest: The Graphic Novel (William Shakespeare)

• Script Adaptation: John McDonald • Pencils: Jon Haward
• Inks: Gary Erskine • Colors: & Letters: Nigel Dobbyn

144 Pages • $16.95

BUT THIS ROUGH MAGIC I HERE ABJURE; AND, WHEN I HAVE REQUIR'D SOME HEAVENLY MUSIC, (WHICH EVEN NOW I DO,) TO WORK MINE END UPON THEIR SENSES, THAT THIS AIRY CHARM IS FOR, I'LL BREAK MY STAFF, BURY IT CERTAIN FATHOMS IN THE EARTH, AND, DEEPER THAN DID EVER PLUMMET SOUND, I'LL DROWN MY BOOK.
ISBN: 978-1-906332-69-3

BUT THE TIME HAS COME FOR ME TO GIVE UP THAT MAGIC. AFTER I CONJURE UP SOME UNEARTHLY MUSIC TO CAST ONE FINAL SPELL, THAT WILL MAKE THEM DO AS I COMMAND, I'LL BREAK MY STAFF AND BURY IT DEEP IN THE EARTH. I'LL ALSO SEND MY BOOK OF SPELLS DEEPER INTO THE SEA THAN ANY ANCHOR EVER SANK.
ISBN: 978-1-906332-70-9

BUT THE TIME HAS COME TO STOP – I MUST CONJURE UP ONE FINAL SPELL.
ISBN: 978-1-906332-71-6

Henry V: The Graphic Novel (William Shakespeare)

• Script Adaptation: John McDonald • Pencils: Neill Cameron • Inks: Bambos
• Colors: Jason Cardy & Kat Nicholson • Letters: Nigel Dobbyn

144 Pages • $16.95

WE DOUBT NOT OF A FAIR AND LUCKY WAR, SINCE GOD SO GRACIOUSLY HATH BROUGHT TO LIGHT THIS DANGEROUS TREASON LURKING IN OUR WAY TO HINDER OUR BEGINNINGS: WE DOUBT NOT NOW BUT EVERY RUB IS SMOOTHED ON OUR WAY.
THEN FORTH, DEAR COUNTRYMEN! LET US DELIVER OUR PUISSANCE INTO THE HAND OF GOD, PUTTING IT STRAIGHT IN EXPEDITION. CHEERLY TO SEA! THE SIGNS OF WAR ADVANCE!
NO KING OF ENGLAND, IF NOT KING OF FRANCE!
ISBN: 978-1-906332-41-9

THERE'S NO DOUBT NOW THAT ALL OBSTACLES HAVE BEEN REMOVED. SO, MY COUNTRYMEN, LET'S GO!
LET'S DELIVER OUR ARMY INTO THE HAND OF GOD AND BEGIN OUR EXPEDITION IMMEDIATELY. AWAY TO SEA, WITH OUR WARLIKE ADVANCE!
I WON'T BE KING OF ENGLAND, IF I'M NOT ALSO KING OF FRANCE!
ISBN: 978-1-906332-42-6

THERE'S NOTHING ELSE IN OUR WAY, SO LET'S ADVANCE
I WON'T BE KING OF ENGLAND, IF I'M NOT ALSO KING OF FRANCE!
ISBN: 978-1-906332-43-3